ABOUT THE NEW WORLD AFRICAN PRESS

The New World African Press evolved over a period of fifteen years. Originally, it began as Elsie Mae Enterprises in honor of my own special guiding light, the late Elise Mae Hadnot-Holloway. Later, Elsie Mae Enterprises was changed to the Boniface I. Obichere Press. This new change was in honor of my mentor, friend, and colleague, who passed from this realm and made his transition to the afterlife in 1997.

Finally, the Boniface I. Obichere Press metamorphosed into the New World African Press in 2000. While the name of the Press has gone through several name changes, its mission and purpose have remained the same. To fill the void and neglect left by the major publishing houses; to publish manuscripts, which focuses on the Diasporic experience in Africa, Europe, and the countries of the New World. While the press is primarily concerned with diasporic issues, it is also committed to publishing non-Diasporic manuscripts and literature such as *Bach: A Fictional Memoir* by Paul Guggenheim.

The New World African Press list of books includes the following. Clarence E. Zamba Liberty, *Growth of the Liberian State: an Analysis of Its' Historiography* is the first in our Diaspora series. Other includes: Herbert H. Booker, *The Noble Drew Ali and the Moorish Science Temple Movement*, and Joseph E. Holloway, *African American History: A Brief Outline, An Introduction to Classical African Civilizations, The African American Odyssey: Student's Manual and Study Guide with Test Combined Volume,* **The African American Odyssey,** and a novel by Joseph E. Holloway, *Neither Black Nor White: The Saga of An American*

Family. Sakui Malapka's *The Village Boy* is the first in a series of novels about Liberia. The second and third novels in this series are *Red Dust on the Green Leaves*, and *The Brightening Shadow* by John Gay.

We hope that you will submit your manuscripts for review by the press. Please mail your manuscripts to the New World African Press, 1958 Matador Way Unit 35, Northridge, California 91330. You can email us at: nworldafricanpress@msn.com.

Joseph E. Holloway, Ph.D.
CEO Editor-in-Chief of the
New World African Press

First New Edition, 2003

Publisher
The New World African Press
1958 Matador Way Unit #35
Northridge, CA 91330

ISBN 0-9717692-3-0

Published by New World African Press,
Copyright 2002 by New World African Press
ALL RIGHTS RESERVED

The New World African Press books are printed in the United
States of America on acid-free paper, and meet the
guidelines for permanence and durability of the
committee on production guidelines for book longevity
of the council on Library resources.

PREFACE TO THE SECOND PRINTING

When I wrote *Red Dust on the Green Leaves* in the early 1970s, I was hopeful that Liberia might continue on a path of reform and national development. William R. Tolbert, Jr., had replaced William V. S. Tubman as president, and it appeared that democracy, unification and economic equality would build on a foundation laid in the early years of Tubman's rule. Tubman had remained in power far too long, and by the end of the 1960s, the country had begun to slip into that pattern of paranoid centralization which has by now become all too familiar across the African continent. Tolbert represented a new beginning, and I was encouraged to think a new era had dawned for Liberia. I believed that Koli ánd Sumo, the twins whose early life story is recounted in this novel, would show how one family could overcome the split between "country" and "kwii". The conclusion is optimistic, the tone upbeat. The beauty, the mature civility, of the Kpelle way of life, by the grace of God and of caring people, would enlarge and enrich the new and domineering world of church, school and government.

In the late 1970s, when the Tolbert regime was beginning to unravel and cracks in the consensus were appearing, I decided to write a sequel to *Red Dust on the Green Leaves*. I called it *The Brightening Shadow*, a title with a double meaning. I drew the title from a marvelous poem by the Senegalese writer Birago Diop entitled *Breaths*. The poem celebrates the deep innerness of reality, where "things are more important than beings," where the dark side is always present, always looming, and yet the ancestors continue to breathe life into a darkened present.

The second novel takes the story of Koli and Sumo several years farther along their roads. Unfortunately, in 1978 these roads no longer appeared so promising or as smooth as they did in 1971. When I wrote the second book, I had a strong presentiment that Liberia could not keep on course that papering over the widening social cracks would not work. I did not know, but subconsciously surmised, that just two years after I completed *The Brightening Shadow* the country would break apart, leading step by tragic step to today's swamp of despair and horror.

The two books speak about the reality of a society in transition, where the division between "kwii" and "country" becomes critical in shaping the fate of the nation. The twins Koli and Sumo grow apart, and yet still maintain respect, even love, for each other. The ties that bind rural and urban society, bush school and western education, subsistence and money economy, micro and macro politics, forest and world religion, unwritten and written law, covert and overt speech are now, however, in the process of being stretched to the point that the lives of the twins can no longer be inter-twined in a harmonious whole.

"From mats to mattresses," as Tolbert defined development is more than a slogan. It is a succinct statement about poverty. When all have mats, no one is poor. When some get mattresses, some go to western school, some sell cash crops, some enter national politics, some become Christians or Muslims, some leave the palaver house for the magistrate's court, some state their ideas in long polysyllabic words instead of in proverbs, then the stage is set for what has now become a class war. That war is hinted at in the first novel, and then begins to brew in the second. In the third, which I am now writing, the war spreads to the dispossessed who know enough to realize that they are dispossessed. That war has been raging across the nation of Liberia for two decades now, a war that can only end when justice is available for all, in short when Koli and Sumo, and all that they stand for symbolically, are once again united.

I dedicate the two books, and the third which is in the making, to the people of Liberia, and especially to the Kpelle-speaking people who, like Koli and Sumo and their families, are attempting to make the best of a very harsh world. God bless them all.

John Gay, July 2002

THE BRIGHTENING SHADOW

BY JOHN GAY

With the editorial advice of

John Kellemu

Photographs by the Author

Cover designed by
Jim Dodson

BREATHS

Listen more often
To things than to beings;
The fire's voice is heard,
Hear the voice of water.
Hear in the wind
The bush sob:
It is the ancestors' breath.

Those who died have never left,
They are in the brightening shadow
And in the thickening shadow;
The dead are not under earth,
They are in the rustling tree,
They are in the groaning woods,
They are in the flowing water,
They are in the still water,
They are in the hut, they are in the crowd:
The dead are not dead.

Listen more often
To things than to beings;
The fire's voice is heard,
Hear the voice of water.
Hear in the wind
The bush sob:
It is the ancestors' breath.

The breath of dead ancestors
Who have not left,
Who are not under earth,
Who are not dead.
Those who died have never left,
They are in the woman's breast,
They are in the wailing child
And in the kindling firebrand.
The dead are not under earth,
They are in the fire dying down,
They are in the moaning rock,
They are in the crying grass,
They are in the forest, they are in the home:
The dead are not dead.

Listen more often
To things than to beings,
The fire's voice is heard,
Hear the voice of water.
Hear in the wind
It is the ancestors' breath.

Each day it repeats the pact,
The great pact which binds,
Which binds our fate to the law;
Acts, to stronger breaths
The fate of our dead not dead;
The heavy pact which ties us to life,
The heavy law which binds us to acts
Breaths dying
In bed and on river banks,
Breaths which stir
In the moaning rock and crying grass.
Breaths which lodge
In the shadow brightening or thickening,
In the rustling tree, in the groaning woods,
And in the flowing water, and in the still water,
Breaths much stronger,
Breaths which have taken
The breath of the dead not dead,
The dead who have not left,
The dead no longer under earth.

Listen more often
To things than to beings;
The fire's voice is heard,
Hear the voice of water.
Hear in the wind
The bush sob:
It is the ancestors' breath.

By Birago Diop. trans: Anne Astik
3000 Years of Black Poetry, An Anthology. edited by Alan Lomax
and Raoul Abdul. New York, Dodd. and Co., 1970.
With Permission.

CONTENTS

BOOK I: THE DEAD ARE NOT DEAD

BOOK II: THEY ARE IN THE CHILD

FOREWORD

This book, like its predecessor, *Red Dust on the Green Leaves,* can cautiously be called a novel. It is a continuation of that book, and as such is a careful reconstruction of Kpelle life in the 1950s and 1960s, based on extensive research. It tells the story of the same two boys, and now also their son. No person and no institution appears as an exact replica of any model past or present, and any resemblance is due rather to an attempt to represent Kpelle life in a single narrative.

I wish to thank once again John Kellemu for his additional help in making sure that this is an accurate reflection of Kpelle life and culture. I must take full responsibility for all errors, of course.

I thanked many persons in the preceding book. I will not list their names again. I can only add the following names, with many thanks for the help these persons provided. I am sure there are others I have omitted. I can only apologize for the omissions.

My hearty and sincere thanks, for the help they have given me, go to Suakoli Bomosii, George Browne, Jerome Bruner, Curtis Campaigne, Jack Down, Gerald Erchak, Jack Goody, Harry Greaves, Sr., Jordan Holtam, Kiapeh Jackson, Emmanuel Johnson, Flumo Kerkula, Gene LeVan, Barbara Lloyd, Charles Mulbah, Peter Mulbah, Ken Nichol, John Nuumeni, Sandy Robertson, Kerkula Sergeant, Herbert Spirer, Bobby Sumo, Andrew Wager, Karen Wiken, Pauline Willby and Edward Yarkpazua.

Again I acknowledge my immense debt to the Kpelle people, particularly those in the villages of Gbansu and Balama. It is to them, and to all parents, Kpelle or otherwise, who know that their dreams for themselves are only fulfilled in their children's lives, that I dedicate this book.

John Gay

BOOK I

THE DEAD ARE NOT DEAD

I: HEAR THE BUSH SOB

Koli shouted, "Hey! You, boy! Stop!"

No one paid attention.

The boy had caught the bag Koli had thrown down to him from the top of the truck, and was off and running, running as fast as he could, threading his way through the press of market women carrying pans of rice and cassava on their heads, men with high piles of folded lappa cloth, boys selling gum and cigarettes.

Koli jumped down from the truck, but he was too late. The crowds on the street closed after the boy. Koli ran, but soon saw it was useless. His heart sank. The boy could have ducked into an alley between the stores or gone up the hill behind any of the houses.

The boy had seemed friendly enough when he'd helped Koli climb on top of the truck in Salala. The white man had paid for the truck fare, and he had said goodbye in Salala that morning, and Koli had told his problem to the boy.

Koli had said, "This white man took care of me all through elementary school, and now he's sending me to high school in Muhlenburg."

"Huh," the boy had responded. "You'll never see him again, and you won't make it to high school. If the man's going to America like you say, he'll forget you."

"No," Koli had shot back. "He promised me. He gave me a letter to take to the church office in Monrovia, explaining the whole situation. He himself had been called suddenly to go back to America, to go to school again. But he told me that, the white lady at the church office would know what to do. It's true, he said he forgot to tell the lady anything about it, but the letter is supposed to explain everything. He asked her to give me work for the rest of December and all of January, and then send me to Muhlenburg, and he'll pay for it. He told me that when he gets back, he'll find me almost ready to graduate. He said he's really sorry he forgot to tell her, but there was so much business with his ticket. Besides he even gave me money and some clothes to take to school, and I've got them in my bag here."

Koli remembered, kicking himself, that he'd shown the boy

the new clothes and the five dollars. He'd seen the boy's eyes light up at the sight of the clothes and money.

"What a fool I was," he thought, "to show him what I had. I ought to remember what my father Flumo told me, that monkey shows leopard how to catch him by talking so loud in the bush. Anyhow, at least I kept a dollar in my pocket, and I've got the letter to the white lady at the church office. She'll help me. He said so."

But then Koli remembered. He felt in his pocket to make sure, but he knew it was no use.

He said aloud, but no one even turned to look, "The letter's in my bag, and so the boy's got it now."

He looked around again, thinking that he might try to chase the boy. But he saw quickly it was no use. The boy hadn't even been gone a minute, but there was no way to find him.

"What'll I do next?" thought Koli. He looked around for someone to help him, someone to stop the crowds and bring the boy back, someone just to tell his troubles to and get advice-the white man, his father Flumo, his step-father Yakpalo.

"Yakpalo would know what to do. He's the town chief. But he's not here. No one's here, the white man's gone, the letter and the money he gave me are gone, my clothes are gone." Koli came as close to crying as had since he had finished the bush school and had been initiated as a man.

He stood blank and confused for a few moments. The only person to notice him was the car boy for a bus going to Gbarnga. "One more seat to Gbarnga. Where you going, boy?"

Koli pulled back and started walking from the bus stop. He got his thoughts together. "I'll have to go to the mission house and talk to the lady. But all I've got is the dollar the white man gave me, and the clothes I'm wearing. And I'm sure the lady won't believe me without something to show who I am.

"Maybe I can go back to Salala, to the school. But no, that won't work. The other teachers have all gone away for the long vacation. Besides, they probably wouldn't help me, because they didn't like the way the white man cared for me, even going with me to my village. Anyhow, I don't have enough money to get back there. All I've got is my dollar. No, I've got to go to the mission house and ask the lady to believe me."

It was a long walk from Waterside to the mission house, on the beach in Sinkor, where people were just beginning to build modern, kwii houses, those white, grass-surrounded houses with too many windows. Koli started walking up the hill, but he was still so confused that one kwii boy laughed at him. "You want me to show you where to go, country boy?" Koli moved faster. He might even lose the dollar, if he let someone else in his life.

He passed a tailor shop, but stopped at the next door, and looked hungrily at the man eating rice and soup. He felt the dollar, but decided not to spend any money yet, and so walked up to Ashmun Street. There he saw the President's Mansion, with that frightening garden of fantastic stone animals next to it. Koli always shuddered when he saw them. "What do they all mean? Is there some kind of secret society behind the high fence? What do they do to people there?" He didn't want to think about it, and turned his eyes away, to look at the house itself.

"The President lives there. He'd help me if he only knew the trouble I'm in, just like the old president helped stop the quarrel between my real father Flumo and my step father Yakpalo. I don't remember too much about it, but they always tell me how the president was in Gbarnga, how he gave me to Yakpalo to help Flumo make up for shooting Yakpalo's son.

"They say this new president is trying to settle the big quarrel between the country people and the Americo-Liberians here on the coast. He wants us all to be one big family in Liberia, just like Flumo and Yakpalo are now members of one. family." The idea made Koli feel good inside, but then he remembered the kwii boy down on the Waterside who had laughed at him and called him "country boy."

"It'll take a long time, " thought Koli. "And I have to finish high school first, if I'm going to help my people be part of the family that matters in Liberia. Otherwise they'll just keep on laughing at us, and never give us what we need. No, that lady at the mission has to help me."

Koli walked down Broad Street, leaving the President's Mansion behind. He was about to turn up Center Street, when he saw a group of boys clustered around a signboard. It was a huge

5

picture, showing a strong white man fighting what looked to Koli like a leopard. There was a beautiful white girl standing nearby looking frightened, and a black man lying on the ground half dead. The sign over the poster said "Tarzan Fights Again." Under the sign it said "Ten Cents," and the other boys were talking about whether they would go to see the film.

Koli thought of going to see the film, and thought of himself as the black man. "I wouldn't be lying on the ground like that. I'd find a way to fight that leopard, and maybe I'd even take the white lady for my girl friend." But Koli realized he couldn't fight leopards or go to high school or do anything, if he didn't get to the mission house. He turned away, and walked up Center Street, past rows of shops.

"Who buys all these things?" Koli asked himself. But he knew the answer - it was successful kwii people who bought them. He saw a white lady, with a long skirt and a blouse covering her neck and arms, walk into a tailor shop and come out with a large bundle of clothes.

She saw that Koli was watching her, and told him, "Keep your eyes to yourself." She walked to the street, asking herself, "Why don't these country people work harder in order to get things for themselves instead of just hanging around Monrovia hoping for someone to give them things? If this were my country. . . ." Koli couldn't understand the rest as she got into a waiting car.

Koli wondered, "Maybe this really is her country. The white people are always running things - at the Salala school, in the shops, at Firestone, and even here in Monrovia. True, in my village black people like my fathers Flumo and Yakpalo are in charge. But what do they have? Just a few thatch houses in a small village. And even here in Monrovia all that the country people have are these ugly zinc-roofed houses, without the zinc even nailed on, just lying there held down by stones. And just look at all this trash and garbage lying around. When my uncle Saki came back from Firestone to visit our village last year, and threw paper on the ground, Yakpalo fined him one chicken for making the town look ugly. But here no one takes care of anything. If I get through high school, I'm going to find a way for us to live a better life, find a way for us to live the way these white people do."

6

Koli walked past the cemetery to the end of the road, where he saw the army training camp and the prison. He had heard stories of what happens to people who didn't do what the president wanted. The white man in Salala had told him how one country man had written something against the president in the newspaper, and then had been forced to clean prison toilets with his bare hands while being beaten with sticks the whole time.

Koli thought, "When we do something bad up-country, the chief at least knows how to treat us. I remember when Saki's little brother stole the chicken from Saki's enemy Tokpa, Yakpalo forced him to make five mats to give back to Tokpa. He couldn't make them all himself, and so Yakpalo sat with him and helped him. Things are sure different here."

Koli turned left past the army camp, and walked on the road toward Sinkor, where the mission house was located. He passed the place where they were beginning to build new government buildings. "What are they for?" asked Koli. "Don't they have enough already? Saki tells me that they just take money from country people and use it to build these big houses here in Monrovia, and they don't give us anything in return."

Next on his left Koli saw Liberia College. It was just a few old two-story buildings, but there the most powerful people in Liberia went to school, not the powerful white people, of course, but the Liberians who ran the government. "Maybe I'll go there instead of Hopewell College, after I finish high school - if indeed I get to high school."

Koli was looking at Liberia College and thinking, when a car almost knocked him down. It was big and black, and had a flag on it. He saw two fat men in it, who looked at him and laughed. One of them leaned out the window, after the car stopped, and shouted, "Go back to the bush, boy."

But the other quieted him, and motioned for Koli to come nearer. He wore a black suit, a tall round black hat and a black necktie. A chain and signboard hung around his neck.

"Boy, come here, I've got something for you," he called, telling the other man to be quiet.

Koli remembered those stone animals at the President's Mansion, remembered how the other boys said people like these

7

men might kill a country boy for medicine. So he ducked off the road into the bushes between him and Liberia College.

The men laughed and drove off.

He turned around and saw a young man watching him. Koli felt so small and stupid to have that man see him being afraid.

The man spoke, and he surprised Koli by speaking in Koli's own Kpelle language. "My name's Jonathan. My friend, what are you afraid of?"

Koli could only point to the black car, now far down the road.

"Why were you afraid of it?" Jonathan asked again, smiling in a friendly way. Koli didn't know how to answer. He knew he should be afraid of this stranger, but somehow his manner was different. He wanted to speak, to be comforted. He really thought all of the stories he had heard were stupid lies. But, just as the stone animals in the President's garden had frightened him, so did that black car and those two men in black suits. But he couldn't say all that yet to someone he didn't know, even though he felt inside he wanted to trust him. He could only answer, "I don't know. I was just afraid."

Jonathan smiled again and Koli felt better. "I understand. We're all afraid of those people. But don't worry. I'm Jonathan, and I can show you how not to be afraid. You see me, and I'm just a country boy like you. And here I am, a student at Liberia College. Do you want to be a student, too?"

Koli relaxed a little, and laughed also. "Not until I finish high school." He hadn't even started high school, and his letter was gone - but he couldn't say that to the student. "I've come to Monrovia to go to high school."

Jonathan said, "Good. You can do it, I'm sure. But maybe you want me to help you."

Koli was still afraid, but his fear was melting fast. Jonathan seemed different from all those people who laughed at him and stole from him. Koli hesitated a moment, and then said, "No, I'm all right."

Koli turned and walked away. The young man called after him, "If you change your mind, just come here and ask for Jonathan. Everyone knows me. I can help you go to school." He said it and laughed again.

8

Koli answered, "Thanks, Jonathan. If I need help, I'll come back. But I think I'm all right."

He looked to his left, and saw behind some trees beyond Liberia College the mat and thatch houses of the village where Bono, his mother's brother, lived.

"I'll spend the night there if I have to," he thought, but I know they can't help me." Bono had come to Monrovia to help build the port, and had stayed on, getting occasional jobs with construction companies. His wife Sua was selling rice in the market. Koli's mother Yanga sent her the rice to sell, and she would send the money back through Koli's uncle Saki, who worked at Firestone.

The houses thinned out as he walked along the road out of town. He saw another village and a few fine kwii houses under construction before he turned right where he remembered the mission house to be. He walked to the ocean toward the large grove of coconut palms, with the big mission office behind the trees. He wondered why they bothered to have palm trees, since they never seemed to pick the coconuts.

He walked to the door and knocked. A middle-aged white woman answered and listened with some difficulty as Koli told his story.

When he had finished, she answered, "I saw Vernon yesterday just before he was leaving to go back to the United States. He did tell me last year about a little boy he was helping, but he didn't say anything about his going to Muhlenburg. No, I'm sure Vernon would have sent a letter, or would have told me himself. What you say about losing the letter doesn't make much sense to me. Are you sure you didn't just wait until he was gone, and then come to me with some story you made up?"

Koli strained his ears and his brain to hear what the lady was saying, but she spoke too fast and in too difficult a way for him to understand much of it. He could only tell that she didn't believe his story. He tried again, "Please, he did give me a letter, but that boy stole it from me. If the white man was here, he'd explain everything."

"But he isn't here," she answered. "No, young man, all I can do for you is to give you his address, if you want to write him a letter."

Koli took the address, written on a sheet of mission paper, but in return Koli felt that he was giving back to the white lady whatever hope he once had. He was now sure he would never make it to Muhlenburg. He asked himself aloud, "What good would it do for me to write the man, now that he's gone?"

The lady seemed to understand how Koli felt, but didn't seem able to reach out to him. Koli was sure she had never been up-country, had never seen the real Liberia. Salala was probably just a story told her by the other missionaries. Koli could see how embarrassed she was just to talk with him.

She thought to herself, "Look at him, he hardly knows how to dress, and he has no belongings at all. The only thing I can do is to give him an air letter." She explained to Koli, "All you need to do is write your message on one side, the address on the other, and then mail it."

Koli looked confused, and the lady obviously realized that he had no idea about mailing a letter. "How can these people ever hope to enter the twentieth century?" she asked herself, but she put the thought out of her head. "It isn't right for me to think that way. I should help this boy. But how?"

Koli took the address, took the air letter, and left. She had been friendly, hadn't laughed at him or beaten him. But there had been a kind of wall around her. She was clean, white, kind - and totally out of touch with him.

He stopped outside the mission house, and could see that the lady was watching out the window to see what he would do. He thought for a moment, "Maybe there's some one working here at the mission house who speaks Kpelle, and who can help me talk to her."

He hesitated, started to turn back, and then realized, "What's the use? Anyone who works here would just agree with the lady, if only to keep his job. It's better to try something else.

"Let me think. I can't go back home yet. I haven't any money, and it would be too shameful to go back without something to show for the trip. My twin brother, Sumo, would just laugh at me, and my fathers, Flumo and Yakpalo, would say they told me so, and tell me to go work with the men who are starting to cut the bush for the new season. And Kuluba - I can't go back to her yet. I gave her to Sumo, and with her I gave up my son. If I had stayed at home, I could have married her, but that's over now.

"Maybe I should try to find that student - Jonathan was his name. He even spoke Kpelle to me. He says he can get me into school."

"But without money," Koli realized, "I can't even go to any school. First I have to get a job and start over again." Koli walked back toward town, no longer with the hope and vigor with which he had left his village two weeks earlier, nor even with the courage he had felt when he had left Salala that very morning. The long walk from Waterside to the mission house in the hot sun had tired him, and the clear impossibility of entering school this year had weakened him still further. He thought of all the possibilities - he could try to sell gum and cigarettes on Waterside, he could join boys like the one who had taken his bag and steal for a living, he could go to the port, where his uncle Bono had once worked, he could tap rubber at Firestone. Each possibility sounded worse than the last one.

"One thing is sure," Koli knew. "Only my family will help me." Koli went to the shabby mat house his mother's brother Bono had built behind Liberia College, to see what hope lay there.

But Bono couldn't help him. "Koli, you know I can't get regular work at the port or anywhere. You have to know someone to get a job. And who do you know? Only me, and I'm no one. The only thing that keeps us alive is the little money my wife, Sua, gets selling rice. Stay the night, and we'll feed you. But if you want work, go to Firestone. Maybe my brother Saki can help you. After all, he's also your uncle. You can read and write. Ask Saki to find you a job doing office work."

Koli's spirit lifted somewhat at that thought. "That might be the answer," he responded. "I'll try it."

Bono's wife, Sua, came back from the market with some fish she had bought from the Kru fisherman at the beach. made rice and soup for supper, and heated Koli bath water. He slept the night there, and felt better by morning. He left after a quick breakfast of fried cassava, glad he didn't have to live in such surroundings, dirty and crowded and ugly.

He went to Waterside, after spending ten cents and two hours

11

to find out more about Tarzan, the leopard and the white lady. At the bus stop, he thought for a moment he saw the boy who had stolen his bag, but realized he was wrong. He fought off the drivers and car boys who wanted him to go to Gbarnga, to Kakata, and down the coast to Bassa, and chose a battered small truck, with a frame built over the back, which was looking for one more passenger to go to Division 45 at the center of the Firestone plantation. Koli's uncle Saki lived about an hour's walk from there, in one of the workers' camps.

The price was seventy-five cents, and Koli took his place. The car boy now said they must find still another passenger. Koli couldn't see any space for another person, but the driver didn't want to lose his profit for the day. The last man to come was fat and drunk and carried a goat and a chicken. He stepped on Koli's feet, and almost put the goat on Koli's lap. But they managed to get him on board, and the bus started.

The truck edged its way out of the city, almost as if the driver didn't want anyone to see it. Through Sinkor it drove, and then on into Congo town. Koli was beginning to feel safer and easier now, when suddenly he heard a howling noise from down the road. The driver swung off the road and parked. Two policemen, riding on powerful motorcycles, roared past them, faster than Koli had thought possible. Behind them was a black car, much longer than the one he had seen yesterday, when the fat man had called to him. A flag flew from the car, and inside it sat the President and his wife. Koli recognized the President from the pictures.

"If only he knew about me, he would help me," Koli once again thought. But the car flashed by, and was gone. Now finally under way, the truck turned inland, as it passed through the sandy barren stretches of Paynesville, where scattered trees competed with the tired coastal soil, and old mansions on pillars alternated with coastal villages. The last signs of the ocean were left behind. Rubber trees, and still more rubber trees took their place.

As the truck left the main road to Gbarnga, and entered the Firestone plantation, Koli wondered when he would ever go home again. It was mid-afternoon. One or two tappers were cutting the thin slice of bark to make the latex bleed into their cups. But most were walking to the collecting stations, each carrying two buckets

12

balanced across their shoulders with a pole. Koli watched carefully as a white foreman at one station was weighing the latex, checking off the workers, and dismissing them. Koli shuddered, telling himself, "I hope I never have to tap rubber."

Just at that moment, as the truck slowed down to turn off at the market, a car which looked like the missionary's passed on its way to the airport road. A white man was in the car talking to a friend.

"That looks like the white man on his way to the plane. I thought he was leaving yesterday, but maybe he was delayed." Koli tried to lean out of the truck to call, but the fat man with the goat got in his way.

"I'm sure that was the man," Koli felt, even though he couldn't see him clearly. But then the car picked up speed, and was on its way - gone.

The truck stopped at the market, which was closing for the day. People were folding up the cloths they had spread out, piling together the cooking pots, pouring the unsold rice back into large bags, trying to sell the last few pieces of bread, eating oranges to relieve the thirst of a long day, pushing trash aside without picking it up.

A white woman, with two crying children, came out of the big store where the white people bought their food, and walked to the market just as Koli was getting out of the truck. She bought more oranges than she could possibly need, and motioned for Koli to carry them for her. She pointed to her car, a small yellow station wagon.

Koli thought to himself, "Her children could carry her oranges. Why don't they? All they want is for their mother to give them candy." Koli didn't know the woman, but he carried her oranges just the same. She reached the car, took the oranges, pushed her children into the back seat with the food she had bought, gave Koli one cent, and drove away.

It all happened so fast that Koli didn't have a chance to think about it until the lady was gone. It was obvious to the lady that Koli would want to work for her. Moreover, Koli had done it. "What kind of world is Firestone? Do the white people own everything?"

Koli turned away, and saw that the fat man was looking at him and laughing, laughing so hard he could hardly stand up. Koli felt the blood rising in his face. This man had pushed a goat on his lap, had kept him from calling to the white man, and had laughed at him. But Koli turned away. He had too far to go before dark to get into a fight now. And he was too tired.

He walked east, away from the low sun that cast such long shadows from the rubber factory and from the beautiful houses where the white people live. He crossed the green, carefully cut fields which led up to the river and the swamp. Beyond the swamp were rubber trees, more rubber trees, where the shadows had consolidated into an early night. Koli quickened his step, so that he could find his uncle before nightfall. He knew the way, but wasn't sure he could find it without light.

There was no moon, and so it was almost completely dark when Koli arrived at the workers' camp. His uncle lived in the third house in the fourth line. "What a curious way to arrange houses," Koli thought. "It makes no sense to have all these lines and rows, just like boxes in a store. How can people know who are their friends and family when they live like this? Why can't people who are related or friends live right next to each other?"

But Koli found the house easily enough. He slipped into the habits he had learned at Salala, feeling as if he were doing the multiplication table again. His uncle Saki was, fortunately, at his house. He saw Koli and made him sit down.

"What are you doing here?" Saki asked. He seemed to want to say more, but stopped, waiting for Koli to speak. Koli didn't know how to answer, didn't know how to say all that had happened to him since yesterday morning in Salala. Yakpalo or Flumo could have helped him pour out his story, but not Saki. It seemed so terribly long ago that the white man had given him the letter, the dollar, and God's blessings on his future at Muhlenburg. The truck ride to Monrovia, the stealing, the long walk, the disappointment at the Mission, the return to the bus stop, the ride to Firestone, the man with the goat, the lady with the oranges - the two days had been too much for him.

Koli wanted to tell his uncle what had happened, but no words would come. His eyes filled with tears at his realization that

14

the whole dream had been empty. He could say nothing. Saki, too, could find nothing to say, but fortunately he seemed to understand. He, too, once had had his dreams. He, too, had been unable to cope with a harsh world. And he understood.

II: THEY ARE ALSO IN THE HUT

Saki took Koli to get a job. He introduced him to the same white man Koli had seen yesterday evening checking the tappers as they brought in the latex for weighing. "What can you do?" the man asked Koli.

Koli thought fast. "I can read and write, and can check how much the tappers bring in to the collecting station. I saw you yesterday from the truck, and I am sure I can do the same thing."

The man smiled, "It'll be a relief to get off that job. I had a country boy doing the job before, but he took his pay at the end of December and didn't come back. It's now half way through January and I'm tired. I want another boy to help me. The job is yours, if you're honest and careful. But one mistake, and you're out."

Koli promised, "I'll try to do it right, if only you show me exactly what to do." The man promised to pay him seventy-five cents a day, which was more than his uncle Saki had ever made. It sounded like a fortune to Koli - but money, glad as he was to have it, was not school.

The job was easy, but Koli had to be careful. Every day he started at the main warehouse and collecting station in his division, and made a list of all the men who reported for work that day. He made sure each one had a knife for making the new cut on the trees that were to be tapped, collecting cups to attach to the trees if any were missing, buckets to carry the latex he collected from the cups, and the pole for carrying the buckets.

When the men were out tapping the trees or collecting the latex, he had to enter the names in the book for the division, and then record for the day before how much each man had brought. He knew that he had to be accurate, since the total weight for all the men on his list had to be the same as the total which his division sent to headquarters. The job took him all day, especially at first, when he still was unable to do it the way the white man wanted.

For the first two weeks, the white man was with him much of the time, to make sure the work was being done properly. The white man always checked to make sure he recorded the right

16

weight beside each tapper's name. But after a while the man relaxed and let Koli do it alone. The tappers must have been watching for that, because, early in February, Sulongteh, a Kpelle man from his mother's village, came to Koli and asked him to change the weights recorded in the book.

"I need more money, because I want to buy a cane mill. If you change the numbers so I get more latex against my name, I'll give you half of what I earn. Besides we are both Jorkwelle Kpelle men, and I know your fathers and mothers. I even remember when you first tried to run away to school."

Koli said, "The white man always checks the books against the total weight."

Sulongteh answered, "That part is easy. Just take a little off the weight of each of those Bassa men. No one will ever know about it."

Koli tried to argue, but the tapper pushed him hard. "If you don't do it, I'll get you. I'll complain that you're stealing latex and selling it in Kakata on Sundays. I can always fix it so that some is found in Saki's house"

Koli agreed, but he was afraid he might get caught. He had to find a way to get away with cheating the Bassa tappers. He knew he couldn't do it to his own countrymen. The trouble was that the tappers would watch the scales as they weighed the latex, and so Koli had to change the records the next day in the warehouse.

He thought, "I can do it. I'll try to write down a light weight for one man and a heavy weight for Sulongteh when they bring the latex. But if anyone is watching I'll have to do it at noon the next day."

He soon found the men he would be able to cheat. There were four Bassa men in the team, and he could take a bit from each on successive nights, and give it all to Sulongteh. This way Sulongteh would build up a good reputation, and get a bonus for doing good work.

Only once did Koli come near getting caught. He was rubbing out two entries for the previous night's latex, when the white man happened to see him at it. "Oh, I made a mistake last night and I'm fixing it."

The white man looked at him strangely, and began to check

over his work. He saw other places, on previous days, where the record was corrected - almost always with the same men. "What's wrong? Don't you know these people?"

"Yes, I mean, no. I get these two mixed up sometimes."

"Be careful, now. I'll have to check your work more closely. Besides, isn't this one the man who got the bonus last month for the highest total? Are you sure he earned it, and it wasn't your mistake?"

Koli denied knowing about any bonus and added, "Sulongteh is always coming to the collecting station with the fullest buckets of anyone. You should come and see for yourself."

Koli went to Sulongteh that night and warned him that he had to get fuller buckets than anyone else for the next several days without any help from Koli. The white man would be checking. The next night the white man was indeed on hand as the tappers came in. Fortunately for Koli his countryman had the fullest bucket, and likewise for the next few nights.

"I guess he earned it," admitted the white man. Koli breathed easily again - but didn't go back to cheating until another week had passed. After that, he did his erasures very carefully so that no one could tell.

It was now March, and Koli had been paid twice. He was eating Saki's food, and sleeping in Saki's house, and thus was able to save almost all the money he earned. It was time to visit home, and time also to go back to Salala and see if the new teachers would help him go to high school. Koli waited until the last day of March, took his third pay, and then told to white man he would be away for two weeks.

"Why didn't you tell me earlier, if you knew you were going home? I could have made plans for a substitute."

Koli hadn't thought of that, but knew he had to go. He thought fast, and then said, "I just got a message that my mother is very sick. Please excuse me this time."

The white man turned away, saying to himself. "These people have more mothers than my cat has kittens - and they're always sick. I don't believe it, but what can I do?"

Koli went to the Firestone market the next day, and bought carefully. He found a headtie for his mother, Yanga, a pack of shotgun shells for his foster-father, Yakpalo, and a kwii pipe for his real father, Flumo. He found a small shirt and trousers for his son. He thought a long time about Kuluba, and then decided not to take her anything. But he took for his twin brother, Sumo, a length of iron spring he had found in the wreck of a car by the side of the road. He knew his brother was already doing blacksmith work, and could use the iron to make hoes and knives and cutlasses for townspeople.

Koli then found a bus going to Kakata. He packed his few belongings together very carefully, and vowed not to let anyone touch them on the bus. He had learned to trust no one. In Kakata he got down from the bus, took the iron off the roof, and waited for a truck to go up to Salala. A gas station had just opened in Kakata, so that cars and trucks could fill up before heading up-country, and not have to rely on what they had brought from Monrovia.

The trip back to Salala was easy enough, but Koli became more and more nervous. He still had hope that someone at his school would help him go on to high school, even though he realized that only the one white man had taken real interest in him. The other teachers had thought him too much of a country boy. The other white missionaries had their own favorites, and the two Liberian teachers paid attention only to the sons of big-shots.

His reception was as he had expected. School had finished for the day, and some boys were on the ballfield in front of the classroom building playing soccer. They stopped when they saw Koli walk up, and crowded around him to ask about Muhlenburg. There was nothing Koli could say. He thought for a moment of lying, of saying that school was fine. But he knew the truth would get out soon enough, and he would then appear even more foolish than if he told the facts now.

He told the boys, "I've decided not to go on to school just yet. I'm working at Firestone, as a clerk, just to earn some money before going back to my studies." ("A clerk," he thought, "I'll have to know a lot more before I can be a clerk.") He continued, "I just wanted to stop to see my old school before going home to bring presents to my family." This retort at least stopped the laughter, although he could see from their eyes that some of this year's sixth graders didn't quite believe him.

The boys quickly told him the news. The white man who had helped him had gone to America, and the word was that he would stay there for three years, some said five. There was a new white man in charge, and most of the teachers also were new. Only the old pastor who was trying to translate the Bible into Kpelle, and one of the Liberian teachers, the one who always gave high grades to the paramount chief's children, were left from last year.

"A lot of good they will do me," thought Koli.

But it was worth a try. Koli went to the white man's house, where the new principal lived. The man was playing with his children behind the house, two little boys, thin and sickly looking. Whenever he saw boys like those, Koli could understand why people at his home thought that whites were devils. They didn't quite look real, with their fancy clothes, their thin legs and arms, and their leprous-looking skin. The mother kept trying to protect them from the sun, which Koli couldn't understand.

"Who are you?" the man called when he saw Koli coming around the house. "If you're selling something, we don't want it."

Koli tried to answer, but the man called again, "If you want to see me, why didn't you come during school hours? Can't you see I'm busy with my family now?" He turned to wife. "They always come when I'm tired and the kids are sick. Why don't these people let us alone?" he complained.

Koli was confused by the reception and tried to speak But the man had already turned away to warn his children to stay in the shade. Koli started: "But, sir. . . ."

The man cut him off. "Are you still here? Please come in the morning. I'll be in my office."

Confusion turned to anger. Koli wished to himself that the missionaries had let the Kpelle people alone in the first place. "Maybe Sumo is right. Why do they have to make their lying promises, and then abuse the people they make the promises to? Why don't they stay in their own country if they're going to act this way, instead of coming here and hurting the people who own the land? White people are all alike."

But Koli could find no one to tell how he felt. He turned in his confusion and anger and left. He went to town, to the house where the relatives lived who had housed him so many years ago when he had first arrived in Salala. They at least would receive him as one of the family.

His people, too, asked him questions. He couldn't lie quite so freely before them, because he knew that Saki would come this way soon and tell them the whole story. So he had to admit that he had lost his bag and the all-important letter in Monrovia, and so had not been able to go to school at Muhlenburg. He told of his new job, and of his desire still to go to school.

The head of the house, Flumo's brother, told Koli, "Forget school and settle down. You can find a good wife back home."

But Koli wouldn't give up so easily. He thought, "This kind of talk from illiterate people always makes me want to go the other way." But he kept quiet that evening. After all, he realized he had very little yet to show for all his schooling. The next day Koli went back to the Salala school. He saw the new white man teaching, and had to wait two hours before he came out of the classroom. Fortunately the man didn't seem to realize that Koli had been at his house the night before. In the school office, he seemed to be all business, all friendliness.

Koli thought to himself that the man was either a liar or selfish, to change himself so completely from home to school. Maybe the thought moved into Koli's voice, because somehow the conversation did not move easily. He explained to the white man that he had been a student last year, had in fact been seven years at the school, and had graduated from the sixth grade.

The principal was polite, but clearly was not interested. He had not put anything of himself into Koli's education. He explained to Koli he was busy trying to reorganize the school. "The former principal spent too much time running off into the bush and hardly kept up the school. The buildings are falling down, the students don't know anything about discipline, and all the old teachers, well almost all, have left. I'm sorry, but I really don't have the time to do much for you."

Koli realized that he was just another reminder to this man of what had to be changed. He tried again, but the man merely let Koli talk himself out, about how he had lost the letter, about how the other white man had promised he could go to Muhlenburg, about the white man's trip to Koli's village.

Finally the man said, politely but plainly wanting to get rid of Koli, "The only thing you can do is to write him. Here, I'll give you his address."

Koli had heard that before. He hadn't done it, not only because he didn't understand the business of mailing letters, but because he had somehow hoped he would get help from the school. But now even that hope was dead. He took the address, not saying that he knew it already. Koli guessed, "I might as well write the man. It probably won't do any good, but I'll try."

The principal sat there, waiting for Koli to go. Koli asked again if there wasn't anything the school could do for him. "I was here for seven years. . . ."

The man nodded as if he understood, but said, "The school now has to do something for the next group of children. It educated you and now you must make your own way in the larger world."

The only answer Koli could think was so bitter it would have earned him a good beating from Yakpalo. Koli knew the principal's kind of talk, and knew it meant nothing at all. When they sacked someone at Firestone, they talked that way to him. Koli could only force himself to say, "Thank you," turn around, and go. Now he was completely on his own. He would have to go home to his village and explain everything. And that would be hard.

Inevitably, the visit home was a disappointment to everyone. Even Koli was disappointed, but in a curious way. His failure to enter Muhlenburg was greeted with general relief, and now everyone assumed he would stay at home and live a sensible life. Koli had expected, even hoped, that his family and friends would be sorry for him, even though he had feared at the same time that they would laugh at him for losing his chance. On the contrary - they took it as a matter of course. All the tears and pleadings of his departure only three months before had been forgotten, now that Koli was home.

Koli's father, Flumo, even went so far as to make tentative arrangements with a friend in Yanga's village for a girl to marry Koli. The girl had come out of bush school with Koli's sisters, and for many reasons seemed to be the right person to marry him. Flumo had been sure nothing would come out of the white man's promises, and this time Flumo had been proved right. He had rehearsed the scene often before Koli's return, and so it was no surprise to him when Koli came walking from the forest with presents for all.

Koli's foster-father, Yakpalo, had shown a bit more surprise, since as the town chief he had half hoped for Koli to be his people's link with the kwii world which was pressing on them more every day. Koli's mother, Yanga, had been simply relieved, glad to have her boy back. His twin brother, Sumo, was glad, both that Koli had been away long enough for Kuluba to forget him, and that Koli was back to take the place assigned to the two of them in the cooperative work group. Sumo had found it difficult to work at the blacksmith shop and collect the medicines he needed as an ambitious medicine man and zoe, as his people now called him, and at the same time to take his share of cutting the forest for the new farming season.

When Koli had been home only a short time, he saw how difficult it would be to leave. He relieved Sumo five days in the work group. It was the least he could do. He was assigned to the young men's group, and was given the nastiest jobs. It was true that he could not cut a small tree with one quick blow of the cutlass. It was also true that he got tired more quickly than the other men, since he had spent the last seven years in school. Thus, he was put under Tokpa in the cooperative work group. Tokpa was Yakpalo's nephew who had fought with Saki some years before and who still nursed a grudge for having been forced to apologize and humiliate himself in public. Tokpa was now expected to become the next head of all the men's cooperative work, and at this time had already been made leader of the young men in his group, the first step up.

Tokpa had no love at all for Koli. Ever since his fight with Saki, he had been down on all of Flumo's family. He had looked for ways to cause trouble for them. For instance, had enticed Flumo's wife, Yanga, had enjoyed several nights with her, not only for the pleasure of a woman not his own, but also because he knew it would hurt Flumo. He didn't bother Sumo, because Sumo was proving his vocation as a zoe and medicine man by acquiring more powerful medicines every year.

Tokpa knew he was himself a member of the water society. He had been told this by his dreams. He had gone under the river at night, in his dreams while he slept, and there he had learned to control the rain. His power had cost him his three children, who had died of fever and worms. He worried that Koli and Sumo might also be his children since he had slept with their mother during the year before they had been born. But he was not yet sufficiently certain of his own power to challenge Sumo.

So, when Koli came back to the village, Tokpa saw a chance to make more trouble and get the satisfaction of revenge. He knew Sumo would not interfere if Tokpa gave Koli a hard time in the work group. Flumo was no longer of any real importance in the village, especially since he had shot and wounded Yakpalo's son in the forest. Moreover, Yakpalo would not interfere because he liked to see Tokpa keeping discipline tight among the young men of the village.

So it was always Koli who was told to cut down the wasp nest in the bush and who was thus covered with stings on his head, arms and legs. It was always Koli who was placed where the knifelike saw-grass was thickest. It was always Koli who had the smallest piece of meat from the pot, or perhaps no meat at all, when the men stopped at mid-morning to eat. It was always Koli who was fined for talking or singing when the men made the hard drive in mid-afternoon to finish cutting the bush. It was always Koli who was asked to buy more cane juice for the group when the supply ran short, just because he had come home with ready cash.

Five times out in the bush in eight days was too much for Koli. He felt that it was only because he was visiting home that the work group went out so often. Tokpa had persuaded the head of the men's work group to call out the group because he said the rains would come soon. The leader increasingly relied on Tokpa, because he himself was getting old and knew he would have to give up the job. He could still do a full day's work, but often that work consisted of marking out the parts of the forest to be cut rather than actually cutting it himself. Tokpa carried the bulk of the work, and received the bulk of the respect and admiration.

24

Koli resented it most when the women of the village sang and clapped as Tokpa showed off his skill at cutting the forest. When the women arrived to give water to the sweating workmen, Tokpa would push the others aside for a moment. The drummer would see what was coming, and would leave the other men to play with doubled intensity near Tokpa. Tokpa would flash his straw leggings in the air, sound the bells that hung from his waist, look to each side with unfocused blank eyes, and then suddenly, as from nowhere, slice a good-sized tree down with one blow.

Koli had to admit that he did it well, that he had earned his right to wear the leggings and the bells, but he resented it all the same. It was even worse when Koli had been leaning against a young tree, and Tokpa, as was his right to do to anyone caught leaning against a tree, cut it out from under Koli, almost cutting his arm in the process. It would not have been so bad if he had done it privately, but all the men and girls were watching, and laughing.

Koli knew he would have to tell Saki all these happenings. Saki remembered Tokpa and their fights all too well. He didn't trust Tokpa at all, and would just as soon have seen him die as live. Saki was aware that Tokpa in his dreams belonged to the water people, and he hoped he might one day have an accident at the river.

Sumo had used Koli's arrival to get out of the work group and devote his full time to working iron, making tools, and learning medicines. Indeed, the happiest person at Koli's arrival had been Sumo, to whom Koli had brought the car spring from Firestone. It had given Sumo an independent source of iron, and soon he was getting orders for cutlasses and hoes. But Sumo had not been grateful enough to Koli for taking his place in the work group, Koli thought resentfully.

Yet Koli realized that Sumo had all the power of the two of them, the special power of a twin which Koli had rejected when he had gone off to school. If he did favors for Sumo, then Sumo would help him in return. And if he did not help Sumo, then he must fear for his own safety. Koli thought to himself, "These medicine people can be more dangerous to their own family than to outsiders."

In fact, Sumo's medicine was most impressive. He was practicing what old Mulbah, the head zoe of the town, could do. He was learning to put his hand in a pot of boiling palm oil. Mulbah would set up his pot on a fire in the center of the village, heat it to boiling, put his hand in another pot which contained water and leaves, and then plunge his hand up to the wrist in the palm oil. He would then challenge the other men in the village to do the same. No one dared to accept the challenge, even though all could see plainly that Mulbah's hand was in no way harmed. No one dared, that is, until, during Koli's visit, Sumo told Mulbah quietly that he would like to try.

If it had been any other person, Mulbah would have let him burn himself if he liked. But Mulbah himself had already shown Sumo medicines, and in fact had been the one to recognize Sumo's powers in the first place. So Mulbah called Sumo aside and told him not to try the trick at that point. It was better to learn it in secret, and then show people later. Later in Koli's visit, Sumo had performed the trick in public for the first time, and the people in the village had been most impressed. Koli realized all the more that he must be careful with his brother.

Koli wanted to be on good terms with Sumo, and so promised that he would bring him more iron. It would be easy to get enough iron around Firestone, because there were so many wrecked cars and trucks. As the roads improved and increased, and as more cars came into Liberia, there were more accidents.

Koli was sorry to see that his father's elder wife, Toang, was getting old now, and increasingly sour. Her only living child, Lorpu, had been divorced from her husband, another nephew of Yakpalo, and Lorpu had gone off to sell rice and cassava in the Gbarnga market. Toang resented this disappointment. "Toang's attitude won't help our relations with Tokpa," Koli realized.

Toang had hoped her grandchildren would grow up in the village, but Lorpu had taken her two children with her to Gbarnga. Her husband was trying to sue to get the children back again to the village, but so far without success. People said that Lorpu was sleeping with the chief in Gbarnga, and that he had prevented the children from being returned to their father, as they should be. Tokpa was threatening that, if the children did not come back, he would make sure that Kuluba's child would find himself in trouble one day. Koli feared this, but felt that Sumo's medicines were enough to protect the boy, his natural son.

Koli's own mother, Yanga, Flumo's younger wife, continued to be strong, and still looked young, another reason for her older co-wife, Toang, to be angry. Toang had once tried to kill the twins by witchcraft when they were young, as everyone knew. People still feared Toang, but Sumo's power was enough now to keep her away. Sumo was still young, but old Toang knew she could not hurt him, although she could try to turn Sumo against his twin, Koli. And there were still times when she tried to revenge herself on Yanga. She had helped Tokpa succeed, even recently, in his night-time affairs with Yanga, in order to keep the anger alive between Flumo and Yanga. She promised Tokpa to give love medicines to Yanga whenever he wanted her. Tokpa knew he could count on Toang for help.

Yet Tokpa was an important man, admired and feared by most of the people in town. It was he who made the medicine to drive away rain when they burned the forest. It was he who brought home the biggest load of fish from the big river to the east. It was he who could cut down a tree with one blow of his cutlass. However, all his own children had died, and he could never again have living children. It was the price he had to pay for being a water person and for driving away the rain. Thus, Koli and Sumo were sure Tokpa had helped kill their sister's child.

All these things made Koli glad finally to get away from home and return to Firestone. He went directly to Saki, who questioned him closely about how he had managed to get away from the village without making enemies.

"It wasn't easy," admitted Koli. "I had to make a lot of promises, especially that I would not go to school anymore, and that I would come back in time for the harvest and the next bush-cutting season. I had to tell my father that I'm not yet ready to marry. I had to say that I was no different from any villager going to Firestone. And in order to make Sumo happy, I had to promise him not only more iron but also contacts with Bassa medicine men. But the worst problem was Tokpa, who is doing everything he can to hurt our family."

Saki was ready for revenge on Tokpa himself. Saki told Koli that during his absence he had had quiet conversations with Mogo, a Bassa water man, to find out how he could have Tokpa drowned. Saki was all the more determined to finish off Tokpa, once he heard how he was reviving the old quarrel in his actions against Koli. "The Bassa water man works as a tapper in our division," said Saki, "and is perhaps my only Bassa friend."

The only problem Saki raised was that recently Mogo had been given a hard time by the white head of the division for not bringing in enough latex. "Mogo swears that he brings as much as anyone else, but his recorded weight is always low. This has kept Mogo from concentrating his full attention on the problem of making water medicine for me to kill Tokpa. Only in the last two weeks, the time you've been home, has his weight come back up to standard."

Koli realised, of course, that Saki's medicine man was the same Bassa man he was cheating to help Sulongteh. However, he decided to let Saki's comment pass and keep quiet about it for now.

Saki was determined to take advantage of his friendship with Mogo, and told Koli of his plans for the two of them to work with Mogo, so that Mogo could help Sumo with his medicine also. Saki insisted, "You have to agree to help Mogo some way. Perhaps, since you weigh the latex when it is brought in, you can put extra weight on top of Mogo's latex, to give him a break."

Koli realized from this that his deal with Sulongteh was still a secret, but that didn't help him much now. He had to find a way to satisfy Saki as well as Sulongteh, and Mogo was the man in the middle.

Saki asked also about his wife, who had deserted him three years previously. She had stayed with Flumo that terrible year when there had not been enough rice, and the twins were just beginning to eat real food. But Saki had come home too little. Life had become too difficult, and thus she had gone to Gbarnga to sell produce in the market. She had been the one to welcome Koli's older sister, Lorpu, there, when she had been divorced. However, Saki did not mind too much, since his wife at Firestone had remained faithful to him and had borne him four children, two of

28

whom were alive and growing well.

Saki had not been back home for almost a year now, and was glad to get the news from Koli. The village was still his home, even though he rarely went there. He no longer served as town drummer, since he was there too infrequently. But he knew that he could not live at Firestone forever, and that he would go back eventually. He did not know what his children or wife at Firestone would do - that was their problem. But for him, he had to keep up with the news at home.

Koli was himself glad to be back at Firestone. Even without the humiliations brought on him by Tokpa, he felt he had no real future in the village. His son, Ziepolo, was now sitting up, but was as frightened of Koli as he would be of any stranger. It made Koli feel even more remote from the village. He would earn money at Firestone, take some of it home to his father and mother, make contacts for Sumo, and eventually he would save enough to go on to high school. He was still angry at the matter-of-fact reception of the news that he had not been able to go to Muhlenburg. He was now all the more determined to go on to school, even if not there. He would earn some money for now, and by next year he would try again.

Saki encouraged him in his determination, because he saw that Koli already was making more money than himself. Saki planned to use that money as soon as Koli accumulated some savings. Indeed, he smiled quietly to himself when Koli talked about saving money for school. He knew better than Koli when it came to handling of money, but he didn't want to spoil the dreams which impelled Koli to work hard. Soon enough Koli would have to give up the dream, and then Saki would help him use the money in ways more useful to Saki himself.

III: THE HEAVY LAW

"I know she's a Bassa girl, but that doesn't matter. I like her, and she's pretty. Besides, she knows how to type, and she's teaching me so I can get a job in Monrovia and go to high school at night." Saki didn't at all like the idea of Koli seeing this girl, Eva Brown. He knew that Brown wasn't her real name, and he was sure both her mother and father were Bassa. She worked in the warehouse as a typist and clerk, and Koli saw her every day when he filled in his records.

They had just been friendly at first, but now, in the heavy daily rains of September, so much heavier than Koli ever remembered up-country, their friendship had developed fast. Sometimes, over the noon hour, when the white man had driven home to eat his dinner, and there was no one else in the hot, rank warehouse, Koli and Eva would substitute something else for food on an old mattress at the back of the stockroom.

Once they had almost been caught, when the white man came back early from dinner. They had dressed quickly and come out to the office, breathless and a bit confused, just as he was calling for the third time, "Koli, damn it, where are you, Koli?" He looked at them, laughed, and then went on to the business. He had to take Koli with him early that day, because the rain had blocked some of the roads, and they must go by foot to the collecting stations.

One hot afternoon, Eva asked to see the records for rubber-collection. She pointed to a Bassa name on the list, and asked, "Why does Mogo always have such a low weight for the day."

It was the same Mogo that Koli had come to rely on when giving extra weight to Sulongteh, his countryman who had forced Koli to alter the weights. Koli knew now how he could have gotten around Sulongteh's request, but he was now too deeply involved to back out. Besides, he had come to count on an extra dollar now and then when he needed it.

But now came Eva's request, and it confused things for Koli. She said, "Mogo is my uncle, and is about to be sacked for low production. Besides, don't you know that Mogo is a powerful medicine man? It would be bad for you if anything happened to him."

31

Koli felt himself pressed hard. Mogo was the only Bassa man in his group now, and the others were all Kpelle. One had left early in the year to go home. Koli had cut down the reported production for two other Bassa men, but they had been dismissed in July because they brought too little latex every day.

The other Kpelle men in the division, including Saki, had figured out by this time what Sulongteh and Koli were doing, and so Koli couldn't change his tactics and cheat them. Mogo was himself too tied up in his medicines to notice the light weights. It seemed to Koli that Mogo was almost crazy sometimes because of the medicine business. Last year, he had been to Gibi mountain, just east of Firestone, to learn the really strong Bassa medicines, and it had affected his mind. It was easy to cheat him, because he never looked at the weights Koli recorded. However, his powers were now more than before feared by the other men.

Eva pressed the case. "Surely you could alter the figures a bit, just to help me. If you don't, I might not be there some noon when you want me. I might even report to the white man that you pay more attention to me than to your work, and this would get you into trouble."

As if to show her point, she turned away when Koli tried to hold her, tried to tell her not to get involved in business that was not hers. "Of course, it's my business. He's my uncle, and you - well, at least you say you love me. Now prove it."

Koli said, "I'll have to think about it. I'll tell you."

Her response was, "Maybe tomorrow I'll tell you some other things, if you don't say the right thing."

Koli was relieved that the white man came in at that point, because he could get out of what was fast becoming too hot an argument.

That night Koli discussed the matter with Saki. Saki repeated his dislike and distrust of the girl. "I'm sure she has other boyfriends here and back in Bassa country. She's already been pregnant once, so the other men say, and spoiled her pregnancy by going to Mogo for medicine. This is why Mogo is pressing her to help him keep the job. If she doesn't help him, he'll tell about what she did to her baby. But Mogo doesn't understand about weighing latex, and so he's put the whole problem on her to solve. I know

32

this from the other men in the division."

But Koli was determined. He didn't care if the girl had had an abortion. Those noontime meetings were too sweet to lose. So finally Saki told Koli, "The only way is to get Sumo down to Firestone, and work a deal both with Mogo and with Sulongteh. Perhaps Sulongteh will be satisfied if Sumo makes him medicine to get this cane juice mill more easily. I'm sure Sumo knows such medicines."

Koli was more doubtful. "What do sugar cane mills have to do with forest spirits and leaves?" he thought to himself. But it was worth a try.

Koli went to Sulongteh that night and put the problem another way. He didn't mention anything about Eva, but said, "The white man has found out what I'm doing, and is waiting for me to do it one more time so he can sack me."

Sulongteh started to threaten Koli, "You'd better find another way to alter the records." But Koli's answer was, "My brother Sumo is coming soon, and can perhaps make medicine to help you get the money you need in a way that won't hurt either of us."

Sulongteh knew of Sumo's reputation as a twin zoe, and was willing to see what he could do. He had heard just last month that Sumo had chased away the tax collector from his village by making him see a genii at night, that terrible, tall, faceless white thing that can make a man speechless. The tax collector had come to the village in the afternoon, had gone out just after dark to relieve himself in the forest, and had come running back in terror. The only thing he could say was "Sumo, Sumo." The next morning he had left as fast as he had come, taking with him only a small part of the money he had been sent to collect. Sumo had himself not said anything, but he had been seen going into the same area of the forest shortly before dark, armed with medicines, and had come out later, obviously pleased with himself.

Sumo's growing reputation persuaded Sulongteh it was worth a try to have Sumo make him medicine. But he insisted to Koli that Sumo must not charge him. Koli refused, saying that no medicine can ever be given for nothing. Sulongteh realized it was true, but said Sumo must make the price small. Sumo himself had won some of his medicines by paying just a white kola nut for them. Surely he could keep the price down for Sulongteh.

It remained now for Koli to persuade Sumo to come to Firestone, to come to the kwii world which he scarcely knew. Sumo had been on the motor road, had seen the school at Salala, but had never gone further. Koli realized that the only bait to bring him here would be the promise that he might learn about Bassa medicine. The Kpelle always borrowed or bought their strongest medicines from others. The masked figures that danced in the village on important occasions were always from other groups.

As a result, when Koli sent a message by way of his sister, Lorpu, in Gbamga, Sumo agreed to come to Firestone when he had finished making knives for the rice harvest. Koli had found a taxi driver to take the message to Lorpu when next he went to Gbarnga. And Lorpu found a friend who was going back to Koli's village. The message came back in the same way, that Sumo would arrive in about two months.

Sulongteh was not happy with the delay, but now that he was involved with Sumo, he didn't want to go back on his word. "Sumo might do me some harm instead of good if I back out now," he thought. "Once you start with the zoe business, you can't stop. I'll have to be content without my bonus for extra latex for the next few months. But with a little luck I'll get even more money later, when the medicine begins to work."

Sulongteh gave his agreement to Koli the night the message returned from Sumo. For the week it took the message to go to the village and come back, Eva had pestered Koli every day. Koli had merely said, "I'm working on it. I'm trying."

She hadn't been satisfied, but Koli couldn't change his short-weighting scheme until he had some word from Sumo. Fortunately it was still early in October, the month in which the white man threatened to sack Mogo if he didn't increase his production. Koli knew that nothing would happen to the white man for sacking Mogo, since no medicine can hurt a white man. But he feared for himself.

So Koli was greatly relieved when he could tell Eva that he would increase the daily weight for Mogo. He didn't tell her that he was only giving Mogo his proper weight for the first time in nine months. Perhaps she knew that anyhow. Koli had an idea that Eva was sleeping with Sulongteh these days, and she might have found out about Koli's scheme. But she would never tell Koli that she knew, even if she did.

Koli realized, "It is more effective to keep these things a secret. If you tell a person everything you know, then there is no reason for him to depend on you or even to respect you."

Yet it was a risk that Koli was taking, and he knew it. Sumo had to come to Firestone, he had to promise Sulongteh magic for tomorrow and make it seem more attractive than cash in the hand today, and he had to be satisfied with his dealings with Mogo.

He had mixed feelings when Sumo did in fact arrive, because he was not all that confident in his brother's abilities. However, other people seemed to feel Sumo was a real zoe, even though young, and that reassured Koli.

The night Sumo arrived, Sulongteh came over to Saki's house after dark. Koli had tried to persuade him to wait so Sumo would have a chance to negotiate with Mogo, but Sulongteh was determined to get his cane mill.

Sulongteh offered Sumo ten dollars for the medicine, and Sumo almost laughed. "I'm supposed to help you get a mill which costs three hundred dollars, and you offer me ten dollars. Money itself doesn't mean that much to zoes. What will you put on top of it'?" In the end, Sulongteh agreed to add two Firestone lappa cloths and an iron pot for Sumo to take home.

The only difficulty was that Sumo could not find the right leaves in the barren Firestone rubber forests. He had to go back to Kakata, and walk deep into the Bong Mountains between Kakata and the St. Paul River. The forests of the Bong range were well known to be the home of spirits winch would kill anyone not strong enough to stand up to them. But Sumo came back safely, with the leaves he wanted. Sulongteh was impressed that Sumo had gone to the mountain forests, instead of buying what he wanted in the Kakata market. The only thing that worried Sulongteh was Sumo's demand that he should not have any dealing with girls until the medicine began to take effect. Maybe Koli had persuaded Sumo to say this so he could keep Eva to himself.

But Sumo insisted. He said, "The spirit will be jealous, will kill either you or the girl, and certainly will kill any child that might be born."

The meeting between Sumo and Mogo was more difficult. Mogo belonged to the Bassa water society, not just a dream society, but the real thing where men learned to go under water to kill their enemies. He wanted Sumo to join as well. But Sumo had avoided the water people in his own village, primarily because Tokpa was so deeply involved in his dreams in the water business, and also because Mulbah had warned him against it.

Even the stories Mogo told about his own powers frightened Sumo. Only last year, a young man from Firestone had gone to the river to fish. He had called to his friends at the shore that he was going to swim across at a shallow place. He suddenly disappeared under the water, and was not found until four days later. It had been dry season, and the water was slow, shallow and clear. Mogo had been called, and the people who went with him swore that he went under the water for an hour, before he came back up with the young man's body, fresh blood pouring from his nose and ears. Mogo said the young man had been called to answer to the water spirits, who had found he was not being faithful to the laws of the society. The young man had been kept in their village for four days, and then killed just before Mogo brought him back up again, as proved by the fresh blood.

Sumo didn't like water business. He was a man of the forest, and he tried to stay clear of other ways. He even feared that his animal double, the bush hog, the same animal his father had had before him, would be jealous and try to kill him, if he joined the water people.

In the end, he and Mogo parted without really helping each other, except for trading information on a few leaves that the other did not know well. Sumo was relieved, because he wanted to live a normal life with Kuluba and the child he was sure she would have for him. If he had joined the water people, he would have to give the child to the spirits, a demand which his own forest animal would not make.

Saki and Koli then joined the discussions with Mogo and Sumo, and at least one bargain was struck. Koli told Mogo, "I'll make sure the latex you report is higher than before." He didn't tell him he was only giving him what he deserved.

In return, Mogo said, "I'll work through the water spirits in the big river to bring some harm to Tokpa. We Bassa people live along the St. John river where it joins the ocean, and you Kpelle live at the upper part of the river where it divides your country from Mano country. And so we water people of all three groups sometimes work together and sometimes fight each other. My Bassa water spirits are more powerful than the Kpelle spirits of Tokpa, and can hurt him if you let me try. However, I won't kill Tokpa, only keep him from being so important in the village."

Koli was disappointed that Sumo and Mogo had not found a way to work more closely together in medicine matters, but he was satisfied that at least Tokpa would be harmed. As for Sulongteh and his demands for money, at least Koli had bought some time, and at very little cost to himself.

He didn't really believe that his brother could bring Sulongteh enough money to buy a cane mill. Moreover, the white man at Salala had told Koli that, in order to get anything in life, it was necessary to work for it, not rely on foolishness. But it was to Koli's advantage for Sulongteh to believe in medicine, and so Koli did nothing to discourage him. He only pointed out that it might take several months before the medicine would take effect. "And by that time," Koli told himself, "I will be out of here, and back to school in Monrovia."

Everything seemed to go smoothly while Koli laid his plans. Eva was teaching him to type during what little of their noon hours at the warehouse they could spare from the mattress at the back of the storeroom. Mogo was back in favor with the white man. Sulongteh was still waiting patiently for his money. Koli was arranging to be transferred to the trading company in Monrovia attached to Firestone. He would go as a junior clerk and typist to their warehouse there, and help keep the stock records. He had not thought of Eva going with him, and she had kept quiet when he discussed his plans.

But then she told him the news. She was pregnant and was coming with him to Monrovia, where they would make their home, and where she would have the baby, now already four months along. She was determined to have a real home and family this time, and Koli seemed to be a young man with a future. Koli thought hard, tried to find a way out, because he planned to go to school at night. He was scheduled to leave Firestone in only three weeks, start his job at the trading company, and begin night school the week after, on the first of March. His plan was to stay with his mother's brother, Bono, behind Liberia College, and give himself to hard study. He thought, "I can't take Eva. How can I go to school if she comes?"

His first impulse was to say, "Sulongteh fathered the baby. I know, and you know that I know, that Sulongteh has been seeing you at night."

But Eva cried and shouted and said, "I stopped seeing Sulongteh long before you gave me this baby. You know Sulongteh has been very quiet for the five months since Sumo was here, since Sumo warned Sulongteh to stay away from women until the medicine took effect. No, you have to agree that the baby is yours."

Koli thought for a moment, "Maybe I can just leave without telling her. But she knows where I am going, and she'll follow me. I could try to deny any relation, but everyone here knows what we've been doing. Haven't I myself boasted to enough men at Saki's place about her?" He spoke aloud, "I guess I'm stuck. I'll take you with me."

Saki didn't like it at all. He had warned Koli against a Bassa girl. He said, "Now you'll have a child who is half Bassa. The girl can't even speak Kpelle, and so how can she raise a proper Kpelle child? Who will take the child to bush school, or teach him the ways of his grandfathers?"

Saki advised Koli strongly, "Leave the girl." Saki didn't say it, but he was afraid that the support he could count on from Koli when he finished high school would now go to some Bassa people. Saki was reconciled to Koli going on to school by now, but at least he must get something from it in the end.

Koli agreed, "I really should leave the girl, but I can't see how to do it. I have to take responsibility for the child, and besides I still like Eva. Maybe some solution will come along, but in the meantime I have to take Eva with me to Monrovia. Anyhow, she can cook for me and help Bono and Sua at the house. She can learn to speak Kpelle there."

"On the other hand," Koli thought, "she might decide, after living with Kpelle people in Monrovia, that she would do better to go home to Bassa."

Koli thought about staying at Firestone until the baby was born, and then going to Monrovia. But he realized that he couldn't stay much longer, or else Sulongteh would soon be after him to change the weights of latex. No extra money had come Sulongteh's way, and he was no closer to his cane mill than before. He was beginning to say to Saki that Sumo had just wasted his time and money, and had done nothing for him. No, Koli knew he had to leave Firestone.

In fact, it was only two weeks after the argument that Koli and Eva left Firestone for Monrovia. The white man Koli worked for arranged the transfer to the trading company, and Koli showed that he knew enough typing to begin the job. The strongest argument Koli had was that he would go to night school in Monrovia, in order to finish high school.

Yanga's brother Bono still lived in the same mat house near the swamp behind Liberia College. It was nowhere near as good a house as Koli had at home in the village, or in Firestone. It was crowded too close to the other houses, and the area around the houses was dirty. The swamp itself was muddy as well as salty, and so they had to walk up the hill to get water near the College. Koli didn't like it there at all, but at least he was with his own people.

For Eva, it was even worse. None of the women could speak English, and she knew only a few words of Kpelle. She was obviously pregnant, and yet they expected her to do all her own work, as well as help with the house. Moreover, the mat walls leaked, and they couldn't find thatch to keep the roof from leaking. There were three families in the one small house, now that Koli and Eva had arrived.

"You have it easy," Eva told Koli. "You go to the trading company every morning to work, and come back only in the evening, expecting to be fed. And then at night you go to the night school, and claim that man is teaching you something. He's just fooling you, and you're fooling me."

Koli answered, "It's impossible for me to study at home, so I have to stay late at the trading company, or else go to the teacher's house after school to study. Besides, Jonathan is a good teacher, and is a student at Liberia College."

Eva could only take it for three weeks. The other women at Yanga's brother's house thought she was too proud to live with them, and they couldn't understand how a Kpelle man like Koli would take a Bassa girl and have children by her. Eva was accustomed to working at Firestone, and earning her own money. Now she had to sit at home, carry water, cut firewood, wash clothes, sweep the ground, and listen to what she called "the unintelligible nonsense of these uneducated Kpelle women."

At the end of three weeks, she and Koli had another quarrel. Koli had stayed with some of the other students as the night school to drink palm wine with Jonathan, and he had come home half drunk. She had not had any chance to get away from the women at the house for three weeks, and she hardly saw Koli to talk to.

She burst out at him in English, while the other women stood by laughing. "You promised me a house in Monrovia, not this rotten, half-broken shack. You take your fun, and are learning more about the world. I have no decent clothes, and never eat any proper food."

Koli laughed at her, and said, "You have to learn to be a Kpelle mother."

With that she hit him, and the fight started. The other women had to drag her away, and had to quiet Koli down, so that he wouldn't hurt a pregnant woman. They didn't care much for Eva, but they didn't want trouble.

That night she put her few things together, walked in the dark to Water Street, and took a late-night taxi back to Firestone. She said before she left, "I'm going home to Bassa, if I can't get my old job back."

Koli said, "I couldn't care less," and let her go. The only thing he would do for her, confused and drunk as he was, was to give her money for food and the taxi ride back to Firestone. He was relieved to see her out of the house, and out of his life.

It had not been hard for Koli to find Jonathan. He still stood on the porch of Liberia College, still talked to young boys from up-country, still seemed to be so alive and on top of his world. Koli had remembered Jonathan often during the year of his disappointment, his work at Firestone, his affair with Eva, and he was sure than Jonathan would find a school for him to attend.

In fact, Jonathan had started such a school at night, and was busy every week night teaching boys from up-country. Koli could not see that Jonathan spent much time on his own schoolwork, but he still claimed to be a student at Liberia College. He had nice clothes, a small house on the road out of town, beyond the College, and lots of boys around him.

The school met at his house, from 6:00 at night to 9:00. He didn't take little boys just learning to read and write, but had boys from 4th grade up to 9th grade. They all met in one room together, and Jonathan went from person to person, checking what he wrote, dictating to him what to write next, and explaining what he didn't understand. They were twenty boys altogether, and each of them paid Jonathan a dollar a week to go to school.

Jonathan spoke both Kpelle and Vai, and could hear a little Bassa and Gola. He said he came from the interior of Cape Mount County, and had studied at the Episcopal High School in Robertsport. He had finished high school three years earlier, and was now a student at Liberia College.

Koli asked him, "Why didn't you go to Hopewell College up-country?"

Jonathan explained, "I didn't have the money, and so I had to work to stay in Liberia College."

But Koli was curious to know when Jonathan in fact went to school, since most of the time he stood on the porch of the College or worked with the boys at the night school. Jonathan didn't answer the question clearly, but just said "College is like that."

Two nights a week, Jonathan told the boys they shouldn't come to visit him. These were Saturday and Sunday nights. Koli was walking near Jonathan's house one Sunday night, and saw a kwii woman, said to be the wife of a wealthy Monrovia big-shot, come up to the house in a big car. Koli was curious, and went closer, under the banana trees which grew behind the house, to

41

listen. He could hear the woman, who was old enough to be Jonathan's mother, telling him how she loved him.

Jonathan's answer was cool, "O.K. Then prove it by giving me more money."

The woman told Jonathan, "My husband is old and dried up, and I need you to keep me young. Besides, my husband has his country wives on the farm behind Kakata, and doesn't care for me any more. Jonathan, don't reject me. I'll help you with money."

The woman asked Jonathan, "Are you ever going back to school? I'll support you there if you need it."

He said, "I've had enough of that, ever since they told me to leave Hopewell. Liberia College is just a waste of time. I thought about getting in this year, but why should I? I've got you to take care of me on weekends, the schoolboys come during the week, and during the day I have my contacts at the port."

She then told him, "Another boat is due at the port next week. You should plan to go there with me in my car to collect the watches and drugs that will be on board. You can get them out of the port area safely, because I've bribed the guard."

She next asked Jonathan, "Why do you keep on teaching these boys at night school?"

But at that point, a dog found Koli and began to bark loudly. Koli had to retreat from under the banana trees, since Jonathan and the woman began to shout, "Who's there?"

Koli, too, wondered why Jonathan bothered to teach him and the others at night, if he had such big and important contacts. "Never mind," Koli thought. "At least I'm getting a chance to learn from someone who has once been a college student."

A big difficulty was that the school had almost no books. Koli had bought one or two books from other boys on Water Street, but they were old and out of date. They were supposed to be learning science, but the only book Jonathan used was an ancient dirty American textbook, with stories about New York City and winter and dairy cows. Jonathan assured Koli that this was the correct book for seventh grade, even in America, but Koli couldn't make much sense out of it.

For English, he had a book of stories, all of them also about America and all very dull. They had to memorize the stories, since there was only one copy for the four of them in the seventh and eighth grades.

And they had a book which just contained long and unfamiliar words. This was the part of the teaching Jonathan liked best. He loved to spin out big sentences, like "The industrious habitue of mercantile operations inevitably undertakes profitable enterprises," or "Amatory activities encourage dilatory scholarship." Koli and the other boys had to copy the sentences, and repeat them aloud.

Jonathan insisted that the only way to succeed in Monrovia was to use words like these to impress people. Jonathan got impatient when Koli asked the meaning of the sentences or the words, and said the important thing is to learn to say them. When pressed for the meaning, Jonathan would read from his dictionary. "Mercantile," he read, meant "Of or pertaining to mercantilism," and rested his case.

"Mathematics is no better," thought Koli.

He and the other boys spent long hours memorizing definitions of geometric figures. "A rhombus is an equilateral parallelogram," and "The square of the hypoteneuse of a right triangle equals the sum of the squares of the sides." Jonathan said he had no blackboard or chalk, and so he couldn't draw the figures for them. The important thing is to know how to talk about them.

Jonathan taught them about fractions as well. "This," he said, "is one of the most important topics in mathematics. If you take something and cut it into two parts, each of them is a half. And if you take one of those parts and cut it again, then you have three parts. Thus each part is called a third. Likewise if you take one of those three parts and cut it again, the parts become fourths."

Koli wondered how the other parts could be halves and thirds and fourths at the same time, but he didn't ask about it.

The history of Liberia was another important subject. Jonathan told them about J. J. Roberts and the founding of the country in 1847. He told how the people had sold Liberia to the kwii for just a few dollars, and how the kwii had killed so many of the ancestors of the country people with cannons and rifles. Koli asked, "What about the history of my own Kpelle people?"

Jonathan answered, "That's not history. History is what is written in books, and so the Kpelle people have no history."

School went on every night during the week, although usually Jonathan would not be there one or more nights. He would leave the house open, and the boys were instructed to teach themselves. The books were there, and the boys had to bring paper and pencils with them. Koli and one of the other older boys were told to be in charge of the fourth, fifth and sixth graders. Koli was often asked to explain something about arithmetic or spelling or reading English, and he usually managed to remember something they had taught him at Salala.

One night, Jonathan kept them after school, as he often did, to drink palm wine with him. He liked having the boys around him, and he liked them to tell him how intelligent and helpful he was. The boys knew that if they did it properly, they might even get some food after school, not to mention the palm wine.

But this night, he didn't have food for them. He told them, "Now I'm going to give you a chance to pay for your schooling without having to find the money."

He showed them some watches. "I bought these for you to sell on Water Street. All you have to do is go to Water Street and find people to buy the watches. They're cheap, only five dollars apiece."

Koli refused, saying, "I've already got a job at the Firestone trading company." He didn't say what he had heard that night, about where the watches came from. He didn't want to get mixed up in that sort of business. But four of the boys, ones who had not been able to find jobs in Monrovia, agreed to sell the watches.

By the next night, they were able to report having sold four, and they brought Jonathan twenty dollars. But Jonathan hit back at one of the boys. "You sold the watch for six dollars, and now you bring back only five. My friend on Water Street has been watching you, and he told me what you did. Give me the dollar, and don't cheat me again."

The boy didn't know what to say, amazed that Jonathan seemed to have spies everywhere. He admitted it and brought the extra dollar.

Jonathan smiled, "Here, take back fifty cents. Any time any of you boys can make more money than I ask, I'll share it with you half and half."

The school work seemed less important to Jonathan after the boys began to sell watches. They spent time at night discussing how many watches had been sold, and where they would sell the next ones. Some boys began to say that Jonathan should give them a bigger share of the profits, especially since they lost so much of their studying time. Jonathan had to agree with them, so that within a short time those who were selling watches did little if any studying.

Koli and some of the other boys continued full time on their schoolwork, while Jonathan discussed business with the students-turned-salesmen in his bedroom. The boys were soon involved also in selling medicines on the street in Monrovia. Jonathan was teaching them how to persuade persons they met to use these cheap medicines, instead of going to the hospital or the expensive pharmacies. They were told what diseases the medicines could cure, and how doctors cheated them by charging high prices and making them wait long hours. Jonathan taught them how to give injections, and soon they added penicillin (and, Jonathan instructed them, "condensed milk if the penicillin runs out") to their store of supplies.

Jonathan worked on Koli to join them. "You replace the expensive goods in the Firestone warehouse with the cheap substitutes I give you. We'll sell them and split the profits, and no one will ever know."

Koli was tempted by the idea for he knew it could be done, but he was afraid to try just yet. "Let me think about it," he pleaded.

By this time the school year was almost over, and Koli really began to wonder what, if anything, he had learned. He had paid Jonathan a dollar a week for eight months, and now it was December again. He began to worry how he could get into another school, and he went about Monrovia asking people where he might enter eighth grade the next year. He had saved a bit of money, to the extent that living with Yanga's brother would allow, and he thought he might try to go to school full-time next year.

45

But when the schools he visited asked what school he had attended, he told them about the Salala mission school and about the Arthur Barclay Institute, which was what Jonathan called his school. Teachers he talked to said that Salala was a good school, but they knew nothing at all about the Arthur Barclay Institute. He would have to bring a transcript from the school if he was to transfer into the eighth grade at their school. He asked Jonathan about it, and Jonathan, after thinking a while, had Koli type up a statement of the subjects he had studied, and then he gave Koli grades and signed his name, with an almost unintelligible flourish.

But when Koli took the paper to other schools, the teachers and principals almost laughed, and said it was no good. He had to have a regular transcript, approved by the Department of Education, showing that he had been to a proper school. The only school which would consider him was the Modern Life Academy, also a night school and also meeting in a private home in a back street of Monrovia. And they said he must accompany the transcript with a ten-dollar registration considered.

Koli realized soon enough that he had wasted his year. No one else knew anything about Jonathan or about the Arthur Barclay Institute. He had learned only how a piece of paper could be utterly worthless. He could see now that Jonathan had just been using him and the other boys, at first to make money for himself, and then later to help him with his business. He knew now that Jonathan was just a rogue, not a person to help country boys, not a teacher, not a student at Liberia College.

At least Koli had done his job. He had kept away from any more girls like Eva, and had lived with his family behind the College. He had learned how to type better during the year, and the people at the trading company trusted him to keep records. His boss laughed when he found out how Koli had wasted his time in Jonathan's school. He asked him, "Why didn't you come to me for better advice? Now you'll have to start over again in the seventh grade, this time at a real school. You must have saved some money, at least a hundred dollars, since you're earning thirty dollars a month. Surely, you don't have to spend that much."

It was in fact true, although the amount he had saved was nearer seventy-five dollars. With that, Koli could enter a proper mission school in seventh grade. He had his record from Salala, and surely they would at least give him a good reference to continue school. The world seemed brighter again. The money was safe - Koli had made sure to save it at the company, since in Monrovia he couldn't even trust his own family not to rob him.

But, when he arrived home that night, he found his older sister, Lorpu, waiting for him.

"There's trouble at home," she said. "You have to come with me tonight. And bring money - a hundred dollars, if you have it. Your father, Flumo, is in trouble."

"What happened, another shooting accident?"

"No, he was walking in the forest, and he stopped to rest on the way home in Yakpalo's rice storage kitchen. The kitchen was full of newly-cut rice. Flumo was hungry and tired, so he stopped to cook some cassava root. He built a fire, but fell asleep waiting for the cassava to cook. Somehow, the fire jumped to the wood pile and it set the entire storage kitchen on fire. The whole year's harvest went up in flames, and Yakpalo has taken the case to the elders. Flumo admitted what he did, and has thrown himself on Yakpalo's mercy. Yakpalo said that Flumo should send for you and Saki and get you to help in the matter.

"Flumo asked Sumo to go get you and Saki. But Sumo said he didn't know Monrovia, or even where you were living. Sumo turned to me as older sister to come down to get the two of you. I've already seen Saki, and he agreed to bring twenty-five dollars. But that isn't enough. We need at least a hundred to buy a cow. We need a cow because Yakpalo says he had enough rice in the kitchen to make at least twenty-five bags. He'll have to start all over to build a new rice storage shed, and he needs food for next year. You'll have to help."

Once again, the dream was over. Koli had to be loyal to Flumo and Yakpalo, the one his real father, the other his foster father. He would have to withdraw all his saving. Koli couldn't understand his bad fortune. He thought, "If it is a good thing for me and my family that I go to school, why does it never seem possible?"

IV: LISTEN TO THINGS MORE THAN BEINGS

It seemed to Koli that all he heard was complaints when he arrived back in the village. No one was grateful to him for giving up all the money he had saved during the year in Monrovia. No one felt he had done anything strange by sacrificing his last chance to go to high school. Instead they complained that he had broken his promise to return for the next bush-cutting season.

Even his twin was down on him. Sumo said, "I've had to leave the blacksmith shop and my medicines to work with the young men's group because you didn't come back earlier. And why haven't you sent any iron since your last trip? What happened to all the iron you said you could find along the road? Why didn't you bring any this time?"

What was even worse was that Flumo appeared so old and beaten. The burning of Yakpalo's rice kitchen seemed to be the last in the series of misfortunes that had broken over his head in the past several years. Flumo seemed not able to take any more. He thanked Koli for the money, but there was no ring in his voice. When he went to the blacksmith shop, it wasn't to seize the hot iron with his tongs and beat it into cutlass or hoe. It wasn't even to sit and joke with the men, drinking palm wine and telling half-true stories about the women of the village. Now he sat on the edge of the group and hardly spoke. The other men felt it too, and the joking yielded to serious talk and the serious talk to silence when Flumo sat there too long.

Koli remembered how, when he had been very young, it had been different at the black smith shop. He had come there not long after his father had shot the leopard in the forest. How Flumo had half-danced his way back with the news of killing it with his new shotgun! Though the memory was tempered by the recollection that the same shotgun later wounded Yakpalo's son, Koli remembered how he had often sat outside the shop and listened with affection and admiration as his father told the story for yet another time.

He remembered how once Flumo had returned to the cutlass he had been working on, now that the iron had become red again. He had taken up the red, spark-showering cutlass blade, and with a look of mock ferocity and anger at the other men, had rubbed the blade against the roughened hard callous of his foot and then had waved it in the air as if to threaten the others. Koli had been frightened at the smoke and smell of flesh from his father's foot, but nothing had happened.

No longer would Flumo attempt such a trick. The callous had thickened instead on his heart and spirit, and he seemed insensitive now to both the pain and the beauty of life. Somehow, he seemed much older than when Koli had left almost two years earlier. Koli had known even then that his father's importance had lessened in the village. He was still chief of his quarter, but more and more often cases did not remain with him, but went on to Yakpalo to be settled. Two years ago, he had been able to work a full day, had still laughed and drunk his palm wine, had still worked alongside Sumo in the blacksmith shop. Now, Koli wondered, "Who is this old man that I hardly know?"

Even Yakpalo felt it, and when the time came for Saki and Koli to produce a hundred dollars to buy a cow for sacrifice, he seemed almost embarrassed about the demand. Old Mulbah, the medicine man, would take the fire from the land by killing the cow and dividing up the meat by quarters throughout the village. He would pray the ancestors to take the evil eye from the land, and then cook and eat a portion of the meat where the rice storage kitchen had stood.

The village elders and the family discussed what to do after that. The rest of the family and others in the town would help Yakpalo and his family when they needed rice until the next harvest. And all would work together to rebuild the kitchen.

Flumo's last words on the matter, his apologies to Yakpalo, and his thanks for not pressing the matter to the limit, were almost too quiet to hear. Koli worried that Flumo was forgetting the issue at hand, for the old man drifted off into a long story of the rabbit who lost his way in the forest. "The rabbit heard singing behind a hill, but when he reached the place, he saw no one. Again, he heard the singing, and went beyond the next hill, but saw no one. The third time, when he heard the singing, now from a new direction, he knew something was wrong. He went silently through the bush, leaving the main trail. There he looked out on

50

leopard, sitting quietly on the branch of a tree, and saying to himself, `I will eat rabbit, will eat rabbit, will eat rabbit - if only I can find him.'

"The song started up again. Leopard sang most beautifully, urging rabbit, 'come - there is a feast here.' But he did not tell rabbit that the feast would be rabbit.

"Now, rabbit was old and tired. He was hungry and had been wandering in the forest for longer than he could remember, without a meal. He thought, 'is it better to die of starvation here in the forest, or to be eaten by leopard once and for all? At least leopard might give me a plate of rice to satisfy my hunger before pouncing on me.'

"So rabbit retreated, until he once again heard leopard singing the song of invitation. He then walked into the clearing before leopard's tree and showed himself, weak, thin, dirty, and helpless, expecting to be eaten at any moment.

"Leopard started, as if to leap from the tree, but checked himself. He, too, was hungry, but it would only insult his hunger to eat this scrap of hair and bone. He could only say in disgust, 'Thorn-bush grows when cotton-tree refuses to fall on it.'

"Leopard eased himself down from the tree, picked up rabbit in his mouth, and shook him until rabbit feared he had no bones left at all. Leopard told rabbit, `At least tell me where I can find some real meat.'

"Rabbit, in his fear, told where his children were hiding. The scraps of leopard's rice were on the ground, and leopard kicked them to rabbit, who ate them, more out of confusion and fear than hunger. And then leopard left, to eat what and where he might that night."

Yakpalo had been tired, had been waiting impatiently for Flumo to finish, so he could arrange the building of the shed. But he paid attention as soon as he saw where the story was going. He saw Flumo, old for the first time. The hundred dollars was really the substance of Koli and Saki, but the greater shame, the greater loss, was that of Flumo, who had done wrong, and had not been able to repay it, had not even been fleshy enough to eat.

The hundred dollars which had been given to buy the cow seemed now to Yakpalo the price of defeat, not only Flumo's

51

defeat, but the defeat of Koli and Saki, and even the defeat of Yakpalo himself. The other men were looking at him. beginning to realize how no one had come out ahead, how everyone had lost.

But Yakpalo recovered himself, realizing that if he didn't end the matter, rabbit might even persuade leopard to find food for rabbit. He said, to close the matter, "Some people are like the intestines of porcupine. When you are about to throw them away, they seem a good food. But when you try to eat them, they are a bitter thing."

And then, to turn the corner from defeat to reconstruction, he said, "Umbrella tree - you can't burn it, it doesn't give fruit, its leaves are no good for thatch, it won't give shade, but at least you can use its poles for building."

The family prepared to leave the palaver house outside the town elder's house, where they had discussed the matter. Yakpalo had not insisted on a court case, despite his initial intention to sue Flumo for the loss of his rice. As a result, they had gone to the elder to provide a friendly ground for discussion. He had done little more than bless the occasion, and let the principals talk it out. If matters had become serious, and hot words had passed, he would have had to intervene to make sure the discussion did not destroy the village. A house palaver is different from a court case, because in it no one really wants to hurt anyone else in the end, for fear of future repayment.

But before they left, the elder had a final word to say. "I am nearly ready to finish my time as elder of this village. I can no longer do a full day's work, and other men will soon take my place. Before Koli and Sumo were born, I was acknowledged as the strongest and bravest and hardest-working farmer in the village. But now, like rabbit, I'm old and tired. There are others, too, in the village who are getting old, others like me and rabbit."

"But," and he paused for a moment to let his words sink in, "Leopard also can grow old. And if leopard eats all of rabbit's children, who will care for leopard when he cannot hunt for himself? Does not leopard know that he must be father of all the animals, now that they have given him their children? If rabbit tells leopard where his children are, then leopard must care for those children, not eat them."

Yakpalo turned again, annoyed that he was once more stopped from collecting people to build the rice kitchen. He insisted, "Leopard has already cared for all his children, and is still caring for them, but they must help when the food is gone." The elder didn't answer, but instead gave his blessing. The family left the palaver house, the dispute was over, and Koli was without his year's savings.

Koli thought over what he had just heard. The manner of settling the quarrel was so unlike what he was accustomed to in Monrovia. Jonathan didn't speak like that, nor did Eva. But he saw the inside of what Flumo, the elder and Yakpalo were saying. He saw how Flumo had played the game as cleverly as he could, acknowledging the weakness of his position, and trying to turn it to his advantage. At the same time, he was ashamed for Flumo, that he had to beg leopard to care for him, and that he had to use up his children's substance to save himself.

Koli was also impressed by another part of Flumo's story. He thought of rabbit hearing the singing in the forest, and going to answer its call. His first reaction had been, "How foolish of rabbit."

But then he applied it to himself. "I listened to the white man's singing, and went to Salala. What did I find there? I listened again to the singing, and went to Monrovia. What did I find there? What will be the third call, and what leopard will meet me there? Will I, too, have to acknowledge my loss, just as my father before me?"

The next day Yakpalo called to Koli to join the group going back to the farm. Koli, Sumo, Saki, Yanga, Toang and Flumo all went along. Old Mulbah and the elder followed behind, leading the cow for sacrifice. The trail was dry and clean as far as the turn-off to Yakpalo's farm. Koli thought of the many times he had walked on that trail, both as a child and as an adult. They turned off at the big cotton-tree just beyond the stream. There the trail was less clear, because it led only to Yakpalo's area. Here Yakpalo had his small village, and around the village his relatives had their farms as well.

They crossed the small stream on the log bridge that Yakpalo and his people had built. During the height of the rainy season, even the bridge was under muddy swirling water, but now it stood a man's height above a clear stream. It was two logs wide, and tied with vines to trees on either end. Beyond the bridge was the old swamp Koli always hated to cross.

"The dirt of the swamp looks so black and rich," Koli thought. "I've heard that people farther down country are planting sugar cane in such swamps. Maybe I can persuade Yakpalo to do so some day. That seems sensible, a lot more sensible than the scheme now being tried out at Firestone, to plant rice in swamps." Koli had often been told the story of his second year in life, when his mother, Yanga, and her co-wife, Toang, had had to struggle for a whole season growing swamp rice after the failure of their upland farm, just to get a few miserable tins of rice to stay alive.

Beyond the swamp, the trail started to climb, up and out of the lowlands along the river and into the forest itself. Yakpalo no longer farmed these forest lands along the trail, but preferred to plant on the other side of the hill, a good hour from the village. Koli knew that the farm village was not far when he saw the cocoa and coffee that Yakpalo had planted. Both Yakpalo and Flumo sold their coffee in the Gbarnga market, and it brought a good price, although not so high now as it was in the big war when Koli had started school. Cocoa was something else again. Yakpalo had planted a little, the first in the village, and the other men were watching to see if it proved profitable.

Beyond the coffee and the cocoa, they saw the old kola tree that Yakpalo's father had planted when they first came to this area. A medicine rope was tied around it, as if to say to strangers, "Come near me at your own peril."

The lilies were all in bloom alongside the path as they approached the village. Their red contrasted with the green of the forest and the green of the grass that grew along the trail. Goats kept the grass short here, as they strayed from Yakpalo's farm village. Ahead Koli could see the bananas and the two coconut palms that Yakpalo had planted. He looked forward to climbing the trees to bring down some delicious, cool fruit, and it made him feel good to be in the village again.

The village was more built up, more developed, than when he had last been here. He had not returned since he left Salala. His other visits had been too short, and there had been no reason to come this far into the bush. The men's work groups cut their farms elsewhere, since the people in Yakpalo's village generally now worked together to do their own bush-cutting. Koli would have already been called to help, as Yakpalo's foster-son, if he had arrived in the village already. But Yakpalo's people were early this year, and had finished part of the work, far ahead of the other men in town. Yakpalo was working so early because his new farm was in high forest. That meant it would need a longer time than usual to dry, after felling the trees, before burning it.

This village was somehow so much more alive even than the main village, where Koli and his family lived. The chickens seemed to be more numerous and not to be afraid of anyone. The goats had given birth to more young, and one mother had three kids with her. Yakpalo's new wife was busy pounding rice in the mortar, her baby on her back, and the two small children of Yakpalo's second wife were playing and working beside them. And with them was Kuluba, the girl of whom Koli had been so fond, but who was now his twin's wife. Even more disturbing to Koli was that his own son by Kuluba, named Ziepolo, was there with the others. It was a wrench that he had given up Ziepolo to be raised as Sumo's son as Sumo married Kuluba - all a price Koli had had to pay for wanting to go off to school. And there Ziepolo sat on the ground, playing beside Kuluba as she helped winnow the newly beaten rice. Here she also looked beautiful, sharing the beauty of this place that Koli had given up - in return for what?

Ziepolo looked up at Koli, and clearly did not know him. Ziepolo only knew Sumo as his father, and had never known Koli. "My own son, and not one sign of recognition," thought Koli. "What kind of fool have I been?" For a moment, he thought of staying and trying to get her back. "But it's too late now, for Kuluba at least. Maybe I can start again in the village with another girl. There's the one my father brought me before - but no, she's married also by now. I'll have to try elsewhere."

Koli went up to Ziepolo and fished in his pocket for a bit of candy. His eyes met Kuluba's, but quickly he looked back at the boy, and thanked Kuluba for taking such good care of Sumo's son. He gave his son the candy, and went on. "One son here," he thought, "And for all I knew, another one in Bassa." He had made no effort to find out about Eva, after she had left him to return to Firestone. Saki had told him she had passed through and gone home and not taken her old job again.

"What good is it to love these girls and for them to have children, if I can't share their lives?" he continued to muse. He looked back at Kuluba, and realized that she was rounder and fuller, as if she grew by the well-being and peace and richness of Yakpalo's village. It was clear that soon Sumo would have his own child, and would for the second time have the pleasure of being a father. Sumo had stopped to talk with Kuluba, and Koli could see the pleasure they took in each other, and the love which Ziepolo gave his foster-father.

The group didn't stop in Yakpalo's village, but went on to last year's farm, at the far end of the valley before the land rose steeply into the high forest beyond, the forest that separated the village from the big river to the east. It was into that high forest that Flumo had gone to hunt that terrible day last week, and from which he had returned tired and hungry, with no game to show for his effort, only to burn Yakplao's rice shed. Koli could see the forest ahead, from a clearing where Yakpalo's farm had been two years before.

Here on the two-year old farm, there was a broken and already disintegrating storage shed. Yakpalo had kept his rice there before moving during the most recent rainy season to the new shed. Old banana trees still bore their fruit, the pawpaws were almost too high to climb any more, and the cassava's second growth was almost overwhelmed by the return of the low bush.

Koli did not want to go the rest of the way, to see the charred wreck of this year's kitchen. He did not want to see what his father had done. But he had to continue. Beyond the old kitchen was last year's farm, now planted to a second rice crop, to peanuts and to cassava. The peanuts had all been harvested early in the year, the cassava was still in the ground, and the rice was ready to harvest.

Two little boys, Yakpalo's nephews, were there chasing birds with slings, but mostly chasing each other. "No harm," Koli thought, "The noise they are making would keep away every bird in Jorkwelle country." Koli realized that Yakpalo could not have such a great need for food, what with this second rice crop coming up so well. Moreover, Yakpalo's head wife kept her rice in a kitchen in the village they had passed, the very rice that his young wife was beating and Kuluba was winnowing. Koli began to think that perhaps be had been cheated in the settlement of Flumo's fire damage.

They passed the old farm, and there ahead of them was the newly harvested emptiness of this year's rice. The stalks waved free again, with nothing to carry. A few birds were there, searching to see if any rice had been left. The fence the family had so laboriously built to keep out the small animals of the forest was already beginning to break in a few places. And in the center of the field was the charred and blackened witness to Flumo's age and weakness. There was nothing left, and Koli could see that it must have been a big shed indeed, enough to support all the retainers and clients who were moving to join Yakpalo. Koli realized that in fact Yakpalo had not cheated him. His loss had been substantial.

As if to confirm Koli's thoughts, Yakpalo turned to Saki and said, "The rice I needed to build up my village had been there. Just last month, my cousin from near Gbarnga said he would come to live on my farm and work for me. He had worked long enough at Firestone, and Gbarnga had no more empty bush for him to make farm for himself. I had welcomed him, but now he will come and find no rice to eat. I can't turn him back but must find food for him. In the long run, of course, he will help my family grow more food, but the short run is what matters for now."

Only Saki, Koli and Yakpalo were at the farm. The others had lagged behind, the elder and Mulbah still on the trail, Sumo to speak to Kuluba, Toang and Lopu to visit with Yakpalo's new wife, and Flumo - they were not sure where Flumo had gone. When Toang and Lorpu came up, they said, "We haven't seen him either, not after we left the village. He had been there with us, and then had gone ahead."

Koli worried suddenly about his father. "Is something wrong?" He went back along the trail, calling for Flumo.

His father answered when they were near the old storage shed. He had found a heavy pole, once used to support the old shed, and now discarded. He had been trying to carry it, and had fallen with it. He said, "It's still strong, stronger than I am myself, and can be used to build the new shed. Termites haven't gotten into it, the point for placing it in the ground is still sharp, and the notch at the top for tying the cross-beams is still perfectly good. But I can't seem to move the log. I guess I need help."

Koli felt the suppressed love of all these years away from home, nine wasted years, go to his father. He thought, "If I'd helped him before, instead of running away, Flumo wouldn't be like this now. He wouldn't be old before his time, would still be the man I remember from that marvelous day when he killed the leopard."

Koli found no way to say all these things, but instead helped pick up the log. With Flumo at one end and Koli at the other, they carried it to the new site.

Yakpalo saw them coming, and knew at once the story. He knew that Flumo was trying to make up for the damage, was trying to be a man again, and that Koli had tried to help

Flumo asked, "Where do you want the new kitchen?"

Yakpalo answered, "Why, right here, where the old one was. We'll plant the second rice, the peanuts, the cassava and the vegetables here next season, and then bring the new rice from the new farm we're now cutting just beyond here. No, right here will be fine. We can use the old holes, once we clear away the ashes." Yakpalo concluded, "An old rice bag is ugly, but what it contains is beautiful."

Flumo answered, looking up to the sky, "The way the rain builds up in the sky is not the way it falls."

The days of building the new rice storage shed were among the happiest of Koli's life. He and his family slept at Yakpalo's village, and went every day to work on the rice storage shed. They all knew it was the wrong time of year to build a shed. It was better to build it when the rice was ripening in the dry period which separated the early from the late rains. But this was no ordinary occasion. It meant peace in the family again, the rebuilding of more than a rice kitchen. It was making Flumo a man again, even if only for a few brief years, it was bringing Koli and Saki back into the family, and it was showing Yakpalo that indeed it takes more than cotton trees to build a forest or leopards to build a town.

They started by clearing away the ashes and charred wood from the old site. Very little of the roofing timber was actually usable, and that was usable more to make fires at night than to build the shed. None of the thatch survived the blaze. But the holes had been dug straight and deep, and were in good condition. They cleaned out the half-burned stumps of the six main posts that supported the shed, and replaced them with six strong unburned posts, including the one Flumo and Koli had brought, as well as one more from the old shed.

For the other four posts, they went into the forest to cut the right kind of tree. Koli felt the uselessness of what he had learned at Salala, for he hardly knew one tree from another any more. Sumo, on the other hand, named every tree they saw, knew its properties, and defined its uses. Sumo even commented, "The umbrella tree, which Yakpalo rejected for every purpose but building, is good for medicine, if you use the bark in the right way."

They went up the hill, beyond the area where Yakpalo would make his next farm, to find the poles. Koli suggested several trees he thought had the right shape, but Sumo rejected them as wrong for one reason or another. The termites would get into them, or they were too hard to cut to size, or they would put up new shoots when they were put in the ground, or they were not straight enough. Finally, Sumo found the poles he wanted, and the brothers cut and took them back to the site for the shed.

On the way back, Koli asked Sumo, "What do you think I should do, go back to Monrovia and continue my job or stay in the village?" Koli half wanted Sumo to tell him to stay at home, take care of his father, marry and settle down. Instead, he was surprised when Sumo answered, "It's too late now for you to live at home. You have no real place in the village." Sumo was being not unkind about it, just casually matter-of-fact. "You could never find a happy and comfortable slot here, not until there are more men like you, so you can live together and talk to each other."

But - and this came as the greater surprise - Sumo said, "You shouldn't go back to Monrovia, because I want you to help with our son, Ziepolo, when the boy is old enough to go to school. I would never send Ziepolo to Monrovia, not with all those kwii people and their bad ways. Even Firestone is too kwii. But I hoped that our son," - Sumo said "our" when only the trees of the forest were present to hear it - "will have a chance to get some schooling. For you, school will always be a burden, in my view. You'll never really be able to use it. But in the times that are coming, things will be different. Boys like Ziepolo must have kwii schooling, or they'll be left out of the world.

"I don't like it, and I don't want to have anything to do with it myself, but there's no escaping the kwii way. Catch your fish with a trap when the river is low, but go hunting when the rains come," Sumo said. "The water was still low when we were boys. I was surprised when you left the river before the traps went under water. But the water is rising now, and I want our boy to know how to hunt as well as fish."

"Where do I go? What do I do ? asked Koli. "I only had two ideas - to stay here with my family or to go back to the Firestone trading company in Monrovia. I've pretty much given up school, but Monrovia seems the right place to get a good salary."

Sumo answered obliquely. "Yakpalo mentioned you when the clan chief from Sengta near Gbarnga came to see him. That clan chief is a descendant of the woman who was such a powerful chief in the early days when the kwii people arrived in Jorkwelle country. He's also related by marriage to Yakpalo, and visited the village to establish even closer relations between them. Some people are already saying that Yakpalo will be the next chief of our clan, and so the clan chief from the road wanted to make sure they would work well together."

Sumo continued, "Because the clan chief lives on the main road, he wants someone who can read and write to help him. He himself doesn't speak English, much less read or write, and so he feels at the mercy of the kwii, white and black, who come up from Monrovia. Hopewell College has been opened in his area, and he wants to be able to deal with the teachers there, mostly white men. And there are people from every part of Liberia in his village. Bassa, Loma, Mano, Vai, Gola, even Kru from farther down the coast. He needs someone who knows the kwii way to help him manage all these people. And, when he heard about you, it struck him you were an obvious way to do both things at once. He could strengthen his ties with the village and with Yakpalo, and he could have the help he needed. I'm sure you'll hear more about it from the others when we go back to the village."

Koli responded slowly. "I had never thought of such a thing. I have to give it some time to sink in, before I can make a decision. For now, let me think."

He paused, then smiled and said, "Thanks, Sumo, for your advice. You're right. It would be hard for me to live in the village in this generation. Perhaps our son, Ziepolo, will grow up to make his way in both worlds. I hope so."

The brothers brought two poles back with them to the farm, set them up in the holes and went back for the other two. Koli felt good to be talking easily to Sumo, instead of fearing him or seeing him as some kind of mysterious zoe. Sumo seemed more like his brother than he had for years, and it was good. They talked easily about other things, now that Sumo had spoken so freely about what he believed Koli should do. Koli told Sumo more about Firestone, more about Monrovia. And as he talked, those places seemed far away and unattractive. He became increasingly convinced that Sumo was right, that he should remain up-country, where he could try to help his own Jorkwelle people deal properly with the kwii.

The idea grew within him as he worked with his fathers and his uncle and his brother. He thought, "I certainly like it here up-country better than Monrovia. And, if I go back to Monrovia, Jonathan will just be after me again to steal things from the Firestone warehouse and resell them on the streets at prices lower than they cost in the store. I've resisted Jonathan so far, but still - such stealing wouldn't be too difficult, particularly because they trust me to work there after hours. All I'd have to do would be replace what I steal with similar things of lower quality, so that the stock wouldn't be reduced in number. But I'm afraid of Jonathan, afraid he might get me into deeper trouble than merely stealing from the company. No, I don't want to get mixed up with him again.

61

"The towns on the road are better places to live than Monrovia, although they're more kwii than my village. The red dust raised by motor traffic has covered the trees along the road, while the leaves are still green here in Yakpalo's village. But the red dust hasn't completely spoiled the country, not spoiled it in the same way as Monrovia, with its fat kwii and their big black cars, with its easy-talking cheaters like Jonathan, with its hatred and its quarrels." The idea of working up-country seemed good to Koli, but still he let it ripen.

Four days later, when they were almost finished constructing the kitchen, Sumo called Koli to go with him to the big river, to buy some fish there to bring back home. "I've heard a Mano fisherman is now at the river, and he's catching a lot of fish with his big Monrovia net. He lived in Monrovia for a year and worked with the Fanti fishermen from Gold Coast, and now he knows how to use a big net. He can only work in the dry season, when the river is low. He ties the net just before dark from one side of the river to the other, at a shallow place where the river passes over rocks. He then paddles his small dugout canoe along the net early in the morning, and winds the net into shore to get the day's catch. Let's go see him, and get some fish."

Sumo and Koli entered the high forest beyond Yakpalo's farm area. The trail almost disappeared there in the forest, as they were climbing up a small stream bed. They had to cross and re-cross the stream, as they worked their way up to the summit. Then, as they descended the other side, the second stream appeared. People said this one never failed, even in the driest times. Koli asked, "Why doesn't anyone live and farm here?" Sumo reminded him, "There used to be a small farm village here when we were children. It was abandoned after a series of deaths in the village. Fever and blindness seemed to catch people who had never been sick. So the residents decided to leave the place. They came to our town, and asked for another farming area. Now they lived south of the town, still near the river, but well away from their old spot."

There were still signs of habitation where the old village had been sited. There were raffia palms and oil palms along the old trail, making it possible for the twins to find their way without much difficulty. And near the village site itself were still a few struggling banana and orange trees, now untended. The trail led beyond the village site, and down a steep hill to the river. They could hear the water rushing before they could see it below the hillside. At the bottom of the hill, the river was wide and rocky, with the rocks which were normally covered in the rainy season bare to the sun. Small patches of sand shone yellow in the light, just under the surface, and schools of tiny fish passed in formation over the sand. A sudden splash along the opposite bank told Koli and Sumo that some animal had just slipped under the water to hide, perhaps a crocodile or pygmy hippopotamus. Flocks of small water birds were gathered on the rocks, looking for their daily food. The place was peaceful, refreshing, and altogether different from the ocean that Koli found so awesome and unpleasant.

Koli and Sumo sat down to rest on the rocks at the edge of the river, hot and tired from the walk through the forest. The final stretch, where the village had been, was particularly difficult, since grasses and vines had taken over, and the forest had not grown sufficiently high to choke them out. The twins were dirty and their legs and arms were cut from the saw grass. The river was cool and inviting. It was like a return to the time before Koli went to school, when Sumo suggested, "Let's wash in the river before we go to find the fisherman."

As Koli lay on the sand, the water just covering his body and the small fish nibbling at his skin, the clean refreshment of the day, the sun, the forest and the rocks seemed to reproach him for ever having gone to school, ever having persisted in that foolishness by going next to Monrovia. He realized, "In my whole time living with Bono behind Liberia College, I was never this clean and fresh. How can people live in Monrovia, and claim to be happy?"

Sumo came at that moment, and splashed water on Koli, himself fresh and rested from swimming to the opposite bank. "We've been here long enough, and it'll be dark if we don't find the fish soon."

Koli reluctantly eased himself from the water, sat in the sun to dry off, and slipped his clothes on. The river and the sun and the forest and the fish called him to stay, but Sumo was right.

They took the trail downstream, around a steep hill, skirting the edge of the forest. The trail was scarcely more than a hunter's path, but was unmistakable because the water was on one side, the hill on the other. They had to cross several small streams emptying into the big river, but the trail was not difficult. Once, as they came out of a thicket along the trail, a troop of monkeys fled from them through the trees, and another time, they heard what they were sure was the call of an elephant deep in the forest.

Soon the trail opened out, and across the river they could once again see farms, and a small farm village. There was another rocky place in the river, after a long stretch where the river ran deep and brown and silent. At that place, the Mano fisherman had set up his camp, across from the village. He had built a small thatch shelter on the rocks, and was drying hundreds of fish on racks, built chest-high above smoldering fires, fires that were more smoke than flame. The fisherman had chosen the right wood, not too dry and not too green, to make his fire, and the fish he had taken the night before were spread out in the smoke.

Koli and Sumo came to him from the forest side. He turned with some surprise. "Who are you?" he called in Mano.

They answered in Kpelle, and he shifted language. The twins realized that most of his business came from the other side of the river, where his own Mano people lived. Only a few had ever come from the Kpelle people on Koli's side. But he welcomed them, and even spoke enough Kpelle himself to make conversation. He offered them dried smoked fish fresh from the rack, and Koli and Sumo ate with thanks. The fish was delicious, and needed no further cooking. There was fufu in the pot, that pounded and boiled cassava paste which the Mano like so well, and Koli and Sumo helped themselves to some.

After resting a while and accepting the fisherman's hospitality, they stated their business. Sumo spoke for them. "We want to buy enough dried fish to feed our family, and also some to cook for the men who will finish cutting our father's farm in just three day's time. Our father invited some other men to help, because his new farm is so large and the trees so big. So we need lots of fish for them and for us."

The fisherman selected about 20 large dried fish, and put them in the sack Koli had brought. They had to negotiate the price, but in the end the fisherman accepted two dollars for the lot. He then tossed onto the pile their dash, their expected small present. But it wasn't a fish. Rather it was a piece of dried crocodile meat. The twins accepted it with some surprise and also with pleasure. The meat was delicious, but hard to get.

The brothers put the fish and the crocodile meat in the bag, and then started on their way back for Yakpalo's village. The sun was already beginning to move down in the sky, and so there was no time for another swim on the return trip. They moved fast, and reached the almost finished rice shed after it was already in the shadows from the forest trees. The rest of the family was ready to quit for the day from the task of thatching the roof, and were glad to get the fish and the crocodile meat.

Koli was ready to rest when they reached the village. He was beginning to feel the rhythm of life in the forest once more, but he had not totally overcome his city softness. Yanga cooked the crocodile meat in palm oil, cassava leaf and lots of hot pepper, and served it up in a large pot of rice. The family gathered around the pot, as the last light disappeared from the west, and ate the food in turn with their fingers. "It is right for us all to be together," Koli thought.

There was a faint half-circle of moon in the west, following the sun down. It didn't give enough light to make the village alive, but it was an invitation to Koli to stay at least until the moon was big enough to bring a bit more light in his life.

He thought, "I can't remain here, in Yakpalo's village. There's nothing for me to do here, after we finish building the rice kitchen and clearing the new farm. Besides, it's still hard being around Kuluba for too long. But if I take the job Sumo mentioned, with the clan chief beyond Gbarnga, I'd be close to home and at least relatively free of Firestone and Monrovia." Koli went to sleep on that cheering thought.

67

V: THEY ARE IN THE FOREST

The clan chief at Sengta seemed genuinely glad to have Koli as his clerk. Koli had made the decision two days after the family returned from rebuilding Yakpalo's rice kitchen and completing the cutting of his new farm. Yakpalo had approached him about the job the night they finished the work, and Koli had given no sign that he knew about the job. He didn't want to betray Sumo's advance warning. He listened quietly, and said, "I'll have to think about it."

He slept on the matter, and the next day said, "I'll go to the clan chief to make the arrangements. I'm not sure how soon I'll get back, but it won't be too long."

He found the clan chief in his town of Sengta on the motor road, not far from Gbarnga. The chief was lying in a hammock on his porch, wearing a battered black kwii hat and holding a rolled-up black umbrella.

The chief spoke first. "Koli, I want to thank you for volunteering to do my reading and writing for me. I'm glad you decided to show your concern for good government by coming to join me." He sat up slightly and tried to look official.

Koli at once sensed he was being tricked, and responded with a trick of his own. He said, "I'll be glad to read any government mail that you have in your office, and then go on to Monrovia to take up my job again at the Firestone trading company."

The clan chief laughed, "Come on, Koli. You can make more money working with me than in Monrovia. After all, there are taxes to collect, and villages with lots of rice to share."

Koli thought, "That's not what I had in mind. I didn't run away from Jonathan's schemes to cheat Firestone, just to take a job where I would have to cheat my own people." He spoke aloud, "Thank you, Chief, but what I really want is a regular job."

The chief pointed out, "My boy, even if I give you a salary, the only source of the money is the taxes our people pay. After all, our people are protected by the government, and so must pay the government representatives who do the protecting."

Koli looked hard at the clan chief, and asked, "Do you mean there is no government money to run your office?"

"Of course not. We give the government money, not the other way around. We do the people a favor by making sure that some of the money stays here in Kpelle country, instead of letting it all go to Monrovia." The clan chief sat back, looking pleased with his remark.

Koli hadn't thought of it that way, and was forced to grant the clan chief a point. It was finally agreed that Koli would get a regular twenty dollars a month ("It's more than I get for a salary," said the clan chief), as well as a share of the taxes and rice that villages send to support the clan chief. The clan chief was somewhat indefinite as to exactly how much Koli would get, but he assured him, "My boy, you won't go hungry."

Koli didn't like the arrangement, but he had no choice but to agree, he thought. He considered: "What are my alternatives? I can go back to Firestone, where Sulongteh is waiting to get back at me. Or I can go to Monrovia, live with Bono and try to avoid Jonathan. No, it's better to stay here. At least I won't cheat my own village."

The clan chief seemed to know what Koli was thinking when he said softly, "Snake doesn't hunt in his own hole, but snake is never hungry."

The clan chief leaned forward from his hammock. "All I want is for you to be available when I need you. It isn't a hard job. I even have this typewriter which I begged from the mission near town. Here, take it. See if you can make it work again."

Koli took it the next day to Hopewell College, and found a teacher who could repair it. It never did work properly, but Koli learned in time to produce a typed page when the chief needed it. True, some of the letters went up when the others came down, and the left-hand margin had stopped working long ago. But the clan chief was proud when his words could go to Gbarnga or Monrovia, complete with kwii appearance.

Koli went to work. In the first three years, he found that he did many things for and with the clan chief, and he learned much about his own people and about others.

He had to make copies of the decisions on important cases that appeared before the clan chief. If it was a minor matter, the decision would be made verbally and allowed to remain in people's memory.

The clan chief had two soldiers working for him, and he would send these from time to time to arrest a man who had not paid his taxes or who broke some other law. He sent Koli one day soon after he had taken the job to help arrest a man. "He thinks he's some kind of big kwii, and so he refused to work on the farm set aside to grow my rice."

At first, Koli argued he should defend the poor village man, but the clan chief talked him out of his position. He reasoned, "If bush cow lets rabbit eat in peace, then rabbit should give bush cow some of his rice. I protect these people, Koli. They should be grateful."

Koli was of most use when the clan chief had to make decisions relating to the kwii world. The clan chief said, "The white kwii, with a few exceptions, don't understand us Kpelle at all. Moreover, whereas the black kwii from Monrovia understand us Kpelle, they use their understanding to gain personal advantage. We can't start letting our own people think they're kwii, too, or there'll be no one to do the work."

On another occasion a year later, Koli was asked to witness the sale of village land to a Monrovia big-shot. The kwii men had gone to a village near the road to see the chief and the elders. He had wanted to get a large piece of village land so he could make his rubber farm. The people had objected, as did the chiefs and elders of the village, until the visitor began to make them see what was in it for them. He fed them on raw cane juice the whole of one evening, and then offered them each twenty dollars to sign over the land.

The men had agreed, not really knowing what they were doing. Koli thought to himself, "These kwii will keep the land forever, and it will never again be farmed by the village. The chief and the elders may think in their drunkenness that they'll see the land again after it's fallow for about ten years. They ought to know something is wrong with the way the deal was made, but the cane juice fogged their thinking. And so they have signed away some of the best farmland they had. Now I have to prepare the agreement and get the clan chief to sign it. Even the clan chief doesn't know what's going on. He thinks he's so smart, but he himself takes money in place of understanding.

"The white kwii are not so smart," Koli realized. "They get their way by being stubborn and powerful. It's usually possible to get around them, however. Hopewell College has men to watch the houses at night, to prevent stealing. They are supposed to go around with clocks and look at all the buildings. The men agreed to do it, but just go to sleep, and leave one of them to wake up the others. People still take things from the college at night, while the guards sleep - or sometimes help steal."

Only one of the white kwii, a missionary, knew enough to understand the Kpelle, and it saved Koli and the clan chief from a really difficult case.

The white man was walking deep in the forest behind Gbarnga one day, and heard a group of men coming along the trail. He looked ahead, and caught a quick glimpse of raffia. He turned like a flash to the forest and tied a handkerchief around his eyes, to let the party of men pass. It was not allowed for non-initiates to see such things, and he knew it. Yakpalo had been with the men, and had whispered "Thank you" to the missionary for his good sense. He had been greatly relieved that they had not been forced to bring to the clan chief the case of a white man who had seen what was forbidden.

Most of the white kwii didn't even understand when they did the wrong thing, unlike the missionary who refused to look at what he should not see. Koli had gained experience in dealing with these people in the first three years he worked for the clan chief.

It seemed perfectly clear to Koli, for instance, that the missionary who lived not far from the clan chief's court - the one who had opened a school for Kpelle boys - should be held responsible for the death of three boys. When the missionary came to the clan chief, he said only, "The lightning which killed the three boys as they stood under a tree on the mission compound was an act of God, sad and pitiful, but still just an act of God." Koli had to translate and make what sense he could of the missionary's statements.

The clan chief knew the true story. He explained through Koli to the missionary, "Other parents took their children from your school after that, knowing that you urged those three boys to spy on the bush school and tell you what they saw. The boys were discovered, and so the head zoe knew what he must do. He went into the forest, behind the fence, and made lightning strike those boys. He had warned the boys twice against their action, and tried to persuade them to leave the kwii school and enter bush school. You insisted the boys should spy for you - and now they are dead. Can't you see that you shouldn't interfere with our Kpelle ways? Why couldn't you have left those boys alone, either to stay with you, or join the bush school? We gave you those boys, because you promised to take care of them. You've been stubborn and foolish. Now the boys are dead and you'll find it very hard to get other boys into your school."

The white man continued to urge the matter on the clan chief. He had appealed: "Chief, you should stop these superstitious stories about lightning killing boys. Such things can't happen. In my school, the boys are learning a higher truth, learning to escape the heathenism and savagery of the forest."

The clan chief hardly knew what to do next. He turned to Koli, "What do I say now?" he asked.

Koli explained, "I've heard such talk at Salala at school. The only way to deal with such people is to stay quiet and agree - but then do nothing. All white people are like that. You can't talk sense into them, so you might just as well be polite to them."

The missionary continued: "You yourself have said that other boys are leaving the school. You should be concerned that they are losing their chance to know the light, that they will fall back into darkness and error. I want you to make a public statement that the lightning was just a natural occurrence, and that the boys shouldn't worry, should come back to school."

The clan chief was amazed at such nonsense, but he listened seriously, as Koli translated the missionary's words. He said to Koli, "Tell the missionary anything that will get rid of him. He's lucky the zoe doesn't send lightning after him."

Koli thought fast, then told the missionary, "Since it is such a delicate and serious matter, the clan chief prefers to deal with it quietly. He will speak with each of the parents himself. But he asks you please not to interfere in our Kpelle business any more, or else he can't guarantee your safety."

The clan chief knew he had to speak privately with the parents, since they were after him to close the school, but he couldn't tell that to the missionary. In the end, the clan chief managed to quiet both the parents and the missionary by persuading a Bassa man, newly moved to the village, to send his son to the school. He explained to Koli, "The Bassa don't understand about bush school, so let them lead the way to kwii school."

Koli knew his role. He must help keep the kwii people from doing real harm to the Kpelle, and yet at the same time he must make sure that the clan chief took whatever was of advantage to his people. He felt satisfied with his work, and knew he was gradually making himself indispensable to the clan chief. In the three years he had been in the job, he had become accustomed to it, had come to like the clan chief's ways, and had made his life a bit more pleasant by having a schoolgirl, Goma, move in with him. He was, in short, content to remain in Sengta indefinitely.

During these three years, Koli went back to his village several times, and things seemed peaceful on the surface. Sumo was taking more and more of the blacksmith business, and was now almost as powerful as old Mulbah. Yakpalo was working behind the scenes to become the next clan chief of his own particular clan, and was making good use of Koli's relation with the other clan chief in Sengta. The two clans had good relations, and the authorities in Gbarnga would surely look to the long-standing cooperation between Yakpalo and Koli's chief as a reason for supporting Yakpalo's candidacy. Flumo still seemed old, but he was no worse than he had been three years earlier, after the terrible fire.

Tokpa was bidding for power, however, and this was a constant source of difficulty. Tokpa had succeeded the old head of the men's work groups only a year after Koli had gone to work in Sengta. It was also rumored that he had gone much more deeply into the water business, even to the extent of dealing with Bassa water men and joining their society.

Koli was sure this was the heart of the problem. Saki had explained to Koli a while ago that Sulongteh, the tapper, had given up waiting for Sumo's medicine to deliver him a cane mill. He had turned for help to Mogo, the Bassa water man whom he himself had been cheating through Koli's false records. Mogo never learned that Sulongteh had been the cause of his difficulties, and now Sulongteh was trying once more to use Mogo, but in a different way.

Saki had gone on to explain that Mogo had been very disappointed in his earlier conversations with Sumo. Nothing had come out of the relation but the exchange of a few leaves, and Mogo was confused and a bit angry. He had taken the risk of offering Sumo real power if he joined the water society on the St. John River behind Firestone in Bassa country. Sumo had refused it. This had been a blow to Mogo, for he had weakened himself, his own power, by offering to make it available to a man who refused to take it. Knowledge is power, and Mogo had risked making power available to someone who had chosen not to be a colleague.

Tokpa had learned of this. On a visit to Firestone, he had learned of the relation between Sulongteh and Mogo. At Firestone, he had stayed with Sulongteh, and had found out the truth of the matter by questioning Sulongteh carefully, Tokpa saw this as a chance to get back at the whole family, Flumo, Koli and Sumo alike. He saw Saki, his old enemy, as the link. Saki had foolishly - as he later realized - arranged the first meetings between Mogo and Sumo. Saki had been the go-between to persuade Sulongteh to shift his quest for money from Koli to Sumo. And Saki had not been able to deliver on either promise. Sulongteh still had no money for the cane mill of his dreams.

Thus, Tokpa persuaded Sulongteh that he would give him the help Sumo had never delivered. And he himself went one step further to join the Bassa water people. Tokpa justified himself by saying, "The really powerful zoes all move beyond their own people, and join other groups. Wasn't old Mulbah initiated at the Loma medicine town of Malawu, behind Zorzor, beyond the St. Paul River? He earned the right to wear the red robe which he puts on when he wants to show the extent of his power."

Tokpa had heard Mulbah promise to take Sumo to Malawu eventually, but not until Sumo knew more of his own Kpelle medicines. Tokpa had time to get ahead of Sumo. So it was no surprise when Tokpa, himself old enough to be the grandfather he could never become and thus old enough to step beyond the bounds of the Kpelle people, was initiated into the Bassa water society.

Everyone said he learned from the Bassa how to wear a clay pot on his head so he could breathe under water, how to catch a canoe and drag it down with a hook on a rope to catch the occupant and take him to the society's secret fence in the forest, how to kill a man with hot water and put him back in the river and make it appear he had drowned. Tokpa was rumored to share in all these wicked Bassa deeds, and his fear and respect grew in the village.

But then came the blow. Tokpa said to Yakpalo, "I have learned under the water in my dreams that Saki will surely die. I am sorry to report such a sad matter to Flumo and all his people, but Saki has broken the laws of the water."

Saki denied any relation with the water people, denied that he had ever agreed to the laws. "Tokpa is lying," he told Koli when he passed through Sengta on his way back to Firestone.

But Tokpa insisted, "Saki joined the society in his dreams. He has gone out at night, leaving his body at home, gone to the water, and promised never to allow his children to enter a white man's school. And now we all know that Saki's wife at Firestone sent her oldest boy to the new school for workers' children. Saki must know in his heart that he has broken the law. If he had only stayed with us in the village, this all wouldn't have happened."

Saki was confused, uncertain. He explained to Koli, "I certainly have my doubt about the white man's school. I've seen what it has done to you, and you know I'm not convinced it's good. But, on the other hand, I know the power of the white man, and I want my boy to have some of that power. It's true I've dreamed about that school, have even dreamed about the great river that both unites and divides the Kpelle and Bassa people. Perhaps Tokpa is right. I don't know."

75

After Saki went back to Firestone, his normal self-confidence left him. He thought to himself, "I don't have the power to fight Tokpa. Moreover, Sumo will be no help, because he turned his back on the water." He began to brood, fearing that Sulongteh had begun to tell everyone at Firestone the story.

People now turned their backs when they saw Saki, or asked him why he had broken the laws of the water. He tried to get his wife to take the boy from school, but she wouldn't agree. The only answer he could find was in cane juice. At least this stopped him from thinking about the problem. When he drank, he felt good again.

He started showing up late at work, and the white man talked to him once, twice, even three times. Saki would be still drunk when morning came, and would hardly know how to answer the man. This went on for some time and only grew worse with time.

And then, one night, Saki's troubles broke into Koli's growing contentment and peace in Sengta. He stumbled in, dirty, tired and hurt. He begged Koli, "Please pay my truck fare. I have no money at all. The truck is waiting out on the road, and the driver is threatening to have me arrested. I need just a dollar. Oh, please, help me!"

Koli had to do it, of course, but he sensed that something was wrong, and was likely to get worse. He was sure it had something to do with Saki's relations with Tokpa - the old problem again.

Koli asked, "What's wrong, Saki? What's happened?"

Saki poured out the whole story: "I went to work this morning, and I told the boss I would try to do better. You know, I'm sure, what everyone's been saying about me. It's all true, Koli. I haven't been able to stop drinking. I'm too afraid of what Tokpa said. I went out to collect the latex, but I fell with my buckets this afternoon and spilled the latex. I lost a whole day's work out in the plantation. I went to the beer shop and got some cane juice. Sulongteh followed me there. He deliberately pushed me while I was drinking. I know it was deliberate. Sulongteh laughed at me for not being able to hold my liquor. I told him to be quiet, not to trouble me. He laughed even harder, so I swung at him, cracking him hard. He fell, hit his head on a chair and couldn't get up. I tried to help him, but then I saw he was unconscious, maybe even dead. Some men came to get me when they saw the blood pouring from Sulongteh's head. I got scared and ran, ran, ran for all I was worth.

"I picked up a ride right away at the truck stop at Division 45, and left, without even going back to my house, to my wife and children. Fortunately, the truck driver is a Mandingo man I'd never seen before. Give him a dollar and get him out of here. But now you've got to help me! I'm sure Sulongteh is dead, and I killed him."

Koli knew the law. He hadn't been working for the clan chief for three years now for nothing. But he also knew that Saki was his uncle, his own blood, and there was no way in which he could refuse him. What a predicament: on the one hand, he himself would have to go to jail, if they found Saki at his house, but, on the other hand, he had to take him in. He paid the truck driver, who seemed to know nothing of the story, and let Saki in the house.

He told Goma, "Get Saki some bath water," and said to Saki, "I'll go to the Lebanese shop to buy you some clothes. The things you have on are all torn from the fight."

On the way to the store, Koli thought hard. "I have to find a way for Saki to disappear completely, and yet be safe. Otherwise the police will find him, if not at my house, then at our village. And if Sulongteh is dead, Saki himself will have to die in return. Even if Sulongteh is only badly hurt, Saki will be arrested for fighting when he was drunk. Tokpa is surely right - and Tokpa has won this time.

"But if I get too deeply involved, I will lose my job, and very likely go to jail. All my plans to help myself and my village people will fall to nothing. I have to get rid of Saki, at the same time as I help him."

He realized then that the only answer would be to go with Saki, that very night, over the back trail to the St. Paul River, where some distant relatives lived. These people were related to Flumo through his mother's sister.

Koli thought, "They won't know about the problem between Tokpa and Saki. or if they have heard of the difficulty, they won't know its extent. They don't know Saki himself, nor do they know

77

me in person, although they have probably heard of me because I work for the clan chief."

It was a different clan, but in the days of the great woman chief, before Koli was born, its people had given her protection from her enemies. Koli felt it was time to try the same trick again.

When Koli returned from the store with new clothes for Saki, he told Saki, "Bathe quickly, eat the dry rice in the pot, and get ready to go. We're going in the only direction the police would never think of." Koli went to the clan chief, and explained that he had business at home he must attend to, that he had to get seed rice from his mother for Goma to plant, and would be back in a few days. Koli knew that he had to move fast. He had to reach the St. Paul River that night, leave Saki with the people, give them a satisfactory explanation, and then travel to his own village the next day, so that he could cover his tracks with the clan chief.

"It won't be easy," he thought, "but I can get away with it. Lucky no one but Goma has seen Saki, and no one really knows him well here. The clan chief would recognize him, but it was almost dark when Saki got here."

Saki was tired and hungry, but there was no alternative but to go. Even Saki agreed to that, and so, within a short time, he was ready to go. Koli told Goma, "Don't tell anyone - no one at all - about his having been here. No one has been here. Remember?"

This remained Koli's real worry. "What if Goma tells the police? She and I are sleeping together - it's what I get for helping her with school - not that there's any real love between us. I worry that she could be bought by anyone with a higher price. I'm sure she overheard the whole story as Saki told it. But I can't deal with that problem right now. It'll have to wait a few days until I come back from the village."

Saki was almost too tired to make the walk. It had been a long, emotionally exhausting day. And he was by no means as young as he wished he were, or as Koli proved himself to be by keeping up a stiff pace over the barely perceptible trail back to the St. Paul River. Few people now followed this trail. It was easier to go west of this trail, to the large village farther down river. But Koli didn't trust the people there. They spoke Totota Kpelle, and were not really part of his family. Moreover, their village was more in touch with the outside world. Where Koli was taking Saki there was little contact to the west. Contact was more to the east, across the border into French country, where most of their own ancestors had originated, many of them not so long ago. The French border poked down, deep into Liberia, where the St. Paul River crossed from its headwaters in the southern part of French country. "If it proves necessary," Koli thought, "Saki could always escape by taking that route east."

"That is," Koli continued, "if we ever get to the village." He noticed there was no moon and the sky threatened more rain. It was not the full rainy season yet, but a lot of rain had fallen recently and the rivers were high and the swamps full. Koli wished he had already planted his rice, but welcomed the need for seed as his excuse to make the journey.

The trail crossed the watershed between the St. John River, the river that Koli and Sumo had swum and relaxed in, both as children and when Sumo had persuaded Koli to take the job upcountry, and the St. Paul River. At the watershed itself, the trail was steep but dry. However, on each side, there were many small streams and swamps, all larger than they wished. Neither man was familiar with the trail, and they often stumbled and tell into the water. In spite of the risk it implied, Koli had thought to bring with them a schoolboy, young enough not to understand the business with Saki, but old enough to show the way. But all he could do was show the main trail, not the individual details which he knew more with his feet than with his mind.

The worst point came after they had been on the trail for what seemed to Saki a week of continuous darkness, wet clothing and exhaustion. They were on the edge of a nasty swamp, which even in daylight would have been tough to cross in the rains. The schoolboy didn't encourage them when he said, "I saw a small crocodile in this very swamp when I walked to school three months ago."

At that very moment, the darkness somehow yielded to an even more complete darkness, the wind rose, and rain began to fall. It was not the spectacular, lightning-punctuated rain that marked the end of the season, but the dull, hard, cold rain of full rainy season. There was no hope even to find the logs which the boy said led across the swamp, much less keep their footing on them in the slippery darkness. Thus they had to slog through the swamp itself, sinking deeper as they walked. It was not even a clean swamp, but was ripe with muck and rotted leaves and vines which clung to them and filled their clothes, to the point that merely wet clothing would have been a pleasure. The thought was absurd at this point, but Koli wished to himself, "Why didn't I save my money, and buy Saki new clothes at the other end of the trail?"

Twice Saki stumbled and had to be helped out of the deep places in the swamp. Even the schoolboy feared he was losing his way, and would not find the trail at the other side. In fact, when they reached dry land again, the forest had closed them in on all sides. The rain was still falling heavily, and they could see nothing at all, not even each other.

The schoolboy began to be frightened. He said, "I know this country perfectly, but I've never been here before. Maybe some genii grabbed us as we walked through the swamp, and has taken us far off the trail. We'll never find our way now! It's hopeless! We have to go back into the swamp, back to the road."

Koli had to grab the boy and shake him, even hit him, or he would have run off into the darkness, would perhaps even fall into the swamp and die. He shouted, "We have to stay together, or someone will be hurt badly."

Koli began to think of Tokpa and the water people. "The boy might be right, after all. But instead of a genii, it was Tokpa's water people who led us astray, led us to where they can catch and kill Saki, and then do what they wish with the rest of us."

He shook his head. "No! I have to stop thinking that way! It's no good letting the boy's panic catch me."

For Saki was really not much good by this time, and Koli had to watch him carefully. He had begun to shake with fever, after the exhaustion of the day, and his over-heavy drinking of the past few weeks. Koli knew it was malaria, a word he had learned for the disease in school. He had always known the disease and that it caught people when they were too tired.

"Malaria only kills little children and white people," he thought. "Saki is safe enough, but he ought to get some dry clothes, a warm fire, and a good rest. But we are far from that here in the middle of the forest, and we don't know where the trail is."

Koli made the decision, because the other two were either too frightened or too tired to think straight. He told them, "We'll have to wait where we are until morning, when we can easily find the trail. It must be just a few arm-lengths to one side or the other of where we are - but which side is the problem. If we wander far into the forest, we might have real difficulty even getting back to where we are now. On the other hand, when the dawn comes, we can see easily along the edge of the swamp which way to go."

It was probably the most unpleasant night Koli had ever spent. The schoolboy was whimpering about the genii, and kept wanting to run away home. Saki was too feverish to be sensible, and just lay against Koli, moaning and shivering. The rain fell, more lightly than before, but it still fell, until almost dawn.

Koli himself felt waves of fear. "The water people will somehow get us yet," he thought. The worst moment, although it was really not dangerous, as Koli realized later, was when an otter came up from the forest and suddenly, as if from nowhere, nuzzled them to see what they were. The boy was unable to speak from fright, and Koli was badly shaken. Fortunately, Saki was too far gone to notice the animal.

Dawn came slowly and painfully. The rain had stopped by that time, but the forest and the swamp steamed with mist, and the sky was heavily overcast. It was some time before they could see far enough along the edge of the swamp to know where the trail left it and entered the forest again. When they were able to see, they realized that they had strayed almost the width of a small rice farm to the right of the trail, as they slipped and stumbled through the black and mucky waters at night. They had to work their way back through the dense forest to the trail. This was secondary growth, not uncut forest, and so it was thick with vines and creepers and saw grass. Koli somehow had to laugh to himself, "Surely Tokpa would be glad to see me again where the saw grass is thickest."

They arrived back at the trail, and once again started to walk toward the St. Paul River. Saki was better - the fever had left him, although Koli knew it would be back again by nightfall, and so they must not lose time. The boy was over his panic, and was once again showing them the way. They found a small stream coming down from the hills ahead, and stopped to drink and wash out their clothes. They were still thoroughly soaked, but at least they did not have to walk in the mire and filth of that swamp.

The climb to the watershed was itself very tough. The trail climbed up and up, getting narrower and less visible all the time. They had to cut back several times, to get around fallen trees or large boulders. Moreover, it was heating up fast, and now instead of being cold, they were sweating profusely. Koli feared that Saki's fever was coming back again, but Saki assured him, "I'm still all right."

At the top of the climb, they entered a small bush village. The women were still in the village, though they said, "Our men have gone to cut and pile the brush on the farm which we burned two weeks ago. We moved up here from the St. Paul River and its villages to make our farms, and to get away from the crowds at the central village of the area."

Koli had to laugh, "A crowd to these people means fifty houses. Here, they have five houses, with mat walls, and nothing on any side but forest."

Saki insisted he could go no further. He had to stop here and rest.

The women said, "You can stop and rest, and if you have to, you can stay here until you're better." Koli talked with them, and found that they knew his mother, Yanga. One of them had come from his part of Jorkwelle country, and had enjoyed Yanga's hospitality once or twice.

But they asked, "Why on earth are you and your friends here, and why did you come at night on that nasty back road?"

Koli had to think fast. The only thing he could think of was to tell half the truth. "Saki broke the law of the water people in the St. John river, and is running away. He was told by the zoe that it is safe in the St. Paul watershed, since there the Bassa water people can't come. This village is the first village beyond the watershed, and he'll be safe here. He was at Firestone, but he can't go back there, since the water people will catch him. And he can't even go to his own village, since the St. John passes nearby. I agreed to help Saki, and bring him to a safe place near the St. Paul. Perhaps this is the place." Saki was too tired and weak to do more than agree quietly.

The women answered, "We'll have to ask our big man, Dabolo, when he comes."

But Koli could sense there would be no real problem. He took Saki aside and said, "You'll have time here to get yourself together, and shape a future for yourself. If Sulongteh lives and recovers, you can eventually go back to Firestone, and make your peace. But, if Sulongteh dies or can no longer work, you can escape from here, if you have to, into French country. And no one will know you were here."

Koli added to himself, "Except for the school boy and Goma, no one on the road or in our home village knows where Saki is or even that he has passed through. The school boy understands nothing, but Goma is another matter. She can be mean and might just decide to tell the story in public. I'll have to solve that problem when I get back to work. But how... ?"

In the meantime, they could only wait until the men came back. The women got them bath water - a second bath felt good - and helped them wash and dry their clothes. They then cooked rice for them, and made them welcome. Saki fell into a deep sleep almost as soon as he had eaten, and Koli was glad.

The men came back after one of the women had gone to inform them of Koli's arrival. The head of the village was Dabolo, a strong, older man who had brought the others with him. Three of the women in the village were Dabolo's wives, and he had built three of the huts himself. There were two other men, who were his clients. They had come, not unlike Saki, after failing to make it elsewhere. One had a wife, but the other was single. Dabolo had given him his third wife for the time being, and expected the man to raise up children for him.

Saki looked like another client to Dabolo, and so he said, "I'm willing to accept you as my worker, for as long as you want to stay. You only have to do your share of the farm work, since I'm determined to clear the forest and plant cocoa and coffee after I finish piling and burning the sticks for my rice farm. I need extra hands." He looked at Koli as if to ask him to stay also.

83

Dabolo continued. "I came here from the big village on the river that you were probably aiming to reach. I'm the younger brother of the chief, and I'm tired taking my brother's orders. We had almost come to blows several times recently, and so I felt it was better to make my own village. I'm glad to have it small to start with, since there won't be the conflicts we knew in the big village.

"I myself worked at Firestone for two years before I took my second and third wives. I hated every minute of it, and wanted to get back to my farm. I even walked to Monrovia once before I was married, just to carry some big-shot's rice to the coast. I saw a man fall and die, his chest burst from the pain and the pressure of carrying more rice than he could manage. I stopped on a kwii farm near Monrovia, and saw a kwii, a black man like myself, beat his servants like they were slaves. I never want to go back there again, as long as I live.

"Here in the forest, on top of this mountain, I am free and I am my own man, and so are my people." He turned to Saki: "No, I won't ask you any questions. Just stay and work, and no one will know about it. The two men working with me also ran away. No, don't deny it! One look at you told me the truth. I don't even care if you killed a man."

Saki's visible jump at the word made the big man smile slowly. Koli realized he had guessed the whole story, and that it would be no good to repeat the business he had told the women.

Dabolo went on, "No, it doesn't matter if you killed a man. Just do your work, stay quiet, don't go to the big village at the river and get drunk, and you'll be all right. You can even expect to get a woman of your own. I'm negotiating for a fourth wife, and you can have her."

It was almost too good to be true, but then Koli realized that Saki himself was becoming a kind of slave as a result. He had no choice, and at least the area was clean and free - no red dust, and no police. But also there was no escape, and both Koli and Saki knew it.

Saki took Koli aside to talk to him. "Will you be sure to come get me if Sulongteh recovers? I don't dare leave the village until I know the story in full."

84

Koli promised, "I'll come back as soon as I have the story, but if Sulongteh is badly hurt, or even killed, you must stay where you are, and not try to come out. I'll send a message to you to keep low, lest you get in trouble further. Otherwise, you can take a chance and go to French country, where you know no one and no one knows you."

"It isn't bad, this place," Koli thought. "Saki could do worse. The big man Dabolo seems honest and straight forward enough. Saki will have to work hard, will have to cut the man's farm for him, take care of his village, accept a woman and raise up children, and not get credit for anything. But the man is clearly wealthy, and is clearly on the way up. If Saki does well, he might be able to move up too, provided he stays on the farm for a long time to come."

Koli left Saki there, tired and confused. The big man asked no questions, not even Koli's or Saki's name. He didn't ask where they had come from, or what they had done. He simply accepted Saki, and told Koli goodbye.

His last comment was, "If you yourself ever need a place to stay, you shouldn't forget this village. There's always room for more."

Koli was still tired, but his clothes were dry, and he had eaten a good meal. He knew he should start early, so that he might reach home that very night. Once he was beyond Gbarnga, he wouldn't have to worry about getting lost on his own trail - he knew it well enough to walk it blindfolded. But he worried about being seen crossing the main road and coming from the wrong direction. In any event, he must go now, and push hard to get there before nightfall.

He first arranged for the boy to go back to Sengta with some villagers who were going that way. Koli then asked for help in directions. With the help of the women, Koli didn't take the same route, since he didn't want anyone to see him in the clan chief's town. "On the other side of the watershed, the trail branches, and the lefthand fork will lead you to Gbarnga. It's a clear trail, better than the one you followed last night, and you'll be able to reach Gbarnga well before sunset. But you must hurry. There's a small village half-way where you can stop for food."

85

He set out at a rapid pace. He cut wide around Gbarnga to avoid being seen, and crossed the motor road just before dark.

Once he was back in the forest, he headed for the trail to his village, and found it not far below Gbarnga. It was late now, almost dark, and so he was less likely to meet people who might recognize him. He walked fast, so that he might be home before his family went to bed for the night. There was still no moon, and that made walking difficult, but he felt he could make it home all right.

He slipped silently through the village next to his own, Yanga's village. There was no trail around it. He remembered having been stopped there so many years ago, when he had first run away to school. He didn't want to be stopped this time, but now he was older and was able to take care of himself.

He reached his mother's house after she had gone to sleep. "On a dark, moonless night, with rain in the air, there is nothing to do in a village," Koli realized. "I myself would sleep early if I were here. I'm glad I don't have to stay here. There's more life at night in Sengta, although not so much as in Monrovia."

He stopped at his mother's house, and knocked at the door, calling, "It's Koli."

A response came, frightened but still welcoming. "What are you doing here at this time of night?"

Koli thought fast. His story had to match with that he told the people at the clan chief's village. He said, "I left the village yesterday evening to come home to see you, but was caught by fever. I'm not sure who were the people I stayed with, since I came by the back road, not through Gbarnga. I slept the night with strangers in a small farm village, and waited until late afternoon before starting again. Even so, I had to sit down on the trail several times before reaching home. I'm very tired, and still a bit feverish, but the chills and sweat have gone away now."

His mother let him in the house, and found him some dry rice left over from the evening meal. He wanted to sleep, and gave a good imitation of someone just recovering from illness. It wasn't hard for him to do so, because he was so very tired. He hadn't slept at all last night, in the forest in the pouring rain. And he was in fact still chilled from that night out. He let his mother put him to bed, and give him some leaves to take with his rice and palm wine.

He went to sleep, realizing that his plan had succeeded, and that Saki was safe for now. He thought, "There's only Goma in Sengta who knows. How can I keep her quiet if there is any trouble?"

VI: THE VOICE OF WATER

Koli woke up the next morning to find confusion already swirling around him.

A soldier in a red cap was at Yakpalo's house, asking for Saki. He announced, "Sulongteh has died. Saki knocked him over, and he died from falling and hitting his head on a table. Saki is missing, and I've been sent here to find him."

Yakpalo frowned and asked innocently, "Why do you look for him here?"

"You know that Kpelle people run back to their home villages when there's trouble at Firestone! Besides, Saki was seen running from the drinking house toward the market, but no one has seen him since, not even his wife. It is thought that he might have taken a truck and gone to his home. I want to know if anyone has seen him in the village."

Yakpalo asked, "When exactly did it happen?"

The soldier replied, "Late in the afternoon, the day before yesterday."

"Who were the witnesses?" Yakpalo continued.

"Sulongteh's friends who were at the bar," the soldier replied. "The case is clear, and Saki is wanted for murder."

Tokpa was on the edge of the gathering crowd of people, listening very carefully, but saying nothing. Koli came up to the group, and he listened equally carefully. Koli knew Tokpa's part in the matter, and he feared him. He believed Tokpa might even be able to read his thoughts, and so he wondered how much Tokpa might guess about his own role. Sulongteh had merely been used by Tokpa to get back at Saki, and through Saki at Flumo, Koli and the rest of the family.

The soldier eventually turned to Koli and asked, "What do you know about it?"

Koli denied knowing anything, and said, "I've been traveling since the day before yesterday, and was caught by fever in a farm kitchen between here and Sengta where I work."

The soldier was suspicious. "Why were you traveling at just the time Saki was running away?"

Koli said, "I came home to see my family and collect some rice to plant on the farm I'm making near Sengta." This much was true, at least, and Koli was relieved to find a reason for having gone home.

He explained, "I was given a spot in the forest, and paid a work group of women to clear the forest, and then a group of men to gather the sticks after I myself had burned the farm. Now I have to get seed rice in order to have the farm planted. My mother will give me the rice."

Koli tried to turn the attention from himself by asking, "What really is the problem about Saki? I came to the gathering late, and heard something about Saki hitting Sulongteh at Firestone. What happened?"

All the while Koli was talking, he saw Tokpa looking at him strangely. Koli feared Tokpa, feared his knowledge, feared his suspicions, feared whatever medicine he might have that let him see deeply into Koli's lies. But Koli knew he could rely on Sumo to help him, knew in fact more about Tokpa's recent activities than Tokpa thought he knew. He thought to himself, "I mustn't give away my knowledge cheaply, since it gives me real advantage."

Koli thus looked back at Tokpa, and asked him, "What's wrong? Do you know something about Saki and Sulongteh? After all, weren't you at Firestone more recently than anyone else in the family?"

Tokpa was clearly caught off guard. "How do you know about this?"

Koli's answer was, "Anyone at the clan chief's court knows who comes and goes, particularly so important and clever a person as you. It's the clan chief's business to be aware of what's happening, and I merely listen to what is said at the court."

It also happened to be true that the clan chief at Sengta, in laying his plans to be on the right side of Yakpalo in the next election, was watching Tokpa very carefully. He had discussed with Koli Tokpa's trip to Firestone, although of course he did not know anything of Tokpa's relations with the Bassa water people nor his most recent quarrels with Saki.

Koli had hit home, had used the knowledge he had acquired from Saki, and had combined it with casual information at the clan

89

chief's court, to put Tokpa on the defensive. Everyone in the village, including apparently even the soldier, knew about Tokpa's quarrel with Saki. Thus the challenge came back to Tokpa, just at the point where he had thought he might find something through attacking Koli.

Tokpa's quick answer was, "The hawk flies over the chicken's village to learn what is happening, not always to steal the babies."

It was a good answer. Tokpa admitted his quarrel with Saki, openly and honestly. He asserted his strength as opposed to Saki's weakness. And he denied that he had any wrong intentions. Koli was impressed, and was for the moment at a loss for words.

A voice behind Koli gave the response. "Yes, but the hawk who spreads his wings too wide makes an easy target for chicken's owner." It was Sumo, who hadn't seemed to be there just a moment earlier. Koli was grateful that his brother could find the right answer, even though it meant that the battle had been joined between two zoes.

Tokpa laughed, but the laugh came out as slightly forced. He admitted, "It's true hawk shouldn't fly too often, when chicken has to hide behind a kwii man's rifle."

Sumo countered, "Chicken may live with the kwii, but his owner is the forest, the same forest who also owns the river." Koli was afraid now, since Sumo had openly challenged the power of the water people, and had made the challenge in the name of the forest.

Tokpa's reply was, "Without the water, the forest would wither and die, and so the tree, even if it owns chicken, should beware lest lightning or wind should strike the tree and it then fall into the river and die. In that case, hawk will swoop down and find the chicken that lies hidden under the upturned roots of the tree."

Yakpalo intervened, since he did not like the force of the challenges. He knew that Saki was the focus of the problem, and that Sumo and Koli were defending Saki against a strong attack from Tokpa. And yet he wanted to keep Tokpa's friendship. He needed him and feared him. Without Tokpa's help, promised only a month earlier, he might lose the election to the post of chief of the clan which included their village. The clan chief's position was soon to be filled by an election, since the old clan chief had died recently. Yakpalo was caught, and so he changed the subject.

He turned to the soldier, and asked "Why did you decide to come all the way to this village for Saki? Did anyone actually see Saki come up-country? Had any truck driver been found who would say that Saki had left Firestone? If not, why do you trouble honest, law-abiding people? Don't you see that you're just stirring up old quarrels here, quarrels which were settled with prayer and kola nut many years ago? I agree it's the job of the police to find Saki and bring him to justice, but they shouldn't poke under a man's bed to find the snake that never entered the house. It seems more likely to me that Saki would have tried to escape into the mountains behind Firestone."

The soldier responded that he was just following orders. He had visited the clan chief at Sengta, and the clan chief himself had urged that he check Yakpalo's village. Koli stiffened inside himself when he heard that the soldier had been at his clan chief's office, but he also realized, "Obviously no one told the soldier about Saki's passing through my house two days ago."

Nonetheless, questions remained in Koli's mind. "Does Goma know Saki at all? Did she see the soldier come to the clan chief?" Koli had some space to move now, but he must cover himself carefully.

Two old men had been playing the board game of malang near Yakpalo's house before the soldier arrived, and Koli had noticed the position on the board. "It's like my own case right now," he thought. The first man had a one-move advantage over the second, but, if he lost the initiative, he would lose the game. "It's like that with me. I am slightly ahead, and Tokpa has been outfoxed and diverted with Sumo's help. But Tokpa has ways of finding out about Saki. I have to get back to Sengta soon, and cover myself against his next moves."

The soldier asked more questions. Yakpalo responded, "Saki hasn't been here in the village for several months, in fact. No one knows, or at least says he knows, anything about Saki's movements in the last two days. You yourself checked the villages along the trail from Gbarnga, and you say no one has seen Saki come this way."

91

The soldier responded, "I'll go back to Firestone, and report that I found nothing here. But the hunt will continue, and, I warn you people, if any of you keeps back information about Saki, you will be held responsible for the murder of Sulongteh, too. After all, it's not just the police. Remember that Sulongteh was also one of your family, and his spirit will come back to trouble any of you who don't help find Saki."

Koli hadn't thought of that. "I guess I'm getting too kwii," he reflected. "Perhaps Tokpa will also be in touch with Sulongteh's ghost. Perhaps the result will be that Sulongteh will not only show Tokpa where to find Saki, but will tell him about my part in his escape.

"No, I mustn't think like that. Didn't the white man at Salala tell me such ideas were all nonsense? I wish I believed more in what the white man had said. If only that white man had been more reliable in the first place, I might be able now to rely on his words. Maybe in fact the old people are right, and Sulongteh's ghost will be walking tonight."

The soldier said, "I'm leaving now to go back to the road and travel down to Firestone."

Koli thought fast and said, "I'll walk along with you. Just let me collect my rice from my mother, and I'll go back to my job."

Yanga began to protest, "You just came last night, and you've been sick!"

But Koli said, "I have to get back. The clan chief is expecting me for business, and I need to take the rice to the girl who will plant the field for me. I'll be back in a few weeks. Besides, I want to keep the soldier company." '

Sumo and Yakpalo, too, looked amazed that Koli would arrive and then leave so soon. Tokpa openly asked, "What business do you have with the soldier that you can't stay even another day with your people?"

Koli stuck to his story, "It isn't business with the soldier, I've got to be back at work." He couldn't say that this was a necessary move in keeping ahead of events before they overtook him. "To win the game, I've got to stay a move ahead," he thought.

The soldier got himself ready to be on the trail to Gbarnga, while Koli stopped for a quiet word with Sumo. "I can't explain just now, but someday soon you'll understand why I have to hurry. Please explain to Flumo and Yanga that it's very important to all of us that I hurry back to my job." Sumo asked, "Is it something to do with Tokpa, or maybe even Saki?"

Koli answered, "Yes, but be quiet about it. I can't explain just yet. Don't worry. Saki's all right. But watch Tokpa very carefully." Sumo answered, "OK, Koli, I'll trust you. But it isn't enough just to be a kwii man to beat Tokpa at his game. You have to trust our Kpelle ways a bit more. You think you can do it yourself. But don't forget the people here, or our ancestors. One tooth doesn't make a mouth, Koli."

As he walked along with the soldier, Koli reflected, "It's remarkable for Sumo, in fact, to trust me. He's right about my trying to go my own way as a kwii man. There's a lot I've done and said that must prove me untrustworthy in the Kpelle way. Sumo may not know how to read and write, but he knows a lot I don't know. I used to think him stupid to stay back in the bush while I went off to school. I know better now, and I'm glad he reminded me of it. He seems closer to me now than I guess I deserve. It wasn't for nothing that we grew up together, that we are twins. Now maybe I can take a share of being a zoe, admittedly a kwii zoe, but still a zoe."

Koli made a point of walking openly through Gbarnga. He stopped at the German store and bought the soldier a cold beer. He couldn't afford it, but it seemed worth it. He mustn't let the soldier leave with the least suspicion that Koli knew anything. He talked naturally and calmly, about the new road beyond Gbarnga to the north, about the president's latest visit up-country, about the troubles they all had still with the kwii in Monrovia.

It was only just before he turned to leave the soldier that he said, "I'm really sorry to hear this business about Saki. I personally hope Saki won't have to suffer for what he did, but I can understand that you are just doing your duty."

That comment seemed to relax the soldier still further, seemed to lead him to accept that Koli's frankness showed he knew nothing about Saki's whereabouts. The soldier admitted, "People in Firestone don't really believe Saki came up-country. They themselves would have run into the forest near Gibi mountain, if they had been in trouble, and tried to hide there. In fact I was sent to Saki's village really only to lead Saki to relax his guard and show himself somewhere in the Firestone area. Soldiers are waiting there with instructions to catch him if they see him."

Koli's wits sharpened and his senses quickened at these words. He realized, "This soldier is playing a game with me, trying to catch me off guard, too. I'm sure he still thinks I know something, and I think his friendly talk is just a trap." But Koli tried not to show that he realized the game had doubled and redoubled back on itself. He smiled wryly and said, "I have to wish both you and Saki good luck. Good luck to Saki since he's my uncle, and to you since you're doing what you know is right to do."

He laughed slightly as he told the soldier on parting, "If I see Saki, I won't tell you, because I'm sure you'll have seen him first."

"If you won't watch out for Saki, then watch out for yourself. Don't forget - before python eats red deer in the forest, he checks for driver ants," the soldier replied.

Koli was troubled, as he waited at the truck stand in Gbarnga to catch the next vehicle going toward the clan chiefs town. "Did I let something slip past my guard? What does the soldier know? Am I, Koli, python, red deer or driver ant, in the soldier's eyes? Or was the soldier just spreading his net in the hope that something might fall in, be it python, red deer or even driver ant? I'm sure the soldier knows nothing about Saki's hiding place, but I must be careful."

He found a taxi waiting across from the German store in Gbarnga. It belonged to a Mandingo man from French country who had come to Monrovia and bought an old car there. He drove it back to Gbarnga, and was now running it as a taxi. Its headlights didn't work, and the tires were almost as thin as leaves, but it could still ply the road from Ganta to Salala and back. The driver did not dare take it further toward Monrovia, lest he be arrested. He had bribed the police here, but down country he didn't know anyone.

Koli got in the taxi, but had to wait almost an hour until the driver had a full load of six, two in front and four in back. The car was finally filled with two Hopewell College students who had gone to Gbarnga for a day away from campus and a chance to shop for some kwii things. They spoke English, neither being Kpelle, and Koli sat quietly, listening, without giving the impression he could understand. At first, their conversation was unimportant and uninteresting to him. This teacher had newly come from America, that student had left after winning a scholarship to go abroad, the football team had defeated the Liberia College team.

Then Koli's attention was caught.

It was caught - of all things - when they began to talk about Jonathan!

One said, "Jonathan was arrested last month in Monrovia, and had to face charges of theft. What a joke! He claimed to run a school, but really he was just using it to recruit boys to sell stolen goods for him. Jonathan's godmother, a real big-shot's wife, took care of him. She pleaded for him in court. That must have been a sight! She bribed some official, and Jonathan was set free.

"And this is the best part," the student continued. "The condition of Jonathan's freedom is that he take a serious and responsible job up-country, to help the 'tribal people.' They said he had to come to Gbarnga this month, where he would have to work as a clerk to the tax-collector."

The other student laughed, and said, "It's like setting a hawk to watch the chicken-house! Country people, watch out!"

The students were dropped off at the gate of the college, and the taxi went on with Koli. He knew he'd run into Jonathan sooner or later - worse luck! "I'm sure Jonathan will remember me, and I'm sure he'll try to use me for his own purposes. He'll try to use me to profit from the local people."

He shrugged, saying to himself, "Let him come, I'm older and smarter now, and I won't be fooled again!" He ground his heel into the gritty floorboard of the taxi in silent emphasis.

The taxi slowed to a stop in front of the clan chief's court. Koli paid the driver 25 cents, and got out. He was dead tired, but he had to make a good show. He went to the clan chief's office, and announced, "I'm back. I brought the seed rice I need for my farm. Thanks very much for letting me go home on such short notice."

The clan chief asked after Yakpalo and Flumo and Tokpa, and didn't seem at all suspicious where Koli had been. He then asked casually, "Did you hear about Saki?"

Koli's response was equally casual. "A soldier came to our village looking for Saki, and he and I returned together. No, Saki hadn't come that way, and no one had seen him." The clan chief accepted Koli's statement, apparently at face value.

Koli asked, "Please excuse me a little longer, so I can go home, leave the seed rice, bathe and have some food. I'll be back in the afternoon to work."

The clan chief agreed, "There's nothing very important to do, only a letter from the provincial commissioner in Ganta to be read and answered." He held out the letter.

Koli went over, picked up the letter and scanned it briefly. It said something about a new clerk for the district tax collector.

Koli thought of warning the clan chief about Jonathan, but decided against it on the grounds that his connection with Jonathan might get him into trouble. He only said, "I'll read it more carefully when I get back." He handed back the letter.

At home, he found Goma back from school for the day. "She's so pretty, so desirable," thought Koli. "And yet she doesn't think of anyone except herself."

The first thing she asked Koli was, "What did you bring me, lover?"

He showed her the seed rice to plant, and said, "We'll share it, if you help on the farm."

She shook her head and frowned. "That's not what I mean. What did you bring me from the store at Gbarnga? I give you what you want. You're supposed to take nice care of me." Fortunately, Koli had thought ahead, even when he was with the soldier. He had picked up a head tie and a bottle of beer at the German store, and he gave them to her. He realized he couldn't be too careful.

She seemed satisfied with his gift, and went to cook Koli some rice and soup. She was old for school, being mature already four years. He thought, "I'm not sure why she doesn't quit school and marry. I guess she's content to live my kind of kwii life, and enjoy what I can give her. She doesn't study hard, but neither does anyone else at that school. She's in the sixth grade now, and will be finished soon, if she doesn't get pregnant first." That thought worried Koli, but not very hard. "That's her business," was his first thought, reacting just as he had done when Eva had become pregnant.

But at once he remembered it wasn't the same game at all. Goma might know more about Saki than he wanted her to know. As if she read his thoughts, she asked, "Who was that man you went off with two nights ago? What kind of trouble is he in?"

Koli thought fast, and then said, "It's not women's business. Forget it."

She pressed him harder, "Come off it, Koli! I know he was in trouble. And if you don't tell me, I'll try to find out. And you might not like that."

Koli thought of beating her to keep her quiet, but realized, "She's too dangerous to allow loose if she's angry. She could lead the police to me and then to Saki." So he simply replied, "OK, he's a relative of my father's from Monrovia. He lived with them near Liberia College. He was caught sleeping with his friend's wife, and just got away in time. The friend threatened to kill him, and so he needed to find a place to hide. He asked me for help, and I suggested a place in the bush where he could be safe until his friend forgot the matter."

Goma laughed, and asked, "Koli don't be stupid. Why did the man say he was Saki, just from Firestone, and needed to be hidden? Why do you lie to me? What are you afraid of?"

Koli realized she had figured out what had happened, so he had to admit, "1'm afraid the police might come and question you about Saki. If they do, you need to have a good story. If the police find out that either of us knows something, and didn't tell it sooner, we'll be taken to jail. You have to be as careful as I am, lest that happen. You're involved because you know everything. I can protect you by not telling you where Saki really went."

Her response was, "I can find out any time I like, just by asking the little boy who guided you. You shouldn't think yourself so big that you can treat me like a child also. You ought to know that the policeman in town likes me, and wants to sleep with me. If you don't satisfy me, I'll just leave you and go to the policeman. And then I can't be responsible for what I might say to him. So you had better make sure you bring me presents from time to time, and take good care of me. Already I have to do too much of the work, and I want a little girl to help me."

Koli was tempted again to strike out and hit her, just to keep her quiet, but he stopped. She might say too much. And, even if Koli denied what she said, people would be suspicious. He could only say quietly, "I have to trust you. I'll treat you as nicely as I can. But you should remember that if you ever do anything to me, everyone will know you betrayed me, and you'll never have peace again. Moreover, my brother Sumo would get you in the end. You know that Sumo is a powerful zoe. The best thing is for both of us to forget the whole issue. I'll take care of you. Just you be quiet and respect me.

"As for the boy, he knows nothing. I was careful to say nothing in his presence. So the only way the news can come out is by you. And if it comes out, it's true that I will be finished, but you'll then find out that life won't be easy for you, either, even with your policeman friend. He'd know you are a betrayer, and that knowledge would beat you in the end."

The exchange ended by Goma asking, "Just take care of me, Koli, and don't worry about me." Koli knew he had won a temporary victory, but still worried about the future.

A year passed with no word from Saki, after Koli had sent him a message that Sulongteh had died. Koli heard indirectly from the big man, Dabolo, that Saki was well, and was living with the big man's new wife. Koli was worried only that Dabolo knew exactly how to send Koli a message. Might he be a threat in the future?

Saki's disappearance was also largely forgotten in his own village, particularly during the election for clan chief of Yakpalo's clan. There had been two candidates, but the other man, from a village near Palala, received little support. When the elders from all the villages involved in the election had lined up to vote, Yakpalo had received 830 votes and the other man only 297. Yakpalo's rival tried to protest, but the Provincial Commissioner overruled him. "The people have spoken," he said.

It was a time for real rejoicing in the village, since now they would begin to have some privileges that other villages had enjoyed in the past. Yakpalo announced he would keep his headquarters in his own village, and the government allowed him to do so.

Flushed with his overwhelming success in the lopsided vote in his favor, Yakpalo wondered after the election why he had ever enlisted Tokpa's aid at all. As Yakpalo's nephew, Tokpa had offered beforehand to make special medicines to defeat the other man, and Yakpalo had accepted.

The problem was that now Tokpa could expect special privileges for having helped Yakpalo win. In particular, he would expect Yakpalo to be hard on Flumo, Sumo and Koli. However, Sumo had also made medicine for Yakpalo, and Tokpa knew it. Thus, Tokpa could not expect too much privilege. He had had to stay quiet after Saki's disappearance, lest he draw attention to himself in the matter. But now that the issue seemed largely forgotten, he could begin another attack on the family he had grown to hate so heartily.

Tokpa's anger had grown during the year. He had contacted Toang, Flumo's older wife, to make medicine for Yanga to sleep with him. At first, he thought Toang's medicine had worked, for Yanga came to him as planned. But instead of accepting his lovemaking, she began to ask why he treated her boys so badly. He became angry, and Yanga left his house before anything could happen. It made him all the more determined to get revenge on Flumo and his family. "The business of Saki might be forgotten," he thought to himself, "but I'll find another way."

Even Goma seemed to have forgotten about Saki, although Koli remained afraid of her for her knowledge. She was failing her sixth-grade work again, and Koli thought, "It'll be the same situation as with Eva. Why she isn't pregnant I can't understand. Surely, she will be soon, and I'll have to support her or else run away. And I can't run away, since she'll use the business about Saki against me."

But matters were out of Koli's hands. What began to make a difference was the Liberian lady, Sarah, from the Seventh Day Adventist church. She made friends with Goma, during the second year after Saki's disappearance, and even Koli could see that the girl began to change.

Koli thought, "Sarah isn't just another white missionary." Koli had little use for these people. "The white man who found me in the first place and took me to school never even wrote me a letter. True, I never in fact wrote him the letter I always intended to write. Too many things happened in the meantime. But at least the man might have tried to find out about me."

But Sarah seemed different. In the first place, she wasn't a white foreigner. She was a Kissi woman from the north of Liberia, where she had been a hospital worker. She had come to work at the clinic in Gbarnga, where she translated what the patients said to the foreign doctor. She came on weekends to Sengta to preach, and to hold services on Saturday. She seemed to think that praying on Saturday was much better than praying on Sunday. Koli never understood why, even though Goma began to go regularly to her church on Saturday. But Koli could see that Sarah was different.

He thought, "She means what she says, for one thing. If she tells the people she'll come to their village for prayers, they can count on her. If you are sick, she'll get you to Gbarnga."

The most important thing to Koli was that Goma went regularly to church on Saturdays. However, he heard that Sarah told Goma, "Just sleeping with a man is wrong. You should find yourself a husband, and stop living unmarried with Koli. I have a husband myself, and marriage is a good thing."

Koli himself could only laugh. He had failed so often. But now that Goma started spending more time with the church people than home with Koli, Koli wondered what he must do to keep Goma with him, and to protect himself from trouble over Saki.

One Saturday afternoon in the heavy rain, Goma came back from church, and told Koli, "I'm leaving you unless you marry me. I've lived with you all this time, and never once did you talk about getting married, not even now that I've quit school. I now know that living like this is sinful, and I don't want to do it any longer. I'm tired of cooking your food and making your farm - and I want children. Probably God has prevented it because of the sins we are committing."

Koli had heard talk about sin before, and it confused him. He asked, "Isn't it a sin for the white missionary to break up families by telling a husband to get rid of his second or third wife? Isn't it a sin for a boy to be told that his father's ways are foolish?" Now someone was accusing Koli of sin, and he didn't like it.

Goma continued, "I don't know about other sins, I know what we are doing is wrong. I have a friend in the church. I'm going to live with her and her parents, and now try to do the right thing in my life for a change. If you ever want to see me, you should start coming to church. It wouldn't hurt you to pray, to think of God and not just of yourself."

Koli tried to laugh inside himself, but it didn't come easily. This was the third time he had failed with a woman.

True, it might make his life easier to have Goma out of his way, but inside he didn't like it. He was fairly sure she wouldn't bring up the business about Saki now that she was joining the church. It wouldn't help her with the church, and they would probably say it was sinful to bring a report against Koli. At least, he hoped so. What worried Koli more was that he couldn't make a success of his relations with women.

Koli didn't want to be deceived again by church people. He had trusted the white man at Salala, and had been let down. It was true that Sarah was a Liberian, from farther up-country than himself. But that didn't help Koli believe her, because surely she was just part of the same white man's system.

And yet, he thought, "Goma invited me to the church to meet the people. Praying is more than I can do, but I might at least attend the church. It might give me a way to go on seeing Goma."

He put the question aside, however, because Jonathan came to see him in Sengta.

Jonathan reached for his right hand, shook it, properly snapping fingers as the handshake ended. "It's great to see you, Koli, after so long! I heard you were here, Koli, and you really are here! When I heard you were here, I wanted to come tell you about myself. You left Monrovia very angry with me, but I've changed now. I'm sorry I treated you so badly before, but now I'm here to help all of us country people. You're Kpelle, and I'm Vai, but we have to work together."

Koli ignored the allusion to working together. "Why haven't you finished college?"

101

Jonathan said, "I now plan to go to Hopewell College. But first I have to do some work to make up for the money I lost in Monrovia."

Koli thought of asking him how the law case had come out, but he decided against it: "Let him pretend if he wants to. All Jonathan will do is lie, and so it's useless to discuss the law case or the fact I know he used to go to Hopewell. I'm not going to fall for his stories again, however!"

"This time," Jonathan continued, "I've come to talk about something new. I've made friends with some students at Hopewell College who came this year from East Africa. These students are great people, and they're opening my mind to the truth about Africa. . . ."

"Truth?" Koli interrupted.

"Africa soon will be free from the white men that have dominated her for so long, and now I'm part of a real movement for freedom and justice in Africa. In fact, these students are going to Ghana in three months for a conference on just that topic. They want me to go with them to learn more about this wonderful new movement."

Koli was confused. Jonathan always did this to him, he talked so fast and confidently, usually a little beyond Koli's grasp. He had heard of Ghana, had heard of Kwame Nkrumah who had set his people free. He had heard also of Sekou Toure, just across the border into French country. He thought, "Now they call it Guinea, but I don't know why."

He said to Jonathan, "But this surely has nothing to do with Liberia, which has been free and independent for 111 years now? Only last month they celebrated the day, as they always do, and I joined the others in praising Liberia's freedom."

But Jonathan asked Koli, "Do you really believe Liberia is free? Don't you know what those people in Monrovia are doing to the country people? Haven't you heard what they did to me, Jonathan, by accusing me falsely of all sorts of crimes? True, we sold a few watches cheap, but they weren't anybody's watches really."

Koli knew perfectly well what Jonathan had done, but he didn't think it worth letting Jonathan know. Jonathan had clearly made up his mind that he had not been treated fairly. It had taken some help from the East African students to shift the story the way he had, but facts had never bothered Jonathan once his mind was made up about something, Koli remembered.

Jonathan went on about what these students said. "Just the other day, one said, `Liberia is just a colonial outpost of the United States. It is hardly even a country of its own. Didn't Firestone buy the country for ninety-nine years back when the British and the French tried to take it over? What do Liberia's leaders ever do to help their own people, when it comes to a choice between American interests and the interests of the country people?' And I agree with him. You know all about these things, Koli."

Koli had to half agree, even when he remembered that Jonathan was the source. He did know that when he was at Firestone, he and the other men who did the work got almost no pay, while the white men lived in beautiful houses and hardly did any work. He still remembered the white lady at the market who had made him carry oranges for one cent.

But Koli asked, "What has this to do with me? Even if Liberia isn't completely free, there's no hope for people like ourselves except to work with the government we have. Already both of us have good jobs, and have a chance to work up the ladder. We're making decent money, and, as the clan chief once told me, 'Snake is never hungry.' What I'm doing is hard on some people, and what you're doing is even worse, but we have to live, and all that we earn is going back to help the country people in the long run. Besides, the government protects the people, and has to get something for its work."

Jonathan laughed at Koli for his ideas. "Don't you understand that one day there will be a change, a real revolution in Liberia? These East Africans came here to make friends with the poor people, the real people, of Liberia, and help them form their own revolution. Someday they will take over the country, in the name of the country people, and they will throw out all the Americans, the missionaries, and, most important of all, the Americo-Liberians."

Koli wondered where this talk was going to lead and how it was going to touch him personally.

"And now I need your help. I want you to loan me some money, at least as a way to thank me for all the effort I put into your education. It wasn't perfect, of course, but you would never have gotten this job if it hadn't been for the education I gave you. You'd never have known how to work with a clan chief, how to advise him on dealing with white people, Liberians and country people. You'd have just remained a little country boy from behind Gbarnga. And now I need your help. I know you're making good money, and I know that you can afford to give me some help.

"I need the money to go to Ghana with the East Africans. We'll take taxis and buses overland through Guinea and Ivory Coast, until we reach Ghana. Guinea will be independent of France by that time."

"What does that mean?" Koli asked. "Isn't Guinea French country?"

Jonathan replied, "No, Koli, it will be free, truly free. We can travel from Ganta to 'Nzerekore in a free country, and from there through Bouake to Kumasi and finally down to Accra. And there, in Accra, will be the greatest gathering of real Africans you can imagine. People from north, east, south and west Africa, leaders of their people, men who will overthrow the colonial yoke - all will be there. And Liberia can learn from them what to do next.

"If you can just loan me some money, even fifty dollars would help, then you'll be glad later. Not only will I be sure to return the money, but I'll make sure that you are on the inside of the movement when it gets under way in Liberia. You have the beginnings of a good education - I made sure of that - and the movement needs you, just as you need the movement for more education."

Jonathan sweetened it ever more "There is a group which meets in Gbarnga, behind the tax office, in the dance hall there. On the front it is a school, but behind the school we have ideas and plans. The East Africans come from Hopewell at night and on weekends to teach in the night school. They are even persuading some of the white teachers at Hopewell to join them in the teaching. It makes things look better, they say. But after the white teachers have gone home for the night, they remain and have beer with the students, mostly grown men who want to improve them-

104

selves. At this time, we hear their real ideas, their ideas about a truly free Liberia, where Americans and their slaves, the Americo-Liberians, no longer rule.

"I want you to come along to the evening classes. You will be able to learn something, not only about mathematics and English and history at the regular classes, but also about freedom and revolution and socialism at the discussions held after the classes. This is the chance of your life, the chance to be part of a new country. If you loan me the money I need, then you can come to these classes without having to pay anything."

Koli wasn't sure whether to laugh or cry at all these words. He wasn't sure if this might be just another scheme to sell stolen watches, stolen medicines, or stolen ideas.

"And yet," he thought, "It's a chance to go to school and have Hopewell students and teachers as my teachers. Moreover, Jonathan is making more sense this time than he did in Monrovia. I think the Americans and the Americo-Liberians are hurting us. I've seen them do it at Firestone and in Monrovia."

Koli said, "I want to think about the matter. I understand what you're saying, but I'm not sure if it's what I want just now. Isn't there a danger that the government might find out about what you're doing? The man who opposed the president in the 1956 elections is still in jail, and is likely to stay there a long time to come. The president has made speeches about this. He said, `I'm against all those who want to destroy Liberia with strange and confounded ideas, ideas of communism and godless devilry.' Our president really wants to help the people of Liberia, and besides I don't want to go to jail for nothing."

Jonathan laughed again - it bothered Koli that Jonathan would always laugh at such times. "There's no danger," Jonathan said. "Why, there are lots of government people who know about our plans. I don't want to name any names just now, but we have supporters in high places. And the revolution will come soon, very soon. No, there's nothing to worry about. But if you want to wait a bit before deciding, I'll come back."

In fact, Jonathan returned the following Saturday, and took Koli to drink a beer at the Lebanese store. They talked about old friends, about the days in Monrovia, about Eva and now Goma, about which was worse, the Lebanese or the white people. Jonathan bought Koli a second beer, and added a bit of cane juice to strengthen it. By this time Koli was beginning to feel relaxed, was beginning to think, "Maybe I misjudged Jonathan in the first place in Monrovia. He talks so well, and he has such good ideas. Perhaps I should help him a bit."

Jonathan bought Koli a third beer, and mixed in a strong lacing of cane juice. Koli felt better, even though when he tried to stand, he found he couldn't make it to his feet alone. Jonathan had his arm around him and was praising him to the skies. It made him feel good.

Fortunately for Koli - as he realized later - he had only saved thirty dollars. He had sent some back to his family last month, for them to buy rice to tide them over until the harvest. So he had only thirty dollars to loan Jonathan. He was not quite sure how Jonathan managed it, but it wasn't long before the thirty dollars was in Jonathan's hands, and a small booklet from East Africa was in Koli's hands in return. It was all about someone called Karl Marx, and about how he would lead the people of Africa to freedom. Koli had thought the whole idea of the movement was to get rid of the white people, and here was another one, named Karl Marx.

Koli promised "Jonathan, I'll look at the book later. My eyes aren't working too well now. No, I won't show it to anyone else, without your permission. And I'll come to Gbarnga to your night school next week."

"It isn't every day," Jonathan insisted, "that you have the chance to better yourself and improve the life of your fellow Kpelle people, all in the same action."

Koli found it difficult getting home. It was dark, and rain was falling again. The road seemed different to him, and he fell into a pool of muddy water.

What was worse was that he met Goma on the street. She started to ask Koli when he would join her at church, and why he hadn't come that day, when she realized that Koli was drunk. That was too much for her.

She almost shouted, "You lie, you cheat the soldiers of their proper pay, you won't pray, you refuse to marry a girl you've lived with for all these years, you tried to take the law in your own hands in a murder case - and now you're drunk! God will punish you for all you've done, and are now doing."

Koli wanted to tell her to be quiet. People would hear her, and might know what she was talking about. But somehow his head was spinning too much to reach out to her, and get her to be quiet. He could only somehow realize that she was right, and yet he couldn't admit it to himself. He had too many ideas to deal with for one day, and his head wouldn't hold them all. He slipped again, and half fell against her legs. He reached out to hold her, and noticed that she felt good to him.

She hesitated, realizing that if she pushed Koli away, he would fall into the mud. Besides, she still cared about him enough not to want to hurt him again. She let him lean on her, until he caught his balance again. But somehow he didn't let go, didn't go on walking, as she had thought he would. He stayed next to her, holding on now to her waist and arms, just looking at her. She couldn't see him clearly, it was too dark for that, but she knew he was looking at her. He was drunk, wet, muddy and sinful. But still she felt something of what had brought her to him in the first place.

She could only say to him, "Come, let me get you cleaned up, and then maybe I can talk sense to you."

Koli half-followed, half-led her back to his house. There was no light at the house, for Koli had gone out early in the day. No one had moved in with Koli to help him after Goma had left, and he was alone in his two rooms, now dirty and smelly. He had bought some dried meat in the market earlier that week, and was still eating the same palm butter he had made for himself. The meat had not been fresh in the first place, and now it smelled rotten. It had rained too much all week for Koli to wash any clothes, and what few things he had lay dirty on his bed and on the floor.

Koli knew what Goma would say and think when she lit the lamp and saw all these things. Somehow, he hoped she would just leave him there in all his dirt and drunkenness just as he also hoped she would come in with him and put him to bed, join him in bed.

He realized, "That can't be. She's too practical for that, too much concerned to do the right thing, now that she's joined Sarah's church."

Goma lit the light, and started to help Koli put things in order. She was angry at him, he could see that, but she also couldn't help laughing. She said, "When snake sheds his skin, at least he pushes it out of his hole." Koli looked so foolish and pathetic, she couldn't bring herself to be more angry than that.

"Koli, this place is awful," she said. She threw the rotten palm butter and meat out the door for the chickens to eat in the morning, and found some clean rice for the two of them.

Koli roused himself to say, "I don't have any soup to put on it, but at least there's palm oil and greens."

Goma went to the Mandingo man at the next house, and begged for some water so sweetly that he unlocked his well and let her take two buckets. She said, "Tomorrow, I know I'll have to go to the stream and get more, but it's too dark and wet now."

The Mandingo man laughed at her for coming back to Koli again. She insisted, "I haven't done anything of the kind, but I'm just helping him get himself together." But her statement didn't carry the ring of conviction.

She knew what she had to do. She thought, "I'll help Koli clean up and get something to eat, and then go back to Sarah. Yet I can't leave Koli this way, he needs me. I have to show him the right way to live, have to bring him to the church, have to get him away from bad company."

She continued to herself, "You can't make fire in wet wood, but dry wood will cook the food. I have to dry Koli, outside and inside, and one day perhaps he'll be willing to marry me. I do like him, even though I can't really explain it. If I were at all sensible, I'd have just let him slip into the mud and lie there, but I couldn't do it."

By the time the rice and greens were ready, Goma had cleaned the house enough and made sure Koli was himself clean enough to be satisfied with her work. Koli was still drunk, but was coming somewhat to himself. She set the rice on the table, poured the hot palm oil and cassava greens over it, and made him eat. She took her own portion, finished it, and said, "Koli, now I'm going home."

Koli tried to stop her, remembering how good she had felt against him as he picked himself up from the road. "Stay with me, sleep with me, love me again."

But she refused. "I've found a better way than falling in the mud, than mixing with rascals from Monrovia, than lying to the police. I don't want to come back to you, unless you too find that better way I told you about."

Koli ate what she brought, tried again to stop her, but found even that was difficult for him. His head was beginning to hurt, and he realized that really he just wanted to sleep. She had built a fire in the center of the house, to warm the water and cook the food, and it took the chill of the night rain off the room. Koli's eyes had trouble staying open, and the only sensible thing he could do was to admit defeat. He promised her, "I'll try to live better, if you promise to come back to me." He barely remembered when she left the room, and hardly knew anything until the Mandingo man's roosters wakened him the next morning.

VII: THE THICKENING SHADOW

Koli heard that the president would travel up-country, to hold an executive council in the far interior. He expected all the chiefs to meet him in Gbarnga after he returned from the council, and then to go with him to open a new village school at Balataa behind Hopewell College. The school had been built there in Balataa by a group of American boys and girls, in Liberia for a school holiday. Koli had watched them at work, and couldn't understand why they should come to Africa to waste their time doing hard work, and for no pay. He was sure they would get something out of it in the end, and that the Kpelle people would lose.

But at least now there was a new school. The school in the clan chief's village was already overcrowded, and this new school would make it possible for children behind Hopewell to learn to be kwii without walking all the way to the clan chief's village, even if they could find a space there, which was itself unlikely.

Koli thought, "I wish I'd been born later, wish I could have gone straight through school in my own country. Now other children will get that chance. Jonathan was right that we country people may have been exploited - I now think I know what that word means - by not getting a chance for an education when the kwii people of the coast could always get their children into schools and colleges."

Jonathan had gone to Ghana with the East Africans, and had returned just two weeks before the school was to open. He was full of excitement and great plans for Liberia as he talked to Koli at the night school in Gbarnga.

"The conference was," he said, "a turning point in my life. I see now that I have to give myself to a new Liberia, a new Africa, and I want you, Koli, to join the movement as a full member." Jonathan's fresh enthusiasm on top of his old, winning charm won Koli over, making it hard to remember the old parcel of lies.

Goma, however, tried to stop Koli. She had persuaded him to attend church for the last three Saturdays, and now she had come back to be with him at his house. Sarah didn't like Goma's returning to Koli before they were properly married, but she decided to wait and see.

Koli felt pushed by both Jonathan and Goma (behind whom stood Sarah). So it was a relief to go home to his village for a few days, especially since he went there on the orders of the clan chief. Koli didn't want to lose Goma again, but he was impressed with Jonathan's greater power and strength after his trip to Ghana.

"He really might have changed his ways," thought Koli. "The trip to the village will give me a chance to think over what the two of them have to offer. Sarah is troubling me these days to make a 'decision for Christ,' as she puts it. It's hard enough to make a decision for Goma or for Jonathan, without bringing in other people."

So Koli took the message to Yakpalo about the opening of the school. He told Yakpalo, "The president will come back from the interior in four days. When he comes, he wants you and all the other chiefs present. I'll walk to Gbarnga with you and there we'll meet the president's party and go on to Balataa."

For a few days, he could let his mother, Yanga, take care of him before returning to the necessity for decisions. "Life is getting too complicated." Yet even Yanga didn't leave him alone.

"It's been six years since you went to work in Sengta, and you aren't married yet! Your brother has two children now, and where are you? Why don't you let us find you a girl from my village? You've got a good place to stay now. Why not?"

Koli didn't to think about it yet. He told his mother, "Just wait. I'll find a good Kpelle girl in Sengta. I might even marry Goma."

Flumo had largely given up even the pretense of work these days, and Sumo was supporting him. Yanga and Toang were still active in the village work groups, and as a result they had enough rice and some to spare. But Toang herself was weakening, and depending more on Yanga to do the work for the two of them. Their old jealousy had faded.

The rivalry between Sumo and Tokpa was still the most serious issue in the family.

Three weeks ago, Tokpa had drunk too much the night after the women's work group harvested his rice. He had been boasting how wealthy he had become, now that the water people were helping him. He said, "The forest obeys me, just as the land and

111

trees are always at the mercy of the water." Sumo broke in and said, "Tokpa you yourself are at the mercy of the water, and someday you'll be sorry. You should realize that the land and the forest are the father and mother of the waters, and without them there would be no water."

Tokpa responded, "Sumo, you don't know what you're talking about. I, Tokpa, know the water is father of the forest."

Tokpa was silent for a moment, smiled slightly, and then became direct. "What do you know about your own parentage?"

Sumo began to speak of the leaves, the trees, the bush cow, to which he owed his life. But Tokpa brushed proverbs said, and told Sumo, "Ask your mother, Yanga, who is the father of her twins."

The group went silent. Tokpa had gone too far with this one. The young ones turned away, but listened hard to hear what would happen next. The old ones knew what Tokpa was talking about, and were hurt inside that he had chosen to reopen old wounds. They knew that Yanga had been sleeping with Tokpa in secret off and on before the twins were born, and even often after that, although they knew Yanga had rejected him recently. They also had guessed Tokpa had slept with her, not so much for love of Yanga, but to hurt Flumo and his family. And, that now he was striking out against all of them, and in particular at Yanga for her coldness.

And now here was the accusation that many people thought had been buried forever. Flumo was fortunately not present when Tokpa broke the rules of discourse, broke through the veiled hatred of almost thirty years, and diverted the attack from the family as a whole to the boys themselves and to their mother. He knew that if Sumo's parentage were cast in serious doubt, he might be discredited as a powerful zoe. Moreover, if Sumo had to admit Tokpa as possibly his father, then Tokpa would gain an authority which would show that Sumo had always been in the wrong in fighting Tokpa.

Tokpa did not get away with his attack this time, however. Yakpalo stepped in.

Yakpalo was in Tokpa's debt, but he also was Tokpa's uncle - his sister had been Tokpa's mother. Because the relationship between them existed, Tokpa had to respect it. So when Yakpalo took Tokpa aside, harshly and quickly, Tokpa had to follow.

Tokpa would have preferred to fight it out with Sumo then and there, but he followed Yakpalo. He didn't really know if Sumo and Koli were his children or not. It didn't really matter very much. Tokpa had no living children of his own, and his vocation as member of the water society prevented him now from having any.

Yakpalo took Tokpa outside, and pushed him against the wall of the house. "You fool," he said. "The only person you'll hurt in the end is yourself after you kill Flumo with shame. The village is too small for this sort of thing."

Tokpa was about to answer when Sumo came out of the house, determined and clearly enraged. He started to push past Yakpalo to get at Tokpa, when Yakpalo stopped him and said, "Tokpa made a mistake, and wants to say something to everyone in the house." No one else had left yet, and Yakpalo half pushed, half pulled the two men back inside Tokpa's house.

Tokpa knew what Yakpalo wanted him to do, but he couldn't say it directly. He could only say, "There are monkey people. They know how to pick ripe corn, but they don't know how to carry it."

Everyone knew he was referring to the chimpanzees from the forest who had stolen ear after ear of ripe corn from Tokpa's fields, but had dropped each one as they went to pick the next one in the field. They ended by taking one ear each, and leaving a trail of already harvested corn for Tokpa to pick up and take home.

Tokpa went on to say, "I, Tokpa, am like monkey. I knew how to start the fight, but I didn't carry it right. I spoke nonsense, and I hurt Yanga, who had no business to be hurt." He concluded, "Monkey drunk is a fool, but don't mistake monkey sober for monkey drunk."

Sumo controlled himself, for he knew that Tokpa had scored a glancing blow, in referring again to Yanga, even in denying the force of his earlier reference. He responded, rather lamely, "It's hard to tell the difference between monkey drunk and monkey sober. Both fight the same way." Sumo knew it was a weak answer, but he was still too shaken by the reference to his mother, and to the possibility that Flumo was not his actual father.

Yakpalo stopped things by pulling Sumo out of Tokpa's house and walking with him half way back to his own house. Sumo asked, "What did Tokpa mean by his words?"

Yakpalo answered, "He was drunk, and didn't know what he was saying."

"Who is my father?" Sumo asked.

Yakpalo answered, "Flumo, of course."

"Did my mother have any other lovers?"

"Certainly, don't all women have them?"

"What does Tokpa know?"

"Nothing, most likely, or else it would have come out long ago. He is just guessing, just to insult and hurt you. Don't take it seriously. Most likely Tokpa's own mother, my sister, had her boy friends too, but no one is asking whether Tokpa belonged to her husband. Don't worry about it."

The situation was still not quiet when Koli arrived at the village. He had hoped to find some rest, and some escape from decisions, but Sumo called him aside the first day of the visit, and told him what Tokpa had said, how he had insulted Yanga in front of all the people in his house.

"Did Flumo hear about it?" was Koli's question.

"No, he doesn't go out much these days," said Sumo. "Anyway he mostly sits at home and talks to himself. No one would tell him anyway."

"What about Yanga?" Koli continued.

Sumo replied, "She heard all about it from the other women. It was only luck she wasn't there at the time. She'd been home getting Flumo some food, and didn't go to Tokpa's house after the harvest. But she doesn't seem to take it too seriously."

"What do we do now?" was Koli's question. "We can't let Tokpa go on like this. He's out to get both of us, even at the cost of ruining himself. He's probably jealous that Flumo has children, while he has none of his own. Even if he had them, he would have to kill them or let them die, if he is to go on being his kind of zoe."

"If only Saki were still alive, or still in Kpelle country. . . ," began Sumo.

"Why?" asked Koli.

"He could prove that Tokpa led him to fight Sulongteh, now that Tokpa has shown how far he is willing to go to destroy our family."

Koli stopped a moment. Sumo wondered what was wrong. When Koli started to speak again, he seemed to force out the words. "I told you a long time ago, Saki is all right. I asked you to trust me until the time came to talk about it.

"Saki is alive, is in Kpelle country, and can come back here if it is wise for him to do so," Koli continued. "I know where Saki is now, and I can get him back here, if you can arrange to prove that Tokpa's spirit forced Saki to do what he did."

Sumo was quiet, then said, "You helped him, didn't you? You know, you can go to jail, too? I thought you had done something, that time when you told me not to worry about him but to trust you. But I didn't want to ask you about it because the time wasn't right."

Koli told Sumo the whole story of spiriting Saki away to Dabolo's village deep in the forest.

Sumo turned back to the subject at hand, "Yes, I can get the right kind of evidence against Tokpa. He gave himself away that night last week, by speaking too loosely. He's probably telling the truth, that Yanga had boy friends before we were born. That doesn't matter much. Even if Tokpa himself were our real father, still it's Flumo who brought us up. But what Tokpa did was to show he's willing to destroy us. Just let's be quiet about it, and wait until I arrange the medicines. Then I'll tell you to bring Saki here. You'll see what we can do to Tokpa."

Yakpalo also spoke privately with Koli about the affair. He warned Koli, "Stay away from Tokpa and don't cross him. It would do no good, and might harm everyone. Let's use these few days as a family together, and not create more trouble."

Koli agreed. "There's no point," he thought, "in risking what we hope to gain later, by taking too quick action now."

Yakpalo also wanted to talk about young Ziepolo. "Sumo mentioned that he wants Ziepolo to go to kwii school, and I think he may be right. You'd be the right person to help find a school for Ziepolo, and take care of him after that. Perhaps this new school that the president is opening would be the right place. Balataa isn't

115

far from Sengta, and if you live near Balataa you could walk to work every day and also let Ziepolo go to school. I've heard from Yanga and some others that you are going to marry Goma. I'm pleased with that, because Goma comes from a good family. Moreover, Goma can help with the house and with Ziepolo."

Koli listened to all this, and wondered if he had stepped into a trap. It all seemed to fit together all too well. He wondered if Yakpalo knew Sarah, and was about to ask what Sarah had to do with all this, when Yakpalo said, "I met this preacher woman from Kissi country. She told me about you and Goma, and she said that you are almost certain to join her church. She even tried to get me to become a member, but I'm not interested in the white man's God, at least not yet." Koli had to smile, realizing that the trap had indeed by set by Sarah, and that she was clever enough to use Yakpalo as bait.

There wasn't really much Koli could do but agree. Ziepolo was his own son, even though raised by Sumo. He wanted Ziepolo to go to school, and there was no other way to do it but for him to go with Koli. The school at Salala was beginning to charge the students money, and they had to bring food with them, and besides Ziepolo was too young to go to such a school without family to take care of him. Their relatives in Salala would always give him a bed and a meal the first few days, but things were getting tougher now on the motor road, and they would not want to take care of another child besides their own.

So Koli knew he had to take the boy and raise him and put him in school. And he had to have a woman with him if he was to do it properly. He supposed his mother would find him another girl if he asked, but he liked Goma. So the result would be that he would marry Goma, and to marry Goma he would have to join Sarah's church.

Yakpalo and Koli went the next day to talk to Sumo and Kuluba about Ziepolo's schooling. Sumo had not discussed it with Kuluba before, and so he had to be a bit cautious. He had to give the appearance of not wanting the boy to go to kwii school, but then allow himself reluctantly to be persuaded by Yakpalo. Koli had to stay on the edge of the discussion, since Kuluba was reluctant to let the boy go with him. It raised too many old memories for her of how Koli had loved her. Fortunately it had been almost nine years since then, and she now had two children of her own. One had been born not long after they fixed Yakpalo's rice kitchen, and the second just this year. She thus didn't mind as much losing Ziepolo now as she would have even last year. "But why must it be to go with Koli, of all people?" she thought in her heart.

But the only question she asked out loud was, "Who will be Ziepolo's mother, when he needs someone to cook for him and care for him?"

Koli thought twice, and then said, quietly, "I'm going to marry Goma in a few weeks' time. I have to join the church first, and then we'll be married."

Yakpalo smiled when he heard Koli's decision. He knew that the trap had closed successfully, and that Koli was caught. He was also pleased that Koli was man enough to recognize when he was trapped, and take the only option available to him.

Kuluba looked visibly relieved. She had always been afraid of Koli, afraid that he might try to revive what had existed once between them. She thought, "Now he'll marry, and will no longer be such a threat to me and my marriage to his twin brother."

She asked Koli, "What I don't understand is marrying in a church. Won't you give Goma's family the white cloth and money that you should pay to get married?"

Koli's answer was, "Goma's people will be treated right. I'll still pay bridewealth for Goma, but we will also go to the church to have the preacher marry us. It means a special promise to God to live in a Christian way, and not have more than one wife."

Yakpalo had to laugh now. He asked, "Is this what Sarah wants me, Yakpalo, the clan chief, to do? I have four wives now, and might take another, if I'm not getting too old for that. Am I supposed to get rid of three of them? It's pure foolishness. I can't understand why these Christians insist on a man having only one wife. How can a man be wealthy, and give his family the right kind of love and care, if he has only one wife? Especially now that I'm the clan chief, I have to live in a way fitting of my position."

Yakpalo spoke directly to Koli. "And are you thinking of having only one wife?"

117

Koli tried to avoid the question. He knew he would have his girl friends, especially if Goma became pregnant. And he knew that if she didn't become pregnant, he would have to marry another girl in order to have children. But he didn't want to say all this in public, since he knew Sarah would refuse to let them be married in the church under such conditions. So he just said, "If the ground hog can't break through the fence, he will try to dig underneath."

Yakpalo smiled that Koli was at least becoming a Kpelle man, and learning to speak in the right way. He laughed when he warned Koli, "Watch out lest the ground hog find another trap under the fence and be caught for the second time!"

So it was agreed.

Ziepolo was told that he would be going to live with his new father, Koli, and go to school.

Ziepolo had been out to Gbarnga twice before, and found the idea of the road attractive to him. He was afraid of the trucks and cars and white people he saw there, but he wanted to find out how they lived, and learn to live in their way.

Koli felt somehow sad and empty inside himself, as he saw how easy it all was for Ziepolo. He thought, "With me, it's been a struggle every step of the way. I had to run away to go to school, was caught and brought back, had to fight for the chance to return, and was almost stopped half way through. What's worse, I never had a real chance to go to high school. And now Ziepolo is going, with everyone's blessings, as if it's nothing more than going to live with relatives. And there's no reason why Ziepolo can't go on from that school to high school, and even to college, if he does well in his studies. It somehow isn't fair - but it's too late now for me."

Koli's thoughts continued as Sumo and Kuluba told Ziepolo what he'd have to take to school. "At least I've got a job and now I guess I've got a wife. I should be satisfied and see if my son, Ziepolo, can go farther than I have. If he makes it, it's almost as if I made it. What's that I heard Flumo say once? `You can't eat all the cassava. Some of it has to be buried again for next year's crop.' Maybe I'm the cassava that has to be buried."

Koli remained for three days and let these decisions become part of him before they left for Gbarnga. There Yakpalo and his chiefs and his family met the president, then went ahead to Balataa to wait for him to open the new school to which they would now make such a great personal commitment through Ziepolo.

Yakpalo, Sumo, Koli and Ziepolo arrived at the school well before the president and his party. Only the most important officials were able to ride with the president, or in one of the other black cars that followed his.

Already a large crowd of Balataa people had gathered in front of the school building, and along the road. The Bassa people who lived between Balataa and Hopewell College were drumming and singing beside the road. Three tall Mandingo chiefs from Gbarnga were standing with their followers, impassive and impressive in their long robes, their heads tied with gold and silver cloth. White teachers and missionaries were at the school, standing on the platform. One of them, newly arrived in Liberia, was photographing the people in the crowd. He passed by Yakpalo and his family, as if they were not worth looking at twice. He seemed to have eyes only for the strangest-looking people in the crowd.

Then a cloud of dust appeared on the road where it left Hopewell College. At the head of the dust was the president's black car, and presumably behind it, although obscured by the dust, were the other cars in the procession. The president had to lead any line of cars, lest the red dust fill his eyes and nose, as it filled those of his followers.

The car drove to the bottom of the hill below the school, and there it stopped. The other cars pulled up beside it, and the people got out and started to walk up the hill, the president in front and the others behind him. He wore a white, open-collared shirt, and smoked a large cigar. He seemed much more human than Koli had remembered from the occasional parade of big shots in Monrovia.

The president was followed by members of his government, one of them obviously unshaven and drunk. Then came the paramount chief from Gbarnga, and the provincial commissioner from Ganta. With them were the important officials from Hopewell College, including the head of the church that ran the college. He was a light-skinned American - Koli had heard them called "Negroes." To Koli he was just another white man.

The president walked up to the platform, and took his place at the center of the row of officials. He spoke a few words about the importance of education, all in English. Yakpalo looked inquiringly at Koli, who translated what the president had said.

The president then asked for the key to the schoolhouse. The Balataa chief, another relative of Yakpalo and a descendent of the famous woman chief of thirty years earlier, gave the key to the clan chief who had hired Koli. He gave the key to the paramount chief, who gave it in turn to the provincial commissioner. He then presented it to the head of the church who gave it to the head of the college, who finally gave it to the principal of the school.

The head of the school walked to the door, and opened it, with thanks to the president and other officials. He said, in English, that this would be a great occasion for the people of the village. Koli whispered the translation to his family, and particularly told Ziepolo, "This means you. Look carefully, for your life will change here."

After a few closing remarks, the president and his party left, faster than they had come. They climbed back in their big black cars and went off into the scarcely-settled cloud of dust that had risen when they arrived.

The crowds began to leave, when Ziepolo asked Koli, "Who was the white man pointing the box at all the people? What was he doing? What would happen to the people?"

Koli laughed, and told Ziepolo, "Don't worry. The box was a way of capturing people's faces and putting them on paper. I've shown you pictures in books, and these are made in the same way.

"Only the old people are afraid of the box, and say it will take away their spirits. Last week I heard some old women complaining that the same white man had taken away their faces when they were crossing the Hopewell College grounds. They were carrying fish nets with them, and were returning from a hard and unsuccessful day of netting the few fish that remained near the motor road. This man pointed his box at them, without even asking them. They had threatened him, but he had pretended not to understand, and had gone ahead to take their pictures."

Ziepolo said, "I want to meet that man, to see the pictures he took of the people at the school."

Yakpalo and Koli warned him to be careful of mixing with white people, but Sumo said, "Go find out for yourself. I have given you medicine to protect you against witchcraft, and so you needn't worry. I prepared the medicine from leaves and bark, burned them in palm oil, and then slit open your wrist, to put the medicine permanently into your body. But you must never touch a lime, lest the medicine be spoiled. If you avoid limes, you'll be able to see a witch coming to hurt you, regardless of how well disguised the witch might be."

"But, medicine or no medicine," Ziepolo said, "I want to find out more about the white man's world. The one who took the photographs got into a car with the others to go back to Hopewell College. It's only a short walk, but they went in a car. Are they so old and sick that they can't walk for themselves? Or is this how they show their importance?"

Koli laughed. "You'll find out. But you'll have to wait for a chance to meet the white man for himself. In the first place, you don't know a single word of the white man's language. In the second place, you're still very small, and you'd be afraid to walk by yourself to the white man's home. In the third place, you have to get settled with me and Goma, after the rest of the family has gone back to the village."

Goma was glad to see Koli come back. Her eyes were alive as she asked, "You look different. Have you accepted Jesus as your Lord?"

Koli had no idea what those words meant, and he didn't really think Goma understood them either, even though perhaps they meant something to Sarah. But Koli at least knew what he had to do next. He told Goma, "I want to join the church, and I'll believe whatever you believe. I know what I have to do, and I'll do it."

Goma was obviously happy at Koli's statement. She could tell from the way he said it that he had been trapped into this position, and was not at all sure he liked it.

"But, trapped or not," she thought, "Now he'll marry me, and I can face Sarah again. Sarah was so unhappy when I moved back in with Koli, and she told me she would pray for me to stop sinning. All I want is to marry Koli and stay in the church. It's given my life a kind of meaning I've never known before."

Yakpalo seemed not to want to see Sarah. He had been upset by her demand that he lead the way for his people into the church.

He respected Sarah, but saw no reason to leave his own ways, and particularly not to leave his wives.

But it wasn't Sarah this time who came to him, it was Goyakole, whom the church people now called Joseph. He was the leader of the zoes in a village an hour's walk into the forest from Hopewell. He said, "Now I've become a Christian, and I hope you'll do the same."

When Yakpalo asked about his wives - he knew Goyakole had three of them - Goyakole wouldn't answer directly. He only said, "Bush hog doesn't scratch when he's in a thorn bush."

Yakpalo knew Goyakole well, knew that he enjoyed palm wine, and, in these modern days, cane juice, knew that he was proud of his three wives, knew that he cared very much about his position as head zoe. He said, "I can't figure what you want with Sarah's church, unless perhaps you have ideas of marrying Sarah too. But Sarah already has a husband, and doesn't seem likely to leave him. No, there must be something behind all this, and I want to know what it is."

Goyakole insisted, "It's because Jesus is my Savior now, and has shown me how to live properly. I've given up my evil medicines, although not, of course, the good ones. No man is so foolish as to throw away what he has that is good. But Jesus brings stronger medicines now, medicines that will help people improve their lives. Don't you see how things are changing on the road? Can any of your people make a truck or write a book or give injections?"

Yakpalo tried to say, "Our sons will learn these things, and soon do them for themselves."

But Goyakole hit back with his same argument. "It's only by knowing Jesus that our children can learn to be kwii. Look at Koli. He became a Christian when he went to Salala to school. He's done well. But as soon as he dropped it, after he finished school at Salala, his luck turned. I know all about Koli, about how he spoiled his chances by getting mixed up with bad people at Firestone and then in Monrovia. Now he has a chance again. Goma just told me that Koli would join the church and marry her. Watch that young man now. He'll make a success of himself again,

122

and find a way for Ziepolo to go even farther in his own life. Jesus will help him."

Yakpalo didn't feel ready to make any commitments himself, but said, "I'll watch. And don't forget, Bush hog should watch out for the thorns. The church will find out about your three wives, and throw you out if you don't give them up."

Yakpalo and Goyakole walked down the hill from the school into Balataa. The hard dry season sun burned easily through the haze of dust left by the cars of the president and his party. The Mandingo women had gone back to selling dried fish along the road. Children were playing where the president had driven. Hopewell College farm laborers, off work for the day to see the president, were talking in small groups in the open area between the shops. A policeman had stayed behind to drink a beer at the Nigerian's store, and argue with the local government tax collector. Two college students, who had remained over the long vacation to work in the college storehouse, were drinking beer at the Lebanese store. The school was open now, and the visit of the president, his only one to Balataa and probably his last for a long time, was over. Nothing seemed very changed.

Yakpalo met the chief of this clan, the chief who had hired Koli to work in Sengta, at the bottom of the hill. The Balataa chief then approached the two of them for advice. "I have a problem with students from Hopewell College. They come to my village with money, and find local girls to sleep with. Most of the students aren't Kpelle, and some aren't even Liberians. And now two of these girls are pregnant. I don't know how to manage it.

The clan chief and Yakpalo tried to advise him, but there wasn't really much they could say. "The kwii are taking over everywhere, and all we can do is to go along with it. Look at the school the president opened today. The children who go there will grow up to be like those Hopewell boys. They won't care for their parents any more. And you won't be able to protect the village against them."

The clan chief's advice to the Balataa chief was, "Hold onto what you have. If your own children go to school, let them go, but try to keep control of them. On the other hand, you should resist with all the strength you have any other changes. If you have to

123

agree in words with these changes, do it, but undercut those who are bringing the changes. Otherwise, nothing will remain of Kpelle ways."

Goyakole had a different view. "My idea is to join the people who are bringing the changes, and benefit from the changes as they take place. I've become a Christian, because I know that the real force behind these new things is the man Jesus. I've never met him. In fact, they say he's dead, and has gone to be with God, because he's really God's son. But he has the power of God, stronger than any of our Kpelle ancestors or spirits or medicines, and will make the world into a new world. And I, Goyakole, want myself and my children to be part of the new world, and on the right side of things. And, just to show I'm serious, my own son will enter the new school when it opens next month."

The conversation stopped for a space when Goyakole said that. The school had been opened officially by the president. But no one had really given much thought to who would actually attend the school. People were uneasy about it, and each person hoped that the other would send his children first, wanted to wait and see what would happen, and was very doubtful that it would really be good for the Kpelle people.

But now Goyakole had made the first move. Yakpalo said next, "I've brought along young Ziepolo, Sumo's son, to go to the school. Ziepolo is standing there with Koli, who is talking to Sarah near her church. And look at Sumo under the big cotton tree, talking with the village medicine man, as if to show he's given up his boy to the new world."

Goyakole and Yakpalo looked to the Balataa chief, as if to ask him what he would do. The chief only smiled, smiled that open and friendly but concealing smile he was famous for.

Yakpalo thought, "He could say that rice grows from palm trees, smile at you, and you don't know whether he believes it or not."

The chief smiled, and said, "My two sons are also going to start at the school."

One of the boys had the orange flower from a cotton tree and was spinning it on a piece of vine. The other was chasing a girl across the open space between the shops. Yakpalo could only ask himself, "Is it with such boys that the change will begin?"

The men turned and looked back up to the school, newly painted white and shining in the still dusty mid-day sun. The red roof seemed strange in this village of thatch houses. But the school was outside the vine that had been drawn around the village so many years earlier, after the war between Wolomian and Biito, when the original village had been burned down. Yakpalo, Goyakole, the clan chief, the Balataa chief, Koli, Sumo, Ziepolo, Sarah, Goma and the rest of the village people were still inside that vine. But this white, red-roofed building seemed to shrivel that vine, and break it open once and for all. The president had come and gone, and now it was up to the village to live with the change that the president had brought.

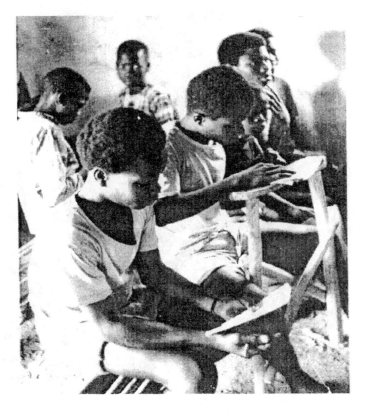

125

126

VIII: THE ANCESTOR'S BREATH

When Koli married Goma, not long after the president opened the school, they left Sengta to be closer to Ziepolo's school. It was a compromise, so that Koli wouldn't have too far to walk to work and yet so Ziepolo could walk to school easily. The village was on the edge of the Hopewell farm, not far off the main road. Ziepolo walked on the back trail alongside the Hopewell farm, and from there to school every morning.

Ziepolo's first day at school was somehow not what Koli had expected. It was different from Salala, where the white people had run everything. Here in Balataa there were two teachers, one for the children who could speak some English and one for those who knew no English at all. Both teachers were Liberians. The teacher for the kwii children was from Monrovia, even though she could speak some Kpelle. The other teacher was a young man from Gbarnga, who had gone halfway through high school but then had quit. He was Ziepolo's teacher, and he lived in Balataa where he had the boys work on his farm. He demanded that they help him, since he said that, for his part, he was helping them to be kwii.

Ziepolo came home the first day saying that he had learned to say "Good morning," and that he had been beaten for saying it too many times. He asked Koli and Goma, "Please get me a pair of brown shorts and a brown shirt, as my school clothes. If I don't wear them starting next week I won't be allowed in school." He also asked for a copybook and a pencil, which Koli bought for him at the Lebanese store.

Koli's new life seemed to go smoothly for a month until Jonathan met him.

Jonathan laughed when he found that Koli had married. He came to the clan chief's office on tax business, and found Koli there writing a letter to the paramount chief.

Jonathan's reaction to Koli's news was, "I thought you were a sensible man, not one to get caught in churches and marriages. Don't you know that the world has changed now? The only people getting married these days are either the big-shots from Monrovia who can afford a big party and fancy clothes, or up-country people who are too stupid to move with the times."

Jonathan continued, "You've lost your chance to be a part of the new movement, unless you come to your senses and stop being such a homebody. I had hoped you would come to Gbarnga this Saturday to an all-day meeting, where those of us who went to the Ghana conference will tell people about the changes coming to Africa."

Koli tried to say, "I have to go to church with Goma," but Jonathan looked at him so hard and unbelievingly that Koli had to turn away his eyes, half in shame and half in amusement.

"Jonathan is too funny," Koli said to himself, "And probably right as usual. I don't know what I want to do. What they're going to be doing in Gbarnga sounds interesting, but, if I go, it will cause trouble with Goma. We've only been married now a short time, and I made a promise to come to church every Saturday. If I go with Jonathan, I've got to think of a way out of it that would satisfy her. The only thing is to say that the clan chief asked me to go to the meeting, to find out what is happening."

But Koli was afraid to ask the clan chief to give him the order to go, because the clan chief himself didn't like these new ideas. Koli thought, "He's just satisfied to do what the government says, and he's afraid of new movements which might upset the president. So, I'll have to lie to Goma, and say that the clan chief told me to go, and only hope Goma won't ask the clan chief about it." He went to the meeting in Gbarnga, not to church, drawn from one unknown to another.

The meeting was just enough beyond Koli's understanding to confuse him hopelessly. The other men were talking about a new constitution for Liberia - or was it for Africa as a whole? Liberia would be part of a free and independent and united "pan-African" nation, where all men all over the continent of Africa would be free and equal. In his confusion, it only seemed to Koli that what they really meant was that these East African students from Hopewell would be telling other people what to do, and at the same time trying to persuade them they were free.

Another man at the meeting, a teacher at the mission in Gbarnga, asked the question Koli had in mind. "What does it mean to be free, if we are just taking orders from Nkrumah in Ghana"? Moreover, how does it differ from the situation now, when we take orders from the president in Monrovia? At least, under the present system, we can see the president in Monrovia once in a while, but we would never see this man Nkrumah. Maybe you students are just fooling us with your talk, and want to run things yourselves."

Jonathan answered the question himself, motioning to the East Africans to wait a moment. He started to tell the story of one of the East Africans. "Do you know that Zedekiah here walked from his home in Kenya all the way across the continent, after he had suffered terribly when the white men killed his family and burned his home? He came to Liberia, the country named for liberty and freedom, only to find the same suffering here. He found that the kwii from Monrovia are just as bad as the big shots from England who were running and destroying his own country. He doesn't want the people of Liberia, the true people, the common people, to suffer any longer. Now there is a black man, Nkrumah, who is offering us a new choice, a new way. Zedekiah came here to Liberia, to Gbarnga, to bring freedom."

The mission teacher asked again, "Why then does Zedekiah study at the white man's school, Hopewell College? What is he after there, if he really wants to bring freedom? And why is this same Zedekiah going after Kpelle girls at night, if he wants to help the Kpelle? I've heard stories about what that man is doing."

Jonathan's answer was surprising even to Jonathan. He said, "There won't be any difference between Kpelle and Vai, between East African and West African, in the new Africa. And so it's in the interest of pan-African unity-making one nation of all Africans - that Zedekiah is making friends with girls as well as men. You shouldn't mistrust what Zedekiah is doing. How can Zedekiah have suffered so much at the hands of others, only to bring that same suffering to the Kpelle who have taken him in? If anyone has any complaints they should just bring them to me, Jonathan, and I will see where the truth lies."

"For now," Jonathan continued, "The job lies in organizing the people of Liberia to throw off their colonial masters. With the help of the East Africans, and with the help of some Monrovia students who have seen the new light, we will write a new constitution for Liberia, so that when the revolution comes, Liberia will be a good country."

Koli was less and less clear what they wanted from him at this point. He didn't feel smart enough to understand all this talk. He was letting his thoughts drift, when suddenly Jonathan called on him. He said, "Koli here has volunteered to give us financial help. He works for the clan chief in Sengta, and has access to the money we need for our work. He has a good salary, and will surely help the cause. Moreover, he might be able to persuade the clan chief to cooperate with the movement - whether the clan chief knows it or not!"

The group laughed at that, and Koli had to laugh too. He knew what the clan chief thought of people like those who attended the meeting.

Jonathan now told Koli, "We are counting on you for help with money. You have shown we can trust you by loaning the money for me to go to Ghana. I haven't forgotten the debt, and when the new constitution comes into force in a free Liberia, you will be repaid enough and more to make up for your loss. But now we need more money, and you can help us get it."

Jonathan turned back to the others and explained, "Koli is the clan chief's clerk, and has access to money in the clan chiefs court. The rice that is collected from the villages goes through the clan chief's office. Court cases involve fines, and Koli is trusted to set the amount of the fines and collect them. The hut taxes come through the clan chief, and there is no real way to check on the total amount. Koli can easily bring enough money each month to keep the movement going. I'm sure Koli will agree, since he too wants freedom and justice for Africa."

Koli listened hard, the words came into his mind, he registered most of their meanings, but he couldn't accept what he heard. The whole conversation had been in English, spoken rapidly and fluently, and Koli cursed himself for not going far enough in school to speak and understand English easily. He tried to speak, but couldn't find the English words to say. He knew perfectly well he couldn't do anything of what Jonathan wanted. He took the only way out he knew: he stood up and started to leave.

Jonathan came over to him, and said, "Wait, Koli. I want to talk to you for a minute. Don't leave until you know what I know."

Jonathan told the others, "Koli and I have to talk over the plan a bit, and will be right back. I'm sure Koli has good ideas, and wants to discuss them privately."

Jonathan and Koli went outside the meeting, outside the hot stuffy room behind the dance hall, out into the hazy dust-filled Gbarnga noon. Women passed by with produce on their heads, coming from the market. A cow had been killed that day by the Mandingo butcher, and a white missionary came by with a basket of fresh beef carried by her servant. Taxis were loading down the street, with people preparing to go to Monrovia. A dog was barking, as if at nothing, in the open space before the tax office. Three large white cow birds were following a flock of sheep.

"What are you talking about, Jonathan? Are you crazy? I hardly understand a thing about this revolution and constitution, and you expect me to find the money to keep it going! Find it yourself! You work in the tax office, and see ten times more money than I ever touch. Besides, I don't really believe you people want to help Liberia. You are just trying to help yourselves, and be the new big shots."

"Quiet, Koli. You will come to understand what we are doing, and you'll never be sorry you helped us. The new Africa I taught you about in Monrovia, the world that will one day be beautiful for all of us - that's what you are building. You can find us the money, because no one would suspect you are in this. People are watching me, and so I can't take a thing, even to help the people of Liberia."

"Jonathan, I won't do it. I'm married now. I'm raising my son - my brother's son, that is. I've promised Goma to go to church and do the right thing. My father is old, and needs me. Find someone else."

"Koli, I'm afraid not. You're going to help us, because I know something you don't know that I know. No, Koli, you can't get away that easily."

Koli stopped and looked hard at Jonathan. "What foolishness are you talking now, Jonathan`? You need more than words to get me to steal from the clan chief."

Jonathan replied, "OK, Koli, you asked me. I'll tell you. I know where Saki is, and I know how you hid him. You don't want people to know about that, do you? If you don't help us, I might just forget myself someday, and tell my friends in the police about it. Saki is safe now, and so are you - if you help us."

"You can't be serious - you don't know Saki, and you don't know anything about him. Saki killed a man at Firestone three years ago, and no one has seen him since. What do you know about that? Maybe you're the one who hid him."

"Koli, Koli - let's be friends. You and I have known each other for a long time, now, since 1951 to be exact, and now it's 1959. You should know by now that I don't lie, at least not when things get serious. I know Dabolo very well. I went back to the St. Paul River last month to collect taxes there, and stopped to see him in his village. He and I have a deal going for land in his area, and I wanted to talk to him. We had a useful night together, and I managed to find out some things while I was there.

"In particular, I met Saki there - you may forget that I saw him at your house in Monrovia, and I don't forget people easily. Saki tried to tell me his name was Nuumeni, and he was from Guinea. I pretended to believe him, but I talked to his wife, and with a little persuasion - I didn't spend your money only in Ghana - she told me that Saki had been brought there by his nephew from the main road. I promised I wouldn't get her in any trouble. It didn't take much effort after that to figure things out.

"Don't worry. I'm the only one who knows anything about these matters. Dabolo doesn't have many friends who come to see him now that he lives so far from the road. He never did tell you anything about his life in Monrovia, did he? He had some business interests at the Port, and we worked together. Now he is arranging to get legal title to some land along the St. Paul river, and I'm helping him."

Koli could hardly speak. His head spun. He couldn't think what to do now, how to get away from Jonathan this time. The deceptions of three years had broken around him.

He spoke again after a moment. "So you'd tell people about Saki, would you? You'd ruin his new life, and ruin my life too? And all I need to do is to steal enough money to keep you and your friends going! If my brother Sumo knew about this, he'd put his medicines on you, and you wouldn't live to tell anyone."

"Koli, you are my friend. You don't want to get medicine into this thing. Besides, I've got some more news for you. I think you know Tokpa. Well, he's another friend of mine, and he's at least as good a zoe as Sumo. I haven't wasted my time here in Gbarnga. I know the important people. Tokpa is a water man, and is just waiting for a chance to get back at you and your brother. He doesn't know anything about where Saki is, but he too might find out one of these days.

"Just think about it, Koli. At least, let me tell the people in the meeting that you first have to find the way to do this thing without being noticed. They're waiting in there for you to show that you will stand with them for Africa and for its future. You believe in the revolution, I know that. Don't let a little thing like using the people's money to help them have a better future stand in your way. And you certainly wouldn't want to hurt Saki in any way."

Koli could see no way to move. He had to give in for now, and then hunt a way later to escape Jonathan. "All right, Jonathan. I'll try to find a way to help you with some money. I don't know what else to do. But I'm not going to come to your meetings. I don't understand them, and I don't like them."

"In fact, we don't want you to come. If you're going to help the revolution with money, then you mustn't be too closely attached to it. We just want you to go about your business, stay quiet, go to church, love your wife, and send us money when we need it. Don't worry. We won't tell anyone where we got it."

The others at the meeting thanked Koli for his real interest in justice and freedom, when he promised, "I'll help you with a bit of money from time to time. I'm sure the clan chief will never notice it's missing, and I'm sure you will make good use of it. But I have to apologize for not being able to come to many meetings, both because I have a lot to do in my village, and because people might get suspicious."

Koli's confusion did not lessen when he went home from the meeting. He hadn't been there as long as he had expected, and so there was time to go to Balataa to church before the day ended. He took a taxi from Gbarnga and got off at the Hopewell gate. It was still a long walk all the way across the campus before he could reach Balataa.

He tried to collect his thoughts, but it wasn't easy. He looked at the college as he passed. A herd of cows was eating grass before the main classroom building. Two white men and a black man were standing before an office talking. Students were walking toward the dormitory from the library, and playing soccer on the college field. A group of white children were playing on the brown grass before a beautiful, white-walled, red-roofed house ("Why can't my children have such a life?" thought Koli). College workers from Balataa were repairing windows in the classrooms.

A new black car passed Koli on its way to Balataa, a white man sitting in the back and a black man driving. "Maybe Jonathan and his friends are right," thought Koli. "But then, why are they also students here? I don't understand anything about this business. I only know that Jonathan has me against the fence, and I can't move until I think of what to do next. The only thing may be to get Saki from Dabolo's village, as Sumo suggested, and confront Tokpa with him. But I don't see how it will work out the way Sumo says."

Koli reached Balataa in mid-afternoon. The Saturday service was almost over at Sarah's house. He went in to find Goma, Sarah, Goyakole and the others there, praying, singing and preaching.

He thought to himself, "They seem truly happy and untroubled. They haven't dug themselves into the ground to the point where they can't see a way to dig out again. How can I fight my way back to a decent, happy life? Goyakole told Yakpalo that I would return to a successful life once I gave myself to Jesus in the church. But how?"

Sarah turned to see Koli come in, and then caught Goma's eye in turn. Goma looked back, and a smile came over her face.

She thought, "Koli is my husband now, is a good man, is now going to do the right thing in life. He's given up drinking, has given up seeing Jonathan, has nothing to do with Saki any more, is taking good care of Ziepolo, and has no girl friends besides me. Life is good now, and I thank God for it. I'm even fairly sure I'm pregnant. We've lived together all that long time without my getting pregnant, and so it's clearly a gift of God that now a baby will be mine at last. I'll tell Koli about it on the way back home."

The church service ended as the sun was beginning to ease the intensity of its power. Goma and Koli left Sarah's house, and walked along the path back home. The swamp along the path was low, at the end of the dry season, and they crossed the stick bridge without getting their feet wet. There were new farms being constructed at the far end of the swamp, too many of them, thus allowing too little time for the forest to rest. But the farms would give some rice at least.

Where the path divided at the end of the swamp, they turned left, and followed the edge of the Hopewell property. They passed their own new farm site, where Goma had been clearing the bush with the help of the women's work group from Balataa. Here Goma told Koli that by the time the rice had grown and ripened, she too would be ripe and have a baby.

Koli's world seemed clear and open for a few brief minutes. He had felt something at church, and he enjoyed having Goma with him more than he realized. And now the promise of a baby genuinely his own by his own wife made him feel good and serious, all at the same time. "If only it weren't for Jonathan, all would be well."

Yet Jonathan was still there and Koli had to satisfy him in some way. He managed to remove ten dollars from the hut taxes he collected the next week. He went with soldiers to a village behind the clan chief's village, and counted the houses to be assessed. There were two old women who claimed their houses should not be counted, because their husbands were dead. Another house was no longer occupied, but the owner was still in the village, and he claimed that his house should not require a tax payment. And a schoolboy lived in one, and went every day to Sengta for school. He said he was too young to be assessed, and was living there just for a place to stay.

Koli agreed in principle with each of the claims, but he gave the appearance to all the people that it would be very hard to persuade the clan chief. He commented, "Perhaps if you gave me something to encourage me, I might be able to help you."

He collected six dollars between them. The other four he got by overcharging two women whose husbands were at Firestone, and who didn't really know what they were supposed to pay. He wrote them receipts for the correct amount, but charged them two dollars more than he wrote on the paper. He thought, "By the time their husbands return, these women will have either lost the receipts or forgotten how much they actually paid."

Koli knew he had to hurry, because Jonathan was after him for money. Jonathan had warned that there would be trouble about Saki if Koli didn't produce what he had promised promptly. He said he would be at the clan chiefs village to check the receipts of the but tax money, and at that time would accept what Koli had to give him.

"Jonathan isn't even grateful," Koli thought, when he took the ten dollars from Koli.

Jonathan muttered, "Make sure it's more the next time. It's all right for now, but the revolution can hardly succeed if it depends on such small amounts of money. It's a good beginning, but more had better follow the next time."

Koli asked, "What will you do with all that money?"

Jonathan waved his hands largely, and said, "You can hardly imagine what must be done. The first thing is to buy a typewriter and second to get a duplicating machine. Then we will be in a position to publish a newspaper, as well as print copies of the constitution when it is ready."

But Koli next asked, "How did you print the sheets I've already seen?"

Jonathan explained, "The Hopewell students used the machines at the college secretly. There's a group of students which calls itself Spider, and which has a key to the office where the machines are kept. They usually just put out sheets making fun of students, telling which girls would sleep with any boy who came along. But for a few beers the Spider group let us use their key and duplicate our papers on the Hopewell machines. But this can't go on forever, and the movement has to have its own equipment."

Jonathan continued, "Koli, you mustn't always be suspicious. You'll understand in due time how important your contribution is to the cause. In the meantime you should hustle and bring in more

136

money. You should also realize that I have a second claim on you, in addition to my knowledge about Saki. You've broken the law by taking this money, and I can always just manage to 'discover' what you're doing, if you don't bring in enough cash."

With that, Jonathan thanked Koli again, shook his hand in what he called the revolutionary solidarity handshake, and left for Gbarnga. Koli was shaken by what had happed, and angry as well. He saw that Jonathan himself was becoming a spider.

He thought, "He's weaving a web around me, a web I can never break through. It's bad enough having to bear the weight of breaking the law in the case of Saki. Now I've got a second crime I have to account for, and the same person who insisted on my doing the crime is the one who threatens to betray me in it. And I can never get out of it by saying that Jonathan told me to do it."

Koli was turning the whole matter over in his mind, when Sumo came to visit him. It was Sunday before noon, and Koli had little to do. Goma and Ziepolo were at their farm clearing and piling brush, in preparation for burning when the farm became dry enough. Koli had said he would join them after mending his shirt and trousers. He was sitting and thinking in front of his house, the clothes at his side ready for attention, when Sumo appeared around the corner of the house.

"It isn't really Ziepolo I came to see, although of course I want to find out about him," answered Sumo. "I came to see you, to talk about getting Saki out of Dabolo's village, and back home. Things are getting rough between our family and Tokpa. Just last night Tokpa was drunk again, and was threatening all of us. Yakpalo had to quiet him down, and keep him from fighting me. He's old enough, and to spare, to be my father, and so I have to give him respect, but things are bad. Saki is the only one his age who can fight him properly."

"But what can Saki do?" replied Koli. "He's old and tired now. You didn't see him after the killing at Firestone. I did, and I know he's finished as a fighter."

"I don't want that kind of fighting. I can manage the affair in such a way that we beat Tokpa, with Saki as our agent. As far as everyone else in the village is concerned, Saki is dead and gone. They hardly even mention him any more. What we need to do is to

137

bring Saki back to the village, hide him, and then get the same old argument going with Tokpa again. It won't be hard. He picks a fight with me, if I even look at him.

"What we'll do is this. When Tokpa is drunk, and starts to get wild, you and I will come to his house, and ask him what is the matter. He'll come out after us, probably only in words, and we'll say that if Saki were only still alive, he would know what to do about Tokpa. This will make Tokpa still angrier and he will dig himself deeper into the problem. If we're clever, we can needle him to the point where he'll challenge us to call Saki back again, if we can. At this point, we'll arrange to have Saki come from the bush near Tokpa's house, covered with white chalk and ashes and with his clothes torn, and confront Tokpa."

"What makes you think Saki will agree to do it?" Koli asked. "He's settled where he is now, and Dabolo treats him well enough. This is a big risk he'd be taking. I wouldn't do it if I were Saki. I'd stay where I was."

"That's a chance we have to take. However, I think we can go even a step farther. We can get Tokpa to boast, before Saki comes in, that he was the one whose water medicine made Saki go wild, and kill Sulongteh. Tokpa is so proud of his medicine, that he'll claim to be able to do anything. In return, I'll claim that I can bring Saki back to challenge him. It's worth a try."

Koli began to see that the plan had a chance of success, and moreover that the plan might give him a way to get out from under Jonathan's pressure. He said, "If Saki can be brought back in such a way that the blame is moved from Saki to Tokpa, then my own action years ago in protecting Saki would not be punishable. I'm still worried about the part I played in hiding Saki, and I'm also worried that the police might still try to arrest Saki."

Sumo laughed slightly, and said for Koli not to worry. "The police are after bigger things than that now. I doubt if they even remember about Saki. There's a madman in the Kakata area now. I'm sure you've heard about him. Everyone is trying to catch him, after he killed two people in Kakata. If Saki comes back to the village now, no one will even notice. He just has to be quiet. A few dollars to the Gbarnga police if they hear about him will solve the problem."

138

Koli agreed. "It's worth trying, particularly since the pressure at home on you is getting so great. If you manage to carry this off successfully, you can beat Tokpa, at least for the time being, and strengthen your own reputation as a zoe."

Koli thought to himself, "It'll have the added benefit that I can get Jonathan off my back. But I don't want to mention that to Sumo. There's no point to it just now."

The next thing was to get Saki. Sumo proposed, "You go to Dabolo's village and talk to Saki, to persuade him to come home, while I go home to work on Tokpa."

Koli agreed and left for Dabolo's village the next day.

This time the trip was not so difficult. Koli persuaded the clan chief to let him take time off to do some family business, and said, "I'll be back in less than a week. I've finished with the hut tax collection for now, and there are no letters to be typed, so I can afford to leave for a short time."

On the way, Koli realized that he might have trouble with Dabolo, if the big man were at his village. But, fortunately, Dabolo was away across the St. Paul river. He had hired a man to kill elephants for him, and was there arranging for the man to have a farm and a place to sleep. He had left Saki behind at the village, where Koli found him. Saki was preparing a newly cleared area in order to plant cocoa when the rains came, and had some trees of his own in addition to the large number he would plant for Dabolo.

Koli was amazed to see how in fact Saki had thrived on life with Dabolo. He seemed somehow even younger, and more confident of himself. He had a wife there, and she was pregnant with a second child for him.

Saki was glad to see Koli, but was less pleased with Koli's proposal. "I don't want to leave Dabolo. I believe in the man. And I've settled into the good life for the first time in many years. No one knows I'm here, I'm sure of that."

Koli didn't bother to mention Jonathan's visit. He didn't want to confuse the issue if he didn't have to.

Koli explained the plan of confronting Tokpa. Saki laughed to think of it, but said, "No, I prefer to stay where I am. I don't want to get mixed up in that problem again."

Koli tried every way he could to persuade Saki to leave, and come back to his own village. But the focus of Saki's answer was, "If I come back, I'll lose what I've built up here in Dabolo's village. I have a wife who takes good care of me, and she's about to give me a second child. If I leave, both of my former wives, the one at Firestone and the one who left me to go to Gbarnga, would be after me again. No, let me stay where I am."

Then Koli had to use the one weapon he had, and yet the one weapon he was afraid to use. He told Saki, "Jonathan knows you are here, and will one day tell people about it."

Saki admitted, "It's true Jonathan was here, but I didn't think he recognized me. That makes things different, doesn't it? Maybe I'll have to do what you ask in order to do something about it."

It took the rest of the day to work out a plan. Saki's wife had to be brought into it, because she had admitted to Jonathan that Saki was there. The big question was whether to involve Dabolo, and they decided not to do so. Dabolo was Jonathan's friend, but he was also Saki's protector. It was not clear which choice Dabolo would make if forced into a choice, but they felt he would probably prefer to keep both contacts. Koli felt that Jonathan would not push Dabolo as hard as he would push Saki's wife, if there was a confrontation.

Koli called Saki's wife and explained what she had to do. "You must simply deny you ever told anyone your husband is Saki. He's Nuumeni, who came from Guinea, as far as you know. You must also make sure that Dabolo knows Saki's story, in case he's asked. Tell Dabolo only that some people from Gbarnga were asking about Saki while he was gone, and that you told them this story. You can count on Dabolo backing Saki if there's trouble, because Saki has been doing good work for him. You don't want to lose your husband now that your life is going well. Be careful."

The next step was for Saki and Koli to go as fast as they could to Koli's village, for the confrontation with Tokpa. Saki summarized his contribution to the plan. "I'll appear in the village only long enough to make everyone believe I've come as a spirit to torment Tokpa, and then disappear back into the forest. There's fortunately a waning moon now, and so people won't find me easily. I know the paths around the village well enough I can make a quick escape. It's true the village people also know the paths, but they'll be so amazed that they won't follow me, at least not right away. I can get away, and go right back to Dabolo's village tomorrow night. It'll be a rough walk, but I know the way well enough. Besides, now I'm in good physical condition, after these three years of hard physical work for Dabolo."

Saki reasoned to Koli, "If this plan works, people will believe that I'm certainly dead, and was only called back by the quarrel between Tokpa and Sumo. It'll also mean that there will be no more Saki to interfere with me being the Nuumeni I've chosen to be, no more worry about a past life. Only Jonathan and you will know where I really am, and it won't be possible for Jonathan now to tell anyone and be believed. Moreover, it would cause bad relations between Jonathan and Dabolo if Jonathan insists that Dabolo has an escaped murderer at his village. The plan seems good."

Koli and Saki agreed to start that very afternoon, so that they might cross the main road and reach Koli's village before morning. It wasn't an easy walk, but this time Koli had brought a flashlight, thinking ahead to the possibility that they would have to make a night trip.

Saki took with him his oldest clothes, which he would use for the disguise, and then bury in the forest before coming back to his new village. He and Koli moved as rapidly as they could, following only the back trails and passing through a few small farm villages. They stopped to talk to no one, and only saw a few people out at their fields. By the time they had reached the main road, it was already dark, and they were able to cross without recognition. Two cars passed, their headlights lighting up the bush, before Saki and Koli felt it safe enough to move ahead. They had to walk through the rubber farm of the president's chief advisor, but fortunately no one was out at night.

It was well past the middle of the night when they arrived at Koli's village. The waning old moon had risen, and made it possible for them to walk without using the flash light. But then they realized they had forgotten one thing in their calculations. It was the dying of the moon, and in that thin light the Big Thing, leader of the men's secret society, and his wife might be abroad in the forest.

In fact, Koli and Saki heard ahead of them the deep guttural call of the forest spirit, and the answering flute tones of his wife. The sounds never failed to quicken Koli's heart, but tonight, especially, he knew a moment of real panic.

He said to Saki, "Suppose they find us here, alone in the forest, near the secret fence. What might happen to us? We're both members and can share in the discussions of the Big Thing. But we would be recognized, and our plan would be spoiled."

The only answer was for them to spend the night hidden in the forest. Koli said, "I'll wait until the middle of the morning, and enter naturally, as if I know nothing about the Big Thing's night meeting. You'll have to stay well-covered until tomorrow night, or even the following night, if there's another meeting tomorrow. And it might mean some difficulty in getting Tokpa as drunk and belligerent as we want him, since he's an important member of the society, and will be involved in whatever society business is being conducted."

The singing went on, wild, sweet and tempting, throughout the remainder of the night, with quiet intervals when the matter at hand was doubtless being discussed. Koli and Saki found refuge off the trail in a thorn bush just above a swamp. Saki would have to stay there until Koli came to find him the next day, and so it had to be a place where no one would venture, and where Koli could make his visit to Saki without being suspected. There was a temptation to panic, a temptation borne on the music. Koli almost believed that Tokpa had called out the Poro society to meet them, and that they would be dealt with in that swift and rough Poro justice which they knew was the final court, without the right of appeal.

But nothing happened, and they remained safe. The singing finally stopped, as the light began to show in the sky. The old moon was snuffed out by the dawn and then by the rising sun. And not long after, Koli took his chance to find the main trail and enter the village as if he knew nothing and nothing was amiss.

IX: HEAR IN THE WIND

The first person Koli saw was Tokpa, who was sitting at the edge of the blacksmith shop where the trail entered the village. Tokpa looked somehow tired and confused. Koli thought to himself, "He's obviously been drinking too much lately." He seemed older than he actually was, but it was an old age not tempered with wisdom.

Tokpa called out, "Just like you to come walking in here in the middle of the morning. Where were you last night, when we needed every man in the village to discuss the problems you and your family have caused?"

It was an unexpected attack. Koli answered, "What problems do we cause, that you yourself aren't behind? It seems the last time I was here you were making the trouble, and we were the ones trying to get you out of trouble. Can't the crocodile make his own way in the water without hitting the tree roots on the riverbank? What are you talking about?"

Yakpalo looked out from the blacksmith shop, and told Koli, "Be quiet. Things are more serious than you realize. The Big Thing came out last night because of Sumo. It was said at the meeting that Sumo intends to prepare medicines against Tokpa, and is trying to kill him. The medicines are supposed to be taken from human flesh, provided by the leopard society across the big river. Sumo denied it, of course, but Tokpa brought witnesses against Sumo. The issue isn't solved yet, but whatever way the decision falls, it will be serious. If Tokpa is lying, then he himself will be punished by the Big Thing. If Sumo is lying, not only will the government punish him, but he will be banished forever from the village, and punished by death if he ever returns."

Sumo was in the blacksmith shop also, and looked up at Koli, stopping his work on the hoe he was beating into shape for the planting season that would soon be coming. He looked serious, even troubled, not at all his usual self. His confidence seemed shaken by what he had heard, by what had been said against him in the night.

He said only, "Don't believe any of those lies, Koli. Tokpa knows he can't beat us by fair means, and so he is out to kill us in any way he can. When the crocodile grows old, it will eat anything."

Yakpalo told Sumo, "You be quiet too. The final discussion of the case will be made tonight. We will all be called again by the Big Thing to a serious meeting, a resolution of this quarrel between the two zoes of our village. I still hope that there might be another way out, but the case is serious, no question about that. And so I want all of you to stop putting more troubles in your own ways. Let the truth come out, and there will be no need for any of you to insult the others."

Koli thanked Yakpalo, "You did well in keeping the quarrel from breaking out here in the blacksmith shed, which is supposed to be a place of peace. But, please, I want to talk to Sumo, to find out from his own lips what is going on."

Tokpa started to say, "You'll only learn what lies to tell tonight." But Yakpalo quieted him, and said, "It's only right for Sumo and Koli to talk together."

"Saki is here, and is hiding in the thorn bush above the swamp," was the first thing Koli said to Sumo, after they had gone off together. "But you don't dare go see him now. People will be watching you. Let me take care of the business. This attack by Tokpa is all the more reason why we have to bring Saki into the meeting tonight, because it will show that Tokpa is wrong. The old plan won't work, obviously, since Tokpa most likely won't be drunk tonight, and we can't wait another night. Tonight is our best chance to defeat Tokpa. If we wait he might beat us."

Koli went on to explain to Sumo, "Saki doesn't want to stay here, doesn't have any desire to lose his new identity and his place with Dabolo. He admires the big man, likes the work in Dabolo's village, is very glad not to be part of Firestone any more, likes his new wife and child, and particularly doesn't want to be involved with either of his other two wives. He admitted to me that it's like running away from his other life, but he said that running away seems the best choice at this point.

"Saki wouldn't have come with me at all, if it hadn't been that there was someone who recognized him. He figures that if he is seen to come back as a spirit from the dead here in his own village, and is never seen again, no one would believe the report of the man who saw him. And Dabolo has no reason to give him away, if anyone asks." Koli didn't go on to explain about his problems with Jonathan, which would also be solved by Saki's reappearance from the dead.

Sumo liked the new version of the plan, and felt it would fit in well with what he needed to save himself from Tokpa's lies. "At least one thing is true," said Sumo, "I was making medicine against Tokpa. But the medicine I'm working on is not at all what Tokpa claims I am making. I have never been mixed up with Mano leopard people, and I don't intend to start now. In fact, I wouldn't be surprised if Tokpa himself was trying some leopard medicine against us.

"But the problem," Sumo continued, "is that Tokpa has witnesses who are willing to drink medicine, swearing that I have made a deal with Mano leopard people to buy the genitals and heart of a person they will kill. They say I use these things to make especially strong medicine against Tokpa. I don't know how Tokpa found these people to be witnesses, but they say they will swear at the meeting tonight.

"What I need is for Saki to appear at that meeting, and say he has come from the dead. He must say that Tokpa made him kill Sulongteh, by using medicines against him. He didn't do it of his own free will, but did it because he was forced into it. That in fact is almost true, because Tokpa drove Saki mad before he attacked Sulongteh that day. And next Saki must challenge the witnesses to remember his words, and to remember all their dead ancestors, before they swear their oath. These witnesses too will be visited, may even die, if they drink the water and tell lies against Sumo."

Koli agreed. "It's a good idea, and I think it will work. I'll go to Saki and tell him what he has to do tonight. For the rest of today, he has to stay hidden away in the thorn bush. I'll give him some food and water, when I go to see him. Then Saki will come to the meeting, and hide at the edge of the grove until the time when Tokpa calls for witnesses. Saki will then come out, all covered with white chalk that I'll give him, and make his speech. He'll then disappear into the forest, almost as fast as he came, and head for home, leaving his old clothes on the way."

146

During the afternoon, Koli managed to slip out of town without being followed, to relieve himself. He looked in all directions before cutting into the forest to find Saki, who was waiting, tired, hungry and confused, in his thorn bush.

Saki's initial reaction to the situation was, "I'm leaving and going home now. I don't want to face the Big Thing, and I don't want to get mixed up in an issue bigger than the one that brought me here."

But Koli persuaded him to stay. "You're here now, Saki, and there's no point in going back home without doing what you've come to do. Don't you want to get back at Tokpa for what he's done to you? After all, don't forget - it was the trouble he gave you that made you finally lose control and kill Sulongteh. It wasn't really your fault at all."

Saki agreed finally. "I'll go through with it." He accepted the banana, roast cassava and dried meat that Koli had brought him. He wanted rice and soup, as well as a hot bath, but he knew he would have to wait. He had drunk water from the edge of the swamp, which was fortunately fairly clean. And now he took the white chalk and began to coat himself with it thoroughly, over his whole body. He took the old clothes he had brought, and tore them in every way possible, and rubbed them first in dirt, and then in white chalk. Koli almost had to laugh when he looked at Saki. If the reason for the disguise was not so serious, Saki would have looked comical.

Koli made his way back to the village, after preparing Saki to do his part. Yanga cooked supper for him, but it was not possible for him to eat. Koli was too frightened by what might happen at night. Flumo hardly seemed aware of what was going on around him. He had been to the meeting last night, but seemed not to understand the accusations that were made. Yanga was trying to prevent him from going again tonight, particularly if there were any serious trouble. But he insisted he had to go out whenever he heard the singing of the Big Thing. It hurt Koli to see his father failing so rapidly. He almost hoped Flumo would die before any more troubles fell on him.

The village was quiet that night. It was dark and heavy, and there was nothing to persuade people to sit up and talk. Most of the men had been out half the previous night, and were glad to get some sleep before the next meeting. A few children tried to go out and play in the village before bed, but their parents more roughly than usual brought them in and put them to bed. It was an uneasy time, and everyone felt it, even Flumo, who complained to Yanga, "I don't know what's wrong. Things feel bad in the village tonight."

Koli managed to get a bit of sleep before he heard the singing. In fact, Koli was surprised that the moon had already risen, and he was not aware of it. He had been more tired than he realized from the forced walk of the previous night. But he was glad he had found some rest, since now he could think more clearly.

Flumo, too, had heard the singing, and was rousing himself. Yanga once again tried to persuade him to stay at home, but he said, "I'm a man, and I have to go."

Yanga worried that she couldn't keep him back. "I only hope that whatever happens, I won't lose my husband as well as my sons in one night." She was frightened and confused, and thought, "It was better those days long ago when Tokpa was loving me. I shouldn't have refused him last year, or else I shouldn't have gotten started with him in the first place. All this trouble now has something to do with my foolishness, I'm sure. I should have known better than to believe Tokpa's lies then. Now he's lying again, and it seems everyone in the village believes him. Well, perhaps not everyone. I think I can still trust Yakpalo, and I'm glad Koli is here."

Yanga heard the singing move from the village out into the forest, and she knew the men were going there. She hoped Flumo would not fall and hurt himself on the path behind the fence.

Yanga heard the singing stop, and knew the men would now call on the ancestors to guide them. She thought, "I'm not even sure I believe in all these ancestors they call on. What good have they done me? No, I mustn't think that way. They brought me twin sons, so long ago. And now the twins are in danger. Instead, I ought to ask the ancestors to help us all."

Out of the hearing of Yanga and the other women, the talk moved on to the case at hand. Tokpa repeated his accusation:

"Sumo went to the Mano leopard people to get medicine to kill me. Sumo paid people in Mano country to find and kill a member of his own family." There was a hissing of breath and a sucking of teeth at that remark, which had not formed part of last night's accusation.

"Who was to be killed?" the elders asked. Tokpa had to respond to the question from the society leaders who were listening to the case, in the presence of the Big Thing. This was the critical point now, for a vague, general accusation of medicine murder meant nothing without details.

The talk became quieter now, as if the men wanted to prevent even the trees of the forest from knowing what they were talking about. Tokpa's response was, "Whereas no one has yet been killed, the witchcraft will be directed against some child in Sumo's family. It might be his son, his sister's child, anyone."

The elders turned to Sumo. "You have a chance to answer, a chance to say your own piece and ask questions, before Tokpa brings his witnesses to swear that you are arranging for a leopard murder of a member of your own family."

Sumo pointed out, "Nothing has happened to anyone in my family yet, and so the witnesses had best be careful about swearing to their report of something that might or might not happen in the future. Perhaps Tokpa just planted it in their minds that I'm preparing such medicine. Black deer who does leopard's bidding will be eaten for his pains."

Sumo continued. "Please notice that Tokpa didn't bring the leopard people themselves, just some Mano witnesses. And if these witnesses aren't leopard people, then how would they know about leopard business? On the other hand, if they are leopard people, what business did Tokpa have with them that made them talk so freely to him? Perhaps it's Tokpa himself who is joining the leopard society. After all, he's already half a Bassa man, having joined the Bassa society and given up his proper Kpelle ways to do so.

"Notice also that none of Tokpa's Bassa brothers are here tonight, because the Bassa people don't know anything about Poro, about the truth and honor and tradition of the Kpelle secrets. All they do is make dirty medicine to kill other people through the

149

water, and try to draw in decent Kpelle people to join them. Doesn't everyone know that Tokpa used Bassa water medicine to drive Saki crazy only three years ago, and thus was really the one responsible when Saki killed Sulongteh? He wasn't even honest enough to do the job himself, but found Mogo, a half-crazy water man at Firestone, to do it. I knew all about the matter when I went to see Koli at Firestone, and this Mogo even tried to pull me, too, into the water business. Fortunately for me and my family, I resisted and remained a proper Kpelle medicine man, a proper zoe, so I could be found worthy to go with old Mulbah to be initiated into the deeper secrets at Malawu with the Loma people."

"It's one thing," Sumo continued, "for the Kpelle to join with their Polo brothers in Loma country, and learn the deeper secrets that unite all Poro people, the honest, serious secrets of life and death, of health and sickness. It's another to go with Bassa people, who have never been initiated, and learn the secrets of madness and lying and treachery. Would I ever join a leopard society, which is condemned by all decent Poro members, if I had any hope of ever being a true zoe? Or is it more likely Tokpa, who has already shown the kind of man he is, by what he did to Saki? The real leopard roars in the forest when he has killed."

The judges, one of whom had come especially from Loma country to share knowledge with the Kpelle societies, and who had agreed to sit on this case, asked, "Are you finished?"

Sumo indicated, "I'm done for now, although I might want to ask further questions later. I deny any wrong-doing in this matter, and I've made my point clear that if anyone is likely to do something wicked like this, it's Tokpa."

The judges asked him further, "Do you make a definite accusation against Tokpa in return?"

Sumo's answer was, "No, I'm not the kind of person to make unfounded accusations. It is only spider who talks when he has nothing to say."

This response won Sumo a murmur of approval, since it so clearly, and yet indirectly, challenged Tokpa's apparently reckless accusation, dependent as it was on the uncertain word of Mano witnesses, whom Sumo had so neatly marked as possibly leopard men themselves. The two witnesses Tokpa had brought were

150

clearly uncomfortable with the way things were going, and looked to Tokpa to see what he would do next.

Tokpa stood up to respond to Sumo's questions. "I congratulate you on a clever speech. Your medicine must be working already for you to think of such clever arguments.

"I particularly want to comment on my relations with Saki. It's quite true that Saki and I have never been friends, that there have been fights between us, and that I, Tokpa, have made some medicine to put Saki at a disadvantage.

"But I insist that Saki has done his own deeds, has killed a man, has run into the forest, probably to die. Sumo has no evidence whatever that I caused Saki to behave this way. It seems that it is spider who is trying to roar like leopard. Moreover, Sumo is now bringing up a case where there can be no witnesses, because if a witness appeared it would open the matter again, to the obvious disadvantage of Sumo and his family. On the other hand, my case is one where there are real, living witnesses. Let the judges decide between the two of us, Sumo with his imaginary evidence that doesn't even warrant an honest accusation, and me with a real charge and real witnesses. Let the elders bring the water for my witnesses to drink. May it kill them and me if they don't tell the truth. You will see who is spider and who is leopard."

The water had been mixed in the afternoon by old Mulbah, who was trusted by both sides in the case. The judges then signaled that they were ready for this critical validation of Tokpa's claims.

But before Tokpa could call his witnesses, a torn, white figure walked from the edge of the forest, from the wall of green which skirted close to the grove. There was a cry, and then a hush, from the people. One said, "It's Saki," and another said, "No, it's his ghost - look at him and you can see it." But before anyone could move, the chalk-covered figure, clear and yet indistinct in the moonlight now blurred by high, thin clouds that seemed more a part of the dry season now past than the rainy season to come, began to speak.

"Tokpa, you lie. You know you lie. I am Saki, not troubled by your world any more. You say there are no witnesses. I had to come here to be my own witness, because you have prevented any

151

other witnesses from coming here. It is true I killed Sulongteh, but you forced me into it. You tricked me, badgered me, deceived me, until I was crazy. You told me I would die, because I had joined the water people. You told me I had broken the law of the society by sending my son to kwii school. I never joined the water people, but I was afraid of you, and half believed you. You witched me, so that I drank too much cane juice, and you ruined me. It's true I did my own deeds and killed a man, and thus could never come back to my life here. You killed me in this village, however, since your lies have destroyed my life. You have killed like the driver ants, not like the leopard.

"And now you're trying to do the same thing to Sumo. You tell stories of another society, this time the leopard society. You bring witnesses who are prepared to lie for you, probably even believing they tell the truth, because you have witched them and confused them, just like you witched and confused me.

"But, and now I speak to the witnesses, if they swear on the water that old Mulbah has prepared, then that water will catch them. If they say that the water must catch them if they lie, then it will catch them, and all the ancestors will catch them. The Mano have real ancestors, and we Kpelle have some of the same ancestors. We all know that Wei, the great hero of the stories who was born of the spirits and men, was both Mano and Kpelle. Remember, you witnesses, that the blood that unites you and us, is the same blood that unites Wei with your ancestors and our ancestors. You will not survive if you swear on the water.

"Tokpa, if you go on like this, you, too, will die. You have no children. You are truly driver ant, since you carry your children with you in your lying words. You are not worthy to be called leopard. All you do is kill other people's children to cover your own lack of children. Now those children will come back to you, to get you. This village has needed you, to cut its forest and keep away unwanted rain. But this village doesn't need a madman, a liar and a traitor. Tokpa, watch out."

With that, Saki melted back into the forest, and was gone. The silent men heard everything, because Saki's voice rang clear and familiar on the night air. No stirrings of thunder had interrupted him, and no one in the meeting moved. A few sounds of leaves moving, a stirring of branches, and he was gone. Even the judges made no move to catch him. It was clear to everyone, that Saki had come from the ancestors to solve the case.

The judges turned to Tokpa and his witnesses. Tokpa himself could find nothing to say.

One of the witnesses said, "We didn't know what Tokpa was asking us to say, and didn't understand the case in the first place. We're sorry, but we are confused, and don't want to swear on the medicine."

Another one said, "We've heard so many things about Tokpa, about Sumo and now we seem to be forgetting what really was said. We are only black deer, neither leopard nor spider nor driver ant."

A third witness added: "We prefer to go back to Mano country, to leave this palaver. If the Kpelle have spirits of the dead who come to their meetings, what need have they of living witnesses from across the river?"

The judges did not press the case against them, but let them go. They turned instead to Tokpa, and asked him, "Can you explain what just happened? What was this spirit, this vision, that came to us in the moonlight? What did you do to drive Saki mad, and lead him to commit murder? Can you explain all these things?"

Tokpa's voice seemed old and flat when he answered. "How can I talk now? What you just heard, I heard also. I am not leopard or spider - or driver ant, for that matter. Let this crocodile rest on the river bank, and wait until the sun shines to dry him off. But remember - when the forest shows its secrets, the animals that live there may learn to regret they didn't go to the water to drink."

The Big Thing and his wife sang again the following night, but only a few answered their call. The meeting was reserved for Yakpalo, Sumo, Tokpa, the judges and a few senior elders since the matter had been turned over to the sheep-horn society for discussion in the house of the zoes. Sumo was initiated during the meeting, so he could hear the decision, but it was judged unnecessary to initiate Koli, since he had been outside the core of the problem.

The elders made their decision about Tokpa, and, in keeping with his important and senior position, the decision was communicated to him in this secret session. Had he chosen to appeal, the question would have been taken to the spirit society, that highest of all bodies, half-way between the men's and women's societies, and encompassing not only the Kpelle, but the Loma and other peoples as well.

Clearly, the decision was not to expel him from the village, and equally clearly, Tokpa chose not to appeal the decision. He accepted his punishment. He was too important to the well-being of the people. Even Sumo and Koli realized that much. He was a good worker, and was leader of the men's work groups. Too much of Tokpa was woven into the fabric of the village life, for him to be driven out.

What the decision was, Koli could not guess, and Sumo would not tell. Koli did see, however, that Tokpa refused to drink the next day from the supply of newly brewed cane juice. He wondered if he had been ordered, for the good of himself and the village, to leave strong drink. Even palm wine he refused. He also noticed that Tokpa confined himself to comments on his work. Bush cutting was complete for the season, but the time had come to prepare for burning, and then for cleaning and re-burning the farms. Tokpa wanted to talk only of that, and not of recent events. He deliberately avoided meeting Sumo and Koli. The only interaction between Tokpa and the boys' family was that he sent a hindquarter of red deer to Flumo the next night, with the hope that it would help him feel better.

Sumo and Koli met again after the decision had been taken in secret about Tokpa's punishment. They discussed at length what had happened and what would happen. Sumo said only, "Tokpa has been punished, but in such a way as not to shame him before the other villagers. For the time being he won't be a danger, but such things as this have happened before. Eventually, Tokpa will mount a counterattack. For the present, I have to consolidate my position as zoe in the village, and you have to establish yourself still further as an essential assistant to the clan chief. In that way, we'll be in a stronger position to meet the new counter-attack when it comes."

Koli left that afternoon to return to the clan chief's village, to his family, and to his work. He thought, "Our plan worked better than we could have imagined, but there still remains Jonathan to beware of. Jonathan's first and most important means of attack is gone, unless he can find a way to prove Saki's presence in Dabolo's village. That's unlikely, but still Jonathan is clever. I'll have to be careful."

"The other threat Jonathan made is to reveal how I stole village money. To meet that attack, I know what I have to do. I'll go back to that village, and explain to the women I cheated that I discovered a mistake, and give them back their money. I needn't do it for the people whose names I took from the tax roll, however. What I did was perfectly legal, and everyone does it. The money I received from them was just a gift to me."

When Koli got back to the job, he just waited to see what Jonathan would do, after he had cleared himself with the people of the village. He didn't go to Gbarnga, didn't send any money, just did his work and took care of his family.

As he suspected, Jonathan came over to Sengta not long after, on the pretext that he needed to examine the tax records. He found Koli and took him to task, "Why haven't you sent more money to help the movement? There are many important jobs to be done, and we're falling short of the money that we need to be the saviors of Africa."

"No, I'm sorry, Jonathan. There is no more money here. I just can't seem to locate any. You'll have to wait until I can find some more. It was hard enough for me to return the money to the people in the village where I made mistakes in recording the taxes the other time. It was only because of those mistakes that I was able to give you ten dollars. And I had to replace that money out of my own pocket."

"You did what? You gave the people back the money? And now you say you can't find any more? All right, Koli. If that's how you look at the revolution, don't blame me if you get bypassed when there's a new and free Liberia. And don't blame me either if I slip and tell my friends in the police about Saki."

"About Saki? You mean about a dead man, I'm sure. You're not in touch with events these days, are you, Jonathan? Otherwise you would have heard how Saki came back from the dead two weeks ago in our village. I even saw him myself, as he explained what happened when he killed Sulongteh. No, Jonathan, Saki is dead, and I don't know what you're talking about."

"Koli, you fool. You yourself as much as admitted to me hardly a month ago that Saki is in Dabolo's village, and that you took him there. I know it from the wife that Dabolo gave to Saki."

"I don't know what you're talking about. I never admitted anything. I don't know that village, and I have only met Dabalo once. As for Saki being there, it is too fantastic a story for anyone to believe, now that people have seen that Saki came back from the ancestors in our village. No, Jonathan, you can't get anywhere telling the police about things that no one will believe."

"Koli, you may think you're clever, but you're not. Just wait until I get back to Dabolo and bring Saki out here for all to see. I'm sure Dabolo himself won't want to be caught for harboring an escaped murderer."

"It won't do you any good, Jonathan. No one will believe you, not after what happened. And I'm sure your friend Dabolo won't want you in there troubling the people in his village. They're all Dabolo's friends, I'm sure, including whoever it is that you think is Saki. If you want to keep your friendship with Dabolo, don't go asking him to do silly things like giving up one of his workers, the husband of one of his wives, to the police, on the basis of a mistaken identity.

"Jonathan, I have nothing against your movement. I hope you used the thirty dollars I gave you last year and the ten dollars this year for good purposes. And, don't forget, I know what you're saying in those meetings. I can always tell the clan chief what I know, if I start forgetting myself."

"All right, Koli, all right. Forget it. But we won't forget you. You're still part of us, and we expect help from you. I'm sure you'll bring it of your own free will one of these days. In the meantime, enjoy yourself as husband and church-goer."

Koli thought over these last remarks as Jonathan turned to find a taxi going back to Gbarnga. "I'd have thought myself silly even a year ago to consider being a husband and a church-goer. Jonathan obviously still finds it silly. But I'm no longer so certain

"And now I need your help. I want you to loan me some money, at least as a way to thank me for all the effort I put into your education. It wasn't perfect, of course, but you would never have gotten this job if it hadn't been for the education I gave you. You'd never have known how to work with a clan chief, how to advise him on dealing with white people, Liberians and country people. You'd have just remained a little country boy from behind Gbarnga. And now I need your help. I know you're making good money, and I know that you can afford to give me some help.

"I need the money to go to Ghana with the East Africans. We'll take taxis and buses overland through Guinea and Ivory Coast, until we reach Ghana. Guinea will be independent of France by that time."

"What does that mean?" Koli asked. "Isn't Guinea French country?"

Jonathan replied, "No, Koli, it will be free, truly free. We can travel from Ganta to 'Nzerekore in a free country, and from there through Bouake to Kumasi and finally down to Accra. And there, in Accra, will be the greatest gathering of real Africans you can imagine. People from north, east, south and west Africa, leaders of their people, men who will overthrow the colonial yoke - all will be there. And Liberia can learn from them what to do next.

"If you can just loan me some money, even fifty dollars would help, then you'll be glad later. Not only will I be sure to return the money, but I'll make sure that you are on the inside of the movement when it gets under way in Liberia. You have the beginnings of a good education - I made sure of that - and the movement needs you, just as you need the movement for more education."

Jonathan sweetened it ever more "There is a group which meets in Gbarnga, behind the tax office, in the dance hall there. On the front it is a school, but behind the school we have ideas and plans. The East Africans come from Hopewell at night and on weekends to teach in the night school. They are even persuading some of the white teachers at Hopewell to join them in the teaching. It makes things look better, they say. But after the white teachers have gone home for the night, they remain and have beer with the students, mostly grown men who want to improve them-

BOOK II

THEY ARE IN THE CHILD

I: THE KINDLING FIREBRAND

The next months were quiet for Koli and Goma. Koli heard no more about Tokpa, and Jonathan seemed to accept Koli's new independence, although Koli still feared both men. Ziepolo continued at the Balataa school, and seemed to make good progress. He called himself Stephen now, and Koli accepted it quietly.

Koli thought, "After all, I myself was called John for a time at Salala, and it didn't hurt me at all. A new way of life needs a new name, and if Ziepolo wanted to be Stephen, let him be Stephen."

More troubling to Koli and Goma was Ziepolo's increasing interest in Hopewell College and the white people there. Koli asked him, "Why do you always go to the college after school instead of coming directly home?" Koli had seen Ziepolo and the other boys walk to the campus, with the hope of finding some food at the dining hall, some ripe fruit on the trees at the teachers' homes, some games to play, some small work to do for the students, and he didn't like it.

One day, when the rains had fully started, Ziepolo went to the campus to take oranges from the tree near the house of the white man he had seen at the opening of the Balataa school. Koli heard the whole story later from Ziepolo, and realized, "I can't run his life now. I guess whatever he does is what's going to become of me. From now on, it's Ziepolo who'll run my life. For all too short a time, the son lives in the father. After that, the father lives in the son."

Ziepolo told how he was already up in the tree, when the white man came out and caught him. The other boys who were with him, waiting at the bottom of the tree to catch the oranges he threw down, ran off, but Ziepolo had no chance to do so. The man was too quiet and too quick.

The man took him by the arm, and asked him what he was doing. Ziepolo was frightened, but somehow felt the man's look was not too terrible. He understood enough English by that time to answer, "I want oranges, please."

The man laughed, and said, "You should ask me the next time. This time go back up the tree and pick ten oranges, take five with you, and give me, the owner of the tree, the other five."

Ziepolo, who was still somehow expecting to be beaten, did as he was told, and brought the oranges back down. The man took his five, and told the boy, "Go on now, and come back again if you want more. But don't just go up the tree and steal them. You must ask first. And, before you go, what's your name?"

Ziepolo told him, "Stephen."

"All right, Stephen. Go back to your friends now, and tell them I don't bite people. I see them over there behind the mango tree. And tell them also if they want oranges, they have to ask me."

Ziepolo went down to the mango tree, and found his friends waiting there for him. They were amazed he hadn't been beaten, and asked if the white man was afraid to beat people. "No," Ziepolo said, "He just wants us to ask for things when we take them from his house."

The other boys laughed at him, and one said, "You'll be sorry if you do what the white man wants."

But Ziepolo was determined to try again. So the next day he came again to the white man's house, and asked for an orange. This time the white man wasn't there, only his wife and children.

Ziepolo told Koli later how they had a little boy and an even littler girl. The boy was walking, and the girl was in a small bed on wheels, with the white man's wife pushing the bed. Ziepolo asked, "Give me an orange."

The woman asked, "Are you the boy who came yesterday?"

Ziepolo admitted it, and the woman laughed and told him, "Climb the tree if you want. But you must bring us our share of the oranges. Otherwise you can't come again to the tree."

He was watched by the other boys, who stayed below the house, behind the mango tree. When he came back again with oranges, not having been beaten, they changed their words, and began to call him the white man's friend.

One boy jeered at him, "Why do you want to leave us behind, and go to the white people? Don't you know that if a black man goes to the white people, eventually they do something to harm him?"

Ziepolo was determined to show the other boys that they were wrong. So the next day he went to the white man's house again, to see if he could get some work to do. He had seen the bigger boys in Balataa go to work at the houses of the teachers at the college. He knew that they got work, taking care of the grass near their houses, or planting trees. He wouldn't mind work like that, since it might give him some money to call his own. But it would also give him a chance to get to know the white man, and to learn some more of the kwii way and the kwii language.

He found the white man and his wife together in their house, sitting at their big table. He walked up the steps to the house, up to where he could see through the big glass window into their living room.

He told Koli later, "I'd never seen so many books as there are in the house. And I can't understand why there are so many windows in the house. People can see into the house from any side, and yet the white people didn't seem ashamed."

Koli explained, "White people are different. What they do doesn't make sense to us, but they don't seem to mind. Just be careful, though. You might make a mistake because you don't understand them. I remember at Salala how I cleaned all the grass away from the white man's house, the way we Kpelle do. He was really angry with me, because he only wanted me to trim it short. Why they like all that grass, I don't know. It brings snakes, for one thing. But they like it. You have to do things their way. Be careful, that's all."

Ziepolo explained to Koli next how he stood for a moment at the door, afraid to knock, and watched them at their table. The boy was sitting on a box on top of a chair, and was eating with his parents. They sat at their table, and talked to each other and to him. The little girl was in another chair, with a small table attached to it, and the man reached over from his place to give her food. Ziepolo said, "I'd never seen white people in their own home like this, and I was amazed." He watched them for what seemed to him a long time before they looked up and noticed him.

The man got up and went to the door, and asked Ziepolo to come in. He asked, "Do you want more oranges?" and Ziepolo shook his head to say no.

162

"What do you want then?" asked the white man. His wife had also gotten up to join them, but the baby girl began to cry, and she went back. Ziepolo wondered who ran the home, the man and wife, or their children.

Ziepolo answered, "I want to work."

The man looked at him seriously for a moment, and then asked, "What can you do?" Ziepolo said, "I can take care of the grass and plant trees." The man looked over to his wife, told Ziepolo, "Wait outside on the steps," and then went to talk about it. They stayed there a few moments, but it seemed to Ziepolo forever.

He told Koli later, "I wanted to turn back, run down the stairs, and go back to Balataa. The other boys had warned me that I'd be sorry in the end. But I stayed, because I wanted to find out more about these people, because I wanted to get a job of my own."

Ziepolo told how the man came back and said, "I'll give you some work, but first I want to find out about you. Do you go to school? Do you live nearby? Will your mother and father agree? Are you willing to work hard?"

Ziepolo got lost in the middle of all the questions. He could barely understand what the man was saying, although he found the wife spoke a bit clearer. Ziepolo explained, "I knew from their tone of voice that they wanted me to say 'yes' to all their questions, and I did so. I only hope I didn't agree to anything I'll be sorry about later!"

The woman told Ziepolo to sit down, until they finished eating. They went back to the table, said something to the children, and started eating again. Ziepolo told Koli, "I was amazed at just how much they had on their plates. Not only did they have rice and soup, but they had bananas, oranges, bread and other kwii things I'd never seen before. And they gave them to their children before they ate them themselves. They seemed to be begging the boy to eat, something I just couldn't understand. Why should people have to persuade a child to eat? You and Sumo have never had to beg me to eat. I'm always hungry! But the wife looked up at me, looked down again, and then seemed to understand. She got up from the table, and brought me piece of bread covered with some red sauce, and gave it to me to eat. The man looked impatient for a moment, and then relaxed."

After they finished eating, and after Ziepolo had eaten his piece of bread, and wished hard for another one that didn't come, the man took him out to the yard. He showed him the grass, and tried to explain, "There are two kinds of grass, one which I like and one which I don't like. You must take this knife and dig up the bad ones and leave the good ones."

Ziepolo thought the whole thing foolish, since grass was grass, and worthless in any event. But for the sake of becoming kwii, learning more about these people, and getting some money, be was willing to do it.

The little boy came out to join Ziepolo after a while. First he had to sleep, and then the white man and woman let him come out. He sat with Ziepolo, hung on him, and got in his way. But Ziepolo didn't really mind, since it meant less work to do. The little girl was put out on a cloth to play, with her shirt off to catch the sun before it rained again. Ziepolo told Koli later, "You should have seen just how white she was - all over."

When the afternoon was ended, the white man came to Ziepolo with ten cents, and told him, "You've finished for the day. If you want to come back again, I'll give you ten cents for each afternoon you work. But you must be willing to work hard, and you must make sure that your mother and father agree."

Ziepolo understood only that he was talking about his mother and father, and said, "I'll do it."

The man seemed to realize that Ziepolo didn't really understand, and so he brought his cook out to talk to him. The cook was a Bassa man, but knew enough Kpelle to explain to Ziepolo. The way he said it was, "If you work hard every day, you'll get ten cents, which you must take home to your mother and father."

Ziepolo didn't want to say that Goma and Koli weren't his parents, and so he just said "ye" to that also. If he told the whole story, the white man would never understand.

Koli was both glad and afraid to hear all these things. He told Goma, "I'm glad the boy has a job. It'll teach him to be responsible for himself. I had to learn the same things in Salala. But I'm afraid

164

of what Ziepolo might do next. That boy is too frisky. I believed that white man in Salala too fast, and I believed Jonathan too fast. Does Ziepolo have to make all the mistakes I made, and more?"

II: THEY ARE IN THE TREES

"Stephen, please carry the boy on your shoulders. He's tired walking. I'll carry the little girl. We don't have much farther to go." Ziepolo had worked for the white people over a year now, and had learned to do as he was told. But he still couldn't explain later to Koli why the white family was walking with their children and carrying cloths to sit on, all the way out to the middle of the Hopewell farm.

Ziepolo thought, "When I carry my baby sister at home, the little girl Goma delivered about a year ago, it's for some good purpose like going to work in our farm." Here it seemed for nothing, even though most of the other white faculty members were with them on the walk, as well as a few students.

The white woman explained to Ziepolo, "The teachers have decided to have a small feast on the farm, to give the students something to do on this government holiday. There have been so many holidays this year to celebrate newly independent African countries that it seems good to use one in a different way. We all plan to have our noon meal together out on the farm, and then play games and enjoy the outdoors. A college truck is coming, loaded with the food, but otherwise everyone is supposed to walk."

The problem was the students. Ziepolo had heard them talking as he came to work in the morning. They were saying that the college was refusing to feed them in the dining hall, and was forcing them to use part of their day off to walk in the hot sun for nothing. The students were also complaining about the work they were forced to do in the morning. Some of them had gone to the workshop on the hill behind the college to clean the storeroom, and sort the tools. Others had worked in the library checking books. Still others had been repairing chairs in the classrooms. But most of them were standing near the dormitories complaining, when Ziepolo walked past.

The sun was overhead now, and it was planned that everyone would eat together at the farm when they reached the chosen place. But Ziepolo told Koli later, "Very few students went with the white teachers. I'm sure I would only have gone, if I wanted something from the teachers. I only counted about twenty or thirty students. Probably they were the ones failing their schoolwork or short of money for their school fees."

They arrived at the place where they were to eat. The white man Ziepolo was working for told him, "Put down the boy, so he can run and play."

The little girl was two years old, but she wasn't big enough to play by herself yet. The white woman said, "I'll stay with her for a while, and then I'll let you play with her, Stephen."

The thing that made Ziepolo glad he had come was the food. There was enough and to spare. Even playing the white man's games was not so bad, since they all had lots to eat both before and after the games. The teachers said they had prepared enough for all the students, but since most of the students hadn't come, everyone who was there would have more than enough. The teachers, however, did agree to take much of the food back to the dining hall, to feed the others in the evening.

The little children were tired when they started to walk back in the evening. The sun was still hot, and the young rubber trees along the edge of the road didn't give much protection. Ziepolo had to carry the boy all the way this time, while the mother and father took turns carrying the girl.

Ziepolo told Koli, "I was really surprised at just how weak these foreign teachers are. They get tired so quickly, even on a small walk like that. Some of them climbed onto the truck that was taking the food back to the campus, so that they could ride, although the students had to walk all the way."

When they got back to the campus, Ziepolo realized immediately that there would be trouble. He heard students refusing to go to the dining hall to eat the leftover rice and soup that had been brought back. They wanted fresh food cooked for them, and said that they had not been treated fairly.

Koli met Ziepolo on the campus, as Koli was returning home from seeing the clan chief. He said, "I went the long way around to get back to the village, since I want to see what's happening at the college. Rumors have reached Sengta, and I'm curious to know more. Tell me what's going on."

Ziepolo told him all that had happened on the farm during the day, and then said, "Let's go find out what's happening over there. I see a bunch of students talking."

Koli found there the East African students talking excitedly to Zedekiah, the Kenyan whom Koli remembered meeting in Gbarnga. They then turned to a group of Liberians who came up, and Zedekiah began talking about "exploitation," "racism," "discrimination," "injustice," "poor food," and other matters that seemed remote to Koli.

Koli asked Ziepolo again, "What really went on during the day to make them so angry?"

Ziepolo could only repeat "The students were upset at having to work hard in the morning, and then having to walk a long distance to get their regular noon meal. It really wasn't much of a walk, but these students and faculty both are just fat and lazy."

Koli listened to more of their talk. These were all the same East Africans he had listened to in Gbarnga at Jonathan's meeting, and they were saying many of the same things. Zedekiah spoke for the group, declaring, "Africa is no longer a place for Africans, who now have to dance when the white man tells us to dance. We should show that we are in charge of our own continent, and refuse to do all these foolish things. If we have to stay at this terrible college, and take daily insults, then we should at least be men enough to make our feelings known."

The decision was made by the students not to go to classes the next day. Zedekiah shouted, "We'll stay in our dormitories, until we get promises of decent treatment, with no more forced labor and forced marches. This will be the beginning of our quest for liberation."

Ziepolo didn't really understand what was going on, as he stood with Koli. Koli tried to explain to the boy, but it didn't make much sense to him either, and so he failed. The only thing he could say was, "The white men are running the college, and the black students don't like it."

Ziepolo realized that this was the same complaint the other boys in his school brought when he went to work at the white teacher's house. "Maybe they're right," he thought. "But then where could I get some work to do? No, let me stay where I am."

169

Koli sent Ziepolo to school as usual the next day, having forgotten about the problems at Hopewell. But when Ziepolo arrived, he found the other children talking about how the Hopewell students were standing up for their rights. The teachers had refused to feed them, and so the students were refusing to go to class.

Ziepolo tried to explain how that wasn't exactly true, but an older boy said, "Oh, you're just the white man's friend. We're glad someone is willing to stand up for what's right, and not be walked on. It's a terrible thing not to be fed, when the food has been promised."

Ziepolo tried to tell how they had been fed yesterday, but out on the farm. However, the others laughed at him, and another boy said, "You didn't hear the real story. The students came to Balataa last night, drinking beer, and told us how they had been forced to work, they, the educated leaders of, Liberia's future, indeed of Africa's future. They had been forced to work half the day, and then walk the other half, all for a few crusts of bread."

Ziepolo thought back to the huge meal of rice and soup he had eaten on the farm, and asked Koli later, "Where did these students get their ideas? It wasn't like that at all."

The teachers then called the children to attention, and told them to forget about the foolishness at Hopewell. They were led in saluting the Liberian flag in front of the school, and then the principal gave them a short talk. She was newly returned from the United States, but was herself a Liberian. She only spoke English at the school, although the boys said that she talked Vai at home.

She said, "Those Hopewell students might do any kind of foolish thing, but you're not to pay attention to it. Students must respect their teachers at all times, no matter what color or nationality the teachers are. They must come to school well-dressed, with short hair, must never talk back to their teachers, must work if they are asked to work, and must be glad with whatever they get. Teachers are always right, since without teachers there can be no learning."

And then, as if to prove her case in the most dramatic way she could, she motioned to Ziepolo to come out of the line, and stand before her. "Look at this boy," she said. "His hands are dirty, and he hasn't cut his hair. He doesn't have shoes on his feet, and his short trousers are the wrong color. Let him go home until he can come back to school in the right way. And let that be a lesson to all the rest of you. If you think you can follow those Hopewell students and make trouble for the Balataa school, then you can think again."

Ziepolo was utterly confused and taken aback. He explained later to Goma, "I haven't any shoes, because you and Koli didn't give me any. I don't think my shorts are the wrong color. They're brown like all the other boys' shorts, even though a darker brown than theirs. Here living with you, no one has cut my hair for a very long time, even though I know Kuluba would have done it for me."

Ziepolo watched from a distance as he saw the other boys go into the school. Two of them turned and laughed at him, and made a sign at him he didn't like. He was tempted to turn and run away, to run back home to the village.

He thought, "I was the one boy to agree with the teacher, when I talked with the others before school. And now she singles me out to punish me for nothing at all. What's worse, she doesn't even know who I am, since she's teaching the class which is ahead of me in school."

Ziepolo thought of going back to Goma, but decided instead to go to the college to see the new developments with the students, and also to ask the white man he worked for to help him with shoes and shorts. He felt lonely and confused as he left Balataa, walked down the hill to the Bassa village, and then onto the campus.

He was even more confused when he reached the campus, and saw small groups of students here and there, talking and arguing and even playing. It seemed that almost none of the Hopewell students were at school either.

Ziepolo thought, "Maybe their teachers have thrown them out too." He stopped to listen to one group. He couldn't really understand what they were talking about, but he saw the sign one of them held, saying, "White man, go home."

Ziepolo wondered, "Who would teach them, if the white men do go home? And who would help me get shoes for school, if there were no white teachers?"

In fact, most of the Hopewell students seemed to be just enjoying a second holiday from classes. Some were playing the same game with net and ball that he had played yesterday at the farm. Others were listening to the radio. Another group was cooking over an open fire, saying that if the college wouldn't feed them they would have to feed themselves.

Ziepolo went past the classroom building, where he could see the white man he was working for teaching a group of three students in a big classroom. He was talking loudly, and writing things on the blackboard. Ziepolo stopped to listen, but he couldn't understand one word of what the white man was saying.

Ziepolo told Koli later "I thought I knew some English by now, but obviously I don't know the deep English this man was using. It seemed to me from the students' faces that they didn't understand much either. But maybe it was because they were nervous. The students kept looking out the window, and seemed afraid that someone would notice them. There were two girls and one boy there, and soon the one boy got up and walked out, leaving only the two girls. The white man continued talking, even faster than before, as if he noticed nothing."

Ziepolo told how he walked on past the classroom building. Other teachers were doing the same thing, teaching to almost empty classrooms. There were five students in one class, two in another. "I thought to myself that the principal of my Balataa school wouldn't allow such a thing. She's tough, I said to myself, and then I realized I really admire her for it. The white teachers should have been tougher, and they'd have had less trouble."

When Ziepolo reached the house, he found the white woman at home with the two children. He explained to her his problem at school. She smiled at him, and said, "We have problems at our school, too. What clothes are you supposed to wear, and why don't you have them already?"

Ziepolo tried to explain, "I didn't know what clothes to wear, and no one ever told me about getting my hair cut." The woman said, "We'll help you, but the money will have to come from your pay, if you're going to buy new shorts and new shoes. You've already worked a long time for us by now, and have saved up two dollars, even though you've taken most of your money home."

She then asked him, "Where will you get the clothes?" Ziepolo explained, "There is a Mandingo tailor in Balataa who will sew the trousers for me for just fifty cents. But there's nowhere in Balataa, only in Gbarnga, where I can get shoes."

The woman looked at him suspiciously, and then said, "I'll send you to Gbarnga to buy shoes, and also to buy us some things at the market."

Ziepolo realized he had never gone alone to Gbarnga, never had the experience of taking a taxi without his family or someone to help him. But this was his chance, as he explained later to Koli, to get what he needed for school, and also to show that he could be trusted to do errands for the family.

The woman told him, "I need tinned fish and mantles for the kerosene lamp from the German store, as well as rice and palm oil from the market. I'll give you fifty cents for the taxi, and I'll also give you five dollars with which to buy your shoes, the fish, the mantles, the rice and the palm oil. You must bring all these things back to me safely. If you do it, I'll help you by paying part of the price of the shoes."

She gave Ziepolo the money in a small purse, which she told him to keep very safely in his trousers pocket. He knew that he had a hole in the only pocket in those trousers, but he was afraid to tell her about that. She might not let him go. So he clutched the purse as tightly as he could in his hand, and started on his way.

At the gate of the college, Ziepolo had to wait a long time before a taxi appeared. While he was waiting, he watched the children playing in the village across from the gate. He couldn't understand them, because they were speaking Mandingo and Loma and other languages he didn't know.

When a taxi came, Ziepolo pushed his way in and went in it to Gbarnga. He was the fifth person in the back seat, and so he was not able to lean back at all. He had to sit hunched up at the front of the seat, while two men, a woman and another boy leaned back. He held his money purse tightly all the way, and was greatly relieved when the taxi let him out in front of the German store.

He walked into the store, and was almost too afraid to speak, when the white man behind the counter finally asked what he wanted. He had to wait until three adults did their business, even though they had come after him.

Ziepolo explained, "I need shoes for school, as well as finned fish and mantles for a lantern."

The man asked, "What kind of lantern?"

Ziepolo stood silent, thinking. He had to admit, finally, in a small voice, "I don't know."

"Can you describe what it looks like to me?"

"I've seen the lantern at the white man's house, but didn't look closely. And here I see three different kinds of lantern."

"Doesn't it look like one of them? Point it out to me."

"No, I'd better not. I'll let the woman get the mantles when she comes to Gbarnga herself."

The white storekeeper, whose English sounded strangely different to Ziepolo from that of the white people at Cuttington, showed him a box of shoes, and said they cost eight dollars.

Ziepolo had no idea that shoes could cost so much, and had to say, "I can't buy them, because I only have five dollars altogether."

Finally, the man found a cheap pair of white cloth shoes, the kind the other boys called skates. Even they cost Ziepolo three dollars. He realized that the shoes would take the whole two dollars he had saved, even if the white woman would be willing to give him a dollar more. For a moment, he was tempted to tell her they had cost three dollars and fifty cents, and keep the extra fifty cents to buy his shorts in Balataa. But then he worried that the woman would find out the truth, would tell him to go and not come back.

He took the shoes, and paid an extra fifty-seven cents for the tinned fish. The woman had showed him the tin she wanted, and he bought the same kind. He knew she could have gotten cheaper fish in the other kind of can, but she didn't want that. He asked Koli why anyone would spend so much for food, especially when she could get other food cheaper, but Koli couldn't explain it either.

In the market, he went to the ladies who sold rice, and there he found Koli's older sister, Lorpu. Koli had taken him to her the last time they had passed through Gbarnga together. She worked in the market every day, selling rice that had been sent from the village.

She greeted Ziepolo, and told him "Sit down and talk with me awhile. I'll give you a fried cake to eat. Tell me about your life there."

Ziepolo relaxed in her company, and told her about the problems at Hopewell and in his own school. He told her also, "I'm working for some white people, and the woman sent me to buy things for her house. I've bought some things already. Now I have to buy her rice and palm oil to cook with. I have a dollar and forty-three cents left, and want as much rice as I can get for the money."

He reached his hand in his pocket, and realized that all his change was gone, the forty-three cents as well as the twenty-five cents for the taxi. It had slipped through the hole, and all he had left was the dollar bill. He had forgotten to put the change back into the purse.

He turned to Lorpu, and asked, "What will I do now? I've lost the money I'm supposed to buy rice with. Help me find it."

They walked back through the market to the store, but saw nothing along the way he had come. The money was gone.

Lorpu smiled at him, and said, "I'll help. All you have to do is promise to get me something nice from the white people's house, and I'll replace the money. The white people might leave you alone in the house some day, and you might see a necklace or a wristwatch or something they really don't need, perhaps even some money."

Ziepolo at first didn't like the idea, though he couldn't tell why. Then he realized it wouldn't be too difficult to do what she asked. So he took the sixty-eight cents from Lorpu, and promised her he would try to bring her something one day. But he thought to himself, "I tell Koli and Goma everything that happens. But I don't think I'll mention this one. They might not like it."

He took the bag the white woman had given him, and put in it the twenty cups of rice he bought. It cost him a dollar and twenty cents altogether, leaving him twenty-three cents. He then bought two small beer bottles of palm oil, at ten cents each, checked to make sure the home-made cloth stoppers were in them tightly, and put them in the bag with the rice. This left him three cents, which he would take back to the white woman. He put the shoes in the bag with the rice and palm oil, added the tinned fish, and went on his way back to the road to catch a taxi.

This time he didn't have to wait so long, but managed to find a space in a money bus. He had to sit in the back of the pick-up truck, covered over with a wooden roof. It was a good thing it was covered, because it started to rain heavily shortly after. The road became very muddy, and the truck slipped and bumped its way back to Hopewell. Ziepolo was glad when they finally arrived at the gate, and the rain stopped.

He left the truck, and walked up to the house. He reached there just before the white people were to eat. They welcomed him, and took the bag.

But the woman took one look, and asked Ziepolo, "Why were you so careless? A bottle of palm oil has leaked all over the rice and your new shoes. It's a mess! Luckily, it hasn't all leaked, but a lot of the rice has been spoiled."

Ziepolo tried to argue, "It isn't spoiled. You can still cook the rice and palm oil together."

The shoes were worse. He would have to spend the afternoon washing them to get the red stain out, and still they would never look the same again. Ziepolo had to agree with the white woman when he explained to Koli why the shoes weren't clean and white. "I don't know why I wasn't more careful. It was stupid of me."

Koli warned him that evening. "If you're going to keep your job, you've got to do better. The only thing worse than being careless is stealing. Don't do either one."

Ziepolo went down below the house, to where the Bassa laundry man was washing the white people's clothes. The woman gave him a piece of strong blue Firestone soap, and told him, "Wash your shoes until they're completely clean. I'll take care of the rice. And, after you've cleaned your shoes, you must ask the Bassa man there to cut your hair. You'll have to pay him ten cents for it, because the Bassa man cuts hair strictly for business."

The woman didn't even offer to help him this time. Clearly, she was angry. Koli knew better than to complain, but went and did what he was told. He had to, or otherwise they wouldn't give him money for his shorts in the afternoon.

He listened to the Bassa cook and the Bassa laundry man talking. He couldn't understand a single word of Bassa, and he was sure they were talking about him. But when he got up enough courage to ask what they were saying, they told him in Kpelle, "Today is a bad day to trouble the white man and his wife. They've having too much trouble already from the students."

Koli said, "I've heard about the problems too, and I wonder what will happen next."

The cook told him, "The students forced the teachers to stop teaching, and now no one at all is going to class. I can't understand it, because these students already have everything they wanted, and will get more when they finish their studies at the college."

The laundryman who was related by marriage to the college cook, went even farther. He said, "The students are lazy and disrespectful. They don't even eat the food when it's given to them in the dining hall, but leave it for children and dogs. The best thing would be to beat them all, and force them back to school. If I were in charge of the college, that's what I would do."

"But instead," the cook continued, "the teachers have agreed to have a meeting with the students tonight, and have invited the light-skinned American who is head of their church to come and listen, and then decide the case. It's just pure weakness on the part of the teachers, that they didn't stand firm against the students and put them down in the first place. But now the teachers have put themselves in a bad position, and have had to call their own boss to help get them out of it."

Ziepolo decided that he would have to listen in to that meeting, if he could find a way. He knew where they would have the meeting, since he had come often before to watch the students when they had dances. He and the other boys, if it was a bright moonlit night, would come to the campus to stand outside the windows of the room, and watch the students dance and play. Sometimes a teacher would come out to drive them away, but they would just run into the bushes, wait until he was tired of chasing

177

them, and then come back again. They enjoyed dancing among themselves, and even more enjoyed watching the boys go after the girls at the dances. There were so few girls at the college, that even the ugly ones had someone to dance with.

But this time Ziepolo wanted to see and hear something which was more serious than a dance. He wanted to learn how these students would treat their white teachers, and whether they would get away with all their rough talk. He told the cook and laundry man, "I'm going to try to listen, and I'll tell you tomorrow what I heard."

Koli also had heard about the meeting, and when Ziepolo told him that evening he wanted to go to listen, Koli said, "I want to hear what happens, too, but it isn't right for a grown man to listen in to such meetings, since they're supposed to be for the students. But if you want to go there, it won't cause any difficulty. Just come back and tell me about it."

Thus Ziepolo left home after dark, and walked back to the campus, and along with other boys from the school waited outside the building to listen at the open windows. There was rain in the air and the stars were hidden, but fortunately no rain fell.

Koli had warned Ziepolo to look again for the East African students, to see what they would do or say. He had pointed out the students, particularly Zedekiah, the day before when they were making speeches on the campus, and so Ziepolo had no difficulty recognizing them, when they got up to speak. He couldn't really understand what they were talking about, but he could see the actions clearly.

After a lot of high-sounding, emotional talk from the teachers and other students, one of the East Africans got up, the very Zedekiah Koli and Ziepolo had stopped to listen to the day before, wearing an old coat and looking the very opposite of the well-dressed teachers. He first said some things that didn't seem to mean much to Ziepolo, and then came around to the question of food.

He talked directly to the head of the church and the other big shots that had come from Monrovia. "The college scarcely feeds us at all. Not only did we not get any food yesterday, despite the

178

fact that we were forced to work hard all morning, but night after night we hardly eat."

He then paused for a moment, made sure everyone was watching, and said, "I've brought with me my food from supper this very night. I have it in the pocket of my coat. I don't know its name in English, but here it is."

He pulled out of his pocket a small and tired-looking piece of bread, not even a slice, just a hard-baked lump. "This," he said, "is what we eat at night, and this is what we are supposed to depend on to keep our brains alive when we study."

The students cheered, and even the teachers could hardly keep from laughing at the performance. Ziepolo himself laughed when he saw the student standing there, waving the biscuit in the air, and asking the head of the church, "Can you live on that kind of food?" With that, he sat down, and waited to see what would happen next.

Ziepolo told Koli later, "I didn't understand any of the other speeches, and I doubt if the other people did either. There was too much noise, too much laughter. But finally the leader of the church stood up, and quieted everyone down." He said, "You students are right in some ways. The teachers at the school tried to do something to make you happy at the party held on the farm, but they went about it the wrong way. They don't understand Africans properly, and tried to make you join an activity which only Americans would understand. They also failed to provide food at the dining hall for those students who wanted to stay behind. I'm sure that the faculty will admit their mistake, and will apologize for it.

"But you students were also wrong in refusing to go to class, and in making such insulting speeches."

Ziepolo told Koli, "It seemed to be the principal of our school speaking, when I listened to this light-skinned black American leader of the church. He said that teachers should be respected, whatever they do. Even if they make mistakes, even if they don't understand Africans properly, even if they serve food whose names some people can't pronounce, they are bringing the light of knowledge and must be respected. Our principal talks just like that.

"That church leader went on. He warned the students, 'You must be in class by tomorrow morning, lined up and seated in place, or else you'll be thrown out permanently. I don't want any more nonsense from you. I'll do my best to improve the kind of food you get, and I'll help the teachers understand better how to deal with Africans. But I don't want the very Africans these teachers came to help interfering with my efforts to improve the sort of help they are receiving.>' You should have seen the students when he finished! They couldn't say anything at all!"

The meeting ended quietly, and Ziepolo started to walk towards Balataa. He noticed that the East Africans were walking near him, and he edged closer to them, to hear what they were saying.

He told Koli, "I still found them very difficult to understand, but the main thing I heard was, `We'll find a way to leave this terrible place, where the black man is ruled by white and by those blacks who are their servants.' They were really mad at the church leader. They called him >`the American black man who had become whiter than white,' because he told them to return to class or be thrown out of school. They didn't have any choice in the matter, just like when I was tossed out of the Balataa school this morning. I didn't like it, but I had to do what the principal said."

The next morning, Koli and Goma sent Ziepolo to the Balataa school, hair cut, shoes on, and wearing brown shorts of the right color. Koli watched from a distance as Ziepolo lined up with the other students to salute the flag. He hoped that the principal would at least see what Ziepolo had done. Confused as he may have been by the demands made on him, he seemed to realize that his hopes were foolish, when the principal didn't even seem to notice him.

Koli thought to himself, "Perhaps the only reason she went after Ziepolo was just to show the rest of the children who's in charge. At least half the other boys have long hair, and there are several without shoes. Why did Ziepolo have to spend all that money? Anyhow, he's safe if she gets started again on the clothing business. If Ziepolo is going to do in life what I never had a chance to do, he's going to have to be on the right side of that woman."

That morning Ziepolo's teacher began to teach the children how to use a stick to measure things. Ziepolo had seen these sticks before, and wondered what they were for. Kuluba had taught him how to measure across a floor, by putting his feet end to end. She had shown him also how to measure a table, by seeing how many times lie could stretch his hand from thumb to middle finger. But using this stick was more difficult. It had numbers on it, and by now he had learned to read English numbers. But he had no idea how to use the numbers on the stick.

So when the teacher gave him a measuring stick and told hint, "Measure your book," He carefully placed the number 1 on one side of the book and found the number 8 on the other side. Thus he told the teacher, "The length is eight." The teacher took the stick and hit him across the hand, saying, "The length is seven."

Ziepolo rubbed his hand, agreeing, "The length is seven," although he didn't know why. Other students did the same thing, and the teacher beat them also. Soon they learned that one had to give the answer as one less than whatever the stick said.

Ziepolo asked the white man for whom he worked about it the next day. He seemed in a better mood, now that the students had returned to class, and was willing to talk with Ziepolo. He told Ziepolo, "Stephen, there is one more number at the very end of the stick, called zero. Instead of starting at the numeral one when measuring, you should start at zero, and count from there. Look, Stephen, when you count things, you don't count them until you have them. You can't count length by inches until you actually have inches in front of you. Thus you don't count one inch until you have moved from zero to one."

Ziepolo listened patiently, but the explanation didn't mean much to him. When he had asked Koli about it the night before, Koli had told him, "Begin with 1 and move on until you've finished."

Now the white man seemed to be saying that counting in English is different from counting in Kpelle. Ziepolo didn't know anything about this number zero, and he certainly had never learned anything about it from his people at home. But he thought to himself, "I have to accept it, just as I had to accept wearing

181

shoes and cutting my hair, just as those Cuttington students had to accept going to class if they want to get their college education.

"I guess school is a matter of doing what people tell you to do, and thinking what they tell you to think. I haven't yet been to bush school, but I've heard that it's the same there. Even this white man's explanations are just the same. He just uses up more words making the explanations, and then asks me to accept the result.

"It's easier to plant trees. This afternoon, I'm supposed to help set out baby mango trees, along the path from the white man's house to the classroom building. He's helping a college student who needs to earn some money to pay for his books."

The college student, Edward was his name, was another Kpelle man, not one of these strange East Africans, and Ziepolo could thus talk freely with him. He told Ziepolo, "I've come from farther down toward the coast, and I'm here at Hopewell to learn what the foreigners can teach me. But my family has no money at all to provide me, and so I depend on the Lutheran church for money. But the church didn't give me enough money to pay for all the books I have to buy, almost one hundred dollars worth a year."

Ziepolo told Koli that evening, "Edward and I had to collect baby mango trees around the campus, and then dig big holes to plant them along the path. I'm not strong enough to dig the holes, but at least I could find the sprouting seeds which were everywhere on the campus. Everyone dropped seeds from the mangoes they ate at the end of the dry season, and by now the seeds had sprouted into small trees, and were beginning to put down roots. The white man gave me a small shovel, and I went around finding the best small trees I could. Then Edward took the trees and set them in large holes filled with good dirt."

It wasn't the work of only one day, Ziepolo realized. He also realized that growing fruit from the trees wasn't the work of only one year. He asked the college student, "Why are the white man and his wife willing to spend money to plant these trees, when they won't stay long enough to eat their fruit?"

Edward couldn't claim to understand it either. His reaction was a little different, however. "I'm worried that perhaps the white man does plan to stay a long time. I don't think Liberia should have so many white people here, and I hope that eventually there

182

will be enough of our own Kpelle people willing to do jobs like the one the white man does, so that we can run our own country. You, Ziepolo, why don't you try to be such a person when you finally finish school?

"I was a small boy once just like you. I went to the mission school near my village on the St. Paul river. I had to struggle to find money even to buy a pencil or a copy book. I wasn't as lucky as you, Ziepolo, to find a job which paid ten cents a day.

"But times are changing," he said, "And now things are easier. I did well at the mission school, and was able to go on to high school at Muhlenburg, across the river and downstream from my village. There I was a good student, and was supported entirely by the Lutheran church. As a result, the church sent me here to Hopewell College, and is supporting me by paying for my food, my housing and my classes. In return, I've had to promise to work for the church when I graduate, one year for every year I was in college. They will send me to be a teacher somewhere, to teach children just like you."

The two of them went on working and talking, until the white man came to them, and started talking roughly. He said, "You aren't doing the job right. You started out putting the trees close together, and now you're being lazy by putting them far apart. I've paced off the distance between the trees you first planted down by my house, and they're only five paces apart. And now here, halfway up the trail, you trees are seven paces apart. "Your trees are not in a good straight line either. Look, do this job right."

Edward pointed out that the path wasn't straight either, but the white man said they could straighten that out after they had planted the trees.

As a result of all these complaints, the white man made them dig up the last four trees they had planted, two on each side of the path, and put them in different places. He insisted that they count the same number of paces between trees, and always check by looking back to see that the trees remain in a straight line.

The white man then looked at Ziepolo, and said, "Stephen, you ought to know better by now. Didn't I just finish teaching you about measuring with a ruler? This work is like using a ruler. You start at the tree you just planted, and count zero. Then at the end of the first pace, you count one, and you continue until you reach five paces. I am sure you can do it if you just think about it."

He said something similar to Edward, and then told him again, "Please do the job right. You shouldn't set a bad example for a boy just beginning school. Here you are a college student, and you haven't learned anything yet about accuracy."

After the white man left, Ziepolo raised the whole question of teachers. "Why should we do what they say, even if we don't understand why? I've never seen a forest where the trees are the same distance apart. Why should we plant such a forest here? And I've never seen them grow in a straight line. It's almost ugly to see them marching like so many policemen in a row. But the white man said to do it, and so we have to do it."

Edward laughed, and half agreed with Ziepolo. "It's true what you say, boy. A lot of the things they teach us here at Hopewell don't make any sense at all. They're trying to make us into a different kind of human being, one who does things their way, and not our way. You wouldn't understand some of the things we have to learn about at school here. They tell us about the way people lived so many years ago that even their children's children's children aren't alive any more, and they say we have to remember it. They tell us things we know are not true, like saying that human beings can't make lightning, which they say is caused by clouds. And we have to accept what they say, if we want to get anywhere in their world."

Ziepolo then asked about the events of the day before, when the students had refused to go to school. Edward responded, "Sometimes we students just have to show we are real living human beings. We can't go on, day after day, day after day, just listening to the foreigners, and doing what they say. So when they make us work hard all morning, and then walk a long distance to eat food while sitting on the ground, we have to object. Those East Africans have something good to say, when they tell us we have to learn to run our country. I don't like the way in which they think we should go after these goals, but their ideas are important. When you grow up, boy, you'll have to live with those ideas. I don't want you to forget what you heard here.

"On the other hand, you still have to plant your trees in the white man's way, and you have to put on shoes when he says to put on shoes, if you're ever going to get to the place where you can change things. All of us Hopewell students went back to school today, and we're all measuring our future in the way they tell us to measure it. And you'll do the same thing, if you have any sense."

Ziepolo had to agree, and went back to collecting trees for the student to plant. When it came time to quit for the day, the white man came back and congratulated them on a good job. He told them, "I may never eat from these trees, but you will someday. And when you do so, remember what you did here. You can build your country this way, straight and strong and fruitful. If you don't do it, you'll never have any fruit to eat when you are hungry."

Ziepolo was confused by the big words, but he admitted that he wanted a better country some day. What he couldn't say except to Edward and then later to Koli was that he hoped that the better country he talked about would be one where they could make their own choices, and do things their own way.

ALL AFRICANS UNITE
& FREE AFRICA FROM IMPERIALISM
WE HAVE NOTHING TO LOSE
BUT CHAINS!

III: THEY ARE IN THE HOME.

It was Christmas, the holiday when Christians are supposed to celebrate Jesus' birthday. Ziepolo had been told he could spend the day at home with his family, but he told Koli and Goma, "I want to go to Hopewell to see what white people do at Christmas." As he had often done during school time, he went to church with them in the morning, in the big new church that had been finished earlier in the year.

The worship was so very different from what he knew from Sarah's church in Balataa. The music, for one thing, Ziepolo never could understand.

He told Koli that night, "In Sarah's church we sing, clap our hands, shake rattles, play drums, and feel at home. At Hopewell, a white lady plays the piano, and everyone sings songs from books. The prayers are also written in a book, and don't mean anything to me. I'm supposed to know some English by now. After all, I've been in the Balataa school for two years already. But when I read those prayers in the book, I can't make any sense of them. The words are long and strange, like a different language."

Koli told him, "You won't make much sense out of it for a long time. I went to Salala for six years, and I still don't understand all that much of the deep English. But it's good for you to go, because it's the way to be kwii."

However, Ziepolo had to admit to Koli that the church was beautiful on this Christmas day. He had helped the white woman the day before to gather flowers and branches to put them around the church. The great stone table at the front of the church was covered with flowers and candles, and there were branches of trees over all the windows. It was a grand sight, and Ziepolo asked Koli, "Why can't we make Sarah's church look beautiful in the same way sometime? We never have big feasts in church there, the way the white people do at Hopewell."

After church, the white man, his wife and their two children went to their house, and Ziepolo followed along. They didn't seem to want him there, but Ziepolo was determined to see the rest of what they did at Christmas. He knew they had cut down large

188

branches from a tree below their house, and had set them up the night before in the house. They had covered them with shining strips of paper, colored lights, and beautiful glass balls. The lights worked only at night, when the college had electric power, but they had looked so very beautiful last night when the family was getting ready for Christmas.

Ziepolo had helped them collect the branches, had helped them set them up into what they called a tree, although it was really just branches tied together in a bucket filled with water and stones. He had then sung Christmas songs with them, on the night before Christmas. They were still the same songs from the book, but he had enjoyed being with the family. He couldn't help wondering but didn't ask, what the tree had to do with Jesus, and what the family would do with it.

When he arrived at the house after church, he saw that they had put a great many packages under the tree. The packages were beautifully covered with colored paper and strips of cloth, and looked so inviting to Ziepolo that he wondered what was in them. As the white people saw him looking at the packages, they seemed confused, and then the man went into his bedroom for a few minutes, and came out with a package for Ziepolo. He had obviously just wrapped it while Ziepolo waited.

"Stephen, open it. It's for you, your Christmas present. I can see that you aren't familiar with Christmas giving, and so perhaps you don't understand what we are doing. Any how, this is for you, and these packages under the tree are what we are giving each other for Christmas."

The white man's explanation didn't explain very much, but Ziepolo was glad for the package. He opened it and found a shirt for himself. It looked slightly used, but Ziepolo was glad to get it. Somehow he was disappointed. He had been given a Christmas dash yesterday, along with the cook and washman. Today, he had received a wrapped present, yet clearly this shirt was something the what man had decided to give him only at the last minute when he intruded. He was less upset by having pushed his way into the house than by the meager present he got when he stood there.

The man and woman looked at Ziepolo as if they expected him to leave, but he didn't want to go yet. He wanted to see what was in the children's packages. The boy and girl were tugging at their parents' clothes to hurry so they could open their packages. Ziepolo was sure that they had more than a slightly used shirt, but he wanted to be sure. The man began to tell Ziepolo, "You should go home now."

However, the woman stopped him, and said, "Let the boy stay if he wants."

They started by singing another Christmas song, and then they told the little boy, "You must find a package for each of the members of the family."

He wanted to start with himself, but his mother told him, "Begin with your sister." He really couldn't read anything yet, but he pretended to be able to read, and with his mother's help he gave people packages.

He found a small one for his little sister and gave it to her. She started to tear the paper off, but her father helped her take it off neatly, and then folded the paper to save for next year. In the package was a beautiful new small dress for her. She quickly tried to take another present, but her father stopped her, and said it was someone else's turn.

Ziepolo watched with bigger eyes and emptier heart as each package was opened. There were games, toys, books, clothes for the children, more than he could imagine.

He thought, "How can they use so many things, when they already have more toys and games and books than they can play with?" He thought of his own baby sister, now a year and a half old, with no toys or games or books or clothes at Christmas. "Does this little girl, who has so much, really need all these things?"

Ziepolo had already stolen a few things from the white people to give to Lorpu in Gbarnga. He had promised to do this, after all, because she had asked him to do so in return for helping him. One day, he had given her a tin of fish. Another time he gave her a dollar bill he had found lying on a table. Obviously, the white people didn't need the dollar bill or the tin of fish if they went off to teach at the college and left them just lying around. Lorpu had been so kind - and she was a member of his family - and she

190

needed the things he could bring her that the white people didn't need. Ziepolo didn't always remember how Koli had lectured him on stealing, for this didn't seem to be what he was talking about at all.

The Bassa cook had seen him do it, and warned him to be careful. "One day they'll catch you, boy. And then they'll not only sack you, but have you put out of the school in Balataa."

Ziepolo didn't take his warnings too seriously, because he knew that the Bassa cook also stole from the kitchen. Unlike some of the other teachers, these people didn't lock their food closet all the time. They locked it most days, but they often forgot, and on those days the cook would take a tin of fish or a small packet of sugar to his family.

He argued, "These white people have so much that a few things will never be missed." He was right, because they never seemed to notice.

But the cook had never taken money before. nor any of the many things they kept in the house. Ziepolo's stealing of the dollar bill was the first time anyone had taken money, and the cook was afraid of what might happen.

He said, "You don't know. Perhaps the white man left it there just to test if any of us is stealing." But nothing happened to Ziepolo, and no mention was made of it.

Ziepolo often went to Gbarnga to do errands for the family now, and he would leave these things off for Lorpu. In return for what he was doing for her, Lorpu would have something nice to give him: a few pieces of candy, a bottle of Coca-Cola. That was certainly nice, but it was nicer to know that, by giving Lorpu these things, he was showing the proper respect to his father's sister.

Ziepolo had also taken a few things to Goma and Koli, but didn't say where they came from. He knew that Goma would object if she knew he was stealing from the white people. So he just told them he was bringing presents to the family. He was pretty sure Koli knew what he was doing, but as long as he said nothing, it was all right.

As Ziepolo watched them open their Christmas presents, a plan grew in his mind. "I'm sure that the little girl will forget all about her old toys and games and books, now that she has these exciting new presents. I'll wait a few days, and then, when I have a chance, I'll take one of the old things, maybe even a small old dress, and give it to my own little sister in the village. That will be her Christmas present."

The chance came two days later. The papers, the toys, the colored cloths and the good food of Christmas were put away now. Only the tree remained - Ziepolo wondered why. The mother and father went out in the afternoon, taking with them the little boy, and left the girl to sleep and Ziepolo to watch her. She settled down in her bed for an afternoon rest, and Ziepolo was to sit there and make sure she was safe. The cook and washman had the day off, and he was alone.

Once she was thoroughly asleep, Ziepolo began to look in her room for things the girl would not want to play with again. He went into the closet, and looked carefully. There was an old doll, with one arm broken off. Next to it was something like a small goat, which she used to pull on wheels, but one wheel was missing. Under it was a small book made of cloth, with pages that the girl had chewed. Ziepolo didn't want any of these.

Then he saw what he was after. I was a small brightly-colored doll, just like the little white girl. It was small enough that Ziepolo could put it under his shirt, and not be seen when he left the house. The little girl never played with it any more, now that she had the new things. Ziepolo also found an old dress that was too small for the little girl, and he added that to his collection. Finally there was a book, with pictures of different animals, which had been forgotten in the back of the closet.

Ziepolo thought, "These will be my Christmas presents for my own sister. She doesn't have anything of her own, and now she can play with some nice things, and be happy."

Just for safe-keeping, Ziepolo wrapped them in paper and took them behind the house, far enough so that no one would see, and hid them under a bush. He then returned and waited for the white people to come back. And when they returned, they let him go home for the rest of the day, since they said it was still Christmas.

Ziepolo walked through the farm on the way back, instead of taking the main road through Balataa. He had the presents safely

192

under his shirt, but still didn't want anyone to see him. Also he knew that in Balataa there would be men drunk and playful because of Christmas. They might catch him, and see what he had, perhaps even take them from him.

He reached home, and found Goma and Koli there with the baby. They were so happy with their little girl, and Ziepolo wanted to make them even happier.

He thought hard, and then said, "The white man gave me these things for my little sister."

Koli looked at him strangely, and asked, "Are you sure they gave you these things? You didn't just take them? If you start stealing, you'll end up like Jonathan, and never be the person 1 know you can be someday, if you work hard and are honest."

Ziepolo looked down, then up, and said, "Sure they gave them to me. See, here's the paper."

He knew he had told a lie, and he saw that Koli really didn't believe him, but he didn't want Goma and Koli to give him any difficulty about how he had gotten them. He only hoped that they wouldn't try and thank the white man and his wife. He felt safe in that regard, however, because Goma and Koli had only met the white people once. He thought, "These white people just don't seem interested in how I live. They haven't even been to see Koli and Goma and our house."

After giving his sister the dress, the book and the doll, Ziepolo went back to Balataa to meet his friends there. He found that they were getting ready to play Santa Claus. Ziepolo had not known this game before, when he was home in his village. But here near the main road, the children all enjoyed playing Santa Claus at Christmas.

"This time," they said to Ziepolo, "you must dress up in the old rags and straw. You're a good dancer, and you can lead us to the right houses on the Hopewell campus where we can get some money."

The boys had found an old plastic rain coat, which they put around his waist, and an old pair of trousers many sizes too big, which he wore over his shorts. They covered his head with a paper bag, which they decorated with palm thatch. He wore on his feet rain boots that were much too big for him, but they filled the boots

193

with straw, and tied them on his feet. His hands were tucked in an old shirt, and his neck was covered in straw. Nothing could be seen of his body or hands or feet or head.

Another boy had a drum with him, and played the role of the interpreter, just as the masked dancer in the village always had an interpreter. Ziepolo was supposed to make only unintelligible grunts and noises, while the interpreter would say what he meant, and also play the drum while Ziepolo danced.

They left Balataa and walked to the campus where they would sing and dance for the teachers. The other boys had done this every Christmas, and the masked Santa Claus would bring some money for their own enjoyment. Ziepolo knew the different houses, and who lived in them, and guided the boys to places where they would get a good reception. He knew, for instance, that the man who lived in the house behind the dormitory would just tell them to go away. He hated all this "native culture," as he called it, and would just be annoyed. Ziepolo also knew that particularly the families with children would enjoy seeing them dance, and would give them a few pennies.

They walked from Balataa to the campus in the afternoon. The sun had already gone low in the sky, and so it was not too hot for Ziepolo to walk in all these extra pieces of clothing. Even so, he found it tiring, and had to take off the shoes, the paper bag and the plastic raincoat until they reached the campus. There he dressed again and they went ahead.

But to their surprise they found that another masked dancer had come ahead of them. There was a real Gola dancer, covered in straw from head to toe, going around the campus. The boys admired him, and watched with awe as he did his tricks. But they followed after him nonetheless, and each benefitted from the other. The Gola dancer would go first to a house, accompanied by his drummer and interpreter. He would stride up and down, raise himself up to full height, and sink down to his knees. The interpreter would demand some money, and, if it were given, the straw figure would dance in circles, turn head over heels, and stand on his hands, all without showing any of his body.

When they came to the house where Ziepolo worked the man and his family were home. The little boy was a bit brave, and

194

came out to watch the masked dancer. The girl, however, cried and hid behind her mother, although looking out from time to time if it seemed safe. The man brought out his camera, that same box that had attracted Ziepolo two years ago when he had gone to the opening of the Balataa school, and took pictures of the Loma dancer. The interpreter demanded extra money for this, and the man was willing to give it.

And, as soon as the Loma dancer left, Ziepolo and his group followed behind, shouting "Santa Claus has come." The man and his family laughed, and even the little girl was willing to come out this time. The Santa Claus seemed more her size, and she wasn't afraid. They obviously didn't know it was Ziepolo dancing, and they didn't recognize the other boys at all. "The man and woman had seen those boys almost every day," Ziepolo told Koli later, "and still don't know who they are."

When they finished, Ziepolo let loose a long string of nonsense, mixed with Kpelle comments. He tried to sound as deep and frightening as he could, but he felt within himself that he merely sounded foolish.

The interpreter then told the white people, "The masked dancer is blessing you, and warning you to be careful lest you get in trouble with the spirits." Ziepolo had to laugh as he heard all the things his interpreter was making up.

The man laughed too, and his wife told him, "Give the children some money." He reached into his pocket and brought out a five-cent piece for each of the boys who came along with the party, a ten-cent piece for the interpreter, and a twenty-five cent piece for the masked dancer himself.

The boys went home that evening, and counted their money. They had earned a total of almost three dollars. They divided it equally among themselves, by taking stones, and putting them in piles, one stone for one cent. After they made sure that the piles were equal, they saw that there were three stones left over, not enough for each boy to have one. So they tossed them in the air, and the boys jumped for them, grabbing and shouting. Ziepolo got one, as did two other boys. They then shared the rest of the money according to the number of stones each boy had.

The next day Ziepolo went back to work at the white man's house. The woman asked him, after he had started to work in the garden, "Have you seen a small dress belonging to our daughter? It was an old one, too small for the girl, which we intended to give you for your little sister. But we can't find it anywhere. Have you seen it?"

He lifted his head, pulled himself together as he had so often seen people in his village do, and looked blank. He said, "I know the dress, but I don't know where it might be. Have you looked everywhere in the girl's room? After all, sometimes now she takes things, and throws them around. Maybe she lost it one day."

The woman looked at him suspiciously for a moment, and then the man told her, "Don't worry. Ziepolo obviously doesn't know anything about it. They would ask the washman what he did with it when he last washed it."

The woman didn't seem convinced, but she left the matter. Ziepolo went back to work, frightened but relieved. He thought, "I'll have to wait a while before taking anything more."

IV: THE PACT WHICH BINDS.

After almost a year of cool relations between him and Koli, Jonathan arrived at the clan chief's court, and asked to speak with Koli.

"I've come to do you a big favor, Koli, even though you don't seem to care about us anymore. I happen to know the government is going to build a motor road near your village. I can help make sure the road actually goes right through the village, if you want it. The new iron mine at Nimba needs a railroad, and this road will connect with the railroad near the St. John river, behind the big forest that lies beyond your village. They haven't yet decided exactly where the road will go, and I thought I might be able to help your people out."

Koli almost groaned out his response, "What do you want, Jonathan? When you get big ideas to help other people, there's always something behind the ideas. I haven't got any money now to help you. You ought to know that I don't steal things."

"Forget that business, Koli. It's all over now. You won the last one, and I'm not worried about it any more. Don't always be so suspicious of me. I swear, Koli, this church and husband business have made you sour. And now that you have a little girl of your own, you seem sourer still. What's wrong with you?"

"OK, Jonathan, OK. It's just that I'm sure you have something on your mind, and I'm sure that means something for me to do. I've never yet seen you give any of your favors for nothing."

"In fact, Koli, I do have a favor to ask of you. Some of the East African students at Hopewell are tired of the place by now. The revolution hasn't taken place yet, and their fight for freedom and justice in this part of Africa is failing. They learned not long ago they may have a chance to go to Russia, where they can learn more about the ways to make Africa a good continent for her own children. But we have to check our contacts, if they are to get out of Liberia safely. The government is suspicious of us now, Koli, and we can't do the things we want by ourselves. We need you to help us, and in return I may be able to influence the big shots in Gbarnga to put the road through your village. And if you don't help us, they might be persuaded the other way. It's your choice, Koli, if you want a road in your village."

"Jonathan, I don't believe you. You make promises and you threaten in the same breath. How do I know you're not lying again?"

"If you want to insult me, OK. I don't need to help you. As for proof, you can check with the District Commissioner. But if you do, you'll have to give him a big dash to make sure your village gets the road. If he knows you want it, you'll have to pay - and pay big. But so far, one route is as good as another as far as he's concerned. But it's your business, Koli. Do what you want. Stir up trouble for yourself. I'm sure you're a rich man."

"OK, OK! If I don't believe you, you've got me! If I believe you, you've got me! What do you want me to do, Jonathan? As long as I don't have to break the law, so you can catch me again like you did the last time, I'll help you. But, if you mess me up again, I'll get you somehow."

"Don't worry, Koli, I'm not going to hurt you. All we want you to do is to cross the border into Guinea, and take a message for us."

"Guinea?"

"You know - French country."

"Oh, that's right, it's Guinea now."

"You can go across easily and freely, because you're a Kpelle man, and no one would suspect you at the Liberian border gate. They're watching us at Gbarnga and Hopewell. The president has his spies at Hopewell and they inform him of everything the East Africans and their friends do these days. We could never make the arrangements ourselves.

"What we need from you is this. One of the East Africans - you remember him, Zedekiah - will go to Ganta to visit a friend there. The informers may watch him, but they won't learn anything, because the man he'll visit is in fact just a friend he met in the long holiday, a man who thinks the same way we do, and who will help us. The man said he should come visit him any time, and Zedekiah will do just that."

"And what am I to do?"

"You'll go to Ganta also, and meet Zedekiah early in the morning at the friend's house. There he'll give you a message to take over the border to a man that will be expecting you. Then you must bring back the answer. You may have to cross a second time before you finish, but I'm sure you won't get any trouble. I'm positive you have some kind of relative over there in Guinea, where all those other Kpelle people live."

"That's true, Jonathan. My mother's uncle lives not too far from Ganta, on the Guinea side. I wouldn't mind visiting him, since he's thus my uncle also. I've never been to see him before. Let me go home, and make the arrangements. I might even be able to come back from Guinea with a country cloth for myself, since they say he's a weaver. My mother talked to me several times before about going there, but I've never done so. But, Jonathan, I'm warning you. This had better have no traps inside."

"Thanks, Koli. Nothing's going to happen to you. In the meantime, I'll make arrangements with Zedekiah to meet you in Ganta at his friend's house, directly behind the Lebanese store near the border gate. And I'll try to find out what I can about making sure the road passes through your village. Just think what a great thing that will be - you can have a road, a school, a clinic, stores, all in your own village."

Koli had not taken much time away from the clan chief's office in the past year, and so it was easy to persuade the clan chief to let him have a week off to see relatives. He said, "I'm going home, and am then going to visit Guinea to see my uncle there. I've never met him, but I've wanted to go for a long time. I've also wanted to see for myself what French country is like, under the new government of Guinea."

Koli felt good as he walked to his village. His daughter was almost two years old now, and he thought Goma might be pregnant again. Ziepolo was doing well at school, and was now in the third grade at Balataa. Moreover, Ziepolo had a good job with the white people, and the white people were generous with the boy.

"I'm only afraid that they might find one day that Ziepolo is stealing from them," Koli thought. "I must warn the boy again to be careful, and stop for a while, or he'll be caught. Those things he brought back in the dry season as Christmas presents were stolen. But I've managed to avoid seeing the white people for they might ask about it, or even see the things if they ever came to visit our house."

Also things had remained quiet in the village. In fact, Tokpa had been almost too quiet. During Koli's visits home, Tokpa had avoided speaking to him.

Koli thought, "Either the Big Thing has done a really good job on Tokpa, or else Tokpa has some other plans to get revenge in due time."

Sumo was well and busy, but it worried Koli that Kuluba's last child, a little boy, had sickened and died only three months after he was born. Moreover, their other children were always sick these days. Tokpa may be witching them.

"I should really tell Sumo to let me take their oldest boy with me to Balataa, so that he can get medical care if he needs it. There's a clinic at Hopewell, where Ziepolo goes sometimes, and I'm sure I can take Sumo's boy there also."

Koli's main worry back home was Flumo. "I'm sure that one of these days I'll get a message telling me to hurry home, and be present at Flumo's death or burial. He just sits in front of his house, wrapped in an old shirt even on the hottest days. He doesn't seem to remember things from one day to the next, and almost didn't recognize me the last time I was there. He can see very poorly now, and his skin is covered with white patches, thin and cracked and transparent. At least that's not Tokpa's doing. Old age alone is taking Flumo."

The road was another matter. He met a friend of Yakpalo's on the trail and shared his news. Koli was excited by the idea of having a road to their own village. He thought back to the stories he had heard from his childhood of the days before the first white man had come, of the days even before the Liberian government had conquered his area. He said to the man, "In some ways things were good in those old days. But in most ways, it must have been bad. No one went to school, children died from disease, and, when a hungry season came, people starved."

The man responded, "Now things are different. True, we have to pay taxes, and we have to send laborers to work at

Firestone. But these days no one starves, people can get medical care, and children can go to school. And, the number of people in our village is growing rapidly. It seems that fewer children die now, because they can go to Gbarnga for treatment.

"We're lucky, the man continued. "There's still plenty of farmland around our village, as well as between Yakpalo's farm village and the big river. It's not like the Hopewell and Balataa areas. There, the people can't find enough land to make their farms."

Koli agreed. "The land where my wife, Goma, and I made our farm last year has been taken over by Hopewell. People are planting rubber there now. This year, we had to beg another site, at the very end of the Hopewell farm, but soon even such places as these will come to an end. I know people in Balataa who are having to make their rice farms this year on sites they left to grow into bush just four or five years ago. The way we farm, the land has to be fallow at least seven years before we clear it again. Nothing can grow on these Balataa farms."

Koli spoke again about the road. "It will really help our village. We can have a school, a clinic, stores, easy transportation."

Koli continued, to himself, "If my going to Guinea can make sure that the road comes to our home, it's well worth it. Jonathan has the ear of many of the officials in Gbarnga. They drink together, and Jonathan has probably found out some of their secrets. And I'm sure they know what he knows about them, and thus they're afraid to deny his requests. That's the way Jonathan operates.

"On the other hand, Jonathan could well be caught. And those other officials in Gbarnga would have no hesitation in arresting Jonathan for spying. It would keep them out of trouble, if for any reason Jonathan tried to tell what he knows about them. What a bunch of people! They're so busy fighting each other, it's a wonder they ever get anything done."

When Koli reached home, he talked to Sumo, whom he met at the blacksmith shop at the end of town. He discussed going to Guinea to visit his uncle and he also discussed what he had heard about the coming of the road.

Sumo was suspicious. "What's the use of having a motor road? I don't need it. But I suppose change is coming, and so we might as well take advantage of it."

Yakpalo had taken part in the talks at the Paramount Chief's court in Gbarnga, and had already been advised that they were thinking of building the road through his village. He knew also that they were constructing a railroad from the coast up toward their area.

He told Koli, "The railroad has by now reached halfway to our area, and will be continued after the motor road is constructed alongside the railroad bed as far as Nimba. But the people need an access road, and this is the area they've chosen for it. I myself am very much in favor of the plan."

Koli wondered if the decision had already been made, and if Jonathan was just pretending when he said he would help Koli's village. But still it didn't hurt for him to go to Guinea and visit his uncle. He had long wanted to see the place.

Yanga insisted, "You have to take with you to our uncle a small bag with the best rice we have as well as a knife and cutlass that Sumo's made. And please stop in Gbarnga or Ganta and buy our uncle some kwii presents, so that you don't go empty-handed. After all, you're an important man now, and you must show how an important man can behave. Be sure also to wear your best clothes."

Koli listened to all this politely, realizing that his mother still seemed to think he was a boy. Finally, she sent her uncle a small antelope skin, which she had received as a gift from Tokpa. Koli wondered why Tokpa was still giving the family gifts, but didn't have time to carry the matter further.

In Gbarnga, Koli stopped and bought a small mirror, a headtie and a package of shotgun shells to take to his uncle. He didn't know what kind of man he was, and wanted to satisfy all possible desires he and his family might have.

He then caught a taxi to Ganta, where he was to meet the East African student Zedekiah. The student was staying at a man's home, behind the shops, not too far from the border gate. Koli had been given a careful description of the house, and he found it without difficulty.

"I remember you from that meeting in Gbarnga after Jonathan came back with us from Ghana," said Zedekiah to Koli. "You promised you would help us with the cause then, and at least you did a bit for us. However, Jonathan told us later you weren't really interested in helping anymore. Have you changed your mind now about helping Africa?"

"I don't like the way you put that," answered Koli. "I love my country just like the rest of you. It's only that my first job is to take care of my family. I'm not as free as you students, who don't have to worry about children and jobs and houses. But I still hope that we can have a better country here to live in, and I wish you well in all your own home countries."

Koli didn't want to get mixed up with this student. He remembered how smoothly he had talked in that meeting in Gbarnga, and he had heard from Ziepolo about the speech he gave with the biscuit at Hopewell.

He thought, "I don't trust him at all. I just want to get the letter and take it across the border. I want to make sure Jonathan doesn't mess up our village getting that road."

But Zedekiah insisted on talking still further. "Koli, tell me about your family, about your wife and children, about your village. I've heard from Jonathan about the new road, and I want to know how it will help your people."

Koli answered briefly, trying to avoid involvement. He was sure the man would lead him into some kind of trap. Finally, Koli said, "I have to go, if I'm to get across the border this morning."

Zedekiah gave him the letter to carry, and told him, "Keep it very secret, so that the Liberian border guards won't see it. When you're across the border, you must go into the first village and ask for Kerkula at the main shop. Kerkula will be expecting you, and will give you a reply to bring back through the border when you've finished seeing your uncle."

At the Liberian border, the guard asked to see what he had brought with him. Koli brought out the knife, the cutlass, the rice, the skin, the headtie and the shotgun shells. At the sight of the shotgun shells, the guard told Koli to wait, and went to get his superior officer, who was at headquarters in Ganta.

205

"What are you doing with these things, my man?" asked the major, when he came to the border. "Don't you know that Guinea is a dangerous country? Are you trying to start some kind of revolution over there? If you take these things across the border, you'll be arrested just as surely as if you were to bring a rifle back from Guinea to Liberia. I should really arrest you myself."

"I didn't know there was any problem, major," answered Koli. "I'm just going to visit my uncle across the border, and these are a present for him. If I shouldn't take them, I'll leave them here and pick them up when I come back."

"That's not necessary, my man. What you should do is just give them to me, and I'll forget about the fact that you have broken international customs and military agreements. Besides, you are supposed to have a passport and documents if you want to go into a foreign country. Where are they?"

"I was told that we Kpelle people could cross freely just to visit our relatives in Guinea. Passports are only for official business."

"That's true, my man," answered the major. "But with shotgun shells, your business looks very official to me. What else do you have with you?"

"Just these tools, some rice, a skin and this mirror and a head-tie to take to my uncle, and my own clothes in the bag. Nothing else."

"We'll see about that, my man. I'm afraid I'll have to search your baggage and make absolutely sure. It won't take long, and you don't have to fear the search, if you haven't done anything wrong."

Koli thought fast. If the major found the letter, he might read it, and then he would be in serious trouble. He then knew what he had to do.

He said to the major, "Sir, please let me go back and buy another gift for my uncle in the shops here in Ganta. Then you can search my things when I come back, to see that what I have and the other things I buy are all right. Otherwise, you'll have to search twice. After all, I can't go empty-handed to visit my relatives. And since I have to leave the shotgun shells with you, I'll buy something to replace them."

The major hesitated a moment, as if he wanted to inspect the bag anyhow, but then let Koli go. "You come back here and check with me when you're ready to go. Of course, if you don't want any trouble when you go through, you might also leave my assistant here a dollar for the efforts he has put in on your behalf."

Koli left and went back to Ganta, relieved at escaping what might have been a serious problem. As he left, he saw the major and the border guard laughing and dividing the coins he left behind him. He couldn't help wondering if bribery was really the way to run a government. It felt different now that he had to do the bribing.

Koli went into the nearest Lebanese shop, and made a point of trying to buy a gift. He looked at a knife, and then decided against it as also something to make the major suspicious. He thought about a ball, a bag of candies, a hat. He then walked out as if undecided, as if he needed to try another store. He looked around, realized he was not being watched, and then went back to the house where Zedekiah was staying.

"Why are you back so soon? Didn't you find your uncle across the border? Do you have the answer?"

Koli told the whole story, and gave the letter back to the student. He said, "You read me the letter, and let me in turn tell the message to Kerkula on the other side. I'll then bring back the answer by word of mouth."

Obviously Zedekiah didn't like the idea of telling Koli what was in the letter, but he was stuck. He asked Koli, "Can't you hide the letter under your shirt or in your shoes?"

But Koli answered, "The major is suspicious. I'll have to take it in my memory, or not at all."

In the end Zedekiah agreed. He told Koli, "You must ask Kerkula if the arrangements are complete for eight Hopewell students from East Africa to come across the border at night at the farm of his friend in Ganta. The border goes along the river there, and since the rains aren't heavy yet, the students can cross safely. They'll bring with them their clothes and their passports from their homes, and nothing else, no money, no exit visas from Liberia, no official recommendations from Hopewell. No one must know that they're leaving. The contact people from Guinea must be there to receive them in exactly one week, at 1:00 a.m."

Zedekiah continued, "Kerkula must send a message back if these arrangements are satisfactory, and if he can meet the students. If this plan is all right. I'll bring them that night to the farm on the border, deliver them to the contact people, and then return. I myself want to stay in Liberia, at least for the time being, in order to finish some other matters."

Koli left the house, went quickly back to the shops, and in the end decided to buy a flashlight and two batteries to take to his uncle in Guinea. At the border, he met the customs officer, who again sent for the major.

"So you've bought something better for your people have you, my man? I hope it isn't the shotgun itself this time." The major laughed at his own joke, and then proceeded to search everything Koli had brought with him. He went through his small black bag twice, opened the flashlight to check the contents, made Koli take off his shirt and shoes, and felt carefully around his trousers.

When the major finally let Koli go, Koli almost wanted to ask him why he had gone to all that trouble. As if to answer the unspoken question, the major said, "Can't be too careful these days, my man. Some people are taking diamonds through the border, others guns, others books. Moreover, some of these people in Guinea are against our Liberian way of life, and we don't trust them. And when someone like you goes through the border with shotgun shells, I have to do my duty. Why, there are people right here in Ganta who are trying to change our Liberian democracy into communist dictatorship. You probably don't know it, but the house you went into just now behind the Lebanese store is owned by people we are watching. And why, may I ask, did you go there?"

Koli's heart jumped, and he saw that the major knew his heart jumped. "I, I went to see my friend sir. He is staying at that house. But I don't know who lives there."

"Your friend, you say? My man, no one goes there except a bunch of communists. Who do you know that visits at that house?"

"A student from Hopewell College, sir. I knew him from Gbarnga, and he asked me to stop and see him."

"And so you did, and so you're going into Guinea? Look, my man, you just get yourself back to that house, and tell him you've changed your mind and aren't going to Guinea after all. And why does he want you to go to Guinea? No, my man, you tell him you aren't going to Guinea, and let us watch what he does next. Where did you say you work?"

"I work for the clan chief in Sengta below Gbarnga, sir. I'm a clerk for him. He knows I've come here to see my uncle in Guinea, sir."

"Does he know you're hanging around with a lot of dirty communists? I know the clan chief myself, and he wouldn't like it if I were to tell him about you mixing up with communists."

Koli thought hard, and decided to fight back. "What do you mean by communists? I don't know what you're talking about. It's true only that I carried a message to that student.

"I was coming from Gbarnga, and another student asked me to bring the message. I had forgotten it, and brought it to him when I went back to buy this flashlight for my uncle. You can go and check with him, if you want to know the truth."

"Are you talking straight with me, my man? If you're lying, you'll not only lose your job, but you'll go straight to jail. A message, indeed. Probably some communist business. What other student gave you the message?"

"I don't know his name, sir, but he was from East Africa somewhere. He gave me a letter and I left it there. I thought of it when you said you wanted to search my bag."

"Hmm. You may be telling the truth, my man. Anyhow, just let me and my man have something for a beer, after all the hard work you have given us, and you can go through. But don't go around that house again, or you'll be in more trouble than you are right now. If you weren't working for the clan chief, I'd keep you here in Liberia. But I'll do you a favor, if you help me."

Koli slipped the major another dollar, and walked through the border. He had no idea how he would get the message back to Zedekiah, after he had met Kerkula. But he knew he should at least try, or perhaps Jonathan would do something to prevent the

209

road from reaching his village. Maybe he should come back at night, or maybe send Zedekiah a note, so that he wouldn't have to visit his house.

He walked across the bridge and down the road, and there he found the Guinea border post. They, too, searched and questioned him, this time in Kpelle since he didn't speak French, and he answered as much as possible as a country boy would. He knew he must play as stupid as he could and so he spoke only of visiting his uncle. They let him through, and the amazing thing to Koli was that they didn't ask him for any money. He feared he would have to give everything he had to border guards before he was finished.

He walked on to the village, and there he found a shop, just as Zedekiah had told him. At the shop he asked for Kerkula, and within a short time the man himself appeared. He spoke Kpelle, but he also spoke good English. He told Koli to give him the letter, but Koli explained what had happened. The man thus said Koli should tell him the message in English, so no one else would hear.

Koli delivered the message, and the man replied that the arrangement is fine. "I'll have a car in the village in a week to bring the students down to Conakry."

He went on to ask Koli, "How much do you know about the situation?" But without waiting for an answer, he said, "The students will be in Russia within two weeks, ready to get a real chance to learn how to bring the revolution to Africa. And you, young man, do you want to go, so that you can return one day to Liberia and teach people the truth of our great African socialism?"

Koli could only say, "I've often heard about such things as socialism in Gbarnga, but for now I have to take care of my wife and children and my old father. Perhaps some other time."

Kerkula laughed, and said, "I'll get you some palm wine before you go to visit your uncle. But, if you ever want me, just come here and ask for me. I'm working here for a new Africa."

They went back to the shop, and Koli was amazed as he looked around. There was nothing to buy there, only a few bottles of palm oil, some dry bread, and a few lengths of plain cloth. Just across the border in Ganta, a person could buy anything he wanted, but here there was nothing. He asked Kerkula, "Why is there nothing to buy in this store?"

"We don't need all those things here. We're building socialism in Guinea, not capitalism. Our people don't waste their money on foolishness. We work the soil and build our nation, and in the long run we will have a beautiful country. We aren't like you Liberians, some of whom are rich and exploit the rest of you who are poor. Don't think that having things to buy in a store is so great. Someone else gets rich when you buy those things, and the poor man loses what little he has."

Koli listened to the man and politely agreed, but he couldn't help thinking, "It's better to have money and use it, than to have it and just keep it, with nothing to spend it on. And both are better than having nothing at all, neither money nor goods."

But just at that moment, he thought back to the Lebanese man in Salala who had tried to arrest him for breaking that mirror so many years ago, when he had wanted to start school. "Maybe this man from Guinea is right after all."

Koli followed his mother's directions, and found the farm village, but didn't find his uncle. His uncle's wife was there, but she said, "Your uncle has been taken to do road work farther down toward Conakry. We aren't able any more to make our farms and do as we like. Now we have to work for the country, whether we want to or not.

"Liberia is different, I hear, although I'm not allowed to cross the border any more. Your uncle likes the new government, because it's run by Africans and not by Frenchmen. But I'm not so sure myself, because we can't do what we want any more.

"Moreover, I can't buy any of the things that I used to get. Even in "'Nzerekore, there are no clothes, no food, no supplies, in the stores. We used to sell our palm kernels in "'Nzerekore and then buy whatever things we needed for our house and family. Now the government makes us sell our kernels, and we get paper money for it, paper money that won't buy anything at all. We sometimes manage to slip our kernels across the border to sell in Liberia, but it's bad for us all if anyone gets caught."

Koli gave her the gifts for the family, and she was obviously pleased. He noticed that she had no new cloth in the house, and he wished he had brought her at least a lappa to wrap around herself.

"The mirror and the flashlight," she said, "I'll keep until your uncle comes, and the head-tie I'll use now. But I'll have to keep all these presents hidden if any soldiers come around, because they'll take them back to their own families."

Koli spent the night, realizing that he would go back empty-handed the next day. He thought, "These people have almost nothing in the house. My uncle is no longer making country cloth, I'm sure." The loom was standing broken at the edge of the house, and was half covered with vines. He even saw Kpelle medicines lying broken on the floor, and asked about them.

"The government makes us get rid of our medicines," she said. "Even our secret societies, Poro and Sande, can't meet as they used to meet. The soldiers say the societies are working against the government. We aren't allowed to use our old masks any more. Now we just carry them across the border and sell them in Liberia to traders or white people, if the government doesn't catch us first and make us destroy the masks. Things are bad."

Koli was given hot water for a bath, ate rice and palm oil and dried fish, and spent the night. Koli thought, "It seems too quiet here in my uncle's house and village, and even the people in the other houses don't come out to talk. It isn't at all like our villages in Liberia. Something has happened. If this is the socialism they talk about, I'm not at all sure I like it."

The next day he was up early, and out on the road. There was nothing to keep him at his uncle's place at all. He took messages back to his family, and took with him also a small hand mask that his uncle's wife wanted to send to Yanga, Koli's mother.

She said, "The soldiers might get it some day, and I want someone in the family to have it."

Koli reached the border early, and crossed into Liberia without any problem this time. The same customs officer was there, and he sent again for the major. But even though he had to face such men, Koli was somehow glad to get back. It seemed more like home. Even the corruption at the border seemed accustomed and familiar, after the unknown territory of Guinea.

Koli showed them the hand mask which his uncle's wife had given him, and said, "You're welcome to search for anything else. I've got nothing else to bring back. My uncle had gone on to work on the road, and hadn't been at home."

The major laughed him through the border. "Go on, my man. No one ever brings anything out of Guinea worth looking at, except over the river at night. And be glad you're back home. Now maybe you know why we don't want that communism business here in Liberia? And stay away from communists here. I wouldn't be healthy for you to be caught with a lot of communists, my man."

Koli wondered how he would get the message back to Zedekiah. He knew he would be watched if he went back to the friend's house behind the Lebanese store. He thought of going to Gbarnga and finding someone to bring the message back. He thought of finding a person here in Ganta to carry Kerkula's answer.

He was weighing all these plans when he was approached by a boy, probably a schoolboy, judging from his clothes. The boy had never seen Koli before, but approached him and asked, "Excuse me, but I was asked to find you, and see if there is any message from Kerkula."

Koli thought to himself that the matter seemed to be getting deeper and deeper, but he was also relieved. He told the boy, "Kerkula agrees with the plan, and everything is all set as originally scheduled. Please carry the message back to the person who sent you."

He watched as the boy went back through town, and noted that he was going in the direction of the Lebanese store. "Just as long as he isn't sent by the major himself, I'm all right," thought Koli to himself.

He found a taxi going back to Gbarnga, and occupied a window seat. He realized, "I've got to be more careful in the future. Jonathan and his friends have used me. I don't like to be used and I don't like to be in some kind of scheme to get these students out of Liberia. Maybe it means that all those wonderful dreams the students talked about in Gbarnga were just that, dreams. Maybe it means that there's no way in Liberia to have

African socialism. But from what I saw in Guinea, socialism doesn't look like such a good idea."

Back in Gbarnga, Koli looked up Jonathan at the tax office, to report on the trip, and check on the building of the road. Jonathan was there, making out receipts and looking very official before the people who had come to settle matters with the government.

Koli had to wait while Jonathan made out papers for a white man to license his car. Jonathan told the man, "It might be difficult to get the car licensed right away."

The man said, "I can wait. I'm not in a hurry." Jonathan then said, "You might have to come back tomorrow, because not all the papers are in order."

The man asked, "What's missing?"

Jonathan tried to look important, and said, "The inspection certificate is missing. And the only way to get an inspection certificate is to wait until next week when the inspector returns from Monrovia. Of course, I, as principal tax collector in Gbarnga, might find ways to speed things up, if I received some encouragement from you."

The man said, "I prefer to wait until the inspector comes back. Hurrying too much, in order to avoid the proper procedures, always causes more trouble in the end than it's worth."

Jonathan said, "You can have your own way, but if you change your mind, you can always find me here at my office. I'm at your service."

After the man left, Jonathan laughed and Koli had to join in despite his growing anger at Jonathan. Koli knew that Jonathan just wanted his dash.

Jonathan said, "I only wanted to make life a bit more pleasant for myself and affairs a bit smoother for the white man. But that white man is either stubborn or stupid or too selfish with his money to give me something for a beer. Let him come back next week, and try again. Eventually he'll have to give up, and give me what I want."

Koli then explained what had happened at the border, including the part about the major. Jonathan frowned, and said, "Koli, you're lucky. You might have been caught with the letter,

214

and then everyone would have been in really serious trouble. As it is now, we'll have to be very careful getting the students away from Hopewell and up to the border. And I'll have to warn Zedekiah to be very careful and quiet for a while, after we've gotten the students out of Liberia, before trying anything else."

Koli reminded Jonathan about his promise to help bring the road to the village. Jonathan agreed, "I'll do what I can. Things have been made more difficult by this problem with the major, but with a little encouragement I might be able to do something."

Koli snapped back, "Jonathan, you may be able to get away with such talk with that foolish white man and his car. But I've known you too long now. I'm not going to give you a dash just to get what you already promised me. The major in Ganta has nothing to do with a road to my village."

Jonathan laughed aloud. "I was just joking with you, Koli. Don't worry. I'll do what I can. You'll have a road one of these days. And when you get it, don't forget how much I did for you."

V: THE FIRE DYING

Koli met Jonathan in Gbarnga two weeks later. He had gone to see the paramount chief on business, and took the opportunity to find Jonathan in the tax office.

"What ever happened to the East African students?" Koli asked. "Did they go to Ganta, and did they manage to get across the border into Guinea?"

"Everything worked perfectly, thanks to you," answered Jonathan. "Zedekiah is still in Liberia, but he went with the other students at night a week ago, and took them to the meeting place at the border. Zedekiah says his work isn't done yet in Liberia, although he might go out the same way later in the year. It all depends on how they treat him at Hopewell. He says one white teacher there suspects he had something to do with the others going. And you can imagine how angry they are at Hopewell now! They lost some of their best students, and no one knew about it in advance. Zedekiah is clever."

"What about the major at the Ganta border post? Didn't he find out what was going to happen by watching the house where I met Zedekiah?"

"No chance of that. He's too foolish. He did come close to catching us, but his big mistake was to tell you he knew about that house. All we did was move out of there, and find another friend in Ganta. And he had no idea we were planning this escape for the students. We fooled him properly."

Koli turned the conversation to the building of the road. "When are they going to start, Jonathan? And will they really go through the village?"

"I can't really say exactly how soon, Koli. But I know they will start soon. The railroad is halfway up from the coast, and they have to build this road to bring in supplies. Just be patient, and you'll soon find yourself riding to your home in a taxi. It will come."

The construction finally began at the end of the rainy season. The bulldozers and tractors were brought to Gbarnga by the iron mining company and the government, and they began cutting their

216

way back toward the St. John River, following the old trail that Koli had walked so many times.

After school was finished for the year, Koli took Ziepolo with him to visit his village, so that Ziepolo could have some time at home. The white people Ziepolo worked for had gone to the United States to visit their family, and so there was no job for him while they were gone. He would thus spend the entire long vacation with Sumo and Kuluba, and once more get the feeling of real village life.

As they walked on the newly cut road, Koli told Ziepolo, "I had the same experience twenty years earlier, as I went to school in Salala for the first time. We met the trucks and tractors and bulldozers working their way up from Salala to Gbarnga, as my father Flumo and I were walking down to visit Salala. It had been the beginning of a new life then for me, in just the same way that the road will now bring a new life to our village."

They reached the machinery about halfway to the village. The new road had passed the little village where Yanga had been born, and was pushing up the hill into the patch of forest at the boundary between the two villages. Here the workmen were having to cut down large trees, not just the young bush they had met on the way out from Gbarnga.

"It'll be a more difficult job here, and also more destructive," Koli told Ziepolo, "I hate to see some of those old forest chiefs cut down. They've ruled the pathway for all my life, and I always measure my trip home by them. But they've got to go, because the road demands it."

Here the road was an open sore, an unhealed cut across the forest. It was less noticeable in the low bush, where the road appeared not much different from the newly cut farms of half a year earlier. But in the high forest, it seemed more raw and remote, more ugly. The red dirt was exposed, and in the hot sun of December, it was baked dry and hard.

Koli told Ziepolo, "There's no going back. Nothing can ever be planted on such dirt again. I doubt if even the vines and shrubs of the bush could grow on such bare red emptiness. But I'm sure that better things will grow in our village because of the road.

217

Sumo's children can be treated for their diseases at home. They can even attend school there."

The last half of the walk seemed easier and more familiar. The green of the still-standing trees cut the harsh dry season sun, and the earth felt softer. It seemed a shorter walk from there to the edge of the village, where they found the men talking while Sumo was making a cutlass in the blacksmith shop. Koli stopped to greet them, while Ziepolo waited outside and watched.

The talk was all of the road, and of the fact that Tokpa had sold his family's traditional land, which lay where the road would run. Sumo greeted Koli and told him, "The government tax-collector, a clever young Vai man, came to the village to buy land for himself. He brought kwii liquor with him, and managed to get Tokpa drunk, despite the promise the Poro elders had wrung from him not to drink again.

"What confused Tokpa was the kind of strong drink the Vai man brought. It was in a bottle none of us had seen before, and it tasted and smelled entirely different. At first, Tokpa seemed to think it was just another kwii drink, not dangerous at all. But, after he'd started on it, he couldn't stop. The Vai man gave some to Yakpalo also. He didn't become as drunk as Tokpa, but, even so, he wasn't paying his usual careful attention to what was happening.

"The result was that the Vai man talked Tokpa into agreeing to sell his family land, some of the best land in the village. In return he gave Tokpa one hundred dollars and permission to farm the land until the road was finished. Yakpalo called the elders together, and, after they too had shared the Vai man's liquor, they agreed that the land could be sold."

But now, in the sobriety of daylight, Koli could see that the men of the village had second thoughts about what they had done. Tokpa in particular was trying to find a way to get out of the contract. But both he and Yakpalo had put their mark on the paper that the Vai man had brought, and Tokpa had received his money. Even Yakpalo had been given twenty five dollars for his part in the transaction, and so couldn't go back on his word.

Koli knew perfectly well that it was Jonathan who had been here, had come to find his farmland before anyone else had had a chance to choose. "It's a disaster for the village," Koli told Sumo, "But I can't help being glad it happened to Tokpa, and not to anyone else. For one thing, Tokpa has no children to give his land to after he dies. And Tokpa can always find food for himself as leader of the men's work groups.

"The important thing now," Koli told the men in the blacksmith kitchen, "is to prevent the same loss of land happening to anyone else in the village." Koli asked the men where the road would go.

Yakpalo told him, "It will follow the old trail from Gbarnga, and pass right through the center of the village. The road will then turn slightly east after it goes through the village, and will go on from there to pass the new mission which is being built not far from the river. After that, it will meet the new railroad, near where it crosses the big river."

Koli thought back to the time that he and Sumo had gone to the river to buy fish. They had taken the old farm trail through Yakpalo's village and gone over the mountain to reach the river. They had turned south along the river and then passed the old village site, the village which had moved farther down the river after so many sicknesses and deaths. The new village was where the new mission was being built. All that area which had been so difficult to reach, so remote, so clean, and so untouched, would be open to cars and trucks and missionaries - all equally devastating.

"It's a fortunate thing," Koli told Yakpalo, "That your land is well away from the road's future location. You won't be troubled by people coming to buy you out. But, Flumo's land, our land, is directly on the line from the village to the new mission station. I'm worried that Flumo himself can no longer understand what's going on. But he's still head of the family and should make the decisions."

Koli turned to Sumo "We must make sure that no one gets to Flumo without our knowing it, in order to persuade him to give up our land. He wouldn't understand what he was saying in such a transaction."

Koli felt sure Yakpalo would protect him if some other big shot came to cause trouble, unless Yakpalo was caught off guard again by more kwii liquor.

Another change Koli noted was that a small shop had opened in the village. A Mandingo man from Guinea had come with his supplies to set up a business. No relative to the Muslim Mandingo family which had settled long ago in the village to trade palm nuts and kola nuts, he saw the opportunity the road presented. He wanted to be first on the spot, so that when the road came people would be accustomed to doing business with him. His stock was small as yet, but he was trying to accumulate enough money to buy a bigger stock.

Koli went to the shop to buy his mother a present, and found there medicines, shotgun shells, headties, sugar, candies, kerosene, matches, and lappa cloths. He bought a pack of sugar for her, and had a chance to talk with the Mandingo trader. He was young and hopeful, much more of a businessman than the old Mandingo man who had become so much a part of village life by now.

He said to Koli, "I'm afraid I'm not much of a Muslim. I don't bother to pray on Fridays the way the old man does, and I don't want to trouble myself with trading kola nuts. There's more money in clothes, food and household goods." Koli saw also that the young man had brought a sewing machine with turn. He kept it in the corner of the house he used as a shop. Koli asked, "Are you sewing clothes yet?"

He answered, "I've been asked to make a few things, but my big hope is that when they set up a school in the village, I'll make the uniforms for the children. I can also make shirts for men, but so far only one man has asked for a shirt. Let me make you a shirt - cheaply. Just pick out the cloth you like. I want you to do my advertising for me. I'll make your shirt for nothing, if you buy the cloth!"

There wasn't a church yet in the village, but Yakpalo told Koli, "The missionaries from the village near the big river have come twice to preach and pray. They are Baptists, a kind of missionary I've never heard of before. But my son - the one your father wounded - likes them, and went both times to hear them."

Koli went next to see his mother, taking the sugar with him. She, too, seemed older than he had remembered her. Probably the strain of taking care of Flumo had had its effect on her. Flumo was lying asleep in a hammock outside his house, and Yanga was cleaning around him. He looked terribly shrunken and pitiful. Koli called to Yanga, and she looked up, her eyes brightening for the first time that day. He gave her the sugar, and said, "I've come to spend a couple of days at home, and to leave Ziepolo with Sumo and Kuluba, for the long holiday from school."

Koli then took Ziepolo to the house where he would stay. Koli could tell that Ziepolo wasn't happy with having to spend two months here.

He thought, "He's become too used to the life at Hopewell and has already slipped away from our way of life. He goes to school early in the morning, and from there goes directly to the white man's house. He often comes back home to the village only at dark, and he stays just to eat and sleep. He sometimes tells us about his day and what he's done, although less now than he used to. I can understand how uncomfortable he feels here now, but I'm glad that Ziepolo will have two months to get accustomed to village living again."

The next day, men came from Gbarnga to talk to Yakpalo and the people of his village. They would have to help in the construction of the road. A meeting was held at Yakpalo's palaver house for the village elders and leading citizens. What was needed was for the men to clear the brush and cut a wide track along the trail, so that the machines could more easily do their work. Yakpalo asked, "Will the men be paid'?"

The answer was, "No, of course not. They're doing this work for themselves and for their future."

Yakpalo called the elders and leading men to have a private discussion with him. Tokpa, perhaps trying to delay the loss of his land, said, "We shouldn't do the work. Let the government build its own road."

But the other men, with Yakpalo's and Sumo's urging, agreed that they would do the job. They would start the next day, and clear the bush from where the road-building machines were working toward the village.

The next month was a time of hard work for the village people. Clearing the trail was not easy work, and it came at the time when they would normally have rested from harvest. Each day a crew of ten men went out to widen and clear the trail. At a few places they had to cut new tracks through the bush, since the road-builders did not want to follow the old trail, saying it would be easier to cut through this farm or over that hill. The road-building also had to avoid the deep swamps, and so that meant other changes in the route.

It was well into the new year before the people in the village could hear the bulldozers and tractors in the distance. Ziepolo was playing with his friends in the village before going out to collect firewood, when he plainly heard the sound of the engine roaring in the distance. He called to the other boys, and they ran out along the trail. There, beyond the first farm, was the bulldozer ripping away the remaining trees and shrubs. That very day it would arrive in the village.

Koli had been told that the road was arriving that day, and so asked the clan chief's permission to come home to see it arrive. He reached the village in mid-morning, ahead of the machinery, in time for the great event. He was plainly excited, plainly filled with hopes for all the new things of the future for his village.

He greeted his mother and father, but was disturbed to see Flumo sitting up and asking, "What's that terrible noise? What is it, a leopard? Where's my gun? It can't come here in the village if I go out to protect my people."

Flumo got out of his hammock, swayed for a minute, and then managed to stand upright.

"He looks so small," thought Koli. "The machine might run over him without even seeing him."

Koli took his arm, and tried to quiet him. Yanga was on the other side, and she too wanted to get him to lie down again. But he shook them off, and tried to walk, as the noise became still louder. Clearly Flumo had difficulty seeing, and hardly seemed to recognize Yanga, Koli, and now Sumo who had seen the disturbance at his father's house, and had come running. Old Toang, too, who was herself getting feeble, came out of the house to see the problem.

Flumo half walked, half let himself be carried, to the edge of the village where he heard the noise. He was frightened by it, aroused by it, disturbed by it. And, as they reached the blacksmith shop where he had spent so much of his life, first as a boy at the

222

bellows, then as a man making the tools people needed to tame the forest, and finally as an elder watching the work and advising others, the first bulldozer came over the hill. The shock was too much. Flumo lifted his hands as if to shield himself, called out, "The leopard's cub is full-grown," and fell back limp into the arms of his wives and his sons.

He was dead.

Even Tokpa was shaken by Flumo's death. What was to have been a great triumph for the village became a funeral. They all knew that Flumo had been old and tired, that his death was not only expected, but was also a blessing. Had he died quietly, with his family together, and his sons grown to maturity and responsibility, bringing him grandchildren and the riches of a large family, there would only have been muted sadness. Flumo would have been laid in the earth without regret. The words addressed to him as he was lowered into the earth and before the first clods of earth fell on him, would have been words of blessing and benediction, words of request for his favor in the future, words of regret at the harm they had done him in his life.

But now Flumo's death was an omen for the village. He had spoken out, somehow in his death, becoming the zoe he had never been in his life. He had warned once again of the leopard's coming. Flumo, who had killed a leopard in his manhood, and who had warned that the white man would play with the leopard cub as he wished when Koli had gone off to enter high school, this same Flumo had recognized the machines as the master of the leopard's cub, now come to claim their victory.

But it was too late now to turn back. The machines were here. The head operator said, "I'm sorry the old man died. We'll stop work today and tomorrow, until the old man is buried. But we can't agree that we're in any sense at fault. After all, he was an old man, and his time had come. The shock of hearing something strange, and not being able to see it when it arrived, killed him."

The Big Thing came to town that night. The singing began early and remained until the dawn's light had blotted out the high cold dry-season stars. Yanga and Toang remained in their houses, comforted by the other women of the village. Young Toang and Kuluba were there. Even Lorpu came back, after Ziepolo had been

223

sent to Gbarnga to find her and bring her there. Ziepolo remained with his mother and grandmother through the night, confused and frightened. He asked over and over again what it meant that the leopard had come. They had to tell him Flumo's story of how the leopard's cub was the plaything of the white man, the story that Flumo had told when Koli went off to attend high school.

He asked, "Does that mean me now? Am I the plaything of the white man also? Did this machine come to get me, and change me into something else? I know that Koli never had the chance to finish school, and now he's caught between the country way and the kwii way. But I'm going to go farther in school, reach high school and maybe even college. I will do what Koli didn't do. My grandfather Flumo died, afraid of the future. Do we have to be afraid also?"

The women listened to him, but only looked at each other. They didn't really believe in Ziepolo's words. Even Ziepolo only half believed them. The road was bringing only trouble, and the first was Flumo's death. But yet they wanted to believe in Ziepolo, even if they couldn't believe in what he saw for the future. If anyone was to defend them against these changes and these troubles, it had to be Ziepolo and the other children. Even Koli and Sumo were really too old now to be of much help.

Early the next morning, the men walked to the grove of trees near the village where senior men were buried. Flumo had failed badly during his last years, in fact had failed ever since he shot and wounded Yakpalo's son. But he was still the chief of his quarter, an important member of the Poro society, and the father of twins, one of whom was on his way to becoming an important zoe in his own right. He would be given the burial he deserved.

First the grave was dug, in the shade of the cocoa trees that Yakpalo had planted near the village. When it was deep enough, Koli and Sumo brought white cloth that they had bought from the young Mandingo trader, enough to wrap his body and line the grave. No longer could they use country cloth for the purpose - they didn't make enough any more. They carried the body from the village to the grave, and lowered it gently into the earth.

As the body went down, Yakpalo stepped up and tossed a small coin into the grave, and told Flumo, "Prepare the way for me to enter the land of the ancestors, too. I'll follow you soon, Flumo. Greet our fathers for me. And don't forget us here. We are your children. If I have done anything bad to you, forget it. If I have hurt your children, forget it. If I have neglected to respect you, forget it. You are one of us still, and we will always feed you at the crossroads and in our houses. Go quietly, Flumo, and remember us."

Yakpalo was followed by Yanga and Toang, who said their few words, and let him go. Yanga turned away, quietly weeping, but then looked up as if to say her weeping was finished. Sumo and Koli gave their coins to the old man, and bade him farewell. Even Tokpa went to the grave, and spent a long time there, although only the gravediggers and Yakpalo could hear what he said. Lorpu asked forgiveness for not staying in the village, and tossed a larger coin than the rest, as if to say she finally brought back something from her years in Gbarnga as a market woman.

The village elders gave Flumo into the hands of the ancestors, and the grave was covered quickly and quietly. The line of Flumo's people turned back to the village, and there they met the drivers and road-builders waiting. "It's all right now," said Yakpalo. The roar of the machines, that roar of the kwii leopard, drowned any last echoes of the parting words to Flumo. The road was built.

VI: FATE BOUND TO LAW

"Stephen, have you seen my watch? I know I put it somewhere in this room, and I can't find it." The white man had shifted the piles of books and papers in the living room for the third time, and was now getting upset.

His wife told him, "Don't worry. You'll find it soon. Just wait a day or so, and it will turn up." But he didn't seem in a mood to wait.

The watch was by this time safely in Ziepolo's pocket, and he planned to give it to Lorpu that afternoon in Gbarnga. She had been asking him for several months to bring her something big, so she could sell it. She promised him a new pair of shoes as his share of the profit. She wanted the rest to improve her house behind the market in Gbarnga. The roof leaked, and she had no one to bring her new thatch. She could get a bundle of zinc from the Lebanese store for twenty dollars, and she hoped she might sell the watch for at least that much.

"No, I don't know where it is. I saw you wearing it yesterday, but I haven't seen it today." Ziepolo was worried lest the white man check his pockets, but he felt he could get away with it. He had worked for the people a full three years now, and he had found out how to fool them. He didn't take very much, just a bit here and there, enough to satisfy Lorpu, and occasionally give Goma and Koli a present. This was the first time he had taken anything big, however, and he worried about it.

Ziepolo went through the motions of helping the white man hunt for the watch. Finally, he said, "I don't know. I really can't help you any farther. And, can I please go to Gbarnga on family business?"

The white man looked at him suspiciously, but then said, "You may go." He asked Ziepolo to do some shopping for them at the market, and to come back in the afternoon.

It seemed all too easy to Ziepolo. He met Lorpu in the market as usual, gave her the watch, and in return she bought him a cheap pair of shiny black shoes at the small new Lebanese store just beyond the Mandingo church. He did the errands the white man had asked, hid the shoes under the tree after he returned to

226

Hopewell, worked for two hours cleaning under the bananas behind the house, and then went back to Balataa.

It was Saturday afternoon, and the other boys were standing and talking in front of the Nigerian's shop. Ziepolo felt good, and wanted to show off in front of them. He put on the new shoes, and walked up to the group.

"Look at Ziepolo, will you? He's trying to bluff us with those shiny new shoes. Where do you come from, New York City? Where'd you get them, old man?" Ziepolo's friend, the Balataa chief's son, who was also in the fourth grade, pushed him hard about the shoes.

"Oh, I just earn a good salary from the white man, and I save my money. If you weren't so lazy, you could earn something too, and have good clothes."

"Oh, come on, you don't earn that kind of money. What did you steal from these people? It had to be something big." By this time, a crowd of boys had gathered around Ziepolo, and were enjoying the show. Ziepolo felt big now. He was in the top class of the school, and was getting good grades. The Vai principal knew him well, and let him help her with the younger boys who entered school this year. He had a good job and extra money. And now he had shiny black shoes, and the full admiration of the other boys.

He decided to show off still further. "What do you know about how I got these shoes? I know how to do things these days. I'm moving up, and here all of you sit, and do nothing. Come on with me, I'm going to have a beer at the Lebanese store." He knew that the Nigerian storekeeper would never give it to him, but the new Lebanese man probably wouldn't ask any questions. It was at his shop that the Hopewell students went to drink these days.

Some of the younger boys went off to play elsewhere, but Ziepolo's friends followed him to the Lebanese store, where he ordered two beers, and paid for them from his pocket. He drank one, and shared the other with his friends. He felt better and better, and began to boast about all the things he owned, now that the white people trusted him and paid him good wages.

"Sure, but you can't get shoes like that when they pay you only twenty-five cents a day. Come on, Ziepolo. Tell us how you got the money for the shoes. You must have taken something."

227

"Don't tell anyone, you hear. But this morning, there was the white man's wristwatch sitting on the living room table. He wasn't looking, and his wife was out. I just put it in my pocket, and that was that. So easy. And then I took it to Gbarnga and sold it." He didn't bother to tell about Lorpu, and how she was to get most of the money from it. He wanted the other boys to think he was really big.

Ziepolo's friends were impressed with his story, and urged him on. One said he didn't believe it, but Ziepolo laughed, and said he was just jealous. "Why, it's too easy to take things from those people. They never look after what they have. They're always too busy teaching or talking or playing with their children. What do you want me to get for you? I'll get it next week. How about a tin of fish for supper? It's easy."

The beer made Ziepolo feel good, and he bought another one. By this time, there was a small crowd around him, listening to him. But now the laughter was different when they saw he was not used to the beer. He had tasted it before, but this was the first time he had really drunk a bottle of beer straight down.

"Sure, Ziepolo. Bring me a tin of fish from the white man's house next week, and I'll believe you. Until then, I think you're just making all this up. You're trying to bluff us."

"OK, I can do it. You wait until I go there. Those people are such fools they'll never miss it."

The Lebanese storekeeper had begun to listen to Ziepolo's boasting. He moved up to him and warned him, "Be careful, boy. That beer isn't good for you. You can do what you want with your money. But be careful with your words and your drink."

At this point, Ziepolo suddenly began to realize what he was saying and doing. His stomach realized it too, and he felt sick. He got up from the bench behind the Lebanese store where he had been sitting, and had to steady himself. He didn't know that beer could do this also. His stomach made a sudden rush at him, at the same time that he felt himself losing his balance. The wall was a welcome source of strength, but his stomach wouldn't let him stay where he was. He moved along the wall to the edge of the house, turned the corner, and was sick.

228

At this point, he saw Koli and Goma on their way back from church at Sarah's house. He was clearer in his head now that he had vomited the beer, and he saw himself as they might see him, sick, dizzy and confused.

"What's wrong, Ziepolo? Are you sick? What have you been eating? Have you a fever?" Koli stopped, when he smelled the beer. "So, it's beer, is it? What are you doing, trying to be a big man when you don't know how? And where did you get the beer from? Come on, let's go home."

Koli steered Ziepolo away from the Lebanese store, and on to the road to their village. A late afternoon rain had begun to fall, and that helped to clear Ziepolo's head. He had to admit to Koli and Goma that he had been foolish, and had drunk too much without knowing what it could do. Koli couldn't find too much reason to be angry, because he remembered his own first efforts to drink. Goma was disgusted, but realized it wouldn't help to punish him just at the moment. They would have to keep him closer to home, and not let him run so freely.

"The best thing for you, Ziepolo, is bush school," said Koli. "They opened the school behind Balataa three years ago, and next month it will be time to close it to the last group of boys. I've already talked with Sumo and Kuluba, and we've all decided you should go in. Now, I'm sure I was right. You need to learn something about being a proper Kpelle man. If you can drink beer, you ought to be initiated."

Ziepolo let them talk. He knew he was in the wrong. He should have been more careful. But what began to worry him even more was what he had said. He wasn't sure of the exact words he had used, but he knew he had talked too much about what he could steal from the white man. The Bassa cook and washman at the white man's house had told him that if he was going to take things he had to be quiet about it. Now he had given himself away. He could only hope that no one would tell the white man.

In Balataa, the boys had left the store, and most were back in the open space between the shops playing. But one boy, a third grader who had come to Balataa only last year from Loma country, was on his way to Hopewell to work. He had a job with the white family who lived beyond the house where Ziepolo worked, and

229

was expected to return to work that night. They had let him live in the room under their house, and also paid him to wash dishes at night and take care of the children when they went out. Tonight there was a party at the college, and the family wanted him to be there.

The boy didn't like Ziepolo. They had fought twice after school, and Ziepolo had tried to make it clear who was boss.

He thought, "This is my chance to get back at Ziepolo. If it works right, I might even be able to get a job for my little brother with the white man in place of Ziepolo. He's nine years old and in second grade and still hasn't a job. Maybe, if I tell the white people what Ziepolo did, they will let him go, and I can get the job for my brother."

He reached the house of Ziepolo's employers and saw the man walking around the living room, looking under chairs, behind books, through piles of paper. His wife was sitting in a chair trying to read, but she obviously wasn't succeeding too well. The man kept disturbing her. The boy heard him ask her, "Don't you care about the watch? It cost me thirty dollars in Monrovia, and I'll have to get another one."

"Yes, I care, but it's not here. You've looked through this living room ten times now, and you haven't found it. Maybe that trader who was here this morning took it. You talked to him for almost an hour before buying the mask from him. Maybe one of the employees took it."

"You're probably right. I really don't think Stephen would take it, but he was the main person who had been in the living room. The cook was in the kitchen then, although he might have taken it when he was cleaning up after breakfast. The washman was downstairs the whole time."

The boy listened, and then walked up the steps and knocked on the door. His heart pounded as he thought what he was about to do. "I have to make sure no one finds out that I'm the one who told the white man, but I also have to make sure I can get the job for my little brother after Ziepolo is sacked."

"What do you want, John?" The white man knew him, because he often saw him at the next house down the hill. He

230

brought messages from his employers, and sometimes stopped to talk with Ziepolo.

"Uh, are you missing a watch?"

"Yes, what do you know about it?"

"You'd better check with Ziepolo - I mean with Stephen. He was talking about it in Balataa this afternoon. And he had a new pair of black shoes."

"Yes, and what else did he say?"

"That's all I know. I didn't hear any more. Excuse me, I have to go to work. And don't tell Ziepolo what I said."

The boy turned and ran, almost fell, down the stairs. He didn't want to say any more. He didn't want anything more to do with it. He had done what was needed for now.

The white man waited until the boy was down the stairs, and turned to his wife. "What do we do now? I trusted Stephen, and in fact I like him. But if he's stolen the watch, there's no telling what he'll do next. I wonder if he's taken anything else. I never count the cans in the food closet, but it seems they go too fast. We really have to keep it locked. But now what should I do, try to find him in his village?"

"No, he's coming in the morning for church. He promised to be here early, and then work in the afternoon taking care of the children. You can ask him then. Don't rush it. You always want to take things too fast."

"True, but if I go there now, perhaps I can get the watch back before he's gotten rid of it."

"I'm sure it's too late already. He has the new shoes, and so the watch must be gone. Wait until tomorrow."

In the morning, Ziepolo arrived at the house before church time. His head hurt from the beer, and he was worried that the white man might have heard something. But he had to come back to work if he was to keep the job. He knew that other boys wanted his job, and he didn't want to lose it. "Stephen, come here. You know I couldn't find my watch yesterday. What do you know about it?"

"Nothing. I helped you look. . ."

"Stephen, don't lie. I know that you were talking about my watch last night in Balataa. And I know that you bought new shoes in Gbarnga yesterday, new shoes you didn't show us when you came home with our food. How did you get the money for them, if you didn't steal my watch?"

"Be careful. Don't go too fast," began his wife. But the white man went ahead.

"You took that watch, after working for us more than three years. You came into our house, and we trusted you. And now you've stolen something valuable from us. I don't know what else you might have stolen over the years. Come on, Stephen, admit it."

"I don't know anything about your watch. I told you, when you asked me to look. . ."

"You're lying, Stephen, I can tell it. I know you took that watch, and I know you sold it in Gbarnga."

"I don't know anything about..." The white man reached across and hit Ziepolo across the face and stopped his words. He hit hard, and his hand hurt where he had hit the boy.

"Don't hurt him...", his wife began, but he didn't listen to her. He grabbed Ziepolo by the shirt, and shook him.

"Look, you find that watch, or don't come back here again. And don't even try to come back to the Balataa school. The principal and I are good friends. I could tell her in church this morning, if I wanted to, but I'll wait for you to find the watch. And I mean it, don't come back unless you have the watch."

Ziepolo couldn't hold back the tears. He had never been hit by the white man before. He had never even thought the white man could do that sort of thing. Ziepolo considered trying again to deny what he had done, but no words came. He could only turn and run out the door.

He started toward Balataa at first, but then stopped. It wouldn't help him at all to go home. He had to go to Gbarnga if he was to get the watch back. If he just went home, the white man would have him thrown out of school. He might even get the police after him, although he hadn't said anything about police. No, he had to go to Gbarnga and find Lorpu.

But he didn't have any money at all with him for a taxi. He would have to beg a ride, and here it was Sunday. He went down to the gate and started walking. It was at least a two hour walk to Gbarnga if no one gave him a ride.

A car came along, and Ziepolo waved to it. It slowed down, but then speeded up again. The driver laughed at him, and sped off into the distance.

A taxi came next, and stopped, but when Ziepolo said he would get the money in Gbarnga, the driver just told him, "Get the money first, and then think about taxis." He too drove away, leaving Ziepolo in the road.

Rain began to build up behind him, as he walked down the road, past the big shot's rubber farm, past the Mandingo village, past the school principal's house. He looked at the queer Vai letters on the house gate, and thought for a moment of stopping to ask her to help him. But he realized that she would believe the white man and not himself. No, he had to keep on walking.

By this time, the rain began to fall heavily. The road quickly churned up into thick mud, and Ziepolo's clothes were soaked through. And he wasn't even half-way to Gbarnga. It was at least another hour before he would reach there, and he was sure no car would stop for him.

He was right. The long walk to Gbarnga in the rain was just too much, after yesterday and this morning. His head still hurt, not only from the white man hitting him, but from the beer the previous night. He couldn't think of anything to do except to go to Lorpu and beg for the watch. He only hoped that she hadn't sold it yet. But since it was late Saturday morning when she got it, he felt he might be lucky.

A weary three hours after he started, he came to Lorpu's house behind the market. The rain had stopped, and his clothes had dried out somewhat. He found Lorpu there, trying to patch the roof of her house with plastic sheets she had found at the market. Ziepolo could see that the rain had soaked into her house during the morning, for there was a wet place in the middle of the floor. He knew why Lorpu needed the zinc for her roof.

"Ziepolo, what's new with you? Why do you come here, all wet and dirty like that? You look like you walked all the way."

"I did, Lorpu. I had to. The white man found out that I took his watch. I don't know who told him."

"You fool. You must have been talking too much. If you're going to steal anything, you have to be quiet about it. I told you that before."

"I'm sorry, Lorpu. I guess I did tell some boys about it last night. And one of my friends must have told the white man. But now I have to return the watch or I'll be sacked and thrown out of school. Have you still got it?"

"No, Ziepolo, but I can get it. My friend took it to sell it for me. But I don't think he's tried to sell it yet. You're lucky today's Sunday. Let's go."

Lorpu and Ziepolo left her house behind the market, and walked up toward the Methodist Mission. They saw the people coming out of church, well-dressed missionaries and a lot of school children, and some local citizens trying to be kwii. Lorpu laughed at them for showing off, but Ziepolo wasn't so sure. He wished he were at church now with the white people, instead of being here trying to get out of trouble.

Behind the Methodist school lived Lorpu's friend. Ziepolo thought, "She seems to have a new friend every time I go to Gbarnga. The way Goma and Koli live looks better to me. On the other hand, Lorpu always has a bit of money for candy or soft drink. Of course, she doesn't have enough money to put zinc on her house, and she has no one to help her get thatch."

Lorpu talked to her friend, but he was clearly reluctant to give up the watch. She finally had to beg him with fifty cents, and then a dollar, before he would give it back. She took the watch, thanked him, and left with Ziepolo.

"That man! See if I stay with him any longer. The watch wasn't his, but he made me buy it back with a dollar. Anyhow, here it is. But bring me those shoes back again!"

Koli promised he would do it next time he came to Gbarnga, and then asked Lorpu for twenty-five cents to get back to Hopewell. She looked at him as if to refuse, saw how wet and miserable he was, laughed, and gave it to him.

"You cost me too much money, my child. If you weren't my brother, I'd throw you out."

Ziepolo found a taxi and went back to Hopewell. He walked, afraid and alone, to the white man's house. He entered, and found the white man waiting for him.

"Did you find it? Give it to me, Stephen."

Ziepolo took the watch from his pocket, looked at it to see if it was still working, and gave it to the white man. He took it back, wound it, checked the time, and put it on his wrist.

"Now what am I supposed to do with you`? I should sack you now, and get another boy to work for me. I can't trust you with anything any more. You're a thief. I know it now, and l don't know what else you might have taken over these years."

Ziepolo couldn't think of anything to say, and so he stood there, still wet and dirty from the muddy walk to Gbarnga, quiet and miserable. He couldn't even think to himself what he hoped the white man would do. He realized, "If this white man was my own father, he would beat me until the blood came."

"Stephen, answer me. What am I supposed to do now? Am I supposed to keep you here, and see if I can trust you next time? What can you do to make up for this? Do you want to work here?"

Ziepolo looked up, and said, "Yes, I want to work here. Please let me try again. I'm sorry."

"What else have you taken from me, Stephen?" "Nothing. I have never. . ."

"Don't lie," broke in the white man. "I've checked with the cook and washman, and they told me you've taken lots of other things from the house. What's to keep you from doing it again?"

"I'm sorry. I'll work to make it up."

"Are you serious about that?"

He paused, as if to let the words sink in. "If you are really serious, I'll let you stay here, and I'll let you work the next month for nothing. Maybe that will make up for what I've lost. Will you do it?"

Ziepolo said nothing, but just looked down at the ground again. He was glad for a second chance, but couldn't bring himself to say anything.

"Do you agree, or don't you? I'm willing to keep you here, if you work for the next month for no pay, just to make up for what you've done. After that, I'll think about paying you again. Do you agree?"

"Yes, I agree." Ziepolo looked up and then down again, and realized he had to do it.

"Stephen, there's one other thing. You've been coming to church with us every Sunday now, and you say the prayers and even sing some of the songs. We are Christians in this house, Stephen. And Christians know how to live together and forgive each other. How can you steal, when you say you are a Christian?"

"I don't know," was the only answer he could make. He didn't want to say what he had heard the Hopewell students say, that these white people claimed to be Christians, but were stealing the land and life from African people. He didn't want to say that the white people had so much more than his own family that they didn't even know what their employees stole from them. He didn't want to say that Koli had learned from his experience in Salala not to trust white missionaries. He didn't want to say that he felt like the leopard's cub, just the white man's plaything. He didn't want to say that he had tried to be a man for himself, drink some beer, have nice shoes, satisfy his father's sister, but the white man had caught him. He didn't want to say that the only way to succeed for a poor Kpelle boy was to give up the way of life of his fathers and just imitate the white man. He didn't want to say that being a Christian seemed to mean only having nice clothes and a good house.

So he could only answer, "I don't know."

"Stephen, I'll forgive you for all this. And I want you to think seriously about being a Christian. God made you and me both. I may have more than you do, but we both have the same maker and we both have to live in the right way. If you try to do right now, you can make up for what you have done."

Ziepolo went home and picked up the black shoes so he could return them to Lorpu in Gbarnga. After school on Tuesday he was told to go to Gbarnga on the bus to shop for the family. The college now had set up regular bus trips three times a week for shopping, and Ziepolo would go with the other boys that day to buy things at the market for the people they worked for.

236

On the bus, the other boys laughed at Ziepolo. "Why are you taking back the shoes?" one asked. "Don't they fit your feet? Maybe your feet have shrunk since last week. Or maybe you thought you were bigger than you are?"

Another called to him, "Ziepolo, what time is it? Check it by your new watch. Or did you lose it?"

Ziepolo kept quiet. He was just glad that the white people on the bus couldn't speak Kpelle, or they would know what the boys were laughing at. The driver laughed to himself in front of the bus, and when they got to Gbarnga, told Ziepolo to be careful in the future. "Beer and an open mouth don't mix, boy. If you have to do something wrong, keep your mouth shut and your eyes open next time."

Ziepolo went back to Lorpu in the market and gave her the shoes. He said, "I've worn then only that one night in Balataa, and they got a bit dirty and wet. But I've washed and cleaned them as well as I could, and they look all right to me."

Lorpu took them, and said, "I'll return them to the store where I got them. But this is the last time I get you out of trouble."

Lorpu asked Ziepolo what had happened, and said, "You're lucky you weren't sacked, or even worse. You should stop taking anything for a while, lest you be found out and really driven away the next time. But when things cool down after a few months, I'd be glad to get some presents again to show that you haven't forgotten your sister."

Ziepolo did what he was told for the rest of that year. He stayed quiet, and avoided taking anything from the house. It wouldn't have been easy to steal now anyhow, because the white man started locking the house when he was away, and particularly locked the food closet as well as the closet in his bedroom. The Bassa cook and washman blamed Ziepolo for that.

The cook said, "If you hadn't been so careless, things would still be unlocked, and there'd be no problem for us to take a bit now and then."

Koli had heard about the stealing episode from the Kpelle men who worked at the college, particularly the bus driver. He had taken Ziepolo and beaten him hard with a leather belt, and told him, "The next time anything happens, you'll be sent back to the village for good."

But Koli didn't feel this punishment was enough to keep Ziepolo in line. He was determined to get Ziepolo into bush school to teach him the ways of being a man.

Other boys too were scheduled to enter the bush school, in the next village behind Balataa. The men's bush school had nearly completed its course, and would come out early in the coming year. Those boys who had not entered yet, and there were many of them in the Balataa school, must have at least two or three months behind the fence before they could be initiated and become full adults in the Kpelle community.

The chief zoe at the bush school then announced that the fence would be closed next week. The rice harvest was coming in now, and soon people would think about the new bush-cutting season. The zoe didn't want children to be still in the school when it was time to cut the bush. So the word went out that in one week any boy who was to be initiated must go behind the fence.

Ziepolo didn't mind going in. He knew he had to become a man someday, and find his proper membership in the adult world. But he was worried that he would have to enter the bush two weeks before the Balataa school was scheduled to finish for the year. This might give him some difficulty in being promoted to the fifth grade next year.

In fact, on Monday morning after the announcement about the bush school had gone out, the principal called all the children together after they had raised the flag and pledged their allegiance. "I've heard that some of you are going to enter bush school next week. If you do, you'll lose this whole year of school. I can't have children taken out of my school just before exams. I particularly want you big boys in the fourth grade to show the way. If any of you leaves the school early, you'll see. You won't get back next year."

Ziepolo couldn't listen to anything else the teacher was saying in his class that morning. He thought, "I don't know what to do about bush school. I'll have to enter. I know that. But I don't want to lose my place in the Balataa school. I've worked too hard and too long to lose the chance for a kwii education now. Koli had to drop out of school, and now he's only a clerk to the clan chief. He'll never go anywhere in the world, never have a really good house, never become a proper kwii man."

Koli too was determined for Ziepolo to go farther in school, but he also knew he must join the society. He told Goma, "I know now is the time, since Ziepolo is getting older and soon will be really too old to join. Moreover, this stealing business upsets me. Bush school will help straighten him out, so he can stop stealing, or at least stop boasting about it.

"But I don't want Ziepolo to lose a whole year of school, and perhaps even have to go to another school next year, if the principal really throws out the fourth-grade boys who go behind the fence before the exams. I hope she'll change her mind about it."

On Tuesday morning, however, she repeated the same warning. The boys were scheduled to enter the following Sunday morning, and had to spend Friday and Saturday nights at the village behind Balataa in preparation. The only hope Koli and Ziepolo had was to find someone to intervene, either to persuade the principal not to carry out her threat, or to persuade the head zoe to leave the fence open longer.

By Wednesday the matter looked serious. Koli was worried, and Ziepolo began to think what alternatives he had. He decided to speak to the Hopewell student he had planted trees with two years earlier. This student, Edward, was a Kpelle man from down country, and was himself a full member of the Poro. He was now a leader at Hopewell, and had a good reputation with the teachers there. He was himself planning to be a teacher in the rural area, and began to think that he might go on to theological school later, after he graduated from Hopewell.

The main advantage was that Edward was a member of the society in good standing, and in fact had taken some of the higher degrees. Ziepolo told Koli, "Perhaps he can give us some help. I see him often at the home of the white people. He comes not only to earn money but also for help on his classes, and the white man seems to be his good friend. He might be in a position to be go-between with the principal and the chief zoe."

Koli told him, "Why don't you try to see him today after school? See if he can help you."

Ziepolo found Edward at the dining hall after the noon meal. Ziepolo explained the situation, and Edward said, "I can see your problem, Ziepolo. I've heard about it already from other people, as a matter of fact. Aren't there six of you boys in the fourth grade, and doesn't the principal want all of you to finish your exams before you can enter the bush?"

Edward was genuinely concerned about Ziepolo and the others. Ziepolo was impressed, not only because of his interest, but also because he said, "Ziepolo, here's the thing. The people involved have got to realize that both the kwii way and the Kpelle way are good. I'm a Christian, and some day I'll teach Kpelle children. I don't want them to forget their own ways, just as I don't want them to lose the chance to enter the kwii world and be Christians. We've got to find a way to satisfy both sides."

Edward was a leader of the Boy Scouts at Hopewell. This group met every Saturday morning on the campus, and sometimes went out for hikes in the forest or camping trips near the river. Edward taught them about both worlds, the world of the forest and the world of school and books. He often said that was the way God wanted it.

He told Ziepolo next, "Look, you get the rest of the Boy Scouts together, so I can talk to them." Ziepolo went back to Balataa, and found most of the boys, at least those who were Kpelle. He brought them to the campus and there they met Edward at his dormitory. Fourteen boys came altogether, and all but two of them were scheduled to enter the bush on Sunday, and thus to go to the village behind Balataa on Friday night. They all agreed that they wanted to join the Poro, but they also wanted to finish their exams at the Balataa school.

Edward was torn. He was loyal to the Poro leaders. He had to be as a member. He had his own exams to finish, since this was the last week before Hopewell closed for the long dry-season holidays. And he wanted to keep faith with the boys in the Scout troop.

He finally told the boys, "I'll have to find Goyakole and together we'll visit the zoe tomorrow afternoon, after I take my own last exam in the morning. I'm sure if I explain the problem to Goyakole, the two of us can persuade the head zoe of the school to leave the fence open for another week.

"I'll also go to see the principal of the Balataa school, to find out if she'll give the final exams for you boys a week early. I believe in compromise as a principle." Ziepolo wasn't sure what compromise meant, but he hoped that Edward could solve the problem for them all.

Edward went early on Thursday afternoon with Goyakole to the village behind Balataa. He said he would let the boys know by the evening what happened. It was hard for Ziepolo and the other boys to pay attention that morning. They didn't want to repeat those classes over again next year. And they were sure that the principal meant business. When she gave her word, she never went back on it later.

Toward the end of the evening, Edward and Goyakole came back, and first thing Friday morning, they asked the principal if they could speak to her. She left the classroom, and went with the men behind the school to talk. It was the very day they were to enter the house at the village behind Balataa, and the boys were nervous. They could see her there with Edward and Goyakole, arguing, pointing, turning her back, thinking. Then she turned again to Edward, and nodded her head. He then asked her for permission to speak to the boys who were scheduled to go to the bush school.

"It seems all right now," he said. "The fence will remain open until next week Sunday. You won't have to miss a year of school. The principal has agreed to give your exams in class next week, as a special favor to us. She doesn't like this Poro business, and never joined the Sande society herself. But she doesn't want to destroy our Kpelle ways. However, you all must be sure to do a good job on her exams, and do everything she tells you to do. If there's any nonsense at all next week, then the whole arrangement is off." Edward and Goyakole looked at them severely, and then told them to go back to school.

The last week of class went slowly. The examinations were tough, tougher than Ziepolo had thought they would be. He was sure the principal had done it deliberately to hurt them. She had

241

obviously not wanted to yield even one day, but Edward and Goyakole had persuaded her strongly. The only way she could show her authority was to be especially rough on the boys. She sent one home on Monday morning for having dirty shoes, and another on Tuesday for not having cut his hair. Ziepolo made sure to get a haircut from the white people's washman before going to school Monday, and he washed his clothes every afternoon.

Finally the week came to an end, Ziepolo had finished his exams, and he could go to the fence. He would not get his grades until school opened the following year, because the principal said, "I'll only give out the report cards on the last day of school, and whoever is not there will have to wait until next year." Ziepolo realized this too was her way of getting back at the boys who were to enter the bush, but at least that didn't hurt them at all.

Ziepolo went home that Friday afternoon, after telling the white people, "I won't be able to work for you during the dry season. I have to go to bush school."

Ziepolo was surprised to hear the white man say, "We already know about it. We've spoken with your friend Edward who arranged the compromise, and he explained the whole matter to us. But now, Stephen, tell us what bush school is all about, and what you will learn."

Ziepolo said only, "I'm not supposed to talk about it, not now and not afterwards."

The white man responded, "But in that way, none of the knowledge of your people will ever be known outside the secret society. Won't it be bad if all the ideas and wisdom and secrets are lost, when the modern world takes over this country completely?" The white man was determined to learn something about the Poro

Ziepolo was glad the white man was interested, but he was sorry he insisted on asking first about the very area he must avoid. Koli had told Ziepolo that some of the early white missionaries had learned more than they were supposed to know, and had warned him, "Now we Kpelle are being much more careful about giving up our secrets. You must never tell the white people at Hopewell anything you know about Kpelle secrets."

242

So Ziepolo told the white man, "I'm not supposed to talk about it. Besides, if you really want to understand what we do, why not try to learn to speak Kpelle?"

At home, Ziepolo found Koli ready to take him to the village where they would prepare to enter the bush. There, below the village, on the main path leading farther toward the forest and away from the main road, was the fence. It looked somewhat old and tired now, having been in place now for three years. The men had retied the fence in a few places, and had brushed the weeds away from the cleared space before the fence, but still it looked old.

Ziepolo was nervous, even though he told himself over and again, "There's nothing to fear. There'll be some mysterious ceremonies, some strange noise, and then I'll be behind the fence, to remain for only about two months. It won't be so bad as what I've been told about the old days, when boys went in sometimes for as long as four years. True, there are some boys now who've been in there three years, but they don't include educated boys like myself. And surely they'll give me special treatment, as a kwii boy, already finished with fourth grade. Besides, I'm older than some of the other boys who are going in, some as young as just five or six years."

But all this brave front left him, when he had to enter the house in the village behind Balataa on Friday night to get ready. He was told to leave behind his kwii things. He had brought a black bag, with shoes, trousers, a schoolbook and a toothbrush. The leaders told him "These are kwii things, and you must leave them home. Here school is different."

"Why," Ziepolo asked himself, "Am I told to wear shoes when I go barefoot to one school, and am I then told to take them off when I go properly dressed to the next school? The main point of school sometimes seems just to do differently from whatever you were doing before. Kwii school or bush school, what's the difference?"

VII: THE FIRE'S VOICE IS HEARD

Koli took a taxi from Gbarnga to his village to bring the family to watch Ziepolo come out of bush school, Taxis had been running the route now for the year since the road had been built. He had been back there before by taxi, but he still found it difficult to get over the strange feeling of driving in less than an hour the same distance he had walked in half a day so many times,

The village itself was changing fast. Yakpalo now had a proper clan chief's court. His old palaver house had been torn down, and the government had helped him build a four-room zinc house for his business. He lived in the back rooms and heard cases either on the large porch or in the front room of the house. But he, too, was getting old now, and he found it increasingly difficult to attend to all the matters before him. He had hired a young man to be his clerk, although he often said to Koli that he wished he would come back to his own village to do the job.

Sumo was increasingly respected as a leading zoe, now that old Mulbah was really too old to do much but give advice.

Koli envied Sumo as he saw people going to him for advice and medicine. "Why can't I be of real importance, too? He chose his way and he's succeeding with it. In my kwii way, I can't any longer succeed. It's only Ziepolo who can make it for me."

A school had started now, and the people of the village were already building a new school house. The government had agreed to supply the concrete blocks, the windows and the roof, if the people would lay the foundation and bring the sand for the building. School might even be held there this year, if they were to build more rapidly. It was now only one month before the new school year, and the walls were halfway finished.

The Mandingo store was doing well. "The storekeeper is a bright young man," thought Koli, "for he's brought in a kerosene refrigerator to stock cold drinks. He has a good business going, and it was particularly good when the road construction continued back to the St. John river. During that period, the contractors, and then the railroad builders would stop in his store on their way to and from work. He's used the money to good advantage, and seems to be building up his stock. He's constructed a small extension on the store, where he stores the palm nuts, cocoa beans and coffee beans that he buys from the village people. He told me one day that he would try to buy a truck, with the help of his Mandingo friends in Gbarnga. They would each contribute five hundred dollars, and own the truck jointly. Then he could increase his own business greatly, and also haul goods for other people."

There was no clinic yet, but Koli was sure one would be constructed in the near future. The government hospital in Gbarnga sent a nurse there one day a week now, to give routine medicines, and check children's health. Koli was glad that his brother's children had medical care now, and was sure they would all live to adulthood.

More troublesome were the demands being placed on Yakpalo to sell the village lands along the road. Jonathan had already begun to plant rubber and coffee on his farm, and now other big-shots were looking at the area with interest. Koli had heard that Jonathan had promised to find the head of the army camp at Gbarnga a good site, and he was back in the village late in the year to make arrangements. He hadn't succeeded yet, however, and Koli hoped that his people might find a way to resist Jonathan's pressure.

There was now a small mission church in the village also. The mission farther down the road had appointed Yakpalo's son, the one that Flumo had shot so many years earlier, as their evangelist. He had really not been able to work on his farm properly as a result of the shooting. His arm had never healed fully, and it was always weak. Thus when he had been asked to do Bible study at the mission near the St. John river, he had accepted gladly.

Now he was back in the village running the mission, and inviting converts to his new Baptist faith. His father allowed him to seek converts, but didn't himself join the church. Despite Goyakole's urgings, Yakpalo didn't want to get involved with an institution that might make him give up his wives. Besides, Goyakole was a Seventh-Day Adventist and this church was Baptist. Yakpalo tended to agree with the young people that the churches ought to get together and make a common church, before he would think of joining.

Koli had come to bring Sumo, Yakpalo and Tokpa to the closing of the bush school behind Balataa. Ziepolo had been in the school for almost two months, and graduation was at hand. Koli had told Yakpalo he would come to get him in a car, so that he could go in the style befitting a clan chief. Sumo had to come, as Ziepolo's father, and Tokpa deserved the chance, as head of the men's work groups.

Koli told Sumo, "We've got to be very careful not to offend Tokpa these days. Things have seemed to go smoothly for over two years. We may be all right now, and with a little good luck we can be properly reconciled. Let's do everything we can to be friendly. The village needs Tokpa still - there isn't anyone else who can get the work out of the men's work group that he still does - and we certainly don't need enemies."

Yanga and Kuluba also wanted to come to the ceremonies, but there wasn't room for them all in the taxi. Yanga was old now, and so she was given a space. But Kuluba had to walk, and leave her other children behind. "After all," Koli reasoned to himself, "we always walked in the past. Why should she be upset now at having to walk on a familiar trail?"

In Gbarnga, Koli stopped to buy presents for Ziepolo. He would have to train himself not to call Ziepolo by that name soon. His name was to be changed, as is the custom at this time. His new name was to be Tokpa. This name was a gesture of reconciliation toward the older Tokpa which Sumo suggested and Koli agreed to.

Koli bought a new kwii hat, a lappa with a color picture of the president of Liberia, and shoes. Sumo bought the boy a pair of long trousers and another lappa. He would look grand when the new initiates walked bent over in a long line to show their respect to the village and to their elders.

The family arrived in time to see the boys leave the fence for the first time, this time in a line of white, almost-naked uniformity. Koli was surprised, but then realized he shouldn't be surprised, to see that they all wore white shorts.

He thought, "The kwii world has changed even this. Ziepolo - no, I must call him Tokpa now - looks bigger than many of the boys, certainly bigger than I was when I came out so long ago."

247

Koli and Sumo looked at each other with shared pride, that their son was now a man.

The boys then had to wait in a small thatch shed on a farm nearby for the new moon to shine on them. Koli went back to work, while Yakpalo and the others in the family waited with Goma. After four days, the boys were ready, and the family clothed them with their finest new clothes, and brought them into the village.

And here, for the first time that Koli could remember, there was a white man present at the coming out. It was, Koli could see, the white man that Tokpa had worked for when he was still Ziepolo. He had come to take photographs of the event.

Koli wondered, "Did that white man really walk the trail from Balataa? Sure, he had had to walk - there's no motor road here yet." The man had with him Edward, the same student who had persuaded the chief zoe and the principal of the school to reach a compromise. And Edward had been the one to ask for permission for the white man to take photographs.

Koli recognized him, and went up to him to talk. They had never spoken at any length before. In fact, this was the first time Koli had seen the white man away from the college or the Balataa school, and on proper Kpelle territory.

"Yes, Stephen is a good boy. I know he had some problems with stealing, but I think he's gotten over that now. I really think he will be a Christian some day. And I understand that you're a Christian, too, and attend the Seventh-Day Adventist church in Balataa. That's good - you can set the boy an example."

Koli had forgotten that the boy was called Stephen, and told the man that now his name would be Tokpa. The man seemed confused and asked, "Why would he go back to a tribal name, now that he already has a good Christian name, Stephen?"

Koli had to laugh as he tried to explain, "A Kpelle boy has to have a new name when he becomes a man. I myself was once the `good-for-nothing' Kona, then I became John when I went to school, but I really am Koli."

Koli then asked the white man "Please take Ziepolo's, I mean Tokpa's, picture as he comes along in the line. I hear you've got

248

permission from the head zoe to take pictures, and so I hope you won't mind doing this favor for us."

"No problem at all," said the white man. "I'll take several and give you copies of the best ones. And are there any others in your family coming out at this time? I can take their pictures too." Koli checked with Goyakole, and before long the white man had agreed to take photographs of all the boys in the fourth grade, including Goyakole's son.

Koli later overheard the white man saying to his wife, "I wish I could speak Kpelle. I'll surely take lessons if we decide to stay in Liberia another two years. Perhaps Stephen will help teach us. The only problem is time. There's so much to do if we try to teach properly."

Koli wanted to tell them they would teach a great deal better if they understood something about the people they were teaching, but he decided against saying anything. It wasn't his business.

The white man was getting impatient, and even seemed to be about to return home to Hopewell, when they at last heard the gunshot that warned the people to be ready. There came a second shot, an echo of the first, and Koli saw that a third old rifle was being readied to fire. These rifles could no longer shoot to kill an animal. Rather they were charged with powder from the muzzle, and then fired into the air, just to rejoice that new men were now a full part of the community.

Then the line of boys began to move in the late afternoon sun, from a secluded piece of bush beyond the edge of the village. The old man at their head seemed unsteady and even a bit confused, but dignified and reserved, even when the white man knelt at the side of the procession to take his photograph. The boys moved quietly behind him, shielded by their lappas and occasional country cloths, with Goyakole moving up and down the line to keep them in order. Sumo was still behind the fence, arranging medicines for a successful celebration. In the middle of the line was the new Tokpa, crouched down beneath his new cloths, his hat poking unmistakably up from a portrait of the president of Liberia printed on the length of cloth that was over his shoulders.

The line moved to the center of the village, past the newly established mission church, past the Mandingo man's house, past the shop where a young villager sold cane juice, up to the chief's house. There, mats had been laid on the ground along the walls of the houses, and two tables had been set up in the open space before the chief's palaver house.

The Balataa chief, Koli's clan chief, Yakpalo, and the other village chiefs were all seated at the table. Koli saw that Goyakole was still with the boys, organizing them and keeping them from looking up, reprimanding them and encouraging them.

The white man stood at the edge of the crowd, photographing and watching with interest. The village chief called to him to come sit at the main table. He told him, "You mustn't just stand at the edge of things."

The white man seemed confused, and looked to Edward for advice. He was encouraged, and went to sit down. His wife began to follow, but was motioned back. Edward told her, "That's a man's table. You should stand with the women at the side."

The chief then welcomed the boys, welcomed the guests, and said how glad he was on this occasion. It was almost a political speech, not at all what Koli remembered from his own coming out of bush school.

"It must have been almost twenty years," thought Koli. "Our teacher warned us against the changes to come. Now this chief seems to accept and even welcome the changes. I guess having the white man at the head table just shows what is happening."

The chief went on to say, "These boys are now men, now full members of the Kpelle nation. They have proved themselves able to defeat the Forest Thing, even those boys from kwii school who have been behind the fence for such a short time. They are alive again, and everyone should rejoice." The chief then invited the evangelist of the village church to pray for the boys, for the village and for the bush school. The evangelist was a village man who had been trained by the Lutherans to conduct services and prayers at those times when the pastor could not come.

Koli stood up with the rest to pray, and as the evangelist prayed, he thought, "No one mixed in Christianity when I went to bush school. It was a matter then of Kpelle people and Kpelle traditions. I'm not sure I like this change, but obviously Goyakole and Edward are happy about it."

The only person in Koli's party who was clearly unhappy with the idea of having prayers at the coming out was old Tokpa. He scowled and looked off at the line of trees at the edge of the village. Sumo and Yakpalo were just neutral. To them, Koli was the family Christian and could take care of such matters.

After the prayer, Yakpalo spoke a few words for his clan, and then Koli's clan chief spoke also. There was then an embarrassed silence, after which the village chief turned and asked Koli to ask the white man to say a few words. The white man had obviously not understood a thing of what was happening, and so was taken by surprise at Koli's request.

"I, uh, thank you for letting me come here today to be happy with you all," began the white man. "I have been very interested by what I saw, and I am glad I had the chance to take some pictures. I will try to let you have copies of the good ones. I am only sorry I don't understand more of what is happening here. Perhaps I will try to learn something of your language someday. I wish all the boys well, and I pray that God will bless all of you."

There was a scattering of applause after Koli translated the speech, and then the formal program was over. The chief had a bottle of kwii liquor on his table, as well as two large bottles of cane juice. He offered the white man some kwii liquor, but the man said, "Unfortunately we have to go now. I'm afraid that it will be dark before we get home, and so we must go. The sun is already very low in the sky."

The white man turned, and took his wife to go on their way. He was obviously in a great hurry.

Koli had to apologize for the man's lack of courtesy and understanding. He had insulted the chief by not tasting his liquor, which he had brought out of the house partly in order to entertain the white visitors. And he had not stayed long enough to enjoy the feast that would soon be served.

Koli admitted to the company, "The white man and woman don't really understand how to behave in a polite and civilized fashion, but please forgive them for their ignorance. Perhaps someday they will understand."

The boys were finally allowed to leave their places on the mats. They would spend four days in the village, being on display

251

when required, and rejoicing at home with their families at other times. Yakpalo, Koli and Koli's clan chief had to go back to work, but the others stayed on.

Koli went to young Tokpa - he had to get used to that name - and congratulated him on finishing bush school. "You are no longer Ziepolo, but are now truly a man for yourself, not just the old man that your old name suggested."

Tokpa, in turn, went to young Tokpa. He seemed pleased that the boy was named after him. He congratulated the boy, and told him, "You must come for help when you need it. Now that you are my namesake, we must live more closely together and be colleagues. I hope that you will come back to our village from time to time, and not spend all your life in this kwii nonsense, particularly this school and church nonsense. I know that the kwii world has come to stay now, and that you have to learn kwii ways. But you mustn't forget the wisdom and experience of your own people. I'm now an old man, but I am also Tokpa, and I can show you some of the things I've learned in my long life.

"In fact, I hope you will join my bush cutting group, if not this year, then next year. I need strong young men to work with me, and I can show you to handle a cutlass and an axe right, when you're big enough. I'm sure that you'll stop your kwii schooling soon, and come back home where you're needed.

"I'll also help you if you need medicine to make your future more secure. I know the secrets of the forest, but I also know the secrets of the water and the air as well. The real world is more than the forest your father, Sumo, believes in, more than the kwii books Koli has studied, and that you are studying back in Balata. There are secrets and medicines and powers that you also need if you're to get on properly with man and nature and spirits."

Young Tokpa was confused, as he listened to his namesake. "I wonder why my family named me Tokpa. What have I to do with this old man who is my father's enemy? Is it perhaps true that this old man has secrets the rest of my family don't know?

"I certainly don't want to return to my village to live. My future lies with the kwii world. But perhaps this man, old Tokpa, can give me what I need for better coping with the kwii world.

252

The best plan is to bring the two worlds together, and use the best out of each one.

"Now that I'm a full member of the Kpelle people, I'll begin with learning what my own people can teach me. Bush school has been just a beginning, in fact not much of a beginning, since I was there such a short time. The next steps are more difficult, and here Tokpa can perhaps help me make those steps."

After bush school closed, Tokpa had to get ready for the Balataa school again. He was going into the fifth grade now, and had a white teacher for the first time. There was a new group of teachers in Liberia, called the Peace Corps. They were Americans, mostly young, and they seemed to fit right into their work. One of them came to Balataa, and there were three more at Hopewell. They were so different from the missionaries. For one thing, they seemed to enjoy life more, and for another they seemed more to be part of the village.

The Peace Corps teacher in Balataa was given the fifth grade to teach, since he hardly spoke any Kpelle, and since he had a good education himself. The principal continued to teach the third and fourth grades, while two new Kpelle teachers handled the beginner class, and the first and second grades. The beginner class spoke no English at all, and was using this year to get used to the new language.

There were more classes each year, but still held in the same building that had housed two grades four years earlier. They had built partitions in the building, but even so the classes disturbed each other. Tokpa would sometimes listen to the third and fourth grades, when he was bored with the Peace Corps teacher, but usually he enjoyed listening to the man.

The white man Tokpa worked for now began to come to the school to help with their mathematics class. He had planned to go during the rainy season to write a mathematics book for schools, but hadn't done so because his wife had a new baby, another boy. The books had been written anyhow, and he was helping the Balataa school use the books in the first and second grades.

The man had himself begun to learn a little bit of Kpelle, and Tokpa was amused to listen to him struggle with the greetings when he came to school to teach. It hardly sounded like Kpelle, but at least he was trying.

The Peace Corps teacher did better. He had been trained for two months to speak Kpelle, and was still learning. Moreover, he lived in the center of Balataa, and tried to speak with his neighbors. The white man Tokpa worked for almost never came to Balataa except to visit the school, and so he couldn't learn much about the people and their ways and language.

Tokpa liked one thing especially about the Peace Corps teacher. He was more practical than the Liberians in the school. He was interested in farming, and had the boys out working in the swamp on the trail to Tokpa's village, They were learning to grow a different kind of rice, one that grows in the swamp.

The Peace Corps teacher said, "It needs a regular amount of water. You boys have to dig the canals and dams, and make sure that the rice has enough but not too much water."

Tokpa had heard from his fathers that swamp rice was just for old women, and never would produce enough to feed anyone. But he saw that the rice of the Peace Corps man was good. There was plenty of it, and it grew close together. The only problem was chasing the rice birds when the crop matured. The Peace Corps man hadn't thought of that. The boys had to be in school, and there was no one to chase the birds. As a result, in that first year, they got no crop at all. Birds ate everything they grew.

The teacher told the boys, "Now I've learned my lesson. We'll have to find someone to help chase birds when the rice ripens next year, since you boys have to be in school."

At the end of the year, the white man and his family went to the United States again to visit their families. This left Tokpa free to spend the dry season at home again. He didn't mind, because he wanted to get to know his people better.

He thought, "I'm an adult, an initiated member of the Kpelle people, and now I can be more part of the life of the village. Moreover, I want to learn more from old Tokpa. I can't see that the man is so bad, especially now that I share his name."

The old stories about Tokpa were just that to young Tokpa, stories. He had only heard about the bad things he had done, and didn't really believe them. "After all," he thought, "Hasn't the man been really good to me since I left bush school? He even gave me a country cloth and a hat."

Young Tokpa stayed in the village during the beginning of the bush cutting season that next year. He wasn't quite old enough to start using a cutlass for himself, and so he carried the sharpening stone for the men in the field. He felt pleased with himself, because old Tokpa gave him recognition and respect. His father Sumo didn't seem to like it, but there was nothing he could do about it, because old Tokpa was behaving properly these days.

One night, young Tokpa had a strange dream, after finding a beautiful stone in the forest near a small stream. He heard in his dream someone call to him from the forest. He went after the voice, and when he got well away from the village, he found a beautiful woman, who disappeared into the same stream where he had found the stone. He dreamed of the woman again the next night, and the same thing happened, although this time the woman invited him to come into the river with her. The woman was white and dressed in a long white dress. She was very beautiful, and young Tokpa wanted to follow her, but found she would always disappear first and then he would wake up.

He asked the other boys in the village what this might mean, and one of them said, "It means you should join the water people."

Another boy confirmed this, "That was your water woman come for you, Tokpa, come to give you riches and protection."

The first one added, "But you'll have to learn to do what she wants you to. There's only one person here who can tell you the right meaning of what she wants you to do."

"Yes," said a third, "That's old Tokpa, who's a member of the water people himself. You've got to ask him what to do next."

The next night he went to sleep early in hopes of seeing more of the woman and learning what she wanted. But this time, instead of entering the water, she turned into a snake and coiled herself around him. She told him, "Now you have come to me, and are mine. I'll do what you want, if you give me what I want."

He went the next day to see old Tokpa. "What do these dreams mean, and what am I supposed to do now?" he asked.

"You want to follow her, but you don't know how? I know that woman, and I can teach you how to follow her."

255

Old Tokpa was obviously pleased that the boy had approached him, and wanted his help. And he offered that help. "What you must do is to find what she wants you to do. She is the water woman, and she is offering to give you the power to get what you most want in life. You have to decide what it is you really desire, and then give up other things in favor of that.

"In particular, you have to give up playing with girls. Do you have any girl friend now? If you do, then you have to stop playing around with her, because the water woman will be jealous. When she turns into a snake, she can kill you or drive you mad.

"The second thing you have to stop is this church business. I've heard that you go to church with the white people at Hopewell sometimes, and I've also heard that you go to church on Saturdays with Koli and Goma. Don't do it any more. The water woman will drive you mad if you go there. She is jealous.

"But if you do what she asks you to do, then she will give you the things you dream of. If you want success in school, you will get it. If you want power over other people, you will get it. If you want money, you will get it.

"The first thing is to realize that you are now a water person yourself. Your fathers have said some nasty things about me belonging to the water. None of them is true. You can see for yourself that I help the people in this village. I lead the work groups. I make certain people have good crops. I can cut the bush, even as old as I am, better than anyone else. That's because I'm a member of the water society. It hasn't hurt anyone, and the whole village has benefitted."

Young Tokpa listened hard and carefully. He replied, "I really want to be a success in the kwii world, And if this is the way to do it I'm willing to try. I really haven't any particular girl friend, although I've played around with one of the Balataa girls. But she's too young to be pregnant, and so I'm not worried. I'll give her up now, and let the water woman run my life for me. But I don't quite understand what I have to do next."

"Don't worry. The woman will show you what to do, and how to do it. You'll find the way." Old Tokpa assured him that it would all become clear to him. But he warned him, "Don't tell anyone, unless the woman shows you that you can talk to that person.

256

"The only kwii person I think you can truly trust is the man who bought my farmland. Your father knows him. His name is Jonathan. At first I thought he was just a kwii crook, a man out to hurt all of us. But now I know that he is in the water like me, and we water people can work together. He has promised, now that he owns my family land, that he will help me if we work together to develop the land. Jonathan is planting rubber there now, and he says that when the profits come, we will share them.

"And he knows all about kwii medicines. Just look at how successful he is in Gbarnga. He doesn't just believe in one type of medicine by itself. He is a Vai and I am a Kpelle, but we work together and understand each other. I know the Bassa medicine also, and it's powerful medicine. Jonathan can show you the kwii medicine and how to get it."

Young Tokpa was confused by this idea that Jonathan could be a friend. He said to old Tokpa, "I've heard my father speak of him at home, but never in a good way. He says Jonathan is tricky, nasty, a liar, selfish. Now you're saying the opposite. How can you explain it?"

"Your fathers don't really understand Jonathan. Koli has been part of the church too long now, and so he had to decide against Jonathan's way. Jonathan always was friendly to Koli, but it was Koli's choice not to do what he asked. When you go to Gbarnga some day, find Jonathan at the tax office and tell him that Tokpa sent you, and explain what you want. It might cost you a little money, but it will be worth it."

Koli took Tokpa back with him to Balataa at the end of the next month. It was to be Tokpa's last year in the school, and both he and Koli were determined that Tokpa would do well, and then go on to high school.

Koli told Tokpa, "I want you to keep working for the white people, and to save your money so that you'll have enough to start high school, or at least to buy clothes for school."

Tokpa told the white people when he got back, "My father doesn't want me to go to the kwii church on campus any longer. Koli and Goma are Seventh-Day Adventists, and they prefer me to worship with them on Saturdays." The white man accepted that, and didn't insist on Tokpa going to Sunday church with him.

Tokpa, on the other hand, told his father, "I'll be attending the kwii church in order to get ready for high school. So, I won't be attending Sarah's church any more. You needn't worry about me now. I'm almost a man, and will be on my own soon. One of these days I'm going to become a member of the kwii church at Hopewell."

This left Tokpa free to take old Tokpa's advice. He could follow where the water woman led him. But the next thing he must do is find out from Jonathan what kwii medicines the water woman and her kwii followers could give him. The way to find out was to go to Gbarnga on the college bus on a Tuesday afternoon, and then see Jonathan.

When he found Jonathan, he was met with a barrage of questions:

"Your name is Tokpa, my boy? You say Koli is your father's brother, and you live with him near Balataa? And you say that Tokpa is your namesake in the village? I know them both well, and both are good friends of mine. But what can I do for you?"

"Tokpa tells me you can help me find kwii medicine to get ahead in school, and be a successful kwii person like yourself. He says you know about the water society, and can help me find the right medicines for it."

Jonathan was confused. He thought, "Tokpa must be playing some kind of game with this boy. I don't have medicines to sell him. But the boy seems serious enough about wanting to get ahead. I have to tell him something. Anyhow, let me play Tokpa's game," Jonathan decided. "I might even make something out of it."

"I need five dollars, young man." Jonathan spoke with practiced authority. "With that I can get you a ring which will satisfy all your desires. You have to obey the ring, and if your mind or heart shows you what you have to do, then you must do it. But I must have the five dollars, even if I wanted to give you the ring free. The medicine must be costly, if it is to work."

When Koli left, Jonathan laughed to himself. "This is a new game I'm playing. I've never been the kwii doctor before. But why not? If there's five dollars in it for me, and if I can give old Koli something to think about, why not?"

258

Young Tokpa's problem was how to get the five dollars. He thought, "I'm saving every bit of my salary with Koli, so that I'll have enough to start high school next year. I don't dare ask any money back from him. The only hope is to find it at the white man's house. But that'll be tough now that the white man locks his money up in the closet. I'll have to get the key somehow, and take the money out secretly. The water woman will protect me, so I don't get caught."

The chance came a week later. The white man and woman had gone out. Tokpa was left to watch on a Saturday morning while the baby boy was sleeping. The big boy and girl were out playing. He knew that the white man kept the key to his closet in his clothing drawer, and he believed he could find it with a bit of careful hunting. He looked to make sure the cook and washman were busy, and then went into the main bedroom. He was opening the drawer, when the boy came into the house.

"What are you doing, Stephen? You aren't supposed to be in my parents' bedroom. Do you want something there?" "No, it's all right. I was just putting away some clothes I found. Don't worry about it. Just go out and play. I'm staying inside to make sure the baby sleeps all right."

Tokpa realized that was a close call. He had to be careful. So he sat in the living room until he saw the boy and girl run down to play with the two girls at the neighbor's house. Now was his chance. He went back, felt under the shirts in the man's drawer, and there found the key. He took the key, opened the closet, found the money box, as he had seen the man do many times, opened it, found a five-dollar bill, closed it, locked the door, and put the key back. It was quick and easy. But he realized he couldn't do it often, lest they realize money was missing. Fortunately, Tokpa saw at least thirty dollars in the box, so he figured the man wouldn't miss the five dollars this time.

Next week on Tuesday afternoon Tokpa went with the bus to Gbarnga to shop at the market for the white people. He stopped at Jonathan's office, and found him checking over the day's accounts.

"Here is the five dollars you asked for. I need my ring, so I can follow the water woman. Please give me the ring."

259

Jonathan for a moment couldn't remember who the boy was or what he was talking about. But when Tokpa saw that Jonathan was confused, he reminded him, "I'm Tokpa, staying with your friend Koli near Balataa. You said you would give me a ring when I brought you five dollars. Here's the money."

"Oh, yes! Of course.... No, you just wait here.... I'll go bring what you need."

Jonathan for once was at a loss for words. He had completely forgotten about the whole thing after the boy had left. He thought, "I was really just joking with him, but now the boy has taken me seriously! What'll I do?" He thought quickly. Then he remembered.

"I have an old no-good ring I bought on Waterside in Monrovia to give an old girl friend years ago. Hah! Some luck! Before I could give it to my girlfriend, she left me for someone else, and I was left with it. I don't know why I kept it, but I'm sure I did somewhere. It cost me all of fifty cents - a lot of money for me in those days. But maybe I can turn a good profit on it by selling it to the boy!"

"Tokpa, here it is. It may not look like much, but you can see it's old. The power was placed in it long ago. What you have to do is to wear the ring constantly, always rub it before exams and before you need help. And if your water woman asks you to do anything, rub the ring and turn it on your finger, and then do what she says. Above all, never break the rules. I'm sure old Tokpa told you all that."

Tokpa took the ring, and put it on. It fit him not too badly, if he put it on his middle finger. It was old, certainly, but that made it more impressive. He thanked Jonathan, and left. He thought, "This is the beginning of my future. I have dreams, for the woman still comes at night, and I have my ring. I have my teacher in old Tokpa, and I have the future in front of me. I don't need to be afraid of anything any more."

VIII: NO LONGER UNDER EARTH

"I wonder where Stephen is today. I need him here to stay with the baby while we go out this afternoon. He doesn't miss work unless he has to." There was worry behind the white woman's voice.

"In fact, Stephen has been acting a bit strange this year. He doesn't always answer when we speak to him, and he never comes to church with us any more. I honestly don't believe he goes to Saturday church in Balataa either, because he often goes to play with the boys in the village then."

At this point, John, the boy who worked for the people next door, came to the house. "If you're looking for Tokpa, don't expect him. He's sick at home. In fact, he's very sick. I think you'd better go look for him there. He needs you."

"What's wrong, John? Does he need to go to the hospital? Now that they've opened the hospital across the road, we can get him some medical care."

"I don't know what's wrong with him. They say he's gone mad, and is tied up in front of his house. You'd better go and check on it."

The white man looked up from his book and said, "I'll go find out. You stay here with the baby, and I'll walk to his village. I've been there a couple of times, and I think I can find it."

At the village, the white man found that what John had said was true. Stephen was sitting in front of his house, his clothes torn and a strange sly look on his face. His feet were caught between two heavy logs that had been nailed together so that he couldn't pull them free. His hands were tied to his side, and he was tugging at them to try to get them free. His face was scratched, and had been bleeding in several places. The door to his house behind him was broken off the hinges, and the papers which had been nailed to the ceiling were torn loose in several places. The white man recognized old magazines from his house as the source of the ceiling papers, and had to admit to himself that the magazines weren't exactly used the way he thought they would be used.

He tried to approach Stephen, but his mother came out of the house and warned him away. They couldn't communicate beyond greetings, for the white man hardly knew any Kpelle, and the boy wouldn't speak to either of them. He just looked at times confused and at times crafty, searching from side to side as if there might be a way to break the ropes and get loose.

The only thing the man could think to do was to pray. "I've read about praying in an emergency, but I haven't had any real reason to try it myself. But here's the boy who's worked for us almost five years. He's become part of the family. And here he is, cruelly restrained and obviously mad. It almost seems to me that some spirit is in the boy. I've heard stories about country medicine and magic here in Kpelle country, but I can't say I believe them. But the way Stephen looks makes me think some of the stories might have some truth in them."

The white man approached Stephen. The boy seemed to make an effort to bite him, but he couldn't break loose from the rope and the stocks on his feet. The white man reached out to touch the boy. Stephen tried to move away, but couldn't. The man put his hand on his head to quiet him, and then prayed. He thought, "I wish I could pray in Kpelle, but I don't know enough. What kind of missionary am I, if after almost six years I can't speak more than ten words of their language?"

He thought back to the books he had read, as he prayed. "What ought I to pray for? Dear God, help this boy get better, and drive out whatever evil spirit has come into him. I know my faith isn't strong, but this boy needs help. Bring him to you, and make him well. In Jesus' name, Amen."

The white man then looked down at the boy, crouching miserable and pathetic on the ground. He realized that the boy had fouled his trousers, and had even smeared some of the feces on his shirt and face before they had put him in stocks. He wished he could ask questions of Stephen's mother, to find out what had really happened. The only hope was that Stephen himself would begin to calm down, and speak to him.

"Stephen, do you hear me? Can you understand me?" The boy looked up, put on the same crafty look, searched from side to side, and then looked down again. He wouldn't respond.

"I can see that you heard me, and that you know me. I've come to help you. Can you see that?"

263

The boy tried to pull his hands free, looked down at them, and looked up again. "Untie my hands," he said.

"I will soon, but not unless I see that you're going to cooperate with me. You've been trying to hurt yourself, haven't you?"

The boy nodded, and pulled again at the ropes. "Just untie my hands, please."

"I will, but I want to take you to the hospital. Do you want to go with me?"

The boy shook his head, as if to say "No," and pulled hard against the ropes. He kicked his feet out hard against the stocks, and managed to move them a few inches. But then he fell back exhausted, and look down at the ground. He refused to look up again at the man.

"All right, Stephen, I'm leaving. I can't help you if you won't let me help you." The man realized he was gambling that the boy would not let him go. In fact, Stephen looked up with a pleading look in his eyes that denied his refusal.

"Will you go to the hospital, and will you stay quiet on the way?"

The boy pulled again at the ropes, relaxed, and looked up as if to agree. "Help me," he said, "Untie my hands."

"I won't unless you agree to go quietly - and unless you let me pray with you again."

The boy shuddered once more, and the crafty look swept over his eyes. "No," he said. "Don't pray."

"Why not, Stephen? If you don't pray, you won't get well, and I can't help you. Only God can help you." At this point, Koli arrived at the house, bringing Goyakole with him. He was startled to see the white man there, but then walked over to him to talk.

"I thought about coming to get you, but then I didn't know if you would help Tokpa. He's been like this since late last night. We had to tie him up and lock him in the sticks to keep him from hurting himself or us. We are afraid for our own little girl, who has gone to stay at that house there. We don't know what's wrong with the boy. Last night he said something about the water woman, telling him she wanted her chicken, and then he started to tear his clothes and his face. He ran into the house, just pushing the door

264

out of his way, and breaking it, and started tearing down the ceiling mats.

"It was hard stopping him, and it took all of us men in the village to control him, and get his feet into the stocks. But by that time, he was trying to eat his own offal, and we had to tie his hands down before he could do it. It's been terrible."

Goyakole said something in Kpelle, and Koli translated to the white man. "He says that the trouble started when the boy refused to go to Sarah's church, and only went to your church on Sunday. Since that time, he's been acting strange."

"But he told me he'd quit the Episcopal church on campus, because you told him to go only to the Seventh-Day Adventist church. I guess he hasn't been going to either. And just now, the boy told me not to pray over him again. I did it once, and he tried to fight it."

"You mean he talked to you? Good. That's the first time he's talked since last night. You've helped him a bit already, I'm sure." Koli turned and talked to Goyakole again, and looked back to the white man with the answer.

"This is Goyakole, a leader of the bush school. You met him at the coming out last January. He's also a member of Sarah's church. He says that we should pray again over the boy, and wants you to help us. If we pray in both Kpelle and English, God might listen."

Tokpa was listening, they realized, for when they talked about praying, he struggled to get free again, and shook his head violently. He didn't want them praying, it was clear.

"We've got to do it," continued Koli. "He's trying to fight against our praying. But why should he go against the church this way? No, we have to pray over him. Help us."

The white man reached out his hand again, and Stephen made as if to bite it, but he couldn't reach him. He reached over and put his hand on the boy's head, dirty and smeared as it was. The boy shuddered once, twice, and then let go. He looked again to each side, seemed to hunt for something or someone, and then looked down.

"Dear God, we're all here together to pray for this boy. He doesn't want us to pray for him, but we know that he's your child.

265

You know what's in his heart now, and you can heal him. Please, dear Jesus, listen to us, and do something for this boy." The white man finished, and turned to Goyakole, who began to pray in Kpelle. He continued for longer than the white man had prayed, and then stopped.

The white man wanted to ask what he had prayed about, but realized, "I shouldn't ask. It would break the small beginnings of a mood of relaxation that's coming over the boy. I mustn't spoil it by being my usual objective, curious self. That can wait."

He then turned to Stephen again, and asked him, "Will you come with us now to the hospital? It's the only way. It's what you need. Will you come?"

The boy looked up, and said, "Yes." He shuddered again, still looked around him for someone or something he couldn't find, and then relaxed.

"If we untie you, you won't fight or try to hurt yourself? If we take your feet out of the sticks, you won't try to run away?"

The boy nodded his assent. The three men looked at each other, and decided to try to untie him, but he didn't fight it. They untied the hands, and he looked down at them, turned them over, as if deciding what to do, and then put them down. They brought out a cutlass, and pried the two logs apart, and let the boy's legs out of their confinement. For a moment, his eyes began to shift from side to side again, but then he seemed to decide not to fight.

But, even as the white man bent over him again, the boy jerked away from him. Koli and Goyakole leaned quickly over, grabbed him, and tied him before he could move again. Only when they all looked up did they see old Tokpa arriving from the Balataa trail.

The boy looked up with pleading in his eyes to Tokpa, who in turn looked around him at the men standing there. He spoke roughly to Koli, as if to tell him to let the boy go. But Goyakole had enough authority and power, enough presence, not to be influenced by Tokpa. Goyakole was Tokpa's superior in the Poro Society, and Tokpa knew it.

The white man was confused, but also continued to keep his grasp on the boy, while Goyakole and Koli nailed the sticks in again. He listened as an angry exchange went on between the men,

266

but couldn't understand a word. He figured that the old man who had just arrived wanted them to let the boy go, and give the boy to him. But the other two just as firmly refused to do it. They all turned to the boy, who seemed terrified and beaten down. The old man gestured to him, and asked something which the white man was sure was a request for the boy to leave the village and go. Koli and Goyakole seemed to ask the boy to stay.

The boy looked at both, and then relaxed. He was indicating that he would stay here. He looked up at Koli and Goyakole, and then at the white man, as if to ask them to help him. Then he said to the white man, "Let me stay with you. Help me."

The argument with the old man continued, and it seemed that there might be a fight. But then two more men arrived in the village, laborers who had finished work on the Hopewell farm and were home for the day. They went over to the group, and saw that they were needed to protect young Tokpa against the old man.

The result was quick. The old man turned his back on the others, and walked away as quickly as he had come. He was obviously angry, and obviously frustrated.

Koli could only say when he had gone, in trying to explain the matter to the white man. "Tokpa wanted the boy to come with him. He seems to have something to do with the problem, and wants to cure young Tokpa himself. He was angry that we wouldn't let him do it, and left in his anger."

The men turned again to the boy, and the white man asked, "Will you come quietly if we untie you again?"

He agreed with his eyes, although he was obviously torn. If Tokpa had still been there, he might not have agreed so easily. But he had seen the old man run back into the bush.

Once again, they untied his hands and then pried the boards from his feet. This time the boy stayed still. Things seemed safe now, and the men were relieved.

"Look, now we've got to take him to the hospital," said the white man. "There's no time to waste even to change his clothes or wash him. He might change his mind, or slip back to his madness again. The three of us have to get him there now. It's not that far, if we cut across the Hopewell farm."

267

The other men agreed, and made Tokpa stand up, and walk. It was a nervous hour that it took them to get to the hospital, and in through the main door. The hospital had been opened only three months earlier, and was itself unsure of its own routines. The man at the desk wanted to ask Tokpa questions, but Goyakole cut him short.

The man at the desk, not really certain of what he ought to do, responded to the obvious authority Goyakole had shown. He knew Goyakole as an important society leader. He took them into the emergency room of the hospital, and went to call a doctor. The doctors had gone home by this time, but they found one preparing for supper.

The doctor came and examined the boy, and said, "He needs more help than we can give him here. I'll give the boy a strong injection of a tranquilizer, and then you must take him to Monrovia to the mental hospital, and do it right away." He wrote out an order to the mental hospital, and sent them out to find transportation down country.

The white man saw that Stephen would cause no trouble at this point, because of the injection, and so he told Koli, "You go home. I'll do what has to be done, and take him to the hospital." He thanked Goyakole for his help, and asked both of them to pray for Stephen.

He washed Stephen off in the toilet at the hospital, and then went out to the parking place before the building. There, he was lucky to find a taxi that had just brought another patient for emergency treatment which had two spaces for passengers and was going to Monrovia. He put Stephen in the back seat and took the space beside him. The boy promptly went to sleep on his shoulder, and stayed asleep all the way to Kakata. The man was relieved that he wouldn't have any trouble from him.

In Kakata, Stephen woke up when the taxi stopped, and asked, "Where are we?"

The white man explained where they were, what had happened, and added, "We're going to the hospital where you can get some help."

"I can't go there with these clothes. Look at them, they're all torn." Stephen almost whimpered it, but at least he was speaking

268

clearly now. The white man was so relieved that the boy seemed coherent again, that he didn't mind buying clothes for him. Stephen dressed himself, and left the torn rags beside the taxi on the road in front of the Lebanese store where the white man bought him underpants, shorts and a shirt. The boy then got back into the car, and went to sleep again on the white man's shoulder.

It was night by the time they reached the hospital, located about ten miles outside Monrovia, along the old road by the sea. The white man persuaded the taxi to go to the hospital, and wait until he put the boy in. One of the patients was sitting at the door and greeted them. "Have you brought my money? What did you do with it?"

The white man felt, "I'm betraying Stephen to leave him with such people. This man is obviously insane, though probably harmless from the looks of him."

Then a nurse arrived, read the letter from the hospital, and said, "The boy can stay here. You have to promise to pay for his care, and you have to sign a letter of admission for him."

The man thought, "It seems a terrible thing to do to a boy who trusts me, but I can't see any way out. At least, here he'll get some professional help. God willing, he'll come back to his senses and then go back home again."

The white man received a letter three weeks later, saying, "Stephen seems well enough now to go home. You should please come to the hospital and pick him up. The hospital will discharge the boy in your keeping, with instructions to continue the medicines he has been given."

The white man went to the hospital, and found Stephen there, still dressed in the same shirt and shorts he had bought him, but looking altogether different. His eyes were clearer, his face more open, his bearing straight again. The man thanked the hospital, paid the bill, and put Stephen in the college car that had brought him.

Stephen was quiet on the way back, until they were above Totota, once again on the dirt road. Then he said, "I want to talk about what happened, and I want you to help me. First take this ring I got from Jonathan. You must destroy it, because I'm afraid of it now. The ring was supposed to bring me power and success, but it almost killed me."

The white man didn't really understand what was happening, but realized he should keep quiet and just let the boy talk. "I wanted to get ahead, and be a success. The water woman came to me at night, and I knew what she wanted. She wanted me to love her only, give up my girl friends and give up the church. Then if I did what she said, I would get all the money and wealth and fame I needed.

"I followed her orders, and she gave me success at first. I got this ring from a man in Gbarnga, and as a result I was doing well in school this year. I got the best grades in the sixth grade during the first term. The other boys were following me, and I was their leader. I rubbed the ring every time I needed something. It was a good year in every way.

"But then a few days before you took me to the hospital, that old man you saw the day I tried to kill myself came to me and said he had a message from the water people for me. He was right. I had another dream that the water woman wanted me to give her a chicken. The old man said the dream was a message that finally I had to give her what she wanted. She wanted the little girl that had been born to Koli and Goma. He said that was the meaning behind the chicken. The old man said he would help me kill her, because he, too, was supposed to kill the girl and give her to the water people. If I didn't do it, then I would go mad and kill myself.

"I refused to do it, because I love Koli and Goma. And their little girl is my own sister. I even gave her presents. But the old man kept after me. He told me terrible things about the snake and how it would get me. And then he gave me a leaf with medicine on it, I was supposed to put it..."

The boy broke down and began to cry. The white man leaned over him, and put his arm around him. "You don't have to talk about it now. I understand. Just let go, and let God take care of it."

The white man then realized that the driver had slowed down and almost stopped the car. He was listening hard to what the boy was saying. The white man motioned him to drive again, and began to warn him not to say anything about this.

But the driver stopped him, and spoke. "I know this Tokpa, and I know Koli. Koli has to find out about this, before Tokpa does anything worse. No, boss, I have to talk about it. You leave it to me. It isn't any of your business any more. The water business is too serious for you white people to try to solve it."

The driver sped up again, and the white man realized, "I have to get out of this, and let them take care of it themselves. It's getting to be too much for me now."

After they arrived at Hopewell, the driver took Tokpa home, and talked to Koli, who listened with an increasingly serious face as the driver told him what he had heard. The driver said, "Young Tokpa is back now, and will start school and work again on Monday, after resting for the weekend. But you have to do something, and you have to do it now, if you are to prevent more trouble. I advise you to call Goyakole, and get his advice in the matter."

Goyakole, too, was sobered by the facts he heard, and called young Tokpa to him. Tokpa confirmed the story and broke once again into tears. "I didn't want to hurt my sister, and I don't know why old Tokpa wanted me to do something so terrible."

Goyakole told Koli to leave the matter. It was too serious for him, a young kwii man, to try to handle. It had to go deep into the Poro.

He then told young Tokpa, "God saved you this time, with some help, I'm sure, from your ancestors, as well as from the rest of us. Otherwise, you might have killed your sister or even yourself. Be careful.

"There might not be a next time." Goyakole continued, "Those spirits are real, and terrible. Some of them are straight from the devil himself. Jesus came to save all of us from the spirits that were troubling you. A good Kpelle man doesn't play with those spirits, and if you follow Jesus, he'll help you avoid them, as well as help you be a proper kwii. Now, don't lie and steal and play with rings any more, Tokpa. God gave you another chance, and you can't pass it by."

Koli was impressed as he listened to Goyakole talking. He thought, "I guess I joined Sarah's church mainly because I didn't want to lose Goma. Maybe the real reason is because God took hold of me. I still don't know much about this Jesus, but if Goyakole is right and Jesus saved young Tokpa, we ought to believe in him, and not just because we want to be kwii."

Koli's thoughts turned, shifted. "Goyakole said the ancestors helped us. He's probably right. But the children help the ancestors, too. My father, Flumo, never did what he wanted to do. He was really a failure ever since he shot Yakpalo's son. I'm a failure in a lot of ways, too. But Flumo is dead, and I'll be dead some day too, and the two of us - Flumo and I - can only live in our children in young Tokpa and in his children. If they make it, we'll be satisfied."

Young Tokpa was also impressed by Goyakole's statement. He reflected, "I've tried living without God, for these months now, and I've seen where it gets me. I've lied, stolen and almost murdered. And the only way I avoided committing murder was to go crazy myself. No, God is good. I won't forget that again."

Tokpa went to church the next day at Hopewell. He had been away for over three weeks from work, and had been away from church for over six months, all those months after old Tokpa had persuaded him to turn his back on God. It was still a struggle to go back. Things seemed the same, and he realized that even with God's help the church service at Hopewell was not going to be any more clear or interesting.

But Tokpa also realized, "That's not the point. I've been saved now, and I have to give thanks."

He sat with the white man and his family, and was glad to be there. He thought, "Perhaps later in life I'll find out what it all means."

Koli was relieved at the way things had turned out, and he too gave thanks at Sarah's church on Saturday. However, Goyakole was not there this week. He had gone back to Koli's village, leaving a message for Sarah that he had serious business, and might not be back for a week or two.

In fact, it was two weeks later when Koli got the message from Yakpalo that the Big Thing wished to see the men of his village. "You are to come home tonight for an important meeting. You have to explain to the clan chief in Sengta that neither you

272

nor I can be present at the conference with the paramount chief scheduled for today."

The clan chief accepted Koli's word, since the summons came from a higher authority than his own.

Koli arrived home that afternoon to find that the village was quiet, almost too quiet. He asked Sumo, "What's happening?"

Sumo could only tell him, "Wait. Tokpa hasn't been seen for almost two weeks, and the word is that we'll learn why tonight."

Yanga seemed old and tired. She was obviously nervous about what was happening. She had been involved one way or another with Tokpa since the beginning of the troubles, and she wanted to know what would happen to him. Tokpa had been kinder to her since the death of Flumo, but she had remained suspicious of him. She wouldn't be at the meeting that night. It was only for men. But she would learn later what was decided.

She fed Koli, lowered the plaited mat that served as a door, and they went to sleep. It was raining gently now, but the rain was expected to stop shortly. Koli went to sleep, knowing that the singing of the Big Thing would waken him soon enough. But it was toward morning before the sweet singing came. He wakened, and saw that it was clear now, that the old quarter-moon had risen, had paled only the few faintest stars. He went out with the other men to the forest. This meeting would not be in town.

The meeting was short and simple. It seemed to end almost before it began. Tokpa, the word came, was gone. He would not be seen again. And no one should ask what had happened to him. He had misused his powers as a zoe, he had been warned, but he had ignored the warnings. This time, there would be no more warnings. The powers Tokpa had misused had caught him. Tokpa had set the trap, and Tokpa had been caught. The Big Thing had come for his own.

The singing came again, from and through the forest. The meeting appeared to be over. But, before the men could leave, one more message was given, and that was delivered in person.

Saki came once again to a late-night meeting of the society. Goyakole had learned the true story of his disappearance, and had brought Saki back to be accepted once more into his community.

He said to Saki, "You won't be asked to live in the village unless you want to, but you are acknowledged again as one of us. You are forgiven for deceiving us all at that earlier meeting. We see now that you did what you had to do, and that you did it in the best way you could manage."

Saki decided to return to his new life with Dabolo. "I like it there, and I'm growing prosperous. I'll continue to be Nuumeni, severing my ties for good with you people here. But I'm glad to know that in my own village I'm a real person again."

Koli went back to work the next day, realizing that somehow the best had come out of a tangled situation. Much of the damage could never be undone. Saki would never again rejoin the family. There was no real replacement for Tokpa in the bush-cutting group. Yanga's life had been hurt at so many points by the relation she had with Tokpa that her old age would be filled with ghosts and regrets. Tokpa's land was lost to the village, and Jonathan was already planting his rubber and bringing his friends to join him. Nothing was ever as simple as it was intended to be.

And now Koli realized he would lose young Tokpa also, yet not so much lose him as find his own fulfillment in him. The school year was coming to an end. The boy was back in school, and soon would graduate from the sixth grade. The white man he worked for at Hopewell was making arrangements for him to go to high school in the far interior of the country, at a place called Bolahun, where the Episcopal church had a high school. He would be going to school with a lot of Loma, Kissi and Gbande children, but at least one other Balataa boy. Goyakole's son, was going to Bolahun, too, and there was a girl already there in the elementary school from the village at the Hopewell gate.

The first graduation from the Balataa school came not long after. The new school was under construction, next to the old school farther out along the ridge. The ceremony would still be held in the old school. Young Tokpa - he didn't have to be called young Tokpa any more, Koli realized - was dressed in new clothes for the occasion. He was 14 years old now, and too big for the fine clothes they had bought him for the bush school graduation a year ago.

Koli went again to his village, again took his family by taxi to see the boy graduate. It was a repetition of one year earlier - and yet very different. This time the boys walked into the crowded school through the main door. No fence was opened to let through the boys from their confinement. The boys were not bent double, but stood straight in their new shirts and trousers. They were led by their principal, a Vai woman, not by an old Kpelle man. Goyakole was there in the audience, not behind the scenes in the way he and the other zoes had prepared the boys for coming out of bush school. This time the only zoes were the kwii zoes, the principal and all her teachers.

Speeches were given once again, and this time also the big shots sat behind the table at the front of the hall. The clan chief was there, and so was the Balataa town chief, dressed in a kwii suit and tie for the first time in anyone's memory. His son also was in the graduating class, and would go to high school in Gbarnga. He gave the first talk, after the principal introduced the occasion. He seemed ill at ease in his new kwii clothes, but soon he warmed to the event.

He reminded everyone of the opening of the school six years earlier. "At that time Goyakole and Yakpalo and I talked about this school. We decided we would give up our children to the new school We weren't at all sure of the school at the time, but we were willing to see what would happen. In fact it was Goyakole who really shamed me into promising to let my own son attend the school. I might not have done so if Goyakole hadn't spoken first.

"But now the boys are here, finishing their work. I hope all of them will go farther in school, but will also not forget their own Kpelle people in the process. I myself don't really see all that much in kwii school. After all, I grew to be a man without it, and I haven't suffered."

He stopped for a minute and smiled that famous smile of his, to let the people relax and laugh at his remark. The white visitors leaned over to their Kpelle neighbors to find out what he had said.

The Balataa town chief then went on, "You all know the story of the leopard that my old friend, Flumo, young Tokpa's grandfather, told when Koli went off to school. They tell me he referred to the same story on the day he died. It's sad that Flumo died before he could see that the leopard's cub would not just be the plaything of the dog in the village."

The Balataa town chief pointed around him. "Here are leopard cubs - my own, Goyakole's, Flumo's - and they are going to survive and flourish in the world ahead of them. There are other boys, too. I'm sorry I don't know all their fathers, but I'm sure they will succeed in the world, if they don't forget the families which brought them into the world."

The town chief sat down, and the principal of the school stood up to make her remarks in English. She started, "I understand Kpelle, but I'm sorry I don't speak it. You boys, we've had both good times and bad times together over six years. But now you must make futures for yourselves, and then one day come back to make your villages better places. My work is complete with these six boys who are graduating today. Now, I must concentrate on the next group coming up. I even hope that next year there will be one girl in the graduating class, and I'm sorry that this year no girl has been among them."

She then asked the white man, "Would you say a few words on this occasion? You've helped teach arithmetic and you've also helped bring young Stephen to this graduation."

He thanked the school and the teachers for what they had done, and then thanked the children in the school for helping teach him something about Liberia. He said, "I, too, was here six years ago when they opened the school. At that time, I'd been in Liberia only one month, and knew nothing. I don't know very much more now, but I do know at least that it's time for me to learn more. These boys also learned much, and have showed me how much I have to learn from the Kpelle, the Vai and the other peoples of Liberia."

He continued, "The only way in which Africa will grow to be the continent all its people want is for young persons like these boys to lead the way. Moreover, they must lead the way into cooperation with the rest of the world. The day is over when whites can control Africa. From the man sitting next to me, I heard the chief's story about the leopard cub and the dog. I want to say that, in my opinion, the day is over when the leopard's cub will just be the dog's plaything. Rather, the dog of the village and the leopard of the forest must learn to live and work together. I, a white man, am perhaps just a dog of the village, but I am learning to see how the forest might one day be my home, too.

"These leopards' cubs will go on to high school. But they must never stop being leopards, even though at the same time they become citizens of the village and the town. We who are only dogs of the town must still be ourselves, even while we learn the ways of the forest. Only so will this be a better world for all of us."

The boys lined up to walk out of the school after receiving their certificates and the congratulations of the teachers, Tokpa joined Yakpalo, Yanga, Sumo and Kuluba as they left to walk back to Koli's and Goma's house. Sumo was impressed with what he had heard that day. He was even determined to send his own children to the school which had not long ago been built in his village. Kuluba was not so sure about it, particularly for their daughter, but she was willing to listen.

Yakpalo had the last word. "When the cassava root is planted, it's gone. But it's the same cassava that grows again. Koli, your father is dead, but he's not dead. He's alive in you, and you're alive in Tokpa. This kwii world looks new, but it really isn't. The cassava leaves are still green under the red dust that has fallen on them. Listen to the wind blowing in them. Our fathers, your kwii God, all of us, are not just under earth, They are in that wind. Tokpa, you listen to it, also, and never forget us. The leaves may be yours, but we are in the root and in the wind. Remember us, so that your children will remember you."